Z.O.M.B.I.E. GAMES

Written By Ethan Howatt

Font: **Arial and** `Courier New`

Prelude
Z.O.M.B.I.E. GAME PREPARATIONS
Alejandro: Earth's surface: THE CITY
A.K.A
Last City on Earth

My blood pressure was already high, and it was only five in the morning. I normally got up at six, but this morning, I had unwillingly found the truth behind one of the rumors circulating around the king. It was often mentioned as a joke that the king never slept. I might have thought it only a rumor if I hadn't been awakened in the middle of the night and brought to his quarters. Now I knew the truth. It might be definitive proof, but it was proof enough for me.

The king had sent a servant to wake me up just past midnight. To my dream-muddled brain, it took a minute to understand what the man was saying. When I found out it was a summons, my stomach churned. Any summons to the king wasn't usually a good thing. I fidgeted out of nervousness the whole ride there to the king's tower in the middle of the City. I could do nothing but think of all the horrible rumors around the king. Nothing, except maybe a quick prayer to the gods above.

A week earlier, I got a job promotion. Due to some unexpected events in other's lives, no person from the long list of more qualified candidates was available to run the upcoming Z.O.M.B.I.E. Games. How I was the most qualified to run the most watched television show on the planet beat me, but it was terrific. I felt honored for the first day, which turned into a bit of self-delusion about my awesomeness throughout the week. Who wouldn't, though, with all the interviews and invitations that filled my mailbox. It was like the whole world wanted to become my friend.

I had been riding that high for the last week, all the while thinking over what I could do in the games to put my own spin on it. I had to keep it classy, but it also needed to be my baby.

1

Everything was going swimmingly until five hours ago when the king's servant woke me from a deep sleep. The ride to meet the king after that was definitely not in my plans. I really, really hoped that I would make it out of the King's tower with my head still attached. Everyone had heard stories of those who didn't have that luxury.

The hour it took to arrive at the king's study was spent wondering what the king wanted with me. My nose became greasy during that hour as I nervously rubbed at it along with my neck. After the ride, I was escorted through the tallest building in the city and over to the elevator. Finally, I got to the king's floor, where a servant announced my arrival. Instead of having to wait like I expected, I was quickly ushered into the room, where I found a beast of a man scowling down at me.

"Alejandro, was it?" the king sneered at me.

"Yes, my lord," I bowed in respect.

"Why have I brought you here, Alejandro?"

"My lord?" When no response came, I knew I needed to reply with a bit more. My sleep-deprived brain was sluggishly grinding as I tried to come up with something. "I presume it's about… the games?"

"Yes, the games. I need something special this time around." Then, out of nowhere, he asked, "What do you know of the rebels?"

Again, my mind spun. The king had just confirmed this was about the games. Why bring up the rebels? "Not much, my lord."

"Unfortunately, neither do we. They have eluded us, and due to that, I have some major concerns. I would like you to be the answer to them."

"What can I do, my lord?"

"Who are the current participants in the games?"

I rattled off the names of the people that had been provided to me by the enforcers. A list of criminals that would be offered as tribute to the games for a chance to win their freedom and fame.

"I see. Only two on that list should remain. The others don't have ties to the rebels. Keep Kyle and Simon; as for the rest, have them executed."

"My lord?"

"Do not question me!" the king bellowed angrily.

"Yes, sorry, my lord," I bowed deeply, wondering how off his rocker this man before me was. My mind started to work, though. Without the rest of the contestants, how would I have my games? This was clearly what the king was hinting at, so I ventured a careful inquiry. "Once I have them executed, where should I find the new contestants?"

"I don't care how you do it, but get me some rebels. I want the whole lot of in-game contestants to be related to the rebels. Something that will force their hand to show themselves."

I bowed deeply, unsure how I was going to come up with two dozen rebels when the king himself knew little about them. I was dismissed shortly after, with a bad, unfocused picture of what I needed to accomplish and no means of doing it. I was to solve the king's rebel problem miraculously.

So here I was at five in the morning, trying to figure out how to do the impossible. One thing was for sure, though: I definitely didn't feel lucky anymore. That high I had felt over the last week had vanished overnight. Being selected as the Z.O.M.B.I.E. Games coordinator was not a blessing. No, it seemed more like a curse.

Chapter 1
YEAR 2273 A.D.
STAR: Underground Tower #4

I leaned my back against the unyielding, frigid wall, engrossed in reading the digital screen of my info tablet. The dimly lit tunnel loomed around me a mere eleven feet in height and twelve feet in width. Although lights were evenly spaced along the walls, only a handful of them actually worked, their feeble glow barely illuminating the surrounding darkness. Only those creatures accustomed to the absence of light could see clearly in this subterranean maze, and the number of these creatures was few and far between. The tunnels extended deep beneath the earth's surface, unable to support much life.

The darkness didn't bother me at all. Everyone in our group shared this ability, evident by the several young men who casually roamed the area, tending to their own tasks. The ages of these boys spanned from thirteen to twenty-three. One of the younger ones was taking a leak further up the tunnel while others were snacking on some meager rations nearby. As for me, I had already used the bathroom facilities and was now munching on an energy bar while engrossed in an article. I always liked to spend my downtime this way, even though the reading materials available were limited. The only source was the info tablets, which were costly and restricted in their capacity. They only ever held plain text. I had been told that the one I got could hold about 10,000 books on it when I purchased it with my ration chips. What they didn't tell me was how hard it was to get more material on it, as that required sending it up the tower.

A loud hoot broke my focus, diverting my attention from the article to a group of young men absorbed in a card game nearby. They were dressed in the same uniform as me, a plain gray outfit with multiple pockets and reinforced leather on the arms and legs. The players had improvised a card table by mounting a small surface on a gun stand, and one of them was handing out cards to the others who eagerly gathered around. An older boy was busy tallying up the metal chips, which I recognized as ration tokens he had just won in the game.

My attention drifted back to my historical article as I leaned against the wall, as far away from the commotion of the gambling table as I could be. It was my go-to reading material when I wasn't occupied with tinkering on my equipment. However, it wasn't an easy read, with unfamiliar words such as "blinding sun" and "tree branch" that left me puzzled. Nonetheless, I preferred reading history articles since they told of someone's life. I could use my imagination to fill in the blanks for the unknown words. I managed to get through several paragraphs before the sound of curses interrupted my focus once again. I turned my head to see Panther fuming while T-Rex grinned, having just collected a pile of metallic ration tokens.

Panther's frustrated voice echoed through the room. "How do you always beat me? Are you cheating?"

T-Rex just shrugged, "You're just bad luck, Panther."

Panther grumbled, "No, I'm not. My mother gave me a name with good luck—strong enough to beat any other. Look at yours. T-Rex sounds like a bone that a Panther would chew on."

"That's not what my father told me," T-Rex grumbled.

"Well, your parents don't know anything, living on the outskirts," Panther shot back.

"Come on, guys," Cloud interjected, "let's just play the game."

But T-Rex was too focused on saving face. "Hey, Star, what is a panther anyway? Is Panther full of hot air? It probably eats dung or something."

I turned to face them, surprised by the question. "Why ask me?"

"Because you like to read," T-Rex explained while others nodded in agreement.

"Well, I'm not sure," I said, trying to recall what I had read, "but I think it's like a big ant or something."

T-Rex looked dejected, but I continued, "But I read somewhere that they like to lick themselves clean, even their rear ends, so you wouldn't be too wrong."

T-Rex chuckled, "Ha!"

Panther wasn't amused and retorted, "Well, at least I'm not a darkspawn." He used the degrading term for the children of those who lived on the outskirts of the tower and couldn't contribute to society. Their children, like T-Rex, had to provide for them as they had no way to earn their own food rations.

Reed, my best friend since I could remember, had been quietly sitting beside me, stirred in anger. "His parents have been on twice the missions yours have."

He was slender, with short, dirty blond hair and big ears. His eyes were closed, and his head was leaning against the wall. Anyone who didn't know him might think he was napping, but I knew better. Reed was always on edge, anxious, and ready to spring into action at a moment's notice. He had his ears pressed against the wall, listening intently for any sign that it was time to move.

I continued focusing on my article, tuning out the conversations around me. The article discussed the history and science behind zombies, a topic that had always fascinated me. Unlike the fictional zombies of books and movies, these "G-Zombies" were a natural phenomenon. It was fascinating to learn that they were not reanimated dead bodies, as was initially believed when they first swarmed the earth. Rather, they were living hosts infected with a microbiotic ecosystem. These ecosystems, also known as "Zonations of Microbiotic Body Improvement Ecosystems," were initially developed by Canadian scientists in the year 2073 as a means to achieve immortality by enhancing the human body.

However, the spread of the zombie microbodies through humans led to the addition of "Greed" to the front of their name, as their insatiable desire for more micro-biotic matter was the driving force behind their existence. It was incredible to think about the science and technology that had gone into creating these creatures. I couldn't help but feel a sense of awe and respect for the scientists who had achieved such a feat—awe and respect, followed closely by loathing, that is.

As I read the article, my attention was suddenly drawn to movement coming from Reed's direction. I could tell from his body language that he had sensed something. Reed and I joined this group when we were both thirteen years old, and now, four years later, we were among the oldest on the crew. Most of the others were younger, but everyone knew Reed's tendencies. We all reacted to his movement, knowing what it meant. Our playtime was over, and it was time for business.

Everyone quickly gathered their belongings and moved down the hallway, passing through the line of gun stands that had been strategically placed earlier. Satellite, our team leader for this mission, made sure to get the younger boys where they needed to be. It didn't take much effort, though, because they were well-trained. The gun stands were set up in layers, with the smallest boys lying down in front, followed by a kneeling group, and finally, a standing group at the end.

Kneeling next to Reed at the wall, I knew we were in for a long wait. Our position in the second group was uncomfortable, but we were trained to stay in place until given the signal. Standing up too early would put us in the line of fire from those behind us, so we remained still and alert. It was all about precision and timing, and everyone knew the routine. Rushing would only lead to mistakes and accidents, so we waited patiently for the signal to act. As we waited, I couldn't help but feel a sense of unease. Even though we had performed this scenario many times, there was always the chance that something could go wrong. We had to stay focused and prepared for anything that might happen.

The tension in the air was thick as we settled into our positions. Everyone knew the drill; even the group's youngest members were thoroughly trained and ready for action. The flickering light at the end of the long, narrow tunnel cast an eerie glow, making some of the younger boys quiver. I was proud to see them remain focused on the task at hand, remembering my time in the front row. They knew their skills

7

and bravery were vital to the tower's survival and its inhabitants. Every member of the lower tower community had been integrated into the rotational combat unit, which was responsible for sweeping through the tunnels and eliminating any threats that might arise. It was a dangerous job, but one that we had all been trained for and were willing to do in order to protect our home.

The flickering lights played tricks on the eyes, but we refrained from scoping down the tunnel. Only two spotters locked their scopes onto potential targets, but only to track the progress of the G-Zombies that were now spilling around the tunnel's corridor a mile away. The rest of us continued to wait for the signal. This was mainly to prevent the younger boys from accidentally firing at mere shadows, as we didn't have the ammo to waste. While I waited in my uncomfortable crouch, I turned my attention inward, focusing on my breathing. It was a crucial aspect of maintaining steady shots. I took slow, deliberate breaths, letting my worries fade away until they were insignificant. At that moment, all that mattered was my breathing and the bullet in the chamber of my rifle.

At last, the signal was given, and everyone trained their scopes down the tunnel. I nestled my sniper rifle against my shoulder and adjusted my stance to make myself as comfortable as possible. I focused on my breathing, in and out, trying to keep it steady for a clear shot. Peering through the scope, I scanned down the hallway, trying to make out the mark on the wall through the flickering lights. After a few moments, I spotted it and adjusted my aim, calculating the distance the creatures had to cover before they reached it. The approaching horde was a grotesque sight, one we had witnessed many times before. Those of us who had been in this position for as long as Reed and I had were no strangers to it. Even though I hated the sight, I couldn't help but hope that I would have many more opportunities to see it in the future. The alternative, after all, was not something I wished to consider as many people I had known no longer had the chance.

As the G-Zombies drew closer, their deafening groans filled the tunnel, signaling the beginning of the ambush. The small groups that had initially sighted the Zombies had done their part, luring the Zombies to our group while they slowly thinned their numbers. Now, it was up to us to finish the job. We had been mobilized and prepped for this in a matter of hours. Now were shivered in anticipation for the Zombies to reach the mark on the wall. The cold temperatures in the tunnels added to our shivers, but it also slowed the zombies' movements. This was one benefit of being so deep in the ground. It made it easier to pick the zombies off from long distances. We knew every bullet counted in these fights, and that was what most of the prep work was for. Anything to give us an extra edge to make our shots count. We couldn't afford to miss with the tower's limited supply.

The tension in the air was palpable as we aimed down our scopes, waiting for the perfect shots to line up. "On my mark, Team 1," one of the sighters called out, and the tension in the air thickened. The younger boys shifted slightly, eager but also nervous. "Fire," the spotter signaled, and the first row of boys opened fire. I watched as the zombies in the first row crumpled to the ground, and the boys reloaded their sniper rifles, ready for the next wave. Reed and I steadied ourselves, waiting for our own signal.

"Team 2," the sighter called out, and I took a deep breath, focusing on my breathing. Inhale, exhale. I stilled my body, making sure I was as steady as possible before the signal came.

"Fire."

The gunshot echoed through the tunnel, and I watched as my bullet found its target, taking out the zombie closest to my wall. Reed's shot took out the next one, as was the pattern the group used. We counted off the zombies from the walls, each one of us finding our designated number from the wall so that bullets were never wasted on the same target.

"Team 3, fire," the spotter called out, and I felt the burst of heat as the guns erupted just above me. I tried to ignore the

9

fear that shot through me and focused on the task at hand. I hated being in front of a weapon when it was fired, but I knew I had to push past my fear. The world around me wasn't kind to those that couldn't cope. Thankfully, Reed was next to me, and just the thought of having him there calmed me down. Reed always teased me about my fear, but it wasn't malicious like others would be. He always said it was something that made me unique. "It's what makes you, you," he would say, and I would roll my eyes, annoyed but secretly grateful for his support.

As I loaded my rifle, I reminded myself to focus. The two bullets slid smoothly into place as I closed the bolt. I had modified my rifle specifically to fire two shots, the first shot to protect the second bullet from air resistance. This allowed my shots to travel further and penetrate multiple targets at long ranges.

The boys in front of me fired at the command, and I took aim, ready for my turn. Inhale, exhale. The zombie in my sight was small, no bigger than a ten-year-old child. It was a challenge to adjust my aim for its height, but I managed to line up the shot. The bullet hit lower than I had anticipated, taking out the neck instead. Fortunately, the shot was powerful enough to cause an explosive impact, and the zombie's head rolled off.

Any shot that didn't hit the zombie's head was considered a waste. Even if the body was severely damaged, the zombie would keep functioning as long as the brain remained intact. This was due to the specialized microbodies that healed the wounds and repaired the damage. In fact, studies have shown that zombies could even regenerate whole limbs with enough time and resources. However, the regeneration process was gruesome because it involved the attachment of living flesh to the zombie's body, as matter couldn't be created or destroyed. Thankfully, my shot disconnected the head from the rest of the body, so it wouldn't be able to heal anything. Its head would just live, unable to move or cause a problem for us anymore.

As I focused on my task, I thought about some of the research papers I had read. One popped to mind after my poor shot. It stated that a strain of the genetic coding of the lab-created microbodies allowed only human flesh to be used as a resource, thus preventing the disease from spreading to other creatures. Extensive research had been conducted early on to ensure that rats or bugs wouldn't become carriers of the disease within the colony hidden underground. Thinking about how other creatures' heads were at different heights, I was thankful for that small miracle.

Time passed as I fell into a steady rhythm, reloading my rifle, taking a deep breath, aiming, and firing. The shots from the other teams continued to make me shiver, but I tried to ignore them and focus on my own task. Reload, breath, fire, repeat. The zombies kept coming, crawling over each other and moving erratically, making them difficult targets. We waited until they had passed their fallen comrades to take our shots, ensuring the highest chance of a clean headshot.

As the zombies continued down the hallway, I kept track of their progress by the distance they covered. Halfway down the tunnel, they reached an orange marker painted on the wall. It was a sign of how far they had come and how much longer we had to hold out. I hoped that we had enough bullets to make it to the end.

When the time came, there was no need for words. The routine was ingrained in us from a young age. We shouldered our rifles and packed up the stands before picking up our bags that were neatly lined up against the wall. It wasn't a fast process, considering the amount of gear we carried. Ammunition, weapons, and rations weighed us down, not to mention that some of the group were only thirteen years old. Our bodies were well-prepared for this, though, and we quickly made progress.

With everything on our backs, we jogged down the tunnel away from the incoming horde. We weren't running but simply falling back. The older members of our group pushed us to move at a quick pace, drastically outpacing the approach of the incoming G-Zombies. Even with my small frame, I barely felt the strain on my muscles as I kept pace. This was thanks to my training, as my muscles were toned and well-defined due to their extensive use.

Most of the younger boys were in a similar situation, their bodies still developing and lacking the raw power that came with a larger body. No one complained, though, as we were expected to follow the older members' instructions.

The run down the hallway was short, only two miles, but it still took us twenty minutes to cover the distance with our heavy loads. We stopped along the way to paint the start and stop fire points, marking our progress. Once we reached the end, it only took another ten minutes to set up for the next round of killing zombies. I pulled out my tablet and selected my article again, determined to finish reading where I left off as, once again, the waiting began. As I adjusted my seat, a spider caught my attention, and I quickly swatted it away. I briefly wondered what they ate in the tunnels, as I never saw any bugs out here. The only thing in the tunnels were the dead zombie bodies we left scattered around. Other bugs only seemed to live in the tower, but the spiders were different. They were prominent in the towers but also present in the cold tunnels as well.

Chapter 2
THE COLONY
STAR: Underground Tower #4

We made our way through the tunnels, our steps heavy with exhaustion as our fight's adrenaline had warned off. It had taken four intense tunnel runs to take down the massive horde of zombies. This group was larger than any we had encountered before, and it had been a tough battle. When the scout team stumbled upon the horde, they immediately sprinted back to the colony to warn us. I remembered the young boys, only fourteen years old, and their faces pale with fear as they described the sheer number of zombies. One of them had even soiled his pants in terror.

Zombies usually traveled in small groups of around a dozen, but in recent years, larger hordes have become more common, requiring more extensive planning and larger units to handle. Fortunately, most tunnels surrounding the colony were appropriate for this method of hit-and-run. It worked great as long as we weren't in the southern tunnels. That maze was challenging to navigate and required a large number of scouts to keep the area secure. The tunnels there were full of twists, turns, and branches splitting off, making it difficult to anticipate the zombies' movements. It was also an easy place to lure larger groups away from the colony and towards longer tunnels where they could be dispatched. Easy in theory but dangerous in reality.

The journey back from the western part of the colony was a breeze as there were minimal twists and turns in the tunnel. We didn't encounter any unexpected trouble, and before we knew it, we had arrived at the secure entrance of the colony. Although it was still two miles away from the actual settlement, we were greeted by an array of six powerful machine guns and various sniper positions stationed between them. At the end of the hallway, a telescope was set up, enabling the guards to spot any potential threats from afar. We noticed a couple of

13

hefty radios mounted to the wall with cables running back to the tower complex, used to communicate with the other parts of the colony.

Our team leader, Satellite, swiftly approached the guards and briefed them on the successful mission. The exchange was short, and they soon ushered us through the guarded main entrance. I waved at Elephant, a good friend of many in the community, as I made my way to where he stood guard. He gave me a smile and a wink before turning and watching down the hallway, checking to ensure no Zombies had followed us here. The remainder of the journey down the lengthy hallway took another half an hour, but finally, we arrived at a colossal three-foot-thick metal door that spanned the entire width of the tunnel. The doors were already open, thanks to the guards who had radioed ahead.

Walking in the middle of the group, we proceeded through the tunnel at a leisurely pace as everyone needed to go through the screening process before entering the colony. On one side of the tunnel, there was a larger sealed door that led further into the colony, while the other smaller door led to the screening chamber. Our team leader went in first, closing the door behind him. In the screening chamber, he would have to strip down and send his equipment through a decontamination strip while his body was scanned for any colonies of G-Zombie.

These microbodies tended to form small colonies on the skin's surface, making it easy to scan just the outer skin layer. However, they could also dig down deep, ultimately reaching the bone marrow, where they would multiply and spread rapidly throughout the body. This made them extremely dangerous, and even a small scratch could turn lethal in a matter of minutes. It took a couple of days to turn completely after that.

I wished the removal process was as simple as the scanning process, but unfortunately, it wasn't. The whole infected area had to be cut out quickly to give the infected person a chance to survive.

That was the whole point of the screening process: to keep the colony safe from the Zombie microbodies. Once a person was confirmed clear, they could proceed to the next chamber and get dressed, making way for the next person in line.

I had heard stories of unfortunate incidents where people were scratched or bitten and arrived at the scan point. In most cases, the affected area was quickly cut out and burned to prevent the microbodies from spreading, allowing the person to survive. However, for those whose bones were affected, amputation of the entire limb was often necessary. But the worst cases were when the microbodies had already spread too far, reaching the organs or brain. At that point, a difficult decision had to be made by the individual or their peers. It was either risking the danger of turning completely into a Zombie or having to be terminated to keep the colony safe. There was really only one option.

The screening process was routine for our team, and one by one, we passed through it. The upside to having to be screened was that we got back our clothes looking freshly laundered and pressed on the other side. I always found it fascinating how the clothes-washing contraption worked, but I never bothered to investigate further. It was simply referred to as the laundry machine, and that was good enough for me. Besides, with my busy schedule going on numerous missions, I rarely had time to do my laundry anyway. So, it was an excellent convenience that saved me a few extra hours in my day.

The line dwindled, and soon, it was Reed's and my turn. I let Reed go first, and shortly thereafter, I was notified by a blinking light that I was clear to enter. As I entered the screening chamber, I couldn't help but notice how dull and unremarkable it looked. The three walls were identical to every other tunnel wall I had seen, while the last one was an obsidian black with a glossy, reflective surface. I knew that if I stepped closer, I would be able to see my reflection. The floor in front of it was also the same black color, smooth and sleek. In one of the plain walls, I spotted two conveyor belts that continuously rolled, carrying clothing and equipment through the decontamination process.

Without wasting any time, I placed all my weapons on one of the moving conveyor belts before starting to undress. As I took off my clothes, I couldn't help but feel a little self-conscious about my small and lean frame, which was toned from all the training and missions I had been on. Unlike some of the other guys my age, I wasn't bulky or considered muscular, and that seemed to be what the girls preferred. I was toned and solid but not rippling with muscle. From what I had heard, older women usually operated the scanner on the other side of the black mirror, which only added to my shyness. They weren't exactly closed-mouthed.

Tossing my weaponry onto one of the conveyor belts, I stepped onto the icy black surface of the room. As instructed, I stretched my arms out and widened my stance. The silence hung heavily in the air until the crackle of the speaker erupted, instructing me to turn. I obliged and caught sight of the spider in the corner of the room. It had been there for as long as I could remember, but I never bothered it. It probably kept other critters out, after all. Plus, it was too cold to linger, and the line of others behind me wouldn't be happy to be held up.

Continuing my rotation, I found myself staring back at my own reflection on the slick surface. I waited patiently for the scanner to do its work, but as time dragged on, my nerves began to fray. This was taking much longer than usual. My mind started to race, thinking of the worst-case scenarios. Part of me wondered how I could have gotten infected when we had stayed far away from any G-Zombies.

At last, the speaker burst to life again, declaring me clean. I breathed a sigh of relief, but something about the voice sounded familiar. It lingered in my mind as I made my way to the changing room, where my clothing was already freshly laundered and pressed. I again wondered how the machine worked, but only the top engineers were privy to its inner workings. With my weapons and gear in hand, I exited the room as another recruit took my place in line.

16

As soon as I stepped through the exit door, I found Reed waiting for me in the vast open space, which housed a colossal structure in the middle. The tower was said to be three thousand stories high, with numerous offshoots of support beams that jutted into the earthy walls of the cavern. However, due to the dim lighting and the countless support beams, it was impossible to determine its true height from the ground level. The only visible features were the enclosed ramps that led from the building outward, straight into the earth around it, which served as space for growing mushrooms and training. I was told that in the upper tower, there were private villas for the affluent families in the colony. Most people lived and worked in the tower, while the less fortunate and impoverished lived here on the cold ground outside of the tower. This was crowded, though, and many had to live further back in the offshoots of the second northern entrance. There were four entrances, each with its own screening units.

"Ready?" Reed asked, pushing himself off the wall as he had been leaning in a relaxed position while he waited for me.

I nodded and jogged over to catch up with him. As I did, a spider scuttled by my foot, and I tried to adjust its aim for the creature. It easily dodged, and I didn't bother trying again. It was always hard to kill the little creatures.

"What do they even eat?" I mumbled.

"What does what eat?" Reed asked.

"The spiders."

"Other spiders, haven't you seen them drag off their dead companions."

"Not very often."

"Well, that is why you don't see many dead spiders around." Reed wisely continued while he adjusted the rifle on his shoulder. Our quick strides ate the distance from the screening room, heading toward the tower entrance. "Anyway, that was an easy mission."

"I like them that way," I replied, matching his steps.

As we walked, Reed mused aloud, "Why do they keep coming, though?"

17

"What do you mean?" I asked as we maneuvered through the tents that scattered the ground between us and the tower entrance.

"Well, think about how many hordes we have taken out. We must have cleared the areas around the colony by now, but they just keep coming," Reed made it to the entrance first, and the automatic sliding doors opened as he stepped in front of them.

"Based on the math, we have been clearing these zombies out for at least a hundred years. Let's say we average the normal clearing of the surrounding area, and that's 150 zombies a day for the colony. That's a total of..." Reed began to calculate, but I interrupted him.

"5.5 million roughly," I finished for him.

"Right. Now, add in the hordes that we have been coming across, 5000 more every two weeks for the last ten years," Reed continued.

"You're at almost 7 million," I added as we entered the elevator. I pressed the button for the 78th floor, and the doors shut without a sound. We didn't even feel the lurch as the elevator started moving upward.

"Based on only having about 100,000 people living in this tower, we should have cleared out 70 towers worth. Those tunnels weren't meant for people, so that means all those zombies were coming from other places. Zombies can't reproduce, so that means they are just wandering here without more being created," Reed rambled on, but my attention was only partially focused on what he was saying.

As soon as the elevator dinged, Reed and I stepped out into the plush carpeted hallway that stretched as far as the eye could see. Our apartments were conveniently located next to each other, with the closest doors to the elevator entrance. A quick glance revealed a dozen other doors leading down the hallway.

As we reached our apartments, Reed and I stopped outside our doors, closest to the elevator entrance. We had walked down a hallway with a dozen other doors on either side, all leading to the apartments of our fellow tower residents.

Reed continued his earlier topic of conversation, "So my point is, we should be seeing fewer zombies as time goes on, but we're actually seeing more."

I let out a tired sigh, "It's a mystery."

Reed, however, seemed eager to continue the discussion, "Well, it's a problem that the higher-ups have been discussing. Our ammo supply won't last at this rate. We can't get enough gunpowder to reload the casings. Soon, we'll need to start sending out search parties."

This was news to me, and my curiosity piqued, "How did you find that out?"

Reed flashed a mischievous smile, "Ah, I see you're interested now. I'll tell you if you come over for dinner."

I couldn't help but roll my eyes, "You just want me to cook and clean for you."

Reed shrugged playfully, "Can you blame me?"

We often shared meals together, and it made sense since it was just as easy to cook for three people as it was for one. I often cooked for Reed and Wind, his sister. They, in turn, would cook for me as well. The ratio was usually skewed, so I cooked more since I was the better cook.

"I still need a nap first," I said, opening my door.

Reed nodded in agreement, and we parted ways to our respective rooms.

After sleeping for around thirty minutes, I dragged myself up and made my way to Reed's place. I entered the passcode before stepping in to find that the living room and kitchen were deserted. From the sound of snoring, it seemed like Reed was still sleeping. I couldn't help but snort softly, feeling a tinge of annoyance at the situation. I really wished I could still be sleeping, too. Nonetheless, I took a deep breath and decided to be the responsible one. Without disturbing Reed, I made my way to the kitchen and started preparing a meal.

Reed and Wind were fortunate to have a well-stocked pantry, as they were free from the burden of supporting elderly

19

family members. Others in the tower were less fortunate, lacking the abundance of spices, dried goods, rice, and sugar that Reed and Wind enjoyed. My contributions to their provisions only added to our abundance. While I knew the origins of some of the food, such as the mushrooms from a cavern on floor 186 or the beans and peppers on floor 192, the source of the sugar and rice remained a mystery.

I spent almost thirty minutes perfecting the soup when the door suddenly swung open. I could immediately tell it was Wind from the sound of her breathing. I could recognize her presence from a mile away.

"Star, it smells good as always," she complimented, and I felt a flush of warmth spreading through my face. Wind was only two years older than me, and she was a stunning girl with sharp black eyes and a heart-shaped face. Her long brown hair was always well-kept and straightened. I had secretly harbored a crush on her for years but knew she wasn't interested in me. She had recently broken up with her boyfriend, who lived three levels up. They had been together for a couple months, but two weeks ago, she had caught him cheating on her. As she came over to check on the soup, my heart raced. For a fleeting moment, I dared to hope that she might see me differently. Now that she was single, that is. I had to still my mind and remind myself that it would never happen. I knew better than to dream too big. Girls like her didn't go for guys like me.

"Wind," I greeted her with a nod, trying to focus on the soup and not how close we were. I had just finished it and was adding a few final spices, adjusting the flavor until it was a perfect blend.

"Is Reed still sleeping?" she asked, moving to her bedroom and putting her things down in her room.

I nodded, listening to her smooth voice. Suddenly, it hit me why the voice had sounded so familiar over the speakers earlier. It had been hers. I didn't know why it had taken me so long to realize that. But why was it her? Was she one of the scanners now? That didn't make sense, though, but it was definitely her voice. She was too young for such a job.

My mind swirled until it landed on another strand of thought. A chill went down my spine. Had she seen me naked during the scan? I remembered how long it had taken before the all-clear had come. The hopeful part of me questioned whether she had been checking me out while scanning? I quickly scolded myself for even thinking that. Why would she be interested in me when there were plenty of other good-looking guys around?

"What are you thinking about?" Wind's voice made me jump as it slammed me back into the present moment. I looked over and saw her helping by setting the table. "You're awfully quiet."

I flinched a little, hoping she hadn't seen me jump. I tried to cover up my embarrassment and clear my thoughts. "Just tired, that's all. It's been a long day."

"You guys have been having more of those lately. It worries the rest of us," she said with a hint of concern in her voice.

I offered her a reassuring smile. "Don't worry. I've got your brother's back. I'll always make sure he comes home safe."

"I'm more worried about you than him," she teased, and I felt my stomach churn with disbelief. Was she flirting with me? My heart leaped with hope once again, "You cook for me, and my brother just eats part of my portion. If I had to pick one, it would be you."

I couldn't believe my ears. Did she really mean that, or was she just messing with me? I wanted to believe her, but I knew better. "I'll go wake him up so we can eat," I said, doing my best to push the crazy thought out of my head.

.....

After finishing my meal, I left Reed to deal with the dishes and headed back to my room to gather my weapons. Once they were packed, I took a short elevator ride up to the 311th floor. The hallway was more expansive, with carts holding various tools and gears lined up along the sides. This floor was

21

designated for engineers and scientists to carry out experiments and solve problems for the tower. Walking purposefully, I eventually reached a door labeled 311AC. I knocked and waited, hoping to be lucky today. Two people worked in 311AC, but only one of them was pleasant. As the door opened, an elderly man with a wiry white beard glared down at me. I looked right back, and a grin crept onto my face in response.

"Excavator! How are you doing today?" I greeted.

"That depends," he scowled.

"On the scale," I finished, rolling my eyes.

"Things need perspective," Excavator chuckled. "It's a good seven today. Seeing you has brought it to an eight; I haven't seen you in a while."

"Well, I've been showing up every other day, but you were always out. Is everything all right?" I asked.

Excavator shrugged. "I'm getting old, and things just hurt when you get this old."

"Well, you're the oldest person I know, and you're healthier than many half your age," I replied, moving into the room as Excavator shut the door behind me. "So what's your secret?"

"Secret?" he chuckled.

"Yeah, how to live long enough to see grandkids?" I quipped.

Excavator leaned in conspiratorially, "Don't eat the onions," came his whisper.

"What? Why?" I tilted my head.

"Just don't question it," Excavator grinned.

I absently placed my equipment on a back table and began to unscrew my rifle. "But I like onions," I said.

"I said not to question it," he quipped back.

"Fine, I won't," I sighed.

"What do you have there?" he asked.

"I felt like the trigger was getting a little stiff. Figured it needed a tune-up," I answered.

"Well, have fun with that," Excavator said, leaving me to my own devices. Most scouts left their gear and picked it up later, but I preferred to do my own maintenance. Excavator had tried to talk me out of it when I first arrived years ago, but after explaining that if my life depended on the gear, I wanted to know it inside and out. The old man couldn't argue that and had reluctantly agreed. As I had persisted in my desire, he started to teach me when he had time.

I was looking over my rifle when Reed joined me several minutes later. He placed his equipment down next to mine and gripped my shoulder firmly. I looked over at him with a raised eyebrow. He nodded his head at his gear, and I rolled my eyes and reluctantly gave him a shrug. He smiled, stepping back to give me space. I inspected his gear a little more thoroughly than my own, as was the norm. I didn't want to break my promise to Wind, plus he was my best friend.

When I was done, I handed the gear back to Reed, and we walked over to Excavator, who was working on an engine.

"What do you have here?" I asked, almost causing the old man to drop the small wrench that he held in his right hand.

"What did I tell you about sneaking up on people?" Excavator scolded.

"That it was a good habit to have," I replied, still looking at the engine sitting down next to Excavator. I pulled the engine towards me and began examining it closely.

"Did I say that?" Excavator mused before shaking himself. "Well, don't do it to me." That was when he noticed my interest in the engine. "This here is an engine for the bullet factory. I pulled it out and replaced it with a spare, but I've been having difficulty figuring out what's wrong with it."

"Well, it looks like the timing of the second piston is off slightly and might have buildup in it," I muttered.

"You don't say," Excavator mused, looking at the gear. "What makes you say that?"

Excavator and I delved into the engine, analyzing its every component and speculating on the root cause of its malfunction. Meanwhile, Reed tried out the tweaks I had made

23

to his weapons, testing their accuracy and speed. Soon, Reed got board and excused himself, leaving Excavator and me to our tinkering.

Later, when I got back, I sought out Reed in his apartment. I found him and Wind playing a game of cards. I moved over and sat next to Reed and checked out his hand.

"I hope you don't have anything riding on this round." I smiled at him.

"Mind your own business," he scowled back.

I smirked and then remembered we never finished our conversation from before he went to take a nap. "Hey, you never told me where you heard that the higher-ups were sending out search parties."

Wind looked up from her cards in interest, "What is this?"

"He said that we were low on ammo supplies and needed to go out and find resources," I said, pointing at her brother.

"I have my sources," he winked at me.

"It was Rock, wasn't it?" I could immediately tell that I had gotten it right. "How did he know?"

"Not sure, but we should be finding out soon if it's true, and he usually knows before us."

"That's concerning, though." Wind added. "We all knew that supplies were being tightly controlled, but if they are sending out scouting teams, we must be low."

I shrugged, "That depends on how far ahead the leaders are thinking. I wish they kept us in the loop."

"They just don't want to distract us from defending the tower." Wind chimed in.

Reed and I shared a glance that Wind missed as she put down a card, and Reed groaned. "Looks like I win. You're cleaning the apartment this week."

Chapter 3
DEATH IN THE CAVERNS
STAR: Underground Tower #4

Two days later, I was back in the field with Reed and Rock by my side. Rock had been ill during our last mission, but now he was standing tall with his mountainous build, ready to face any challenge that came our way. While Reed tended to be anxious during our excursions, Rock was the complete opposite, living up to his name by remaining unfaltering in front of hordes of zombies. His muscle mass had saved us several times growing up in the southern tunnels, as he would cut through zombies with the sword at his hip. Rock and Reed made a great team, each balancing the other out. Reed kept Rock in check, ensuring he didn't recklessly charge into danger, while Rock provided the group with the necessary momentum to move forward.

At the outset of our group's formation, there was some tension between Reed and Rock. Reed's tendency to be overly careful clashed with Rock's bold and fearless approach, resulting in Rock admonishing him with the biting remark, "Stop shrinking at shadows." During that tumultuous first few weeks, it was my role to keep the group united. But after a couple of missions where they saved each other's lives on numerous occasions, a newfound respect grew between them. That respect grew into a close friendship over the years we had been together. That also equated to becoming killing machines as our close-knit unit functioned seamlessly together.

Our group's rotation had come, and this time, Reed, Rock, and I would venture into the southern district as a three-man team. Our mission was unlike any we had tackled before; we were to venture further south than our usual guard routine to scout out a pocket of caverns. We packed extra rations and supplies to prepare for the fourteen-day round trip. Reed, always cautious, insisted on bringing more supplies than necessary to ensure our safety, and I supported his decision while Rock grumbled about the extra weight. Water was our primary concern. We had a purifier with us to restock whenever we came across any water source. The tunnel system we grew up exploring had a slight incline with a canal on one side to divert any leaks. Those tunnels with running water were the most dangerous since the sound of the water would conceal any noise made by the zombies until it was too late. We would have to be careful to stay supplied with water as well since finding water in the tunnels was a matter of luck.

Our packs were weighed down with all sorts of gear that had been assigned to us for the trip. This added extra weight to our already heavy loads, which included the additional bullets we needed for our mission. Our standard military attire also included a sword that was secured to our waist. The sword's sheath went across our waist horizontally, and the sword was snapped into place to prevent it from falling out. I had read that in the past, people used to carry their swords hanging from their waist, but this had become impractical for running. Therefore, the new placement had become the norm.

Unfortunately, due to the amount of gear we had to carry, we didn't have space for luxury items like my tablet. It had cost a lot of ration tokens to get, and I wouldn't risk breaking it on a mission like this. Plus, I had already read all the history articles it had contained anyway. I hadn't had the time to send it up to get more on it, which would also cost more ration tokens. It was an expensive luxury that most people didn't have.

We weren't alone in venturing further than usual. As we made our way to the southern gate, we came across several other teams getting ready to leave. They also had larger packs, a clear sign that they were exploring as well. We took the time to talk with them, and it became clear that they also had orders to scout out new areas. The sheer number of groups proved the rumor that Rock had told Reed was true. The pressing concern of the dwindling supply of gunpowder for our weapons solidifying into reality. It had always been a limiting factor in our training to combat the G-Zombies. Food and water were not abundant, but only the drive for ammunition would make them send us out.

There had always been a lot of discussion about these concerns, but we didn't have the data that the upper tower did, as they hadn't deemed it worth keeping us in the loop. I had heard many lower tower residents propose barricading the entrances and living with what we had, but that plan was rejected by the higher-ups, the reasons for which were unknown to us tunnel runners. Speculation ran rampant, with some accusing the leaders of withholding important information from us. In contrast, others dismissed the leaders in the upper tower as clueless old fools. Personally, I leaned toward the former, as it was hard to believe they remained in power without good reason. But what were they hiding? News from the upper floors was scarce. Heck, no one on the lower levels even knew how many floors there were.

With our group heading into the twisting and turning southern tunnels, I couldn't afford to have my mind wander. Vigilance was vital in this dangerous place. As always, my trusty sniper rifle was slung over my shoulder, but this time, I also had two pistols on my hips and a semiautomatic rifle with a short barrel and butt ready for quick maneuvering. I made sure to check the battery charge on my flashlight and the spare one, as well as the light on my close-range rifle. Additionally, I carried six spare batteries on my belt. While some of the tunnels were lit, many offshoots lacked light due to damage or age. These tunnels were built to last during the time of human rule on the surface. While some of that technology remained, it was not enough to make this journey a comfortable one.

As I centered myself, the signal that it was time to head out came. Reed and Rock walked towards the exit with stern expressions, mentally preparing themselves. I followed them through the plain door after receiving a nod from the two women stationed at the desk with a computer. They typed a few keystrokes in their logs to record our departure. I gazed at the computer, wishing I could dismantle it and figure out how it worked. It was much more complex than the simple tablet I

27

owned. The applications it could be put to were limitless. At the same time, I was limited to only being able to read a few articles off of the tablet. But computers were highly valued assets, and I knew it was impossible for me to get my hands on one.

It didn't take us long to reach the tunnels. As soon as we did, Rock complained, "So why are we out here?"

Reed replied, nervously checking behind him, "We have orders."

"I meant, why only us? The bottom 250 floors," Rock scoffed. Reed rolled his eyes, clearly annoyed by Rock's constant complaints. "You know why. It's to segregate responsibilities and preserve knowledge. We get trained to fight the hordes, and the upper floors focus on agriculture, science, and history. If they were down here, they'd be killed, and the colony would lose essential knowledge. This is the only way for the tower to progress. We all do our parts."

"But what if one of us is good at something else? Why is Star down here with us? He should be building things, not risking his life out here," Rock argued.

"They don't accept transfers," Reed replied. "It's just not allowed."

"Why?" Rock asked.

"Because it's not," Reed said dismissively.

"That's what the Uppers want you to believe. I overheard that some of the Uppers don't even do anything. We're doing all the hard work down here, and they're sitting lazily up there," Rock said, his face reddening.

I was surprised. I hadn't heard that before, but then again, I usually spent my free time tinkering in the engineering area. "Where did you hear that?" I asked.

"I have my sources," Rock said grimly.

"Probably heard it from Street," Reed commented, referring to the conspiracy theorist who lived on the third floor.

"No, I heard it from some of the elders on the 711th floor," Rock defended himself before he could stop himself.

"What were you doing on the 711th floor?" I asked curiously.

Rock fell silent and didn't respond, so I looked at Reed for help. Reed was less than helpful as he chimed in, "Don't look at me. I didn't go with him. I don't even know what's on any floors above 400." We all knew it took special elevator access to go above the 400th floor.

"It doesn't matter what I was doing up there," Rock said. "What matters is what they keep from us. They have entire floors with people that don't do anything productive. I won't mention some of the things I've seen up there."

I studied Rock's flushed face. I had always been a little envious of his handsome features, but now, looking at his expression, I wasn't sure what to think. There had to be a reason that he had been brought to the upper tower. I knew it wasn't for his brains. But he was claiming to have been somewhere most of us couldn't dream of going. I briefly wondered what they did to him up there before my thoughts returned to what he was indicating. Something was going on on the upper floors that they kept from us, something that Rock had got a glimpse of. I knew him too well at this point to just think he was being paranoid. I didn't know what to say, though, to keep the conversation going. Thankfully, I didn't have to.

"Well?" Reed asked, turning back to Rock.

"Well, let's just say that they treat us like worms. They have a lot more up there than we have down here. They also have some unsavory tastes," Rock said, looking uncomfortable.

Reed seemed to catch on to the fact that Rock didn't want to go into detail. I saw him have a quick inner debate on whether to push it. The part that cared about Rock as a friend won over his own curiosity, and he didn't press Rock further. I could tell that he wouldn't let it drop, though, and would confront Rock later about it.

We fell into a tense silence, lost in our own thoughts. Periodically, we placed devices provided for this mission on the walls as high as we could reach. The devices allowed for remote monitoring of cameras and devices over long distances

29

through the ground. I only knew that because of my conversations with the Excavator. Most groups, if assigned, wouldn't have a clue how they worked but had a general knowledge of them as we constantly had to swap out units. The devices were linked to a sparse camera network strategically placed around the tower. The cameras being the tower's only means the tower could monitor its surroundings. Feed that the people in the lower tower didn't even have access to.

The lack of devices and cameras mounted around the tower's surrounding area to aid in monitoring was a hot topic among defenders. The lack of access to the feed an even hotter one. Some older individuals attributed the lack of devices to a lack of resources. Rock had a different opinion, which he had expressed many times. According to him, the Uppers simply did not care enough about the safety of those below. His recent announcement of being summoned to the 711th floor only reinforced the validity of his beliefs. I couldn't help but believe him.

We stopped for a night's rest in the middle of a seemingly endless straight tunnel. The idea of taking shifts to sleep and keeping watch always made me uneasy, as it meant putting all my trust in Reed and Rock. During our training, we were told chilling stories of teams that were wiped out by a member who had fallen asleep on watch. I didn't want to point out the obvious flaw in that logic - if everyone was dead, how could the story have been told? Clearly, there had to be a witness to survive and tell the tale.

While I had complete faith in Reed's commitment to his duties, Rock's intimidating demeanor and indifference toward danger initially scared me. However, after the first year together, I learned to rely on both of them to keep me safe while I rested. Now, I had complete faith in their abilities as they did in me.

We made it through the night without any trouble and took a break to rest for six solid hours. Once we were all awake, we each had a meal of tunnel rations before packing up and getting ready to move on. As we were packing, Reed asked a question that caught us all off guard. "Hey, I was thinking, how do the higher-ups know about this cavern that we're heading to?" he wondered.

Rock didn't quite understand what Reed was getting at, so he asked, "What do you mean?"

"I mean, it's further than we've ever explored before. How do they have a map that leads right to it? Aren't our maps the most up-to-date?" Reed pressed on.

I mulled it over for a moment before taking a guess. "Maybe they had it in their archive of data leftover from the founding."

Reed shook his head. "If that were the case, they would have had someone scout it out by now. I spent all of yesterday looking through all the shift reports archives in the library. There wasn't a single mention of anyone ever going out farther than three days journey. This one takes seven."

Rock was baffled. "How could you have gone through over a hundred years of records in less than a day?"

"It's cataloged," I replied before Reed could answer. "How many files did you really have to go through? There can't be too many scouting missions."

Reed shrugged. "There were only about two hundred."

"Only two hundred?" Rock was surprised.

"There hasn't been any reason to go out exploring. We've had all the resources we needed on hand. It's only now that we're low on some raw materials that they want us to go looking," I explained. "Why risk it when, as time passes, the number of zombies should have lessened?"

"But they haven't. We've seen more," Rock interjected.

"Not sure. It's just another mystery," I said as we continued deeper into the labyrinth of tunnels.

As we arrived at the cavern entrance, we were tasked with scouting out. I couldn't help but feel relieved that our journey had been relatively uneventful. We had only encountered three zombies along the way, a much lower number than our usual excursions. Thankfully, the small groups were no match for our skilled team of three, or "the tre-o," as

31

we liked to call ourselves. Despite being only seventeen years old, we had years of experience under our belts and handled the encounters with ease.

Upon entering the cavern, we were struck by the stark difference from the tunnels we had been navigating. The familiar hum of artificial lighting was absent, plunging us into a disorienting darkness. Even though the tunnel's lighting was sparse, the fixtures were adequate to maintain our adjusted eyesight. But this cavern was unlike anything we had seen before. It was a gaping hole on the right side of the tunnel, like a wound in the earth. We approached cautiously, our weapons at the ready, as was our custom. We were always prepared for anything that might come our way.

The left side of the tunnel illuminated the cavern with its lights even as we approached the breach in the wall. Slowly, we entered in a triangular formation, with Reed keeping watch on our rear. The cavern's walls were in line with the breach in the tunnel. About twenty feet down, the cavern appeared to open up, but we couldn't see its extent due to the limited illuminance of our flashlights. The ground was made of gravel and had occasional puddles, with water droplets causing ripples when they fell from the sealing. The droplets made a constant, faint background noise that was eerie. Looking up, I saw stalactites hanging from the cavern's ceiling, covering it closely and clumped together about ten feet above our heads. The actual ceiling was another six feet higher up than that. Still, the ceiling drastically changed once we reached further into the cavern's depths.

We cautiously made our way through the first part of the cavern, alert for any potential danger. As we approached an open area, I was stunned by the sheer size of the cavern. While we couldn't see the other end, the walls stretched outward, and the roof rose up at least two dozen feet. A steep slope led down to what appeared to be a beach near a vast body of water. Stalagmites dotted the shoreline, and we could make out sporadic ones further out.

"I've never seen anything like this before," Reed marveled, his eyes darting around the cavern.

"It's beautiful," Rock added, taking in the scenery.

I agreed with them as I scanned the limited area that our flashlights could reach. "How far do you think it extends?"

"I'm not sure, but I'm not going near that water. Can't see what's in it. There could be something hiding," Reed said, shifting nervously.

"A water monster or a zombie?" Rock asked with a chuckle.

"Water monster, obviously," Reed retorted. "Zombies can't hide underwater. They need air as much as we do to survive."

"Well, not as much as we do," I corrected him. "Experiments show that they can last about twenty minutes without it. But they'll also avoid it, although I don't know how society managed to figure that out."

"That's what I meant," Reed sniffed.

"You're right, though. It's a stunning view, but I agree that we need to complete our mission and leave as soon as possible," I said, eager to get the job done.

"Are you ready to deploy the scanner drone?" Reed asked us. Rock and I nodded in agreement and moved to get to work.

I unstrapped my pack and retrieved a long roll of wire, and we made our way back to the tunnel, locating the nearest light on the wall. While Reed and Rock kept watch, I dismantled the light and slowly clipped the wire ends to the appropriate spots in the tangled electrical wires.

Reed grumbled, "This is why we were given this mission. Any group could have done it if we didn't have to do some of the hardwiring. This is what we get for your time being spent on the engineering floor."

I grinned and replied, "Can't help it if I enjoy it," as I completed the wiring. I ensured that I covered it up to protect it from moisture. With that done, I was ready to lay down the charging pad for a drone. Excavator had described how the drone worked, but I had never seen one in operation. Part of

33

me wanted to stay and see it fly, but the initializing sequence would take too long, and I didn't want to risk a safe journey back to see it.

Rock and Reed led the way as we made our way into the cavern for the second time. We walked along the wall, carefully laying down the cable and moving it out towards the center of the cliff. This would ensure that the laydown zone was in an open space for the drone. Once the cord was secured, I got to work connecting the drone dock to the power source. Reed and Rock kept watch over me as I worked, staying ever vigilant. Within a minute, the docking station was properly hooked up, and I placed the drone in its slot. With a single button press, the initialization sequence started.

"All done," I announced, standing up and adjusting my pack on my shoulders.

"Finally," Reed said with a grin. "I can't wait to be back in a warm bed."

Rock nodded in agreement and started making his way back to the tunnel. As I adjusted the straps on my pack, I heard a sudden commotion and a scream. Looking up, I saw Reed's flashlight sweeping erratically through the cavern. It took me a moment to realize that he was running frantically. I noticed that Rock's flashlight was lying motionless on the ground, a couple of feet from a dark mound that I didn't recall being there before.

Without wasting any time, I quickly turned to train my gun on the mound as I quickly scanned my surroundings. As my eyes swept around the ground and my gun positioned toward the mound, its light identifying it as Rock motionless on the ground, I heard a slight noise above me and reacted instantly. My training and instincts kicked in, and I managed to adjust my weapon to pull the trigger as I rolled away just in time to avoid a lunging creature that was trying to land on top of me.

Coming out from the roll, I instinctively pulled the trigger of my gun multiple times as I trained it on the creature. It had landed awkwardly on the ground just two feet away, unable to recover from its miscalculated attack. With my shots at close range, the creature didn't stand a chance. Its head exploded into a shower of gore, leaving the lifeless human body crumpled on the ground.

I didn't hesitate to run after Reed, not waiting to see the body fall. Rock's motionless form only briefly crossed my mind before my training kicked in, knowing it was too late for him and urging me to catch up to Reed. Making the trek back to the base alone would be almost impossible, and I couldn't be left behind. As I closed in on Reed halfway to the tunnel, something caught my attention. A shadow passed between Reed's light and my view. It took me a moment to realize it was a second Zombie, but it wasn't moving like any that I had ever encountered before. In the chill air of the tunnels, all Zombies were slow, only capable of moving at a sluggish pace. The real danger with Zombies was their ability to ambush with quick lunges, but they needed to be in close proximity and in numbers to land a blow with their slow speed. It was one reason why the colony was so deep in the ground, but not too deep. Deeper down, it would be warmer, while the same was true for higher ground.

However, this one seemed different. The Zombie was moving surprisingly fast, even in the cold, and was outpacing Reed. I swiftly brought my gun up to my shoulder, taking careful aim to avoid hitting Reed, and pulled the trigger, firing off several shots at the creature. Thanks to my sharpshooting skills, the shot was simple enough, and the Zombie fell to the ground with a thud, motionless. It didn't even have a chance to see what hit it.

Reed must have sensed the bullets whizzing by him and turned to see the Zombie dropping to the ground. He also must have noticed the group of undead gradually closing in on us as I kept running because his hands tightened around his weapon as he knelt down to take aim at the tunnel entrance. I knew shooting from a distance in that position was his forte and where he felt most confident. He started firing rapidly, taking out the Zombies in rapid succession. I chanced a glance back as I ran and noticed that five that had been closing in on us had dropped dead. However, as they fell, more appeared in the

35

distance, their forms illuminated by the light emanating from the flashlight beside Rock's lifeless body.

"Automatic," Reed called out, but I had already anticipated his request and switched my rifle to full-auto mode. Without turning to shoot, I dropped an item on the ground while continuing to run. Reed noticed, and his gun roared to life, unleashing a hailstorm of a hundred bullets around me into the cavern. The clip emptied in mere seconds, and he swiftly replaced it, tucking the spent clip into his pants pocket. By the time he had loaded the new one, I had caught up with him. Neither of us looked back as a deafening explosion shook the area where I had dropped the grenade.

Without waiting for confirmation, we ran. We went down the tunnel from which we had come as fast as we could. After we had made it down two light hangers, I got a bad feeling and immediately called out, "Sweep and clear, three, two, one!"

We spun around in unison, guns raised, and began firing. I aimed from left to right while Reed took the opposite direction, spraying bullets in an arc. The sound of ten Zombies hitting the ground, riddled with bullets, echoed through the corridor. Reed quickly followed up with another sweep at a lower level, ensuring no smaller zombies were left behind. As Reed reloaded, I watched as more Zombies began to enter the tunnel. We needed to get out of there, and we both knew it. Without exchanging any words, we turned and ran, putting as much distance as possible between us and the relentless horde.

Chapter 4

THE CHASE

STAR: Lower Tunnels

After three hours of running, we were still moving at lightning speed. Despite our efforts, the Zombies were hot on our heels, always lingering just out of range but keeping us in sight. We couldn't seem to shake them off, no matter how fast we ran. It was a strange sight to behold, as we had never encountered Zombies that moved so quickly before. They seemed to be waiting for something, and the anticipation of it all only heightened our fear.

Reed, who was clearly frightened, asked, "What is their deal?"

I knew he was scared, but I didn't have an answer to his question. As we ran, I mulled over the problem, trying to devise a solution. "They are moving like I would if I had numbers on my side without long-range weapons," I finally replied. "They don't tire like we do. All they have to do is wait us out. We have to sleep at some point."

"I'm never sleeping again," Reed declared.

"Me neither," I grumbled back, frustrated that our predicament was seemingly unsolvable. These Zombies were acting unlike any other Zombies we had ever encountered. They seemed intelligent, almost as if they were purposefully trying to keep us on the run.

"We need a plan," Reed said.

"I'm working on it," I replied.

We continued to run forward in silence, our eyes peeled for any escape route. It wasn't until we made it to the end of the next hallway that an idea came to me.

"I have a plan," I announced. "But we need a hallway with two split-offs."

Reed pulled out his map, and after a quick glance, he said, "There should be one another two corridors down if I haven't lost my count."

Thankfully, it was Reed, and I knew I could count on Reed's unwavering navigation skills. He wouldn't lose count when his life depended on it. Just like he knew I would do whatever it took to get us out of this alive. We were a team, and we were going to survive this together.

We arrived at the intersection of two corridors as I finished explaining my plan to Reed. He didn't voice his opposition, but I knew he wasn't thrilled with it. Heck, I wasn't thrilled with it either, but at least we had a fighting chance, unlike poor Rock. Poor Rock, his body left with the zombies to either be consumed or turned. I shook my head and pushed thoughts of him out of my mind, not wanting to dwell on the fact that it could have been me or Reed in his place.

Reed headed down the first corridor to begin setting up while I hung back just around the corner, my machine gun at the ready. It didn't take long before I heard the telltale sounds of zombies approaching from the hallway we had just come down. I tensed, waiting for their noise to come into range so I could assess their distance and prepare to fire.

But then, something unexpected happened. Instead of the sound of footsteps, I heard voices coming from down the hallway. I was confused for a moment, wondering who had slipped in between the G-Zombies and us. I mean, there should only be Zombies wandering the tunnels. That was when I realized that it wasn't other people but the zombies who were talking. And not just any conversation—they were discussing us, their human prey. My heart sank as I listened to their discussion, realizing these were not your average zombies with superspeed. They were intelligent, and they had a plan to take us.

I heard a gruff voice speak first. "Why wa-it?"

A second, smoother voice responded. "I've told you already why."

"But why argg" he coughed up some flem before continuing, "tere only tree? Coudn't you-re have asked for mor-re? That's why-rg I had to get there firg. I needed my leg fix-ed."

"It's a human custom. They limit it to three, so they don't have a chance to fight back when we strike. Normally when everyone follows the plan anyway. That is why we had to split our efforts."

"Still-er dumb. Why arg we allo-ing tese humans to make demands anyway? Tey don't have-er anyting to offer essept for tey're young."

"The queen's doesn't have to listen to a creature as beneither her as you."

"Well, if she did, we-er wouldn't be in tis situation."

"We would have them already if you hadn't messed up the ambush. We should have had all three, but you were greedy and didn't wait until the others were in position."

I realized that these zombies were not acting on instinct but rather under the direction of a higher power. And they had been planning this with someone in the tower. Panic set in as I realized just how dire our situation was.

Suddenly, the sound of the zombies approaching stopped, and I heard a loud smash followed by the thud of a body hitting the ground. The smooth voice returned, barely above a whisper. "Clinglings, so hard to control. I don't even know why the queen puts up with them."

Reed's footsteps broke the silence, and I snapped out of my trance. He was making his way from the first offshoot's entrance to the second. It was time to put my plan into action.

"Something's off," I heard one say, and the undead, or at least what passed for them, quickened their pace. Without hesitation, I stepped out and unleashed a hail of bullets into the oncoming horde. The muzzle of my weapon flashed in the dim light, and I made sure to keep the focus of my eyes away from the blinding light. The smell of gunpowder reached my senses as the bullets flew true. To my surprise, though, some of the zombies used metal scraps as shields, and only two fell to my initial barrage. I didn't bother to send a second and turned, sprinting down the hallway as I reloaded. I breathed in relief as I caught a glimpse of Reed disappearing into the second break-off. Everything was set. I moved quickly and took the first offshoot, pounding hard on the ground so the Zombies would know to follow. As I made my way down the underground hall, I searched the ground thoroughly. Reed had rigged both paths with explosives and a tripwire and shattered the light fixture on the wall near where he had placed the wire. Using the flashlight mounted on my gun, I located the tripwire in the first offshoot and jumped over it. Afterward, I careened down the corridor as fast as I could, the zombies closing in on me with each passing second.

Suddenly, a deafening explosion reverberated through the tunnel, sending me sprawling to the ground. I quickly picked myself up my hands searching for my weapon that had flown out of my hand as I had dropped. As I did, I looked back, searching for any sign of my pursuers. As my hands grasped my weapon, the dust slowly cleared, falling to the ground. I sighed in relief only after it dissipated enough to reveal a heap of debris blocking the path between me and the zombies. It would serve as a barricade against regular zombies for sure, but my pursuers had possessed intelligence and probably could dig their way through.

I didn't know if it would stop them or just slow them down. That wasn't my concern at the moment. I just ran. As I did, I strained to listen for a second explosion, which would signal that the zombies were now pursuing Reed. Luckily, none came, so I pressed on with high hopes. Perhaps the blast had taken out all of our pursuers. Still, I couldn't count on that. They could get through somehow, and I still had several days of tunnel travel ahead of me, alone and vulnerable. There was plenty of danger in front of me. If I could, I'd like to reduce how much by limiting the amount of time I was out here. Being quicker was more dangerous in the short term, but not making it back promptly risked more time sleeping in the open, which was far more hazardous. It was time to move with speed.

I pushed myself to the limit on my way back home, eager to catch up with Reed before reaching the colony. It was a long and treacherous journey, and If I could meet up with him, I would have someone to watch my back, which was crucial, especially after what had happened in the cavern.

As I ran, I thought about all that had happened and what I was facing. It wasn't just the long return journey and the risk of going it alone that troubled me; it was what I overheard from the creatures. If what I heard was true, we were sent out as sacrificial pawns. When I returned, the leaders back at the tower had some explaining to do.

I barely slept for more than three hours at a time, constantly on the lookout for any sign of danger. Surprisingly, I encountered more small groups of regular G-Zombies than usual, but at least they were manageable. Fortunately, I didn't come across any more of those strange ones that had attacked us in the cavern. As they hadn't come from behind yet, I assumed that they had perished in the explosion, which had been designed to cover at least a fifteen-foot area of the tunnel. From what I remembered, there hadn't been that many of them in that area when Reed was setting up the explosives.

The dark tunnel was a place of eerie uncertainty, where every step seemed to carry the possibility of danger. Broken lights flickered and blinked intermittently, casting an uneven and unsettling light that played tricks on my eyes. Each blink seemed to plunge the tunnel into even deeper darkness before the dim light returned, highlighting the rusted pipes and metal supports that lined the walls. The intermittent lighting left large sections of the tunnel shrouded in darkness, with only the slightest hint of light creeping in from the few remaining working bulbs. The blinking lights seemed to dance with the shadows, casting an ever-changing pattern of light and dark that played tricks on the mind. The silence was oppressive, broken only by the sound of my footsteps echoing through the tunnel. The only other sounds were the faint drip of water from the ceiling and the occasional creaking of metal supports. It was as if the darkness itself was alive, holding its breath and waiting for the right moment to strike.

I felt a sense of unease deep in my bones, a primal fear that was hard to shake. The darkness seemed to be closing in on me, threatening to swallow me whole. The broken lights added to the sense of foreboding as if the tunnel was trying to hide something just beyond the reach of the flickering bulbs. Each step was a reminder of the danger lurking just out of sight. It was hard to tell if the shadows were playing tricks on my eyes, but I felt like I could see movement just at the edge of my vision. The darkness was alive, and I was just a trespasser in its realm. The blinking lights were like a warning, a beacon of danger that flickered in the darkness. They created an eerie atmosphere that was hard to shake, a feeling of being watched by unseen eyes. It was a place where anything could happen, where danger lurked in the shadows, waiting to strike.

The days blurred together into a relentless march of exhaustion and anxiety. I barely slept, instead pushing myself to maintain a breakneck pace. I couldn't help but worry about Reed, who had taken a different route, or was he simply faster than I had realized? My thoughts were always consumed with my missing friend and the endless jog ahead. Even when I came to the offshoots, I didn't slow down. Instead, I kept my gun at the ready, scanning each one as I ran by. The darkness and broken, flickering lights only heightened my sense of unease. I couldn't afford to be caught off guard by a zombie lurking in the shadows. Indeed, I faced several ambushes, but their attacks were always sloppy, the zombies failing to predict the trajectory of my fast-moving form. I kept running, firing into the shadows as I went, only stopping to finish off any stragglers that dared to venture into my longer hallway.

As I ventured deeper into the treacherous southern corridors, a day's journey away from the colony and closer to the towering structure, I heard the sporadic sounds of gunfire that were ingrained in our training. My instincts kicked in, and I rushed toward the commotion, assuming the skirmish had already ended. As I drew near, the gunfire ceased, prompting me to tread cautiously. Peering around the corner, I immediately recognized the voices of Stump and Redwood, two veteran tunnel scouts who were approaching their thirties at the ages of twenty-eight and twenty-nine, respectively. They were still actively working as scouts, a rarity for their age group.

Stump turned to Redwood and asked, "Looking forward to retirement?"

Redwood responded with a nod and said, "Yep, almost reached my thirties. Just seven more months, and I'll be on the 500th floor. You mustn't have that much longer than me."

Stump grunted, "Fourteen months. I can't wait to be out of this business."

The conversation caught me off guard. I had no idea people moved up in the tower when they reached thirty. I was about to pop out and ask about it when I heard a third voice coming from the other end of the corridor, past Redwood and Stump. It was Reed, slowly making his way toward the two older men. "Man, I'm glad to see you guys," he said. "You wouldn't believe what I've been through."

Before I could run forward to greet my friend, a gunshot sounded. Reed clutched his chest as blood started to spurt out of the hole that now existed in his body. Redwood lowered his gun, which had been trained on Reed just a moment ago.

"Why?" came the plea out of Reed's mouth.

Redwood replied coldly, "Sorry lad, you weren't meant to come back alive."

He raised his gun again to finish the job, but I acted quickly and fired two short volleys of bullets down the hallway into the two older men. They hadn't even known that I was behind them before they expired.

Ignoring the fresh corpses and the dozen slightly older zombie corpses that littered the ground, I rushed to Reed's side. He was clutching his wound and having difficulty breathing.

"Star?" he asked weakly.

"Be quiet. Let me have a look at it," I said, pulling his hand away from the wound and quickly putting it back. "Keep

43

pressure on that while I roll you over." As I rolled him onto his side to get at his back, Reed yelled out in pain. The bullet had entered around his left lung and passed through the frontal ribs. It must have nicked one on the back, though, as there was a large exit wound on his back. A small piece of bone was still sticking out of the skin at an angle. Blood was pooling out of the larger wound.

Having dealt with accidents all our lives, I wasn't exactly unprepared. Unfortunately, bullet wounds weren't uncommon in the lower levels of the tower. In this case, it was a good thing as it gave me enough training to know somewhat how to help my friend. I quickly took out my knife from one of my many pockets and tore at Reed's shirt. I undid the straps of his backpack and cut him out of his long-sleeved army-issued jacket and shirt. Despite not having all the tools I would have liked, I did my best to stop the bleeding. The location of the wound was scary, and I didn't know if Reed would make it. Still, I put my all into helping my friend. When I finally finished, I knew only time would tell whether my efforts would save my friend.

Chapter 5

GUN FIRE

STAR: Lower Tunnels

Reed lay asleep, his breathing slow and shallow as I sat on the ground next to him, trying to gather my thoughts. It was proving difficult as the weight of the situation was hitting me like a ton of bricks. My mind raced with thoughts. It started off with the need to warn the others in the tower of what had transpired. Initially, I would have as soon as I could get Reed on his feet. But as I sat there thinking, it became clear that it would be pointless to go back. I had just killed two scouts of the tower, and it wouldn't take long for them to realize that bullets, not zombies, had ended their lives. Moreover, these two were planning to kill Reed and me just to make it back from a mission we shouldn't have survived. Something was wrong in the tower, and it was no longer safe. The moment we revealed ourselves, they could very well take us out. There was no telling who we could trust. The more I thought about it, the more I realized what a precarious position we were in. We could easily be called liars and murderers by those who were on Redwood and Stump's side.

I knew I had to come up with a new plan, but what could I do? Reed was in no condition to move, and I didn't even know if he would make it. It seemed unlikely, given the severity of his wound, but I refused to leave him behind. I needed to find a way to keep us both alive and fast.

Realizing that I couldn't afford to waste any time, I got to my feet. I examined our dire situation and started to take inventory of everything we had left. I meticulously went through all of our pockets and packs, as well as the gear and equipment from Stump and Redwood. It wasn't a pretty sight - Reed and I only had five days' worth of food left, and even with the supplies I had pilfered from the dead bodies, we would only have enough for ten days if we rationed strictly. It was clear we needed to find a way to get more food, but I didn't have any ideas on how to do that in the tunnels.

I continued to assess our remaining resources: we had explosives, eight firearms, two gun mounts, ammo, four swords, two sleeping bags, a travel-sized toolkit, ten water canisters with four water purifiers, two lighters, a pack of cigarettes, and two rolls of toiletries. I even stripped the clothes off the bodies of the two men I had killed and laid them out next to their other belongings.

Reed stirred, and I went over to him. He looked up at me and whispered, "Star?"

"I'm here, buddy," I whispered back.

"Why did they shoot me?" he asked with confusion in his eyes.

"It seems like the tower set us up," I replied, gritting my teeth. "They didn't want us to make it back."

"Why?" he asked.

"I don't know," I said, shaking my head. "But we can't go back."

"Where can we go?" Reed asked desperation in his voice.

"I don't know," I said. "But I think our best bet is to head up."

"But they always said death was above," Reed muttered. "The zombies are faster up there."

"Well, it seems like the zombies are pretty fast down here, too," I said bitterly. "Getting out of here is our top priority, but there isn't enough food to last more than a few days on this level. Going up is our only hope now."

Reed nodded and then suggested, "You should leave me. You won't make it with me slowing you down. Without me, you'll make it farther with the food supplies. I can push my luck with the tower. Maybe they will let me come back."

"No," I said firmly. "I'm not leaving you behind. We'll make it farther together than alone. Without someone watching my back, I'm as good as dead. Either we both make it, or we both don't, so don't get morbid with me. You have to get better."

46

"Moving hurts, though," Reed whimpered as he shifted slightly.

"Then I'll carry you as we go," I said resolutely.

"That won't work," Reed protested.

"I know," I said, looking around at our surroundings and then at our meager supplies. A grim smile crept onto my face. "It's time to make do with what we have."

After four long hours, I managed to put together a makeshift contraption that even I looked skeptically at. The wheels were a combination of the light cages lining the hallway and the rubber-coated wire wrapped around them, held together by clothing and tripwire. The axles were made from sniper rifle barrels, and the frame of the cart was built from gun parts, swords, sheaths, belts, wire, and clothing. Although it was far from aesthetically pleasing, it did the job. The front was open, and the back was built up with handles fashioned from the butts of guns. We still had four guns left - two snipers and two machine guns - all assembled and ready for action.

When I finished building the contraption, Reed was still fast asleep. I had to wake him up, knowing that we couldn't afford to stay in one place for too long. We were in a dangerous area, and another patrol could come by at any moment. Although it was unlikely, the fact that Stump and Redwood hadn't returned made it all the more possible. We had to quickly move if we wanted to avoid being caught.

Reed woke up groggily, and I reassured him that everything was alright. I helped him sit up, and he finally laid his eyes on the contraption. He was unimpressed. "What is that? It looks like it's going to fall apart any moment."

"I had limited supplies," I explained. "But don't worry, I've already tested it with my weight. It'll hold just fine."

Reed grumbled, "Well, it beats this unforgiving ground."

I wheeled the contraption over and helped Reed onto it, placing a loaded gun mount in front of him. "There, now you're useful."

"Thanks," Reed muttered.

I checked all the other packs hanging from the cart and shouldered Reed's own pack. As I prepared to move forward, I reminded myself of our goal: stay alive. It wouldn't be easy, but I knew we could do it. After all, we had no other acceptable choice.

With Reed situated in the cart, I took a deep breath and began pushing it forward. It wasn't the smoothest ride, but it was better than leaving Reed and equipment behind. The makeshift wheels rolled over rocks and debris as we made our way through the tunnel.

As we continued down the dark path, I couldn't help but feel uneasy. Every sound echoed, making it impossible to tell where it was coming from. It was nerve-wracking, but I knew we had to keep moving. We couldn't afford to stay in one spot for too long, not with the risk of being caught.

The blinking lights in the tunnel reminded me of our first mission together, when Reed and I, along with a group of other newbies, were tasked with stopping a group of zombies that had gathered along the western tunnel. We were inexperienced and nervous, but we worked together to come up with a plan. We had managed to lure the zombies away and into an abandoned mine, where we trapped them and took them out one by one.

I smiled to myself as I remembered Reed's jokes and laughter as we had celebrated our victory that day. It seemed like a lifetime ago, but it had only been a few years. Since then, we have been on hundreds of missions together, many more dangerous as well. But we had always managed to come out on top, thanks to our trust in each other and our ability to work as a team.

As I continued to push the contraption through the dark and eerie tunnel, I was grateful to have Reed by my side. Despite the danger, I felt a sense of calm knowing that we were in this together. I was determined to get us out of this situation alive, and I knew Reed felt the same.

The sound of footsteps echoing through the tunnel brought me back to the present. I quickly looked around, trying to pinpoint where the sound was coming from. My heart raced as I realized that another patrol could be nearby. We had to move quickly and quietly if we wanted to avoid being caught.

"Reed," I whispered urgently. "We need to pick up the pace. I think there might be another patrol nearby."

Reed nodded, his face grim. We quickened our pace, pushing the contraption as fast as I could without making too much noise. We had to get out of there before it was too late.

Chapter 6
ALONE IN THE TUNNELS
STAR: Lower Unexplored Tunnels

After six hours of pushing forward, my body had reached its limit. Physically and mentally exhausted, I couldn't go any further. Meanwhile, Reed had been sleeping most of the time, except for the moment when we stumbled upon a small group of zombies. As I took them out with precise shots to the head. Reed had briefly woken up and had simply watched before falling back asleep.

In the middle of a tunnel, I gently shook Reed's face. "Hey, wake up," I whispered.

He jolted awake, reaching for his weapon mounted on the cart. However, to his surprise, there were now four mounted weapons, two on each side of him. I had positioned him sideways so he could easily access them—a sniper rifle and a machine gun on either side.

Crouching next to him, I placed a hand on his shoulder. Exhaustion was etched on my face, and I knew that I had to rest. "Sorry, but I need to sleep," I said.

Reed understood and knew how much I had done to help him. "Oh, yeah," he said.

"I wouldn't want to be stuck here with anyone else other than you," I muttered under my breath.

"Not even Wind?" Reed teased.

I smiled and snorted at his mention of Wind. "I'd rather you be out here than her. I wouldn't want her in danger. Plus, you're better company than she is when she's in a foul mood, and I don't have good food to cook here to cheer her up. She would probably always be in a foul mood."

"You're right, I wouldn't wish that horror on anyone," Reed agreed.

Gently patting his shoulder, I hopped down into my sleeping bag that was already laid out on the ground beside the cart. I would have liked to banter just a bit more to ease both

Reed and my nerves, but my tiredness overwhelmed me, and I quickly fell asleep.

However, I was soon awoken by Reed prodding me. "What?" I asked groggily.

"Dude, we have to start moving," he whispered urgently.

Confused, I asked why, but Reed just told me we needed to go. It was then that I noticed he was up and moving despite having been on the brink of death the previous night.

"Did we die?" I asked, my mind racing.

"Not yet, but we will be if we don't get moving," Reed replied.

I noticed the cart was already packed, and we started moving away from the noise. The sound of slow footsteps filled the air, and Reed confirmed that it was the largest horde he had ever encountered from the sound of it.

Making our way down the tunnel, I asked Reed if he was okay with continuing to move. He admitted that he was having trouble breathing, and I pointed out that the bullet had punctured his lung.

"I thought you died if you got shot in the lung," Reed muttered.

"Well, you're not dead yet," I quipped, trying to lighten the mood. "Let's prove whoever you heard that from wrong."

Reed forced a smile and added, "On the plus side, I feel better than I did yesterday. While you were pulling me, I mean."

"If you need to rest, get on the cart," I offered.

That day, the zombies remained out of sight, and as time passed, the clamor died down. We made good progress, putting some distance between us and the horde. However, our luck ran out when we stumbled upon two dozen zombies in the middle of the day. It delayed us and, unfortunately, gave away our direction to the approaching horde. "We've got a problem," I grumbled as I pushed the cart with Reed on it away from the corpses we left behind.

"Only one?" Reed quipped.

"Well, only one that matters for today," I replied.

"What's that?" he asked.

"Zombies don't sleep. We won't survive the night sleeping," I muttered.

"We'll have to take turns then," Reed responded matter-of-factly. "We can sleep on the cart as we move," he suggested.

"Wouldn't that be too strenuous on your body?" I asked.

"Do you have a better idea?" he retorted.

"No," I conceded.

"Then that settles it. I'll take the first shift since I'm already tired. I stayed up all night watching you," he continued.

I nodded silently, knowing that Reed didn't need a response. He was already tucking his head to get comfortable with a rolled shirt. Pushing the cart using the gun stock handles, I thought about how wonderful it would be to have a warm bath, but I doubted I would ever have that luxury again. Reed and I were likely to die in these tunnels. I quickly shook my head at the thought. *No, we will live. Whatever it takes.*

For the next eight hours, I pushed Reed's sleeping body, only pausing for food and drink twice. One of those breaks also led to a small pile of excrement being left on the side of the tunnel. Two other stops were unplanned, one being when we stumbled upon a group of thirty zombies at the end of a hallway. Reed stirred awake at the sound of gunshots, but I instructed him to go back to sleep as I systematically took down the undead before continuing on our journey. I had to be careful as I walked by the dead bodies. I knew from training that Zombies didn't have blood like humans. The microbodies that infected their bodies repurposed their circulatory system, making their bodily fluids thick and paste-like. My training taught me that it took twenty-four hours after the removal or destruction of the brain for the microorganisms to fully die off throughout the body. Without the controlling portion of their ecosystem, their bodies would wither away like any other corpse. The real danger in fighting zombies was the risk of a single scratch or bite that could break the skin and inject small colonies of the zombie's microbodies into an unsuspecting human. These colonies would grow rapidly, slowly infecting the human until the host body was lost to the microbodies.

While pushing the cart, my mind was occupied with thoughts of zombies. My training covered everything from the most effective ways to fight them with a sword to the importance of avoiding even a single scratch. I also had a good understanding of how zombies operated. Unlike humans, zombies didn't require food for daily use, but they could consume human flesh to replace parts of their bodies. They had developed the ability to store excess body parts that they consumed as tumors in case of injury, which could be reabsorbed to replace damaged parts. It was interesting to note that they only consumed humans and not other creatures, although the tower had conducted a few experiments with the limited variety of animals they had on hand. I wasn't sure if this was true for all creatures since the varieties that the colony had were limited.

One of the biggest things we learned was just how much damage had to be inflicted on the head of a zombie in order to kill it. Even with just 30% of its brain mass intact, a zombie could still consume the brains of a human and regrow the rest. But a bullet through the skull usually did the job as our bullets were designed to break on impact and splinter outward causing enough damage to prevent any chance of regrowth. The splintering effect of the bullets was also my cause of concern, but Reed seemed to be doing surprisingly well despite being shot by one. I refocused my thoughts on summarizing what I knew about zombies, determined to use every bit of knowledge I had to ensure our survival.

I thought about how zombies could regenerate their bodies, but it took time. A hamstring could take up to fifteen minutes to reattach, and an arm could take up to a week to regrow, as long as the zombie had the necessary excess mass. I reviewed the sword fighting techniques that were drilled into me during training, knowing that we couldn't rely on an endless supply of bullets. While we were currently low on food, it wouldn't be long before we ran out of bullets, too. I calculated

53

that I could easily take on a group of a dozen zombies with my sword, but we were always taught not to take unnecessary risks, as even a small mistake could lead to infection. However, with our limited resources, I knew that I needed to take on more risk if we were going to survive. I didn't tell Reed about my plan since he was in no condition to help me. When he woke up, I filled him in on our progress and then took my turn resting in the cart.

For three days, I had refrained from using my gun. The goal was to stay ahead of the horde, but unfortunately, they always seemed to catch up during Reed's shifts. These shifts were only three hours long, leaving me with only short and broken sleep. It was taking a toll on me, but I had no other choice. I came across fewer zombie groups than usual, only five in total. The groups varied in size, ranging from six to twenty zombies. Each time, I left Reed behind and unsheathed my sword before approaching the group. The objective was to disable the zombies, which I accomplished by cutting tendons and joints to make their limbs useless. Once immobilized, I quickly and efficiently scrambled their brains by thrusting my sword through their eye sockets and spinning it around inside. Reed was awake for the last encounter and complimented my speed and efficiency.

"Good job," Reed said. "Efficient."

"We can't waste ammo," I replied, shrugging.

"You're right. I'm in no shape to do that, though," he said, shrugging before he realized it was a mistake.

"I know. That's why I haven't asked you to do the same," I replied, grinning.

"I never was as good with a sword as you were," Reed admitted.

"I know, but you might have to use it soon. We don't have a means of restocking our supplies," I warned.

"This won't matter if we don't find any food," Reed stated.

"True, let's keep moving," I suggested, knowing that time was of the essence.

Reed and I had been walking for almost an hour in silence when he suddenly spoke up. "You know, I was just thinking about our days in sword training," he said, his voice distant with nostalgia.

I turned to him, curious. "What about it?" I asked.

"Well, I remember being really impressed by your speed and reflexes," he replied. "You were always one of the fastest in the class."

I chuckled at the memory. "Yeah, I was pretty good with a sword back then," I said. "But it's been a while since I've had to use one in real life."

Reed nodded in agreement. "Same here," he said. "But I also remember how level-headed you were, even in the heat of the moment. That's something that's really important out here."

After another day of wandering, we finally stumbled upon a set of stairs. It was a refreshing change from the monotony of the tunnels, so we decided to take them up to explore. Together, we collapsed the cart and hoisted it up the stairs with us. Since our supplies were running low, it wasn't too heavy to carry. After sixty stories, we reached a different tunnel system that had a different feel to it. The air was warmer, and there was a slight draft coming from one of the sides. As we walked, we noticed that there were more pipes lining the walls than we had seen before.

The pipes were rusted, some with patches of mold growing on them. They were criss crossing each other in every direction, creating a maze-like pattern on the walls. The new tunnel system also had a different layout, with wider tunnels and higher ceilings, giving us more breathing room.

The lighting was also different. The spacing between light fixtures was smaller, allowing the dim light to be that much brighter. There also seemed to be fewer sections of broken lights. With the brighter lighting came a sense of security. We could see further down the tunnel, and it was easier to spot any potential threats.

We continued walking upwind toward the source of air, and we noticed a few alcoves and side passages branching off from the main tunnel. These were also wider than before, which was a new sight for us. We barely resisted the temptation to explore, but we decided to stick to the main tunnel for now since our priority was to find food and supplies.

Despite being on a new floor, we had only encountered one group of zombies after two hours of walking. These ones were quicker than the ones we had faced earlier, so I had to be more careful in my approach. With my sword in hand, I made small adjustments to my fighting style to keep a safe distance from the creatures. Anything to avoid their infectious touch.

Reed spoke up an hour later, "What's that up ahead?" I was so focused on pushing my friend, whose turn it was to rest in the cart, that I hadn't noticed anything peculiar at the other end of the tunnel. I almost chided him for not sleeping when he should be, but then I realized how difficult it would be to sleep with all the strange tunnels and new surroundings. The tension was palpable, and the pressure of staying ahead of the pursuing horde was taking its toll on both of us.

"What do you think?" Reed asked when I didn't respond.

"I can't see it," I said, and he suggested I use my scope. I looked down the tunnel and realized what I thought was the end was actually a partial blockage caused by a single mushroom.

"It's a mushroom," I said.

"Is it edible?" Reed asked, concerned about our dwindling supplies.

"I'm not sure. It's nothing like what they grow in the tower," I replied, and we moved closer to investigate.

"Great! That means one of us has to test it," Reed grumbled, already knowing who that would be.

"Thanks for volunteering," I said, agreeing with him. "At least I'll have a full stomach if it's not poisonous," he grinned.

"Not so fast," I interjected. "Your plan wasn't to eat a whole bunch of it at once, was it?"

"Why not? I'm starving on the rations you've been doling out," he complained.

"You're going to try a very small amount first and see if you get sick from it. Only one small amount today, and then you can try a larger portion tomorrow. If it's not poisonous, you can fill your stomach on the third day," I proposed.

Reed considered it and agreed it was a wise plan. We made our way to the mushroom and began carving out large chunks, filling the cart, our pockets, and our packs.

"Do you think it's nutritious?" Reed asked.

"It doesn't matter all that much," I replied, patting the pocket that held our vitamin pills. "We have another three months' supply of vitamins."

"Still, we'll need to get what we need from foraging eventually," Reed said thoughtfully.

I nodded, pushing the cart forward. We cleared a small portion of the mushroom and took as much as we could carry.

"It's too bad we couldn't bring more with us," Reed remarked. "Hopefully, there will be more along the way."

"That is if it's not poisonous," I said, cautioning him.

"Well, there's only one way to find out," Reed said, popping a piece of the mushroom into his mouth before I could stop him.

"How big of a piece did you try?" I asked.

Reed showed me, and I shook my head. "That's way too much for the first trial," I said, rolling my eyes.

"Well, too late now," Reed grumbled.

"At least you didn't take a full bite," I replied.

"Now all we have to do is wait and see if I'm alive tomorrow," he grinned.

"Don't go dying on me. I've carted your useless corpse this far, and I don't want it to be in total vain," I joked.

Reed gave me a thumbs-up and settled in for his nap on the cart.

Chapter 7
RUDE AWAKENING
REED: Unexplored Tunnels

Gunshots rang out three hours later, jolting me awake. I hadn't heard the sound of gunfire in days and was startled. I quickly scanned my surroundings but saw nothing out of the ordinary. My eyes eventually settled on Star, who had set up his sniper and was methodically loading and shooting. I looked down the hallway and found a horde of zombies making their way to us. I reached for the gun mounted in front of me to help but realized it was the machine gun, which wasn't the proper tool for the distance the zombies were. I grumbled to myself, swapping it out for the sniper. Meanwhile, Star fired five more rounds down the tunnel.

I squinted down the tunnel, my aim all over the place. I spotted the horde of zombies coming down the opposite end of the tunnel, the direction from which we had been running. My sense of direction was disoriented since I had slept through most of our journey. "What's going on?" I asked.

"I came across a group in front, and I didn't see any recent offshoots that we can backtrack to. We'll have to go through those, or we are done," Star explained, continuing to fire and load without missing a beat.

I struggled to dismount the machine gun, feeling self-conscious about my fumbling fingers. I was wasting precious time, and it was taking me much longer than it should have to mount the sniper in place. After finally getting it set up, I called out to Star, "Ready."

"Take the right," Star responded, and our rate of fire increased as we continued to take out the zombies with headshots. But our concern grew as we noticed how quickly we were depleting our ammo. "We won't have enough ammo for this," Star said, stopping mid-shot.

"What can we do?" I asked, fear creeping into my voice.

"Keep firing and taking the right side. I've got the left," Star said, unsheathing his blade. I started to protest, insisting there were too many, but Star simply smiled and reassured me that he would be fine. He then sprinted down the tunnel while I focused on the rhythm of loading, aiming, and firing.

As Star made his way down to meet the oncoming zombies, the left side was reduced in numbers, and the fallen bodies clogged that side of the passageway, helping to funnel the zombies. I missed a beat as I watched Star dance gracefully with his sword, effortlessly taking out the creatures that lunged and growled at him. I noticed many of the zombies had missing flesh, not having the resources to heal their bodies fully prior to this encounter. They were different from the ones that had been attacking the colony recently, which had been much more whole. I wondered briefly at the difference between the creatures but was quickly lost when I refocused on what I was supposed to be doing.

I continued firing, aiming, and reloading, but the rate of zombies dropping was much slower than Star's graceful swordplay. As Star slashed through the creatures, I fired another thirty rounds. It was clear we were running low on ammo, and I worried if I had enough for this bout or would I run out and leave Star to get overrun.

Chapter 8
EXPLORING
STAR: Unexplored Tunnels

My sword went limp in my hand as I stood, my body drained after dispatching over six hundred creatures that craved my flesh. I had no more strength to continue fighting or even move on. The lack of sleep and constant stress had depleted my energy, and I knew my body could only take so much. Though I tried to keep myself together for Reed's sake, I could feel my body giving up on me. I swayed on my feet, feeling like I had reached my breaking point, but then steadied myself and turned to find Reed standing just a hundred feet away. *Had the Zombies pushed me that far back?*

Even as I made my way back to him, Reed loaded his gun on the cart and pushed it toward me. "You alright?" he asked. "I'll be after I sleep," I replied, feeling tired and drained. Reed expressed his awe at my performance, but I knew we could not take such a risk again. Reed nodded in agreement.

"You look terrible," Reed said to me. I shrugged and sat down, asking for five minutes before we proceeded. Reed nodded and went to inspect the best way to traverse the minefield of bodies. After thirty minutes, we made our way across with only two zombies trying to pull themselves towards us. Reed quickly dispatched them with his sword. Once across, I collapsed into the cart and fell asleep without another thought.

I slept for six hours before Reed woke me up, unable to handle the pain his wounds were causing. Moreover, his slower speed had me worried about how close the large horde following us was getting. We had also used up precious buffer space between us and the Zombies in the previous fight. The tunnel ahead of us added to the urgency to wake me up.

"Something's off up ahead," Reed said as I blinked awake. "What is it?" I asked. "See for yourself," he replied. I pulled myself up and looked down a tunnel that was layered with other offshoots and doors. The bright light at the end of the hallway, almost five miles down, was unlike anything I had ever seen before. Not a single Greed Zombie was in sight.

"Take your machine gun and keep pushing the cart, but be ready. I'll take point with my sword," I suggested to Reed. He agreed, and we moved forward together, ignoring the doors that seemed more dangerous than the open tunnel ahead with its offshoots. We moved deliberately, still being pursued by the horde, but we didn't rush down the hallway. Minutes passed, and we passed by fifty doors and six tunnel offshoots. The doors became thicker as we moved down, but no Zombies crept out from the offshoots. Soon, we found ourselves at the end of the tunnel, staring in awe at the view.

A tear in the earth had ripped apart the tunnel, exposing rooms that had been split apart and strong earthen walls on the far side, five hundred feet across the abyss. A strange light came in from above, illuminating the entire area. It was the first time we had ever been exposed to so much open space. We saw on the far wall rooms and tunnels that had been split apart from this side.

"What is this place?" Reed asked. "Not sure, but it's a death trap," I replied. "No kidding. This is worse than the southern tunnels," he grumbled. I nodded but then slumped to the side of the tunnel wall. "We can't keep moving as we are right now either," I said.

"What do you mean?" Reed asked.

"I'm exhausted," I said tiredly. "I've been sleeping only two to three hours at a time. With that and the lack of food..." I shrugged.

"We can't just wait and face them. We don't have the ammo for that," Reed said.

"Agreed," I said, my eyes wandering around our surroundings. The tunnel walls had many more utility lines, and air ducts were scattered along the wall much more frequently as well. The doors could provide some shelter, but we could never outwait a Greed Zombie, let alone a horde. I couldn't pick out a way to keep away from the Zombies. I felt like our struggle had been futile. There wasn't a way out of this. My eyes went back to the open space of the tunnel. If only we could get across, the Zombies wouldn't be able to follow.

Reed sat down next to me slowly, holding his chest. "It's not looking good," he mentioned.

"No, it's not," I replied.

"I guess we'll have to do something crazy. I'd rather jump before the Zombies turned me," Reed said.

"Agreed," I said, scooting over to the lip to look down. It was looking down that got me thinking. It was risky and crazy, but we wouldn't last another day with my energy level. Reed wasn't doing much better with a wound through his chest. It seemed to be too much to have asked for him to recover in a couple days. It was already a large blessing in itself that he wasn't dead yet. But without rest, I wouldn't be able to recover either. "Do you want to take a risk with me?" I asked.

"Will it kill us?" he asked.

"Possibly, but the Zombies won't get us," I replied. "Let's hear it," he grinned.

I explained my idea, and Reed didn't have a better one, so I went to work while Reed sighted down the tunnel we had come from.

Chapter 9
THE GAMBLE FOR REST
STAR: The Abyss

Reed gripped my shoulder as he peered into the seemingly endless void. "Are you absolutely sure about this?" Reed's voice quavered with unease.

"I've already tested it," I reassured him, hoping to alleviate his fears. "It's a long way down," Reed muttered.

I attempted to decipher Reed's facial expression, searching for any hint that he would jump or not. "You said that falling would be a better fate," I taunted him.

"Compared to being eaten by a zombie, yes. But that doesn't mean I want to willingly throw myself to my death," Reed gasped.

I double-checked all of the straps and made a few adjustments, feeling satisfied with the results. I then turned to Reed. "Are you ready?" I inquired.

"I don't think I am," Reed admitted.

"Reed, we need to hurry," I sighed, glancing down the long tunnel. Although the noise emanating from it was becoming louder, I couldn't discern anything with my naked eye. However, time was running out as we needed to descend and anchor ourselves to the wall. Without that anchor, the zombies would likely haul us up. I glanced back at my wavering friend.

"Time's up," I declared, stepping forward and placing my hand on Reed's shoulder. "It will be less painful if you let me lower you down," I added. Reed stared at the hand on his back with wide eyes. "Alright, I'll go," he finally relented, realizing I was about to push him off.

I nodded and assisted Reed as he positioned his legs over the ledge. Although hesitant, he was encased within a sleeping bag that was attached to a metal mesh tubing being used as a rope. A second, longer line served as a backup and was also harnessed around Reed. Finally, Reed nodded and began sliding over the edge. I held onto the tubing that had once been part of a utility line running along the roof of the tunnel. I lowered Reed one arm's length at a time into the murky darkness below. The light that had once illuminated the tunnel had dimmed significantly, putting me on high alert. Although it was still brighter than other tunnels we had traversed, the fading light made it feel like time was running out until total darkness engulfed us. Despite feeling the pressure of the ticking clock, I lowered Reed down slowly, avoiding any sudden movements that might aggravate his still-healing injuries.

If he even will, came a stray thought. I quickly shut down the train of thought that pondered whether Reed would survive such a wound. He had to make it, or else I would be left alone to face death. As I looked over the edge, I saw several lines carrying our equipment, including Reed's open sleeping bag encased in tubing for support. "You're down. How are you doing?" I asked him.

Reed looked around helplessly and replied, "Scared to death. I won't be able to pull myself out in my state."

"I know. I'll be right down," I assured him.

After securing my harness and sleeping bag lines, I lowered myself down to the floor with my sniper in hand. As I surveyed the hallway, I saw a horde of zombies making their way slowly towards us. I quickly stowed my gun in my sleeping bag and slid over the edge, using one of the hanging lines to descend into the darkness.

Reed watched me silently until I reached him, but I gestured for him to remain quiet. "They've reached the hallway. They will be here soon. Our best chance is silence. Let's hurry up and anchor ourselves so they can't pull us up," I whispered.

Reed nodded, and we began rocking our bodies forward and backward to gain momentum. It was a slow process; I forced myself to push away thoughts of the zombies lurking above as I focused on reaching the cave wall. The wall had been partially obscured before, but now I could see the supports of the tunnel below the overhang, with small metal pieces jutting out at odd angles, perfect for our needs. The cable length we had prepared was tucked away in our sleeping bags, ready to be hooked onto one of those metal protrusions to keep us hidden from any zombies peering down.

I swung back and forth, trying to build momentum to reach the wall. It took several swings, but eventually, I was careening past Reed, who was swinging in the opposite direction, our apex only feet from the wall. As I neared the wall, I worried that we wouldn't make it in time. The noise from above was deafening.

Seeing the wall coming toward me, I thought I had finally reached my destination, but as I reached out to grab a metal rod, I misjudged the distance and missed, teetering dangerously on the edge of the swing. It wasn't until I reached the top of the arc in the middle of the abyss and began to slow down that I regained control. After several more swings, I finally caught a metal rod and tied myself and my sleeping bag to it.

Looking back, I saw Reed still swinging furiously. I motioned for him to throw his cable, and he did, though his aim was slightly off. I had to push off the wall to grab the end, only managing to catch the tail with my left hand. With all my remaining strength, I reeled it in as Reed's momentum pulled him away. Finally, I managed to anchor him next to me, relieved that we were both safe.

Reed gestured towards our other bags, motioning for me to grab the attached cord and pull them over, but the thunderous footsteps above us made me shake my head in refusal. Instead, I pointed toward our sleeping bags, and Reed nodded in agreement. We quickly crawled into our bags, pulling the strings tight to avoid being spotted. I cautiously stuck the barrel of my gun out through the small gap that remained.

I didn't have to wait long before movement caught my eye. A head appeared over the edge, scanning the area. My heart pounded with fear as it seemed to look directly in our direction. I silently prayed that the gentle swaying of our bags wouldn't draw its attention. Suddenly, without warning, the creature tumbled over the edge, its body plummeting out of sight. If it screamed, I couldn't hear it over the chaotic noise from above. More bodies followed, at least thirty in total before the deafening pounding sound ceased. The tunnel fell eerily silent, the once bright light source fading, leaving us in darkness. I strained my ears for any sounds of the creatures' impacts below, but all I could hear was the occasional shuffling from above.

I remained vigilant, the proximity of so many zombies keeping me on edge, but the exhaustion from the past few weeks eventually caught up to me. Despite my fear, I drifted off to sleep while still suspended in my sleeping bag.

My slumber was abruptly interrupted by the grumbling of my stomach. It echoed throughout the depths of the abyss, bouncing off the walls as if to signal any creature within miles of my location. I rummaged through one of the pockets of my pants and pulled out a handful of mushrooms, the only edible thing I had on hand. I hesitated for a moment before taking a bite, fearing the possibility of it being poisonous. Reed had been eating them without any issue, but who knows what kind of toxic mushrooms could be growing down here. With a loud growl from my stomach, I took the risk and bit down on the mushroom, relieved to find that it was surprisingly sweet. It was a taste I had never experienced before, and I couldn't help but wonder where these mushrooms had come from. Nevertheless, I continued to devour them, quelling my hunger after four large pieces and a swig of water.

As I finished my impromptu meal, I realized that my bladder was full and needed to be emptied. I released the tightening rope around my sleeping bag's opening, opened the top, and poked my head out into the dark cavern. The strange light that had illuminated the walls the day before had returned, casting a faint glow on the ground. I scanned the area for any signs of danger and was relieved to see that there was no sign of the horde that had been lurking above us before. Reed's sleeping bag was still tightly cinched up, just like mine had been moments ago. I looked out into the abyss and saw that all of our bags were still hanging where we had left them in the open air.

Observing my surroundings, I made a quick decision. There wasn't much of a choice to make. I reached down to my waist and grasped the sleeping bag's fabric, pulling out my belt knife to cut a small hole in the cocoon's wall. It was a tiny slit, but it was enough. Carefully positioning myself, I let out a stream of urine that cascaded down into the abyss below. As I watched the liquid fall, I was reminded of the zombies that had fallen to their deaths the previous night. A fall from such a height was fatal, causing irreparable damage to the body killing both the host and the microorganisms.

I thought I had been quiet, but Reed shifted in his sleeping bag, and his head emerged before I had finished. A brief glance from his sleepy eyes failed to register what was happening. He blinked several times as his gaze followed the stream of urine falling from my sleeping bag. Finally, comprehension dawned on him, and he nodded approvingly.

"Good thinking," he said, promptly cutting his own hole to relieve himself.

"Shhh," I hushed him.

"What?" Reed replied softly, looking puzzled. "Did they come back?" He continued as he sliced a small slit in his sleeping bag.

"Come back?" I questioned, pulling up my pants and zipping them. "What do you mean?"

"They left as soon as the light returned," Reed explained. "Well, the last of them left when the light came. The sounds diminished as time passed. I think they lost our trail," he said.

"It worked?" I asked, finishing up adjusting my pants.

"Yeah, I suppose so," Reed replied, beginning to pee himself.

"You didn't mention that the mushrooms were delicious," I said, studying the location where they were tied off, nearly in the same spot where the zombie had poked its head out the previous night. "I tried them. I was starving and couldn't wait any longer. The rations weren't cutting it," I continued.

"I didn't want to tempt you. They're good, aren't they?" Reed inquired, smiling.

"They are," I agreed, beginning to pull on the cords that connected the hanging supplies to my sleeping bag. "Now, we need to figure out what to do next," I muttered.

"Well, first things first, I think we need a day off," Reed suggested.

"We don't have a day to spare," I countered.

"I don't know about you, but I'm still struggling to breathe. It's a miracle we've made it this far. Resting would benefit us more than blindly pushing forward," Reed argued.

"Agreed. It's relatively safe here for now, and you need to recover. We'll stay here until our supplies run low, but during that time, I'll scout the area," I proposed.

"That sounds sensible. If you can find some more food and water, it could help us survive until I recover," Reed agreed.

I nodded as I worked on the first bag of supplies, pulling the cord attached to it and my sleeping bag to bring it closer to me. I secured it to my sleeping bag's outer cords to keep it stable and supported. The movement made my muscles ache, and I could feel my body protesting. It had been pushed to its limits and needed time to recuperate.

"I think you're right about taking a day off. I'll tie our supplies nearby and then get some rest. I think I need it," I said, yawning.

Chapter 10
REED'S RECOVERY
STAR: The Abyss

As I opened my eyes, I was greeted by an intense brightness emanating from the abyss, a light so powerful that I had to shield my eyes and squint just to see anything. The reflection of the abyss wall felt like it was searing my skin, making my already pale complexion look even paler. I reached for our dwindling supplies, grabbing a bite as I contemplated my next move. Reed was still wrapped up in his sleeping bag, hopefully recovering from his injuries.

Despite feeling energized, I resisted the urge to move and instead listened for any sounds. For five minutes, I strained to pick up any noise, but there was nothing. The horde that had been relentlessly pursuing us for the last two weeks was nowhere to be seen.

Feeling a sense of relief, I decided it was time to explore our surroundings. It took me half an hour to gather all the supplies I needed for my scouting mission. One machine gun was slung over my back, and two swords adorned my waist alongside my trusty belt knife. My toolkit was safely stashed in my bag, which also contained two days' worth of food. With everything in place, I gently poked Reed's sleeping bag with one of my guns. When I heard him grunt in response, I whispered, "I'm going on a scouting mission. I'll be back soon."

Reed grunted a second time in response to my announcement, indicating his understanding. With that confirmation, I released the cord that secured me to the wall and swung out into the open space. Although I still had a cord connecting my bag to the supply bags on the wall, eliminating the need to swing back and forth to gain a purchase next time, I had to be careful not to be blinded by the overwhelming brightness surrounding me as I began to pull myself up using the cord that held my sleeping bag in its cocoon of utility cords. Despite the reduced visibility, I used my muscular arms to lift myself up one arm's length at a time until I finally made it to the ledge where we had previously escaped the zombies. Cautiously, I ascended the last stretch of rope, wary of the possibility of a zombie lurking nearby. Fortunately, when I peeked over the edge, I saw nothing down the hallway.

The brightness from above the abyss made it difficult to see, but I was able to look down the hallway without much difficulty. With a final burst of energy, I pulled myself and my cocoon onto the hard, solid floor. I immediately drew my sword and started to stalk down the hallway, considering what to do next. I had decided that the first thing I needed to do was to find out what was behind the doors that lined the walls. I made my way down to the first door on the right, sword at the ready. After fiddling with the doorknob, I flung open the door, jumping back in anticipation of something jumping out at me. However, nothing came out of the room except for the stale smell of air that had been trapped for a long time. The room appeared to be a recycling room, with scraps of metal and plastic covered in a thin layer of dust.

I moved on to the next door, which had a fresher smell but fewer items inside. The third door, however, surprised me. As soon as I opened it, I heard movement coming from the other end. I prepared myself for a zombie attack, but when I saw the creature cowering away from the light entering the room from the hallway, I was confused. This behavior went against everything I knew about zombies and disrupted my normal fighting strategy. It seemed that the brightness of the hallway from the strange light that shone from the tunnel entrance was bothering the zombie. If that were the case, I would have to reconsider my opinion of the blinding light. I entered the room to face the zombie, and it lunged at me. I sidestepped, cutting the creature's legs around the knee and sending it tumbling to the ground. Dispatching it was easy, as I had done it many times before.

When I looked around the room, I was surprised to see large plastic crates instead of scraps of metal and plastic. I approached one of the crates to examine it, but before I could, I heard the familiar shuffling sound coming from the hallway. With lightning speed, I backed out of the room, scanning both directions for any incoming danger.

The path leading to safety was unmistakable, but a horde of zombies emerged from other tunnels and shuffled their way into the hallway. They kept their distance, yet their eerie shuffling and blank stares made the hairs on my arms and neck stand on end. It was clear that these creatures were waiting for something. As I looked down the tunnel, I realized that it had grown much darker than before.

The zombies inched closer, but thankfully, they remained far down the hallway. I recalled how the first zombie had recoiled from the light in the room earlier, and suddenly, it dawned on me that these zombies shared the same aversion to light. Stray thoughts of where the light came from crossed my mind, and I wondered if I should fear it too, despite its power over the undead.

However, my thoughts quickly shifted to the ever-growing mass of zombies filling the tunnel. I needed to make a decision quickly. My original plan was to explore for a couple of days, but I couldn't risk dying up here and leaving Reed to his fate on the cliff wall. The light was my only hope, and yet it was getting dimmer by the second, seemingly drawing the zombies closer.

I hesitated for a moment, but then I made up my mind. I rushed back down the hallway I had explored until I reached my makeshift harness. Without wasting a second, I tied it around myself and slid into my sleeping bag, beginning my descent. The zombies remained at bay, but I knew I had to hurry before the light disappeared completely.

The light was fading rapidly, and I could feel the urgency to find safety. It didn't even hurt my eyes anymore. I needed to secure myself before the dead hands above pulled me back up. The shuffling noise grew louder as the last flickers of light vanished and darkness engulfed me. Thankfully, I had anchored myself and crouched down with my gun ready. Several heads appeared over the edge, their eyes scanning the

71

hanging bundles. Suddenly, I heard a screeching noise that I had never heard before. It was coming from one of the Zombies that had its gaze fixed on me. I felt hands pulling at my cords, trying to lift me up to my death. However, my anchor held firm and the screeching noise continued in a constant stream for five minutes. The Zombies' mouths hung open, emitting a nerve-wracking sound that shook me to the core.

"What did you do to it?" Reed's voice pierced through the screeching noise from his sleeping bag. "I've never seen one do that before."

"I didn't do anything. They knew we were here all along. They were waiting for me up there," I replied.

"And they didn't get you?" Reed asked, his voice filled with concern. "You're alright, right? Not even a scratch?"

"I'm good. They didn't come close except for the one I found behind a closed door. I don't think they can go through doors," I said.

"It doesn't matter now, does it?" Reed said, his despair evident. "If they're waiting for us, they can wait until we're dead. Time doesn't touch them while we need food and water to survive."

"We'll run out of water first," I added. "Guess you should save your pee."

"Really? Why bother when we're going to die anyway? Might as well just cut the cords and get it over with. The ground below is a quick way out," Reed suggested morbidly.

"None of that," I retorted firmly. "We're going to be okay."

"What do you mean?" Reed asked, his voice filled with doubt. "You're telling me you can take on a horde all on your own with those swords of yours?"

"Have a little faith, man," I grinned at him.

"My sister always said you were crazy," Reed said. Mentioning Wind brought silence to us both. I hoped she was doing well, or at least better than we were. At this point, the colony must have assumed we were dead, meaning Wind would receive the death ration stipend.

Silence enveloped us both as we were under constant surveillance. No Zombies had fallen this time. Three heads stared at us unblinkingly, producing a continuous screeching noise while the shuffling of hundreds of other feet provided a low bass to the soundscape. We watched as hands persistently attempted to tug on the cords connecting the hanging items to the tunnel above, causing a slight rocking motion for both of us. Fear kept us alert for the first few hours, but as time passed, my eyes grew heavy. Eventually, I drifted off into a fitful sleep despite the looming danger. Every sudden jolt from the rocking motion would wake me up, prompting me to peer into the darkness at the motionless Zombie heads, barely visible in the faint light of the tunnel.

I knew they would wait there indefinitely, but I held onto the hope of the mysterious light returning to drive the creatures away, giving me a chance to take care of them. When a shift occurred in the abyss's lighting, I snapped out of my drowsiness and saw the heads' features more clearly. The Zombies' constant screeching had become background noise to me by then, and when the noise abruptly ceased, my gaze was drawn back to the overhanging cliffs. The heads were gone, and the shuffling sound of the creatures moving away grew louder. The light was increasing, and a smile spread across my face; this was the solution to the horde. All I had to do was not make a single mistake.

I quickly made my ascent with fewer items than before, only two swords sheathed in their scabbards and my military protective clothing. I undid my sleeping bag's anchor and drifted out into the open space of the abyss, pulling myself up with my swords on my belt. My training and combat skills made it relatively easy for me to ascend with quick, well-defined motions. The light wasn't blinding yet, making the climb easier than the last time. I reached the top of the overhang in just a minute.

A swift glance showed that the Zombies were forty feet away and retreating. I pulled myself up onto the platform and undid my homemade safety harness, and as I finished, the

73

Zombies noticed me. They looked at me, but no screeching emanated from them anymore. Two of them stepped forward into the lit hallway before quickly stepping back. This movement confirmed to me that they would not enter the light. My sneer widened as I gazed at my enemies.

"Let's play," I growled before moving forward towards them.

I deftly wielded my swords, the deadly game unfolding before me. With each swift strike, I severed arms and tendons, the rhythm of my lunges and jumps keeping the relentless Zombies at bay. The horde pushed forward, but as they entered the light, they struggled to retreat, enraged. It was in those moments that I struck, cutting them down with ruthless precision. As they fell, I made sure to space out their bodies, ensuring their brains were thoroughly scrambled before the Zombies behind them moved forward. The game felt like it had lasted for half an hour, but then something changed. The light suddenly brightened in the abyss, and the Zombies turned and shambled away as fast as they could. Without hesitation, I charged forward, cutting them down with ease as they exposed their backs while fleeing into the side tunnels.

I didn't follow them; instead, I chose to pursue the ones heading further down the main hallway. When they reached the second tunnel, I halted, unwilling to risk being flanked. The light kept them at bay for now, but I didn't know how long it would last. Today's slaughter was over, and all that was left was to clear the tunnel for tomorrow's work.

I made my way back to the ledge, dragging a body by the foot. The brightness of the abyss's walls was blinding, and I shielded my eyes. Once at the ledge, I heaved the body out into the open, leaving me with over a hundred more to dispose of. I didn't make it to the last bodies down the hallway before the light started to dim, but it did so slowly, giving me time to prepare. I anchored myself to my harness and watched as the Zombies filtered down the hallway, getting closer and closer as the light lost its power.

Before they could reach me, I descended the hanging cord, eager to be well anchored before the Zombies started to tug at the cords that held me and Reed. When I reached Reed, he popped his head out of his sleeping bag, relieved to see me back. "How did it go?" he asked.

"Compared to how many are up there, it will be slow," I muttered. "We might have to rethink our ration situation."

"But it's not hopeless?" he asked, hopeful.

I grinned at him. "Not in the least."

Reed looked at me with admiration. "You know, you're like one of those Samurai warriors you used to tell me about from your readings. They were experts in sword fighting and all that. They faced their enemies and even death straight in the eye."

I chuckled. "Yeah, I guess you could say that. But let's hope we don't end up extinct like them," I replied jokingly.

Reed laughed and shook his head. "Yeah, let's hope not."

That night was a repeat of the last, but this time, I felt anticipation instead of fear. I was born a hunter of these creatures, and with Reed by my side, we would be just fine.

Chapter 11
EXPLORING
WIND: Underground Tower #4

"They were shot."

"Shot? Like by one of our own?"

"No one knows why; they were stripped naked, and all their equipment was taken."

The buzz of the tower was all about how Stump and Redwood were found dead a day ago. The buzz dwarfed the missing personnel. My brother, along with his best friend Star, were missing along with all the other groups that had been sent out. It wasn't unusual for people to go missing on these longer trips, but for all the groups to be late. People didn't want to think about what that implied. I, on the other hand, felt like something was off. All the teams hadn't returned. The first group should have come back two days ago. Three other groups should have returned yesterday, including my brother's group. But none had come back.

My mind had been running over the situation for the last seven hours on shift at the lower screening station. I had spent my shift looking through the computer files, trying to find any clue as to what might have happened with Stump and Redwood. I scoured every inch that I had access to in the computer files, but there wasn't anything. What I did find were several files that I couldn't access. These were meant for those in the upper floors. I wondered what secrets those held, but without access, I didn't know what to do, so I just thought about all that was happening for the rest of my shift.

Now that my shift was over and I was walking through the lower grounds beneath the tower, I realized how little people cared about the missing. My brother was much more important to me than the strangeness of Stump and Redwood's demise. Still, I couldn't help but slide into a group of friends to listen.

"It could have been an accident, and they shot themselves." Flower was saying.

"But what happened to their clothes and weapons?" Bridge replied.

"It just doesn't make any sense," Grass replied.

"Unless there are other people out there," Bridge whispered conspiratorially.

Flower scoffed, "Other people?"

"Yeah, we can't be the only ones left," Bridge continued in a whisper. "But it is clear they are savages though."

I snorted at that. "They would have to have had guns. I wouldn't call that being savage. Plus, they came across Stump and Redwood. It's not the best welcoming party. More likely to have shot first."

"True," Bridge conceded. "So, do you think that it is someone new?"

"Not sure, but why were Stump and Redwood there in the first place? They weren't on the schedule," I noted.

"They weren't?" Flower frowned. "That is strange."

"Are you sure? Where did you hear that?" Bridge asked, not liking that I was taking control of the conversation. She loved to be the center of attention.

"I looked at it."

"O right, you have computer access. That is so cool. Totally beats the info tablets we are allowed." Grass smiled at me.

"Blah, those are so expensive and useless," Flower exclaimed. "My brother bought one, which was a total waste of food chips."

"Shh," Bridge hushed us, looking over at a couple of young men our age who were heading to the southern gate. We all looked to see Bomb, Turtle, and Mountain in uniform, ready for a routine patrol. I resisted a snort at Bridges reaction to the young men.

"Stay safe, Bomb," Bridge said with a wave.

Bomb looked over at us and smiled before making his way over. "Good morning to the four of you."

77

I could feel the girls next to me swoon at his attention; his way too-handsome face and broad shoulders were very desirable traits among the girls. He knew he was good-looking though, and it was a real turn-off to me. I preferred the quiet, nice type like Star. Still, he was too young and was my brother's friend. That would just be weird. Still, it was cute, the fact that he liked me. Mountain standing next to Bomb reminded me of Star as well. He was smaller but fast. He was also pleasant whenever I spoke to him. I just needed to find out if he could cook. If he could, then he might be a good candidate.

"Are you heading to the southern gate?" Bridge asked.

"Yes, it's our turn, unfortunately."

"Stay safe, alright,"

Bomb smiled. "Of course, I wouldn't want to let you down."

I leaned over to Mountain, who shrunk back a little, "How do you deal with Mr. Big Shot here?"

Mountain smiled, calming down a bit from his initial reaction of my leaning in, "He only acts that way around girls; he isn't bad otherwise."

"Hey, I was wondering why only Stump and Redwood were out there yesterday. They should have had a three-man team, and they weren't even scheduled to be out."

Mountain shrugged. "Nothing about that makes sense. I haven't heard anything, though."

I nodded, "Well, in that case, be safe."

"Thanks," he replied sheepishly, which was rather cute. Then he whispered, "Is it true that you're running the scanner?"

"Yes, I started a while ago. Why?"

He went red at my words before shaking his head. "No, it's nothing."

I looked at him before realizing what he was getting at and laughing. "O, don't worry. I won't tell the other girls how decent you look."

He went even more red at that. "That's not cool making fun of me."

"I wasn't. All I'm saying is that you are much more attractive than Bomb over there. Just saying."

"Really?"

"Really, really."

"Well, we better get going," Bomb said, cutting off our side conversation.

Mountain nodded and gave me one last inquisitive look before following after.

"Wow, he is so dreamy," Grass replied, looking after Bomb.

I smiled to myself, knowing that he wasn't that great. But the fact that Mountain was going out to face danger without all the information bothered me. All the fighters were. Secrets were being kept from us, and it was wrong. We were the ones putting ourselves in harm's way for them. I really needed to find out what the higher floors were keeping from us. I needed to access those hidden files.

Chapter 12
EXPLORING
STAR: The Abyss

It took us three weeks to clear out the Zombies. Every day, I killed over a hundred of them and threw their bodies into the abyss. But even then, I wasn't making much of a dent in their numbers over the first week. So, I started exploring the rooms behind the shut doors, not because I wanted to, but because I had to. We were running out of water, and I was worried we wouldn't be able to survive much longer.

On day two, I realized we wouldn't have enough water and had to think of a way to keep us alive. That's when I told Reed to start peeing in empty canisters. I did it, too, just in case. It was a terrible thing to do, but we had no other choice. I rationed drinking my own pee as much as I could, not because I had to, but because I didn't like drinking the awful stuff. We didn't actually run out of clean water until day eleven, and it was a bad day because I had to start drinking the yellow liquid.

Finally, after weeks of fighting, the last Zombie dropped to the ground, and I knew I had to find water quickly. I scouted the area diligently until I found it inside a door three corridors down. To my surprise, it didn't take me long to find it. Inside the room was a leak in the wall, and clean water was dripping out into another crack in the floor. All the metal in the room was rusted over, but I didn't care.

That night, I returned to the room with one of our water purifier pumps and used it to fill all the containers we had after rinsing them out several times. Reed rejoiced in earnest when he found out he wouldn't have to drink his own urine anymore.

After another long four weeks, Reed finally joined me on our scouting excursions. Together, we ventured farther than I was willing to alone. I had been hesitant to separate from Reed, which had hindered my exploration. However, after discovering the edible bugs that supplemented our mushrooms, our lack of protein was taken care of, and I felt that I didn't need to explore further without Reed.

With Reed by my side, we began to scout the area with renewed vigor. Since we had no paper to draw maps, we kept a mental map in our heads and left marks and scratches on the walls to distinguish the otherwise indistinguishable corridors and walls of the labyrinth. We also drew as much as possible on the wall next to our home base, recording where we had been. As weeks turned into months, we cleared the rooms and hallways of Zombies, encountering fewer and fewer of them as time went on.

It was strange to me how different the encounters here were compared to the tower we grew up in. In the southern tunnels of the tower, there were always a few zombies wandering, and the hordes only grew over time. Here, we could go days without an encounter, and when we did, it was often only one or two behind shut doors. Very rarely did we come across wandering zombies in the hallways.

During our exploration, Reed and I discovered a lot of odd-looking machinery and other useful items. We gathered metal and wires and worked on our base of operation against the cavern wall, a location out of reach for any wandering zombies. It wasn't exactly a secret, but it was well hidden.

During our exploration, we made a remarkable discovery that would ensure our survival for years to come. We stumbled upon numerous locations where mushrooms were growing and store rooms filled with preserved food, vitamin pills, and old protective clothing that had been vacuum-sealed for over two centuries. Although some of the items had expired, many were still usable, and there was more than enough to last us a lifetime. The only thing we lacked was a source of weapons and ammunition.

For three weeks, we worked tirelessly to gather all the supplies we needed and bring them back to our camp for safekeeping. Under my care, the hanging cocoons had transformed into an entire platform, and Reed assisted me, albeit not as skilled as I was in building. I made sure never to extend the platform too far from the cliff's edge to prevent Zombies from accessing it through the overhanging tunnel. I worked on the platform during the few hours of daylight that penetrated from above, but even then, my time was limited to when the light wasn't too bright.

Reed asked me for the umpteenth time, "What do you think it is?" as he relaxed near our makeshift home, and I replied, "You've asked me that over a hundred times. My answer isn't any different."

He grumbled, "I was just wondering out loud."

I paused my task for a moment to look up at the blinding light from above, which wasn't too bright at the moment, and I could see the cliff walls clearly. However, my vision was obstructed by the overhanging ledge. "Do you want to find out?" I asked Reed with a grin.

Reed sat up and looked over at me, "What do you mean?" he asked.

"I mean, what else do we have to do?" I said, putting down my tools after checking the joint I was working on one last time. I shook the joint vigorously to ensure it was solid before pulling myself over next to Reed. "We've spent our whole lives training to defend the tower. Without the tower to defend and with all our needs met, what else are we supposed to do?" I added.

Reed nodded, knowing what I meant. With no purpose, I felt my hard-won skills dulling with a lack of use. Even the few Zombies we encountered didn't help, as I mostly took them on myself with a sword. Everything felt empty, dull, and meaningless. "We could go back," Reed suggested.

I shook my head, "No, we can't. They will kill us before they would talk to us," I replied.

"You don't know that," Reed grumbled.

I tapped Reed on his chest, where the scar from the bullet's entry point was still visible. "You know it too," I said.

Reed shrugged off my hand, anger evident on his face as he looked back up at the bright light. Although he wanted to go back, every time he brought it up, I would say it was impossible. Without me, Reed didn't think he could make it back. Looking up at the light and wondering at the mystery behind it, his anger dissipated, and he recalled what I had said earlier in the conversation. "What do you mean?" he asked again.

"I don't know how to make it clearer. Going back will..." I began to answer, but Reed cut me off, saying, "No, I meant-what did you mean about finding out?"

I was taken aback for a moment and then pointed to the cavern wall. "Look at how uneven the wall is. With effort, we could scale it," I replied.

Reed examined the wall, seeing handholds where there were rocky protrusions before. Seeing my words taking hold, I reminded him of his past accomplishments. "

"You'd be a natural at it. Remember how you scaled the side of the tower to inspect those cracks in the wall?" I grinned at Reed, reminiscing the memory of him impressing the girls with his climbing skills.

Reed smiled back, remembering the attention he received from the girls, albeit briefly. "But I need the right equipment and lighting to make it up there safely," he replied, his mind already working on the logistics.

"So, you're up for it then?" I asked, eager to explore what lay beyond the walls that scared off the Zombies. Perhaps we could find the source of the light and reclaim the tower with that power.

"I'm in," Reed agreed, and we began planning our expedition. We would need to gather supplies from various rooms, but now we had a clear direction.

I gently shook Reed, whispering, "Hey, it's time." He blinked the sleep out of his eyes and stretched awake. "Star, I want to thank you," he muttered.

I asked, "What is it this time?"

"It's these beds. I haven't slept so well since the tower," he yawned as he spoke. Reed watched me as I also admired my handiwork. I had disassembled a couple of bunks from

83

nearby rooms and installed them in our hovering home. "It wasn't that hard," I said.

"But it made all the difference. The springs make it feel like I'm sleeping on air. I mean, sleeping in a ball in our hanging sleeping bags was actually sleeping on air, which wasn't very comfortable, but the beds..." Reed trailed off, shrugging as if what he was going to say was self-explanatory.

I agreed, and Reed could see how pleased I looked. It was much more comfortable. "Sorry, we couldn't have it earlier. The weight distribution would have been off if we had. Come on, we need to get you up there," I said. I had waited until the infrastructure I had been working on could support the extra weight before installing them, and Reed had heard about it often for the last week.

Reed nodded, and we both pulled ourselves up to the overhanging tunnel entrance. Reed undid his safety harness from below and attached the one we used for his climb. I checked the harness, making sure that it was correctly attached and that the new straps I had added fit correctly. "Looks good," I said.

Reed nodded, walking over to the edge of the tunnel. "Let's do this, then."

I walked over to the edge of the corridor to the hook that held the other part of the pulley's cord. With a quick pull, I gave the cord enough slack to unhook it from the hook. I continued to pull the cord until the cord attached to Reed's harness went taut. With the correct length measured, I re-looped it around the hook for a backup.

"Up you go," I said in the dim lighting from the lights down the tunnel. The abyss, with only a little light from above, allowed us to see what we were doing.

"Ready," was Reed's response as he prepared to plunge into the abyss's open space.

I began to pull, lifting Reed up. We had been working as a team for five weeks. We had decided to attach the line from the tunnel instead of our makeshift platform where we slept. The fewer entrances to our sleeping quarters, the better. We didn't know what we would find above, so it just felt safer to start from the tunnel.

As Reed made his way up the cliff wall, I always stood guard during the few hours of light. It became a routine for us - six days of climbing during the light hours, and on the seventh, we would venture out to gather more cords and supplies we needed to survive.

Chapter 13
EXPLORING
WIND: Underground Tower #4

I tried clicking on the file that had eluded me for the last three weeks. My brother and the others hadn't returned, and I knew the members up in the higher levels of the tower knew more than what they were giving us. It wouldn't take much then to provide more than zero. It wasn't unlike them to keep us in the dark. It had been that way for a long time, but things were off, and I didn't trust them like I had when I was younger. Maybe it was because my entire world was off. I hadn't had one of Star's home-cooked meals for over a month. No, things were not right in the world, and I was going to find out why. I focused on the computer frustration building as I looked at the pop-up that came after clicking the file.

Locked: Enter Password:

Just like the previous million times, I stared at it before trying something.

Access Denied.

"Urg, come on, let me in!" I yelled at the computer as I selected the file again. My fingers flew over the keyboard as I typed in my frustration. *Let Me In!*

Access Denied.

I selected the file again before I sat back, looking at the screen and the words in front of me. Password. Password. What would a bunch of self-centered upper-floor snobs use as a password? … What could it be … What is their password… No, they wouldn't. Right? Well, *it's worth a try.*

Enter Password:

I entered the word 'password' into the slot, and the file opened.

"What in the world? I'm an idiot." I grumbled, kicking myself for not trying it sooner. Part of me wondered why no one had found out the way in before, but then again, it was usually older women who didn't care about computers that were using them. Plus, there wasn't really much to look at on them. It wasn't like we had access to a lot of files. There were probably only ten or so that we had access to. There were another ten that we didn't, and I had just found my way into one of them. After a quick test, though, I discovered that all of the files' passwords were the same. I just shook my head before I started to look through them.

My mood darkened over the remaining six hours of my shift. I couldn't believe what I was seeing. There were records of the families that lived on the upper floors. Over thirteen thousand of them, but only a tiny fraction had jobs. It was clear that the most popular was being in charge, which held two dozen seats at the table. It looked like, besides some of the more minor maintenance and food jobs, the rest of the population fought over each other to get one of those two dozen ruling positions. I couldn't glean why, but the records also had a lot of families in the deceased pile. It really made me wonder what happened on the upper floors. It was clear that they didn't do much and depended on us to keep them safe and fed.

It wasn't until the end that I came across a file labeled Zombie Contract. I couldn't believe the statement, so I selected it out of curiosity. That was when I grew angry. The file laid out a contract to send us to our deaths. It was time-stamped about a month ago at the same time that they had sent my brother out. They had sent him to his death on purpose. He and Star, and now I would never see them again.

"How in the world did they get a zombie to sign a contract, and what in the world are they getting out of this agreement?"

It didn't matter, though, because no one down in the lower tunnels was going to let that stand. Not when they found out. They would be storming the upper floors. I was thinking of doing it myself, but a massacre wouldn't do us any good. No, we needed to do it right. I needed to look at the files more and figure out what exactly they were doing in the upper tower and then plan. Only then should I act. But I had to act before they sent more of us to our deaths.

Chapter 14
ABYSS
REED: The Abyss

I marveled at the abyss as Star pulled me up, and I couldn't help but be impressed by my speed. Star had rigged a pulley system that made it easy to haul me and my supplies up to the highest anchor we had installed. It sometimes surprises me how resourceful Star was in cobbling things together.

I was grateful that Star was the one with me out here. I knew anyone else would have gotten us both killed before making it to the abyss. Together, though, we had everything we needed to survive. While it wasn't what I had envisioned for my life, I realized there was a lot more to living than just killing zombies - which is all the tower wanted from anyone from the lower levels. We were more than just guns and swords. I was good at climbing, and Star was skilled at building. It was fun working together.

I only got to ride for a short while before I had to swap my harness's hookup on the cord. I had to attach it to a part of the cord above the anchor, then unhook it from the bottom hookup. Once done, I tugged on the cord, signaling Star to continue pulling. This time, I had to kick off the wall as I was pulled higher, my momentum always bringing me back to the wall where I would kick off again. It was a strange feeling to kick off into the open space of the abyss. I had to be careful in the dim lighting of the tunnel since Star always tried to get me up to the final anchor before the light appeared. We had a limited working window, and we tried to make the most of it. Without the light from above, it was too dark to make out a path up the wall.

Every time I came across an anchor that signified two days' progress, I had to redo my harness attachment, depending on whether I removed the last anchor or not. I finally made it up to the last anchor, where the pulley system was attached. With three hard pulls on the cord, I signaled Star to stop pulling. Looking up at the opening above, which had become much closer with the distance we had already covered, I estimated that we would breach it in another two days. My climbing time had been increasing, and the further I made it up the cliff face, the longer the dim light existed. Unfortunately, the light also became more intense during a portion when something that burned at my eyes moved across the crack of blue that was above.

Once again, Star had got me up here with a couple minutes to spare, but it was still too dark for me to see properly. After a few minutes of waiting by the pulley, the darkness began to slowly recede as light seeped in, allowing me to continue my climb. I carefully chose my hand and footholds, scanning for any potential obstacles that might cost me precious time. My movements were deliberate and precise as I ascended the wall. Suddenly, a ball of light appeared in my field of vision, blinding me momentarily. After waiting a few minutes for my eyes to adjust, I secured a temporary anchor in the wall and took a quick glance up towards the light. Though I couldn't look directly at it, I could see a plane of blue in my peripheral vision. This was only the second time I had seen the light and the first time I had seen the blue plane. We had deduced that it was the sun based on the stories we had heard and the limited knowledge we had acquired from the archives in the tower.

Star had expressed interest in seeing the sun for himself, but we had agreed that I should finish climbing to the top first. The day's delay wasn't worth the risk of jeopardizing our chance to see what was up there. As I basked in the sun's warmth, my other senses seemed to sharpen, and I felt an indescribable energy emanating from it.

When the sun finally passed over, leaving behind only a blue sky, I looked up in wonderment. Though the blue was still blinding, it provided enough light for me to continue my ascent. With renewed determination, I closed the distance between myself and the light, taking breaks on the available ledges along the way. The climbing had become easier as I neared the top.

Chapter 15
EXPLORING
STAR: The Abyss

I positioned myself at the edge of the precipice, where I had secured the cord to the hook. Knowing Reed wouldn't need me for a while, I started to exercise while keeping an eye on the long hallway below. I began with pushups and sit-ups, completing three sets of each before taking a break at the side of the hallway to consider my next task.

There was always more to do on the expanding cliff house, so I spent the next eight hours alternating between exercising and resting while monitoring the loose cord that led up to Reed, indicating that he was still climbing. Fortunately, the cord eventually became taut, indicating that Reed was ready to descend. Waiting was always difficult for me, but Reed assured me that we would soon see the surface, which was a source of excitement and anticipation.

I released the loop around the hook and slowly released slack as Reed lowered himself down with the pulley system. I felt a tug on the cord, and I knew that Reed had successfully reached the new anchor point. The light had disappeared long ago, leaving only the tunnel's dim glow. However, I knew that the time to bring Reed down was fast approaching before the light faded completely. In the past, we had made the mistake of staying up too late, and Reed had sustained minor injuries. It was essential to get him down quickly.

The descent was quick, and I counted down the anchors, eagerly waiting for Reed's return. When he was still three anchor lengths up, I noticed something strange flying down the tunnel. I stopped Reed's descent and quickly grabbed the rifle I had left on the wall. Multiple metallic objects were flying toward me at breakneck speed. I was unsure what they were but remembered the Zombies that had killed our friend Rock. Without taking any chances, I fired at the closest object, taking aim at its spinning wings. I fired five shots before it was too late. Three of the metallic drones crashed to the ground, but ten more continued to fly around me. Suddenly, I felt a sharp sting in my side and pulled out a dart that had hit me. My muscles began to fail me as I managed to lower myself to the ground before losing consciousness.

Chapter 16

EXPLORING
REED: The Abyss

My body froze when I realized I couldn't descend any further. Quickly, I wrapped the cord below around the metal clip on my harness and undid the loop that held me steady. With that, I used my hands to control my fall, descending quickly and kicking off the wall to fall long distances at a time. Though it was much less controlled without Star's help, I felt like I needed to hurry. My anxiety only increased when I heard gunshots below. Only five shots went off before Star's gun went silent, and a whirring noise came from below. Unsure of what was coming, I quickly grabbed hold of the cliff wall when I came back in contact.

Looking down, I saw five flying objects with their own light source fly out from the tunnel. A bad feeling came over me, and I undid the loop that kept me on the cord. I let go of the cord, free-hanging from the cliff with nothing to catch me if I fell. With limited light, I slowly moved sideways along the rock wall, sometimes having to rely on feeling to get away from the cord. I could see two of the flying things moving up the stone wall, following the cord's path. Climbing up and around a ledge, I hoped I was far enough out of view from the flying objects as they scouted out the cord. I prayed that they hadn't already spotted me.

Even as the buzzing sounds of the flying things approached, I fought the urge to clench my muscles, hanging on to the wall as quietly as I could. They didn't pause near me, which was a relief. My thoughts turned to Star below. Maybe, just maybe, Star had gotten free after firing five shots, and the flying things entered the abyss shortly afterward. It seemed like an eternity as I held on unmoving, waiting, and listening. Eventually, the buzzing things came back down quicker than they had ascended, and I counted the two that had flown by. I waited another minute before I started to make my way back over to the cord, looping it slightly through the harness again and descending in a much more passive manner, making sure to make as little noise as possible.

When I finally made it down to the tunnel, instead of jumping down like I normally did, I shifted my body so that I was upside down. My blood rushed to my head, and it was uncomfortable, but I fought through it as I peeked into the tunnel. What I saw threatened to make my head swim more than the blood rushing to it did. Only one of the flying things remained, and it was noticeably larger than the others, with a wingspan spanning at least six feet. Its body was mostly covered in a sleek, metallic silver material, which glinted menacingly in the dim light. The three cords that snaked down from its body were thick and looked incredibly strong, with metallic clasps that looked like they could grip onto almost anything. The cords seemed to be wound tightly around various parts of a body, making it difficult to see the details of what was being carried in the cart.

The flying thing's wings were long and narrow, with a thin, translucent membrane stretched tightly over a framework of mechanical spars. The wings beat powerfully, creating a low-pitched hum that filled the air. The creature's head was elongated and tapered to a sharp point, with two glowing red eyes set deep in its head. As it flew, the creature emitted a low, whirring sound that seemed to be generated by some kind of internal mechanism.

As my eyes adjusted in the darkness, my heart sank at the sight of Star's motionless body being lifted off the ground by the creature's tendrils. The cords that were clasped around Star's body were now attached to the creature's thorax, and with a swift motion, it placed Star in the cart below. The creature didn't waste any time as it grabbed the cart and began to pull it down the hallway, disappearing from my sight. My mind raced with thoughts of how I could save Star from the clutches of this creature.

My hands itched for my rifle, but I didn't have it on me. I had to wait until the creature was far enough down the hallway before I could lower myself to the floor and rush over to Star's discarded weapons. I grabbed the rifle and aimed down the hallway, hoping to take a shot at the creature. I knelt on one knee, lining up the shot as I steadied my breath. I pulled the trigger, aiming for the joint where a wing connected to the body. My body was braced for the recoil, but nothing happened. I had counted on Star having a bullet in the chamber like he always had. I felt on my person, but I had no ammo, and Star's remaining ammo was on his person.

I slung the useless rifle over my shoulder and grabbed his swords before running down the tunnel after him. I didn't care if the zombies or the flying creature noticed me; I needed to catch up to Star before it was too late. I couldn't bear to lose him. Every time I turned a corner, I marked it on my mental map. The chase seemed endless until we reached the end of my mental map, and the distance between new hallways stretched out.

As the flying thing gained speed, I used the scope to keep track of it. I knew the chase was almost over, and I feared that I would lose Star forever. The next turn I made was more than a mile away, and I ran for all I was worth, knowing that Star or the thing that took him wouldn't be in view, all hope of finding my friend gone forever. What I wasn't expecting when I turned the corner was three humans gathered around the cart and the flying creatures only two hundred feet away. Before I could even call out, the platform beneath them started to rise as the heavy doors slid shut, blocking my view of them.

Desperate to catch up, I banged on the doors with my sword hilt, hoping they would take me with them and Star. But after three hours of fruitless effort, I knew I had to give up. I traced my way back to our home, a home that was now missing its most important piece – a family to share it with.

Chapter 17
EXPLORING

Alejandro: Earth's surface: THE CITY
A.K.A
Last City on Earth

"Alejandro, there is someone here to see you," my assistant said after knocking on the door.

I looked up from my pile of papers strewn all over my desk. "Who is it?"

"It's a city enforcer."

"A city enforcer? What does he want with me?"

"He said he had something you would want to see. He said it would really help your games."

I snorted when I heard the last part. "I've been working on this for months, and some city enforcer thinks he can just walk in and change all that? I get twenty people like that messaging me a day. Send him away."

My assistant nodded and made his way out. I was a little irritated that he had even brought this up to me. He should have been able to get rid of the man himself before wasting my time. I mean, that was his job, maybe I should fire him and get someone who would do their job right.

I leaned over the document I had been examining for the last twenty minutes again. It was a map of the land the zombie games covered with a dozen supply drops we had laid for the games. The locations were for sure, but I needed to determine the number of supplies required. I started writing down some notes, but five minutes later, the knock returned, distracting me.

"What is it now?" I exclaimed.

"Sir, the man won't leave. He said you won't be disappointed. They found something in the tunnels."

"Tunnels? What in the world could they have found down there that I would need in my games?"

"He wouldn't tell me, sir. He said it was for your eyes only."

My eyebrows knitted together at the sound of that after my visit with the King and learning my objective for the games to provoke the rebels into revealing themselves. Still, my interest was peaked. "Send him in, but get a couple of our own men together. I won't have a rebel try and start something here."

"Will do,"

It only took another minute for a man to be led into my office. The man wore the garb of a city enforcer. "Alejandro, it is a pleasure to meet you," the man said, reaching out a hand over the desk.

I looked the man up and down once more before extending a hand. "I'm afraid I am not in the same position. I am a very busy man, and the games are right around the corner. It is only your status of being a city enforcer that I am seeing you now."

"I completely understand; you are a busy man. I won't waste your time and cut to the chase. Yesterday, we found something in the tunnels just below the city. To be more exact, it was a who." The city enforcer pulled out his phone and handed it over. A video was primed to play, and I reached out and pressed play. To my surprise, it wasn't a type of zombie that the man wanted to show me but a human. A human that was surviving in the tunnels. That was amazing all on its own since that was where the majority of zombies resided. But then something sparked in the back of my mind. I had seen this face before. The enforcer seemed to have read my expression. "I see you recognize him as well."

"He was one of the promotional sacrifices for the towers," I asked.

"The one and the same. His group got the most hype as they blew up a tunnel to escape from the zombies."

"It was some heavily edited clips, but they definitely were the most exciting," I mumbled in recollection. The zombies were never clearly shown except for when they

97

jumped on one of the boys. Still, something must have happened for the young man who everyone thought had died in the tunnels to pop up under The City. "What are you going to do with the young man?"

"Well," the enforcer replied. "I was wondering if you wanted him for the games. Help increase popularity and make your games stand out from the rest."

I did like the sound of that, but it was too close to launch day. It would be a lot of work to change things up now. "If you had come to me two weeks ago, I would have taken you up on the offer, but seeing we only have a week…"

"I understand; I just thought you wanted these games to be the best, most popular…"

I paused, looking the man up and down. He really did seem earnest. "I'm sorry but it is just too late in the game."

The enforcer nodded sadly, "Well, I thought I would offer. I won't waste any more of your valuable time. Let me know if you change your mind."

With that, he left me alone. I sat thinking for the next ten minutes dreaming of what the games might be like with such a promotional character in it. Again, my thoughts were interrupted, but this time, it wasn't my assistant; it was someone I didn't want to see. It was one of the king's servants dressed in the identifying clothing. "Let me guess, I'm being summoned?"

The servant nodded, and I begrudgingly stood up and followed after the servant.

"Ahh, Alejandro," the king said when I entered the room. I gave a bow, which the king ignored. "Come here, Alejandro, please have a seat." The tone was way too sweet, and I felt like an ax was going to fall the whole time.

"There, are you comfortable?"

"My lord?"

"That is the thing: people often get too comfortable and complacent. I hope you aren't becoming complacent."

"No, my lord."

"Good, because I've been keeping tabs on the game preparations. I noticed that the public was told that many of the people were part of the rebels, but I don't know if they will believe the web of lies you're spreading. I mean, who is going to want to watch a mother of three be ripped apart from zombies? Not much excitement in that. So how are we going to get the people to watch and, even better, get them to hate the rebels. So I ask again, are you comfortable? Complacent?"

"No sir,"

"Good, so how are you going to resolve this?"

"Well, sir, I have men working on background stories for all the contestants. I have tied murders and crime to each of them, with the rebels as the controlling force. I will release these during the games."

"What good is that if no one is watching?"

My mind raced at that. I mean, it was the Zombie Games; everyone watched it. That wouldn't make the king happy, though. I latched onto the only thing that came to mind.

"We have a special new contestant this time."

"I wasn't aware of any last-minute changes."

"No, I was just informed that it was a go."

"Who is it that would draw the crowd?"

I quickly explained the boy retrieved from the tunnels and his identity. As I spoke, the king's mouth twisted into a smirk of approval. He nodded in satisfaction as he patted me on the back. "Ahh, it's nice to hear that you truly haven't disappointed me. I look forward to the games."

"Yes, my lord."

"I'll also have the test enhancements ready by tomorrow. Expect the shipment to be around two."

"Of course, my lord."

I was dismissed. On my way back, I quickly called my assistant, "Get me the number of that enforcer who came to visit."

Chapter 18
SUNLIGHT
STAR: The Surface

I woke up to a blinding brightness that felt like it was burning my face. It reminded me of the light from the abyss, only much stronger. I rolled over to avoid the intense illumination, but even looking down at the ground was too much for my eyes.

Growing up in the dim lighting of the tower and tunnels, this was the brightest light I had ever experienced. The pain in my eyes sent jabs of pain into my mind, awakening a forgotten memory of a recent period of excruciating pain.

As I moaned out loud, I heard other noises around me, and my mind raced to figure out what was going on. I grabbed my shirt and pulled it over my head, using it as a shield from the blinding light. Slowly, my eyes adjusted to the broken light coming through my shirt, and I could make out movement around me. My senses were overwhelmed, though, and I was unable to process what I was seeing. I waited until my eyes adjusted to the brightness, which felt like an eternity.

When my eyes finally adjusted to a bearable extent, I could see that I was standing on the outskirts of an open plane surrounded by large, rigid, mushroom-like objects. The tops of these objects sparkled and moved like water while green hair grew up from the ground. A backpack and a rifle lay a dozen feet away on a pedestal inside a glass dome. To my left lay a much smaller satchel with a hunting dagger lying on top of it. A blue expanse lay above, and a golden light was so intense that I couldn't look at it.

I took in all this, but my main focus was on a snarling creature moving swiftly towards me. I had seen creatures like this many times, and I was sure they were zombies. It resembled the fast Zombies, unlike the slow ones from deep below the earth. Although cleaner, for a split moment, I thought it was a human. But a human wouldn't come running at me with a sword for nothing, right? I didn't have time to ponder that thought as I rolled to the side, avoiding the sloppy strike. The clumsiness of the strike solidified the thought that it was a Zombie, not a human, before me. No human would be so clumsy with their weapon. It was a scary thought that this new kind of zombie knew how to use weapons.

Unexpectedly, the Zombie didn't follow through with a side-swipe attack like I had expected. The lack of a strike caught me off guard. I had rolled to avoid the nonexistent strike and now found myself wasting precious seconds waiting for its next move. I couldn't afford to wait any longer. With a clear purpose in mind, I made a beeline for the satchel and the dagger on top of it. However, in my haste, I opened my eyes too wide and was momentarily blinded by the intense light. My hands, normally quick and nimble, fumbled as I reached for the dagger, and I ended up cutting my right hand on the blade. I managed to catch the weapon with my left hand but had to delay my rise to my feet slightly.

The Zombie looked at me with a blank expression, but its demeanor quickly turned to anger. I wasted no time, launching myself forward and diving under the zombie's clumsy upswing, just as I had done with the slower Zombies in the tunnels. I sliced at the Zombie's ankles with quick, precise strikes. The creature stumbled and fell to the ground, and I proceeded to carry out my routine kill by slicing at its arms under the armpit before it could turn on me. That's when I realized something was terribly wrong. The body lying in front of me wasn't that of a Zombie but that of a man. Blood sprayed from his wounds, and anguished cries escaped from his mouth.

"Wait, you're not a zombie?" I blurted out, taken aback by the realization that the man lying before me wasn't one of the undead. He was unable to respond, and I couldn't help but replay the events leading up to this moment in my head. He had attacked me first with a sword, but the fact that he was still human bothered me. I had killed before, but only to protect my friend Reed. Now, a man was dying because of me, and I couldn't help but feel guilty.

101

I hesitated for what felt like an eternity, my mind racing with thoughts of morality and ethics. But there was nothing I could do to save him, and it pained me to see him suffer. In a moment of compassion, I did what I would have wanted done for me if I were in his position. I rolled him over, plunged my dagger into his eye, and twisted, putting him out of his misery. It was a hero's death, a way to go that ensured he wouldn't become one of the undead. It wasn't a common occurrence in our colony, but those who received it were honored by all the lower-level citizens.

"Rest well, and may your bones never rise again," I muttered as I finished the ritual words for a proper death. Afterward, I set to work cleaning my dagger and stripping the body of its clothes. The light still blinded me as I looked around, gathering the sword and satchel. I examined the items in the center of the clearing, wondering about the significance of the green ground around the pedestal. As I got closer, a ticking noise caught my attention, and the glass walls of a container separated from each other and pulled away from the pedestal.

I jumped back in fear, my sword coming out from the new sheath I had attached to my waistline. The glass walls stopped about a foot from their original positions, leaving just enough space for me to fit through. Worried that the box would close when I entered, I took a risk and jumped in to grab the items inside, including a rifle. I jumped out as fast as I could, relieved that the glass walls didn't close on me.

Once I was out, the glass walls moved back into place, and the green ground turned red again. The pedestal lowered into the ground, and the glass walls followed it. A red covering closed in a spiral motion over the hole as the glass disappeared out of sight, leaving an angry red surface. I didn't like it at all and quickly moved away from the area.

As I surveyed my surroundings, I noticed a path through the things that sprouted from the ground and a small satchel lying on the other side of the clearing. Uncertain about what was happening, I went to retrieve the other satchel. Before heading down the path, I checked the contents of all the bags.

The satchels contained only two days' rations and a full canteen of water, while the large pack was full of useful supplies, including another set of clothing, two sleeping bags, a roll of tripwire, a sharpening stone, two weeks' worth of food, and a water purifier.

Checking the side pockets, I found two boxes of shells holding two dozen shots each in one pocket and two hard-looking cases in the other. I opened the first case and found a pair of glasses unlike any I had seen before. They weren't clear, but when I put them on, the world darkened to a bearable level, and I didn't have to squint anymore. Intrigued, I lowered the shirt protecting my eyes and slid the glasses back on. The world was still bright, but the glasses helped me see much better than before.

The second case, which was tube-shaped, contained a roll of paper that I unrolled with curiosity. However, I couldn't quite make sense of the green and blue drawings with scattered stars. Perplexed, I rolled it back up and returned it to its container. In a swift motion, I repacked my bag even tighter than before, fitting the contents of both sacks inside. I then slung it over my shoulders and adjusted the straps to ensure the bag wouldn't bounce around. Next, I attached the sword and dagger sheaths to my belt and hefted the rifle. It was time to explore my surroundings.

As my vision cleared, I saw large mushroom-like structures rising up around me, appearing strange and alien. I was hesitant to venture through them unless I had no other choice. However, the clear path that led through the structures seemed more inviting, resembling a tunnel with overhanging growth. I grew up in tunnels and was accustomed to them, making the path even more appealing.

My thoughts turned to Reed, and I wondered how long I had been unconscious. For all I knew, I could be in the afterlife. But the familiar tunnel-like features of the path gave me a sense of normality amidst the unfamiliarity. With my decision made, I set off down the path, alert and prepared for any eventuality.

103

Chapter 19
WELCOME TO THE Z.O.M.B.I.E. GAMES
STAR: The surface
Z.O.M.B.I.E. Games: Drifting Planes

As I walked along the path for a couple of miles, I studied my surroundings. Everything was alien to me, and it made me walk slowly and carefully. So it was a surprise when suddenly a small creature ran out from one side of the path and over to the other. I paused ready for action but nothing came of it and I moved on. My mind continued to wonder at the creature and my surroundings when I stumbled upon a breathtaking view that left me dumbfounded. Everything around me had felt so unfamiliar, but nothing made me feel as vulnerable as when I stumbled my way out of the path onto an open plain that was near the edge of a cliff. To my left, the plain stretched out, while right next to me and bordering the plain was a cliff that led down into an expanse of blue. Below me, the expanse rippled with waves that frothed. It resembled water, but I couldn't be certain. I had never seen water froth, and the sheer amount was mind-boggling. Even as my eyes took it in, I was in denial that so much liquid could possibly exist.

The magnificent view distracted me so much that I didn't notice the group of people staring at me. When I finally turned my gaze away from the water, I was startled to see twenty-two people staring right at me. My first instinct was to raise my gun and aim it at them, but I quickly lowered it when I heard someone yell out, "Whoa, don't shoot!"

Confused and still feeling uneasy, I called out to them, "Where am I?"

The man who had stepped out from the group responded, "You're in the Zombie games."

"Zombie games?" I repeated, bewildered. As I looked around at the group of people, I noticed that each of them carried a satchel like the one I had found earlier. They also had swords or daggers on their belts, but none of them had a gun like I did.

The man grunted, clearly unamused. He directed his words toward the rest of the group and said, "This one went crazy after killing. We shouldn't have waited. We're wasting time. Let's move out."

One of the women in the group spoke up, her voice trembling with fear. "But what if he shoots us from behind?"

The man shrugged nonchalantly. "Doesn't make a difference. We're most likely dead anyway." With that morbid statement, the group started moving away from me, down a beaten path along the cliff face—everyone except for one person.

I watched as a pudgy boy walked towards me, muttering to himself in disbelief. "It can't be," he said as he got closer.

"Can't be what?" I asked, still feeling uneasy about my surroundings.

The boy looked up at me and said, "And your voice..."

I raised an eyebrow in confusion as the boy said my name. "Star, it is you, but how?" he muttered, lost in his own thoughts.

I had to ask twice before I got his attention. "How do you know me?" I asked.

The boy stopped his musings and looked over his shoulder at the others before turning to face me. "First, I need you to answer me," he said, his expression serious. "Why did you kill him?"

I was momentarily confused, thinking back to the multiple dead bodies I had seen. It wasn't until the boy pointed down the path I had just emerged from that I realized who he was referring to. "I woke up down there. When I regained consciousness, I found myself in a clearing with another man. While I was blinded by the sun, he came at me with a sword. I thought he was a Zombie, not just any generic Greed Zombie, but a fast one. I didn't have a choice," I explained, pleading my case. I definitely still felt guilty about what I had done, even though my brain couldn't come up with an alternative solution.

"You woke up in the Killer's Gambit?" the boy asked, surprised. "What about before that?"

"I was in a tunnel, and these flying beasts made with metal came. I don't remember anything after that," I replied, omitting the fact that I was still a bit hazy on the details and couldn't quite recall anything except for pain. I had my own questions, but the one that came out first was, "Why?"

"I'll explain as we walk; we better catch up to the others," the boy said. "What's going on?!" I let it out in more of a growl, causing the boy to pause.

"I'll tell you, but we need to get moving before night hits," he mumbled.

I reluctantly followed the boy, quickly outpacing his heavier strides. "What's happening here, and how do you know me?" I asked impatiently, my frustration evident in my voice.

"Well, where do I even start?" he pondered. "You're going to need a crash course on just about everything," he said with a chuckle.

As we walked, he took a minute to gather his thoughts before continuing. "First off, I know who you are because you were part of the tower experiment. But to explain that, we need to go way back. About two hundred years ago, there was an apocalypse. A scientist had made a breakthrough in science - he had been working on a method to rejuvenate the body, to prevent aging."

"I already know about the apocalypse," I interrupted. "I'm well-versed in zombies and everything that comes with them."

"Well, what you know is only the information that was provided to the colonies," he explained. "You don't know the whole story. The scientist made some mistakes in his studies, and when he tested his method on a human, the human turned into a zombie. The symptoms took weeks to fully manifest, but eventually, the poor guy turned. During the study, the scientist realized his mistake and began working on a cure. Patient Zero was locked away after he turned, and three people were hospitalized due to his attacks. Another person died outright. That's how it all started."

"Everyone thought it was over at that point," he continued. "The experiment was shut down, and the scientist was removed from further experiments. He flew out to his hometown, thinking it was all behind him. But two months later, hundreds of people started turning into zombies. They seemed fine one day and then feral the next. Chaos ensued, and the scientist was brought in for questioning in a remote location. Since he was the foremost expert on the cellular ecosystem he had created, they recruited him to help fix the problem. He worked with a few other handpicked individuals and the military to develop a cure. They only partially succeeded - it was more of a vaccine than a cure.

Unfortunately, by that point, it was too late for most of the world's population. Every scratch, bite, and kiss transferred the disease without people knowing. It made slow progress at first, so doctors didn't realize there was a problem until it was too late. As time passed, the rate of change sped up, and what took weeks to change turned into only a few days."

"The newly made cure was more of a preventative measure than anything else. It stopped the chance of the zombie microbodies from taking hold in the body. With the cure in hand, the remaining 10% of the population fought back against the zombies, but the sheer number of them decreased the population down to 0.1% in just a month. The cure prevented initial infection, but it only slowed down the process of change for those already infected. They couldn't prevent someone already infected from turning into a zombie."

"During this time, a select group of people, including the scientist, came together and created a screening method. They cleared out a single city and built a wall around it to keep both people and zombies out. They screened everyone who came into the city to ensure that no one who had partially turned could make it in. The population had reduced to only 500,000 people according to the history books."

107

"It took another two months before a real cure was developed for those not fully turned. But at that point, the city had been developed and was already at its capacity. The newcomers that arrived from the outskirts were screened and vaccinated but were not allowed to stay in the city. They were carted off to the guard towers built up around the city. Most readily accepted tower duty because it meant they had a chance at life. Some people went back out looking for other surviving groups with the cure in hand, but none came back alive. Only 6,000 people were saved from the outskirts. They were moved to the towers, which was an experiment at the time. You see, the city needed people to reduce the strain of Zombie attacks on them. The underground towers took extensive material to develop, but they worked, relieving almost all of the strain from defending the city. The stragglers to the city didn't mind the towers and thought of it as heaven compared to where they were coming from. They never got to see the inside of the city that they had first turned to for help."

At this moment, the hefty boy was out of breath from talking due to our speedy pace to catch up with the other group. I waited patiently as we slowed down to match the motley crew's pace led by the loud man from earlier. We kept a distance of about thirty feet from them and walked silently for a little while. While I wanted to ask many questions about what the boy had said, I was also trying to digest the new information. The boy had casually mentioned several significant events of which I had no knowledge. The only thing that sounded familiar to me was the underground towers.

When the larger boy finally caught his breath, he continued, "Once the towers were established, they were cut off from the city. This was done in part because if they had kept in touch, the tower people would have realized that they were sacrificial pawns in the larger game of survival. The biggest advantage the city gained from this was that they no longer needed to vaccinate the entire population against the Zombie microbodies. They had a cure to turn someone back if they got infected, as long as they hadn't fully turned. However, their protocols and screenings made it unnecessary to perform that costly preventative measure. That's another whole can of worms, though." The boy scratched his head, "Where was I? Oh yeah, so the city kept tabs on the towers and their residents, but there was no communication. That's how it was until about ten years ago."

The boy paused, and I couldn't help myself, "What changed ten years ago?" I asked.

"The Zombie games," he replied, "but since you're from the towers, I'll have to start a little further back. From the beginning of the city, as a form of ultimate punishment, the city had used banishment. It was a death sentence worse than hanging. They would send people out into the wilds to become prey to the Zombies. They would send them with meager supplies so they would eventually starve if they didn't come in contact with Zombies, but that was unlikely. That is a bit of backstory on the history of the Zombie games, but they didn't become games until later. Several factors drove the formation of the Zombie games. First off was greed. As with all cultures, the rich were greedy and wanted more. They started the experiments that had caused the Zombie apocalypse the first time. They did it a little more cautiously, having learned from the mistakes from before. Second was the unemployment rate.

Technology became abundant, and the decrease in zombie attacks drove people to complacency. Protocols for screenings dropped, reducing the number of lower-level jobs, which increased the number of unemployed people. The population was also on the rise. Tons of other factors came into play, but the biggest was the uptick in crime. Crime rates rose, and people started looking at the rich and powerful, thinking they could take that power away. But you see, the rich and powerful had a way to sway the population's attention away from them. They took a chapter from the Romans and started the Zombie games. It kept the people's attention on others who had it worse than they did and glorified the experiments the rich and powerful performed. The same things that caused the world's end the last time around."

109

At this point, I was getting frustrated. I was only partially following the conversation. I didn't know what the boy meant by the Romans or why a rise in unemployment would cause discontent. I was a youth trained in war. I was good at building and designing, but the terms and meanings behind the words being spouted around weren't familiar to me. I raised a hand at the boy to stop him from continuing.

"Stop shrinking at shadows," I snapped, frustration mounting. "What's this Zombie game all about?"

"We're in it," the boy gestured around us. "We're right in the middle of Zombie territory, and we have to reach the City without getting killed. It's like a survival game. If we make it there before turning, they'll put us up in the winner's quarters," he explained.

I didn't have a clue what the winner's quarters were, but I could only imagine how terrible it could get out here if it was anything like the tunnels. There was too much I didn't know.

"Why aren't there any Zombies around right now?" I asked.

"The sun, obviously," the boy replied, pointing at the sun above. "Don't you know that? Oh, right, sorry. It's strange talking to someone who doesn't have the basic knowledge that you expect," he finished with a sigh.

I glanced up at the blinding sun, quickly averting my eyes. "So that's the sun?" I asked again.

"Yep, I guess it's your first time seeing it," the boy grinned.

"I've heard about it in stories but never seen it before." I pointed to the tall, thin, mushroom-shaped things growing from the ground. "And those?"

"Trees," the boy said, pointing at the surroundings. "Ocean, grass, clouds, sky, rocks. Kyle," he said, pointing to himself.

"Kyle...I don't know what a Kyle is, but I know what rocks are. We had those," I mused.

"Kyle is just a name. It doesn't have any other meaning. We don't use the same naming convention as you tower folk," he explained with a hint of annoyance.

"A meaningless name?" I asked, puzzled.

"I don't know what Kyle means, okay? I'm sure it means something. Most names do," he dismissed.

"So why did everyone else react so strongly when I showed up?" I asked.

"You mean from the clearing," the boy muttered more to himself than to me. "Well, you came out of the clearing with a gun and a large pack. That means you killed the other person in the clearing."

"He attacked me first," I countered. "I thought he was a Zombie, and I was half-blind."

Kyle raised his hands in a defensive gesture. "I'm just stating the facts," he said. "These people don't know who you are, and I only know you from another long story that I'll tell you tomorrow if we make it through the night. Now, about the Killer's Gambit or the thing back in the clearing you came from. The game makers gave the contestants a choice between numbers or quality. At first, everyone fought to the death to gain an advantage with extra gear, but it was quickly discovered by those watching that most were injured or killed during the skirmish. Everyone who watched the Zombie games knew that killing, in the beginning, was taboo. As the years passed, occasionally, someone thought it was best to take the gear by killing someone in the clearing. But those who did were shunned by the group that made it out. It was hard to trust a murderer, and those people would often be killed by the group or would have to massacre their way out. When you walked out of the clearing with the gear, it was clear that you killed the other person. That was the only way the gear would be available to you."

I nodded in understanding, thinking back to the incident with Stump and Redwood. The higher-ups in the tower had made a deal to sacrifice us, which shattered my trust in the tower and the system that was supposed to keep us safe. It

111

wasn't until we found a safe haven that I had the chance to contemplate those thoughts. Now, I was with a group who had to face the decision to kill one of our own for better equipment. Even though I didn't make the decision, that didn't mean the others would understand. Kyle was the only one willing to talk to me, but I wasn't sure if he was telling the whole truth.

"So, the first stage of the Zombie games is the Killer's Gambit?" I asked.

"Yes, that's what the City people call it," Kyle replied. "There are more stages or legs of the journey, like the drifting planes, the Lost City where we have to choose to go through or circumvent, Death's bridge, and the forest."

"Has anyone ever made it?" I asked.

"Yes, but only three times, and the groups were always small. They're held as heroes in the city, but the games only happen twice a year," Kyle said.

I nodded, trying to process all the information. It was like being sent out into the tunnels by the higher-ups in the tower, but this was for sport and entertainment. It was sick, and I couldn't imagine enjoying watching others suffer like that.

"What's the best way to survive this?" I asked, hoping to learn more.

Kyle nodded. "Before you showed up, we were talking, and Gurney over there said he knows where a supply cache can be found. Apparently, he worked for the games three years back. You see, to make it interesting, they stockpile goods and weapons in some places. Every now and then, a group finds one and makes it interesting for the viewers. In most cases, the group finds a map to one of these locations, but we don't need one because he can lead us to it."

"What kind of supplies does he know about?" I asked.

"Gurney said it's fully stocked, or was when it was installed three years ago," Kyle answered.

I wondered aloud, "What's he doing in the games then?"

"It's supposed to be for people who committed crimes, but it's bad etiquette to ask," Kyle replied.

"So, you're all criminals?" I blurted out.

"No," Kyle grinned back. "We are all criminals." He gestured to the group, including himself and me.

My gaze lingered on Kyle, trying to read his expression through the sunglasses. "So, what did I do to end up here?" I inquired.

Kyle pondered for a moment. "I'm not sure. It must have bothered someone that they found you," he replied.

We strolled in silence for a while before I posed another question. "And what about you?" I asked.

"Dude, I already told you it was bad etiquette," Kyle sighed.

Unconcerned about manners, I repeated my question, "What did you do?"

Kyle glanced around warily as if someone might be eavesdropping on us. Leaning in closer, he whispered, "I'm a hacker. I may have stumbled upon some sensitive information, like the background history files about the towers... and you."

My eyes narrowed as I probed, "What did you find out that got you in here?"

"I can't tell you," he responded.

"Why not?" I pressed.

"Dude, I just can't, okay?" Kyle's voice grew harsher as he scanned the area for any sign of danger.

Feeling uneasy, I adopted a defensive stance, scanning our surroundings for any potential threats. "What is it?" I asked, scrutinizing every movement in the field.

"They are watching," Kyle whispered. "They have drones the size of bugs that listen and watch everything we do. That's how they keep tabs on us."

"The city people?" I guessed.

"Yeah," he confirmed.

My eyes darted around, watching the bugs flit from blade of grass to blade of grass. There were so many of them. But before I could say anything, Kyle halted me in my tracks.

"I need to talk to the others," he muttered. "We'll need to stick together to make it through this. And I want to explain everything to them before we reach the supplies. I don't want them to mistake you for a threat."

I nodded as Kyle caught up with the other group, leaving me to walk alone a hundred feet away. His words echoed in my mind as I watched a bug fly close to me. Without hesitation, I snatched it out of the air and examined it closely. There was something off about it, something mechanical. It reminded me of the flying machines that had pursued me in the tunnel before I had ended up here.

"They are always listening," I murmured, recalling Kyle's warning. The bug was a simple design, but the technology behind it must have been incredibly complex. I couldn't help but marvel at the society that could create such a thing. But at the same time, it was a society that derived pleasure from watching people die and be consumed by zombies.

I looked at the small camera attached to the bug, wanting to say something that would make Wind proud or strike fear into the hearts of those who had put me here. But my mind drew a blank, and the moment stretched out. I thought about the dead body I had left behind and Reed, who was either alone in the tunnels or had been captured like me.

Finally, I spoke. "I'm disappointed," I said, crushing the bug in my hand. It was a small act of defiance, but it was enough to express my anger towards those who had separated me from Reed and thought it was entertaining to watch people suffer.

Chapter 20
FIRST NIGHT IN THE DRIFTING PLANES
STAR: The surface
Z.O.M.B.I.E. Games: Drifting Planes

As the group continued ahead, I lagged behind and listened as Kyle revealed my origin story to the others. With nothing to do, I retrieved the small piece of paper from the vial and examined it once more. Kyle had mentioned that these maps were common among groups, and after hearing about our intended path, the significance of the map became clear. Several circles in the bottom right corner marked our starting point, and the blue outline along the right edge denoted the ocean. The crooked line across the page indicated Death's Bridge, while a star in the upper left corner represented our destination, the city. I identified the other landmarks Kyle had mentioned, such as the box shapes for the lost city, a red X near a black arch in the middle, and the small path along the ocean's edge. There was also another red X near the water-land boundary with three tree shapes nearby. I puzzled over its meaning but eventually committed the map to memory, a skill I had honed in the tunnels.

I walked alone, mulling over the map's details until I was satisfied I had memorized every aspect. Only then did I stow it away in my bag. When I looked up, I saw three members of the group waiting for me, including the large man who had been so vocal earlier. Kyle introduced me to Gurney, Nancy, and Trevor as Star, a member of the dangerous Southern underground towers. Nancy quickly urged the group to move on, but as I started to catch up, Gurney, the large man, stopped me with a question. "You're from a tower?" he asked, his suspicion evident. "How did you get out here? How did you get in the games?"

I regarded him coolly. "I come from an underground tower, but I don't know anything about other towers like Kyle mentioned. As for how I got here," I shrugged. "I don't know. I was in a tunnel next to a deep abyss when metal flying things came along and... somehow made me sleep. The next thing I knew, I woke up in a clearing with someone trying to kill me."

The man grunted in response even as I explained. Seeing his unease, Kyle stepped in with a better explanation. "Gurney, think about it. He never showed up to any of the promotional events prior to entry. That's the first time they've ever done that. We were always a man down from the beginning, after, well, you know."

The group nodded in understanding, but I was still confused. Kyle continued, "That's also why they put him with TJ to start with. They knew TJ wouldn't be able to resist a handicapped opponent. Things were getting bad in the city, and they needed something to take people's minds off their own troubles. That's why they spiced up the games this time with our friend here. What better way to get people's minds off their own troubles than a fight during the Killer's gambit?"

"I know that's true," the man said. "But I'm not so sure about this tower crap. No one watches that pathetic drama anymore. How would they get one into the games anyway? I'm just not buying it."

"They were bringing it back, didn't you hear?" Kyle argued. "What better way to promote the show than to have one of their members in the most watched program. It's all publicity."

"That sounds like something they would do," Trevor agreed. "I wouldn't be surprised if they did a couple of other nasty things to those poor people to promote the show."

"That doesn't mean we can trust him," Gurney responded harshly. "He killed TJ."

"He didn't have a choice," Kyle argued.

"How would you know? Did you see it?" Gurney scoffed.

"Well, no. But... Star, tell them what happened," he said. I then recounted the events that occurred without leaving anything out.

"I was wondering about the glasses," Kyle said after hearing the full story. "Can I see those? They look just black. How do they work?" he pleaded.

I hesitated, unsure if I should show them, but eventually decided to show good faith and handed over the glasses. Kyle was amazed by them, and I quickly put them back on to block out the bright sun as I was blind and vulnerable while I had them off.

The group spent several hours discussing various dramatized clips they had seen and clearing up misconceptions about the towers. Kyle explained the different customs in each of the towers, without which I wouldn't have been able to defend myself. As we walked, they discussed whether to trust me or not.

"I say if he can help, which it sounds like he can with his experience fighting zombies, we take the chance and trust him," Nancy said.

"If he stays, he'll be taking point," Gurney grumbled.

"He can't take point all the time. We need him, and that's the most dangerous role," Kyle argued.

"If he is half as good as you say he is, he'll be fine," Gurney countered.

I just listened, watching the bugs fly around as we continued to make progress towards the supplies. I was taking the time to plot how to get through the obstacles ahead based off of the rough information provided on the map. That was when I noticed three trees along the cliff's edge in a nice straight line.

"Hey, Gurney. How much further will it be until we reach the supplies?" I inquired.

He replied, "I'm not going to disclose that information so you can go off on your own."

Kyle observed my eyes and surroundings, asking, "Why do you need to know?"

"I believe we've arrived," I muttered.

But Gurney grumbled, "No, it's between two large boulders."

117

Without hesitation, I hopped off the well-trodden path and made my way through the tall reeds that covered the coastline.

"We don't take orders from you," Gurney shouted, but Nancy had already started to whistle for the others to return. She gestured with her arms, calling the others back.

As I moved forward through the tall grass, my eyes were drawn to the first tree that stood before me. Its trunk was thick and sturdy, its bark rough and chipping, and its branches extended high above me. Looking up, I marveled at how the green leaves flapped in the breeze that was picking up from the ocean side, casting dappled shadows across the ground. As the sun's hard glare softened under the shade, I felt a sense of relief that the brightness was no longer burning at my skin. It was a far cry from the tunnels I was used to, but the feeling of having something overhead blocking the brightness felt familiar and right.

Turning my gaze toward the sea, I was struck by the vast expanse of blue stretching out before me. The ocean was a tumultuous sight, the waves crashing against the rocky shoreline, sending up sprays of foam and mist. The sound of the waves was a constant background noise, soothing and rhythmic, yet at the same time powerful and awe-inspiring.

I watched as birds swooped and circled in the sky; their cries carried on the wind. The salty smell of the sea mingled with the grassy scent of the plains, filling my senses with a heady mix of sensations. The sea's sight and sound were new to me, a reminder of the vastness of the world beyond the tunnels where I grew up.

Returning my attention to the tree, I reached out a hand to touch its rough bark. It was a sensation I had never felt before. Looking around at the golden-green grass that rustled in the wind and the sparkling sea that stretched before me, I couldn't help but feel a sense of wonder at the natural beauty of the surface world.

Kyle appeared beside me, and the others waited at the path's edge. "What is it? Where are we?" Kyle asked.

"The supplies," I replied matter-of-factly.

"How do you know where the supplies are?" he asked, surprised.

I produced the map and handed it to Kyle, who quickly ordered me to put it away. "There's more going on than you know. I'll explain everything later, but hide it now. Memorize it and then eat it," he whispered.

"I already have it memorized. Why would I eat it?" I asked.

"You've memorized it?" Kyle asked, raising his eyebrow. I nodded.

"Every detail?" he continued.

"I could draw it from scratch if I needed to," I replied, handing the canister over again. Kyle walked towards the edge of the cliff and threw the canister with the map out into the open air before the others caught up to us. We they did we made our way from tree to tree and eventually found the entrance.

As I placed my hand on the handle and pulled, there were protests from the others to stop, but I ignored them. The doors swung open to reveal stairs that led down into darkness. It was a tunnel that led underground, and it felt like home to me, irresistibly inviting to someone like me who grew up in the dark.

"What are you doing?" Gurney said, sticking a hand out to stop me before I could descend more than a step.

"You said I was on point, right?" I still grinned. Then, on impulse, I handed the gun over to Kyle. "Point leads and kills anything in the way, right?" With that, I entered the large staircase that led down with a drawn sword and dagger.

I hurried down the corridor, hastily pushing my sunglasses to the top of my head as the light faded. Surprisingly, I could see just as well without them in the dimly lit areas. My eyes quickly scanned the room, taking note of the seven zombies lurking in the shadows. I couldn't help but grin at the sight of them. After killing countless zombies, the handful before me seemed pitiful. I was accustomed to facing hordes of the undead at this point. The zombies huddled away from the

119

entrance, where a faint light filtered in, preventing them from advancing toward me. My knowledge of the power of sunlight against them proved to be true.

With a swift motion, I charged into the room, sword swinging, and struck one of the creatures in the arm before retreating. I toyed with them momentarily, darting in and out of the shadows to maintain distance. After dispatching four of the zombies, I heard a noise behind me. I spun around, bringing my sword up.

"Whoa there!" Gurney yelled, batting at the sword that flew at him, his own blade blocking it. "What's going on down here?" he asked.

"Get back," I grumbled, turning back to the three remaining Zombies. "There's still three of them," I grumbled, turning to face the remaining three zombies. Gurney stumbled backward in fear, reaching for the wall and accidentally pulling a cord. The doors partially shut, dimming the already faint light. I knew I had to finish the job before the zombies could reach Gurney in the darkness. With lightning-fast movements, I sliced at tendons, avoiding the zombies' slashing hands. I took down the first one with a roll, then cut deeply into the armpit of another with my dagger before rolling away from the third zombie.

I lunged in again, my sword flashing as I slowly removed their limbs' ability to function. In no time, all three zombies lay motionless on the ground. The room wasn't completely dark, but Gurney was nowhere to be seen. He must have fled up the stairs when the doors started to shut. I saw it as cowardice, as everyone in the tower could hold their own against zombies. Though there was always a risk of getting infected, no one would have run as Gurney did.

I swiftly eliminated all seven Zombies, ensuring their brains were thoroughly scrambled before finally allowing my muscles to relax. It was at that moment when a voice called down from above.

"Star, you in there?" the voice echoed.

"I'm here," I replied.

"Status?" Kyle's commanding voice resonated through the tunnels. My instinctive response kicked in as I was accustomed to obeying superiors.

"Threat eliminated, no injuries, seven Zombie corpses on the ground," I reported.

"Sweet work," Kyle acknowledged, his footsteps approaching from above.

"There is no way he wasn't scratched," Gurney called out after Kyle.

"You don't know the tower people," Kyle retorted. "I bet Star could take on three times that many and still come out unscathed."

I began searching the room, spotting a dozen bags and several scattered weapons. Kyle descended but halted at the stairwell's edge.

"Star?" Kyle called, straining his eyes to pierce the darkness. I grabbed three bags and brought them over to the stairwell.

Kyle's eyes widened as I finally came into view. I dropped the bags at his feet. "Bring these up."

"How can you see down here?" he marveled. "How do you see above?" I retorted.

"What do you mean?" Kyle inquired.

"The sun blinds me above," I explained, sliding my sunglasses back on.

"Oh yeah, the sunglasses. You look so much friendlier with them off," he grinned.

"Carry them up," I nudged the bags.

I transported the remaining gear to the stairwell, and Kyle ascended with the equipment. We swiftly cleared the room, and I brought up the last two bags myself. As I emerged, I slid my sunglasses back on and discovered the group pointing swords and guns at me while Kyle stood by the opening.

"What is this?" Kyle complained.

"How do we know he isn't infected?" Gurney interjected, clutching a machine gun from the supply cache.

121

"He said he wasn't," Kyle defended, aware of my background.

"Anyone would lie about that," grumbled another man.

I stood there, surveying the group. "Your people must have no honor," I uttered through gritted teeth.

"What do you mean by that?" Gurney grumbled.

"My people would rather die than infect the rest," I declared, glaring directly at the man. "If we were infected by a Zombie and unable to remove the infection, we would kill as many of them as possible before ending our own lives. It was the warrior's death," I muttered.

Kyle stepped in to assist. "They venture into the tunnels, never to return to their tower. They exterminate as many Zombies as they can within three days before taking their own lives."

"We can't trust him," Gurney stubbornly replied.

Kyle tried to reason again, but I raised a hand to halt him. "Proof can be provided," I stated. With that, I stripped down naked, feeling slightly uncomfortable in front of everyone, treating it like the black scanner in the tower entrances. Gurney approached closely and inspected my arms and legs for scratches, finding none. The others watched with uncertain expressions.

After Gurney finished his inspection, he grumbled, "He's good." The weapons that hadn't already been lowered returned to their owners' sides at his pronouncement.

"Thank you," I said as I began dressing again. I quickly clothed myself while several group members examined the equipment.

"Aren't we forgetting something?" I loudly reminded the group.

Everyone turned to me as I reattached the swords to my belt.

"What is it now?" Gurney grumbled.

"You went in with me, or did everyone forget? Shouldn't he be screened as well?" I voiced my concern and was met with murmurs of agreement and Gurney's defensive protest.

"They never came near me," he insisted, his face flushed with emotion.

"How does everyone else know what happened down there? For all they know, you were bitten or scratched down there as well," I muttered matter-of-factly.

Gurney looked around in protest. "I wasn't. They didn't even come close," he defended himself.

Observing as the others closed in, driven by self-preservation. I stood firm with my arms crossed, watching the scene. Eventually, Gurney yielded under the group's scrutiny and reluctantly removed his clothes, revealing a body adorned with old scars, healed over with white scar tissue. Gurney slumped under the group's watchful eyes. My gaze fell upon the small scratch on his leg, a result of the fall in the stairwell.

"Look at his leg," one of the men gasped. "It's still bleeding."

The group tensed, their weapons aimed at Gurney. Acting swiftly, I stepped forward, my voice booming from my petite frame. "Stop!" I commanded. "Put your weapons down," I yelled.

"But he's been infected," argued a blond-haired man.

"Infected? Infected with stupidity, just like the rest of you," I retorted angrily. "I was down there and can attest that the Zombies didn't get close to him. You're all blinded by fear. He is not the enemy. The enemy is the walking dead, the ones who inhabit the bodies of our loved ones," I pointed to the setting sun. "Time is our enemy," I lowered my hand, staring intently at each of them. "The enemy is the one who sent us here to die as entertainment. The enemy is the one who made a man believe that killing me would improve his chances in the Killer's Gambit. And fools are those who bought their lies. We are not each other's enemies. Don't be fools who turn against one another," I continued.

"You're not entirely correct," a smaller woman interjected, stepping forward. "They didn't provide you with all the information when you arrived here. Kyle explained that you

123

were from the tower project and woke up in the Killer's Gambit. So, you don't know what you're talking about. We are enemies of each other."

"That's not true," Kyle chimed in. "That's a rumor spread to divide us, saying that only the first three survivors will be the winners. Well, just so you know, five people made it in the last games."

This revelation shocked the group, and the blond man asked, "How do you know that?"

"I met them," Kyle explained.

"You met them?"

"If that's true," someone pondered out loud, "then everything changes. We should be working together."

"But how can we believe him?" another person questioned.

"Hey, Gurney, you worked for the games. Why didn't you mention that? Is what he says true?" attention turned to Gurney, who slumped further in the spotlight. Not only Gurney, but I also noticed Kyle's uneasiness, his eyes darting nervously toward Gurney.

It took Gurney a moment to respond, "I don't know. I was part of the prep team. I never dealt with the winners. It didn't happen very often," he muttered.

I observed Kyle relax upon hearing Gurney's answer. Clearly, there was something Kyle didn't want the group to know about.

"How do we know he's telling the truth?" another voice questioned, redirecting everyone's attention to Kyle.

Kyle puffed out his chest, projecting confidence as he declared, "I am Kyle Pecoraro, son of Lorin Pecoraro."

The group audibly gasped, and someone couldn't help but ask, "Why are you in the games?"

Curiosity piqued, I stepped closer to Gurney, who had already dressed, and inquired, nodding towards Kyle, "Who is he?"

"He is Lord Lorin Pecoraro's seventeenth son. I thought he looked familiar," Gurney answered.

Still trying to grasp the situation, I turned back to Kyle, hoping for a clearer explanation. He kept it short, yet I didn't understand a word of it. By then, I didn't care anymore because I noticed the lowering sun.

"Kyle!" I called out, raising my voice to get his attention.

Startled by my tone, he responded, "What?"

"Whatever this is, we can wait until we're safe. We need to set up camp before the sun disappears," I asserted.

Confusion clouded Kyle's face as he questioned, "What do you mean?"

"I mean, we need to organize our sleeping arrangements," I ordered.

Realizing the approaching darkness, Kyle looked up and suggested, "Okay, but all we need to do is set up camp. We can light a fire here and keep watch."

"You want to sleep on the ground?" I exclaimed. "Where the zombies can reach you?"

"According to history, we're far from where they should be, so we shouldn't encounter any," a voice chimed in.

Another voice asked, "Where else would we sleep?"

I pointed to the hole from which we had just gotten the supplies.

A girl's voice from the crowd joined the conversation, stating, "I don't want to sleep in that hole, and tonight will be the first Changing."

"I'll sleep down there tonight," I pointed to the hole again leading to the underground room, "and tomorrow, I'll sleep there." This time, I pointed to the cliff's edge. "It's the safest option, even if there isn't much risk. I'd rather be safe than sorry. You are all welcome to join," I concluded.

Kyle raised an eyebrow at my words but didn't question further. Convincing the rest, especially two of the women, took some effort. Still, once they realized everyone else would be down there, they agreed to come along.

As a group, we made our way into the confines of the underground stash. I had moved the bodies of the dead zombies to the side, ensuring no one would be in close

125

proximity to them. Although it wasn't ideal to sleep next to the zombie corpses, it was the only option without alarming anyone else. After closing the doors behind us and bolting them shut, only a faint light seeped through, allowing me to navigate the room relatively easily. Others struggled, bumping into objects and each other in the absence of light. I helped them settle into their sleeping bags before curling up next to Kyle.

I couldn't contain my curiosity any longer and asked, "You mentioned a Changing tonight? What does that mean?"

In a somber tone, he responded, "Earlier today, I mentioned that these games are essentially a cover for human experimentation. They want to test the effectiveness of their concoctions on us. Tonight might be a painful experience, and we'll all wake up a little different."

Curiosity piqued, I pressed further, asking, "In what way?"

"We were given choices, but I'm uncertain about the specific changes they've made for you. It could be something subtle, like developing thicker skin or increased speed. Alternatively, more advanced powers are possible, such as telepathy or heightened senses like enhanced hearing, sight, or smell. Or, if they went all out, who knows? You might discover the ability to control insects with your mind or even sprout additional appendages. I'll explain more later. Just be prepared for something to change tonight. And when you feel terrible, well, that's supposed to be normal," he muttered.

Feeling a sense of powerlessness, I questioned him further, "So there's nothing we can do about it?"

"Nope," he replied simply, leaving no room for hope.

"Well, in that case, see you on the other side," I grinned defiantly in the darkness. With those words, I rolled over, ready to embrace the uncertainty of the night's sleep.

Chapter 21
REED'S DISCOVERY
REED: The Abyss

I awakened from my slumber, peering into the darkness. A faint glimmer illuminated the walls of the abyss. The light had appeared and vanished twice since Star was taken away by those peculiar metal creatures. As I gazed at the brightening cave, my thoughts drifted away from self-pity and toward the possibilities that lay above. Perhaps, just perhaps, that light held the key to my salvation. Fueled by this hope, I reluctantly emerged from the cozy confines of my sleeping bag.

Taking in the surroundings of the platform that Star and I had called home for the past few months, a wave of loneliness washed over me. Star would have found solace if it had been I who had been taken, but I relied on companionship to keep going. Without it, I felt adrift. It became clear to me that I couldn't stay here. I needed to keep moving, even if it meant facing the imminent threat of a zombie horde.

However, I wasn't reckless in my decision. I took the time to prepare, packing a large bag with supplies, food, bedding, and weapons. I left behind what I couldn't carry, using it as a cache for future use. With a final glance at the makeshift floating home, I ascended the cables that supported the platform, leading to the opening of a long tunnel. Peering down the tunnel, I saw no sign of zombies or flying metal creatures as far as my eyes could see. With this assurance, I hoisted myself up, unfastening my harness from the platform and securing it for the ascent. Gripping the anchor rope tightly, I began pulling myself upward.

Although slower without Star's assistance, the pulley system facilitated a relatively swift ascent up the abyss walls. As my arms strained with effort, I couldn't help but marvel at how Star accomplished this task day after day. In the past, I had relied on my own climbing skills on rocky terrain, which demanded careful precision. However, utilizing the pulley system gave me a sense of urgency despite being in a relatively safe position. The desire to ascend quickly pushed me to exert extra effort.

One arm's length at a time, I steadily progressed up the wall. By the time I reached the apex of the pulley system, the cavern was bathed in blinding light. I secured a new length of cord to the wall anchor I had previously placed and surveyed my surroundings. The shifting slope of the wall offered numerous handholds and ledges for a brief respite. Mapping out a mental path, I resumed my ascent up the cliff face. Engaging in physical activity helped momentarily distract me from the loss I had suffered and the sense of insignificance that engulfed my existence.

Scaling the rocks like a nimble spider, I advanced with each grip and foothold. I tracked time by the brightening light until a blinding orb traversed the sky, forcing me to pause. Finding a secure ledge, I shielded my eyes from the intense glow above. It wasn't until the orb disappeared beyond the opposite side of the abyss's opening that I resumed my climb. With the fading light urging me onward, I took calculated risks, surpassing my usual level of caution. The urgency to reach the top before darkness consumed my very being. Alas, I couldn't cover the remaining distance as the light continued to wane. I halted on a ledge, resigning myself to the fact that time was slipping away. Surprisingly, even after fifteen minutes, the faint light persisted, casting a subtle glow on the rocky terrain. Encouraged by this glimmer, I made a daring decision to press on.

Time slipped away as I continued climbing relentlessly for two hours, yet the light stubbornly persisted. Regrettably, the length of cord I had brought along proved to be inadequate. Out of habit, I secured the end, all the while casting my gaze upwards toward the short distance separating me from the mouth of the opening. It was a mere thirty feet away, and the path appeared relatively safe. Without allowing any second-guessing to seep in, I unfastened my harness and embarked on the final leg, free-climbing the remaining distance.

The possibility of a fatal fall didn't even cross my mind, consumed as I was by the burning desire to reach the summit. Speed propelled me forward, perhaps recklessly so. It was this haste that caused my hand to slip, and I felt myself losing grip, descending slightly. In a desperate frenzy, I clawed at the rocks until my hand found purchase in a groove.

My body jerked, and a cry of pain escaped my lips, but I refused to let go. Blinking away tears that threatened my vision, I focused on finding secure footholds, then carefully extracted my injured hand from its temporary sanctuary. Blood stained my hand and arm, evidence of the jagged surface that had cut me. Anger surged through my veins, momentarily numbing the pain, as I begrudgingly completed the final few feet to the surface.

Once there, I hauled myself onto the top, rolling away from the perilous edge. Gasping for breath, I turned my gaze upward, greeted by the expanse of a vivid blue sky. A softer, less blinding light drifted toward the horizon, captivating my awe-struck stare. I felt infinitesimally small in the face of such vastness, as tiny specks of light scattered across the celestial canvas. It took a moment to tear my eyes away from this celestial spectacle. When I did, I gradually turned my head in the opposite direction, away from the abyss, and beheld a towering wall a hundred feet from where I lay.

Every aspect of my surroundings appeared peculiar and alien, but then again, I had spent my entire life beneath the earth's surface. I lay there, taking in the strange sight for an extended period before grunting, pushing myself into action. My first order of business was attending to the wound on my hand. Extracting a spare piece of clothing from my ample pack, I tightly wrapped it around the injured area, staunching the flow of blood. Retrieving the rifle secured to the side of my pack, I surveyed the area using its scope. I directed my focus toward the wall, peering up to the top, but only the vast expanse of sky with its dotted lights greeted my eyes. At ground level, about a mile away, a dark patch stood out on the wall, capturing my attention for future exploration. The fissure in the earth, housing

129

the abyss, snaked along the edge of the wall. Shifting my gaze to the opposite side of this ravine, my eyes met the sight of majestic mountain peaks, their summits adorned with glistening white. The beauty of this panorama failed to distract me from my objective.

Sweeping the land with a watchful eye, aided by the scope of my rifle, I sought any sign of zombies, but none were visible.

Intrigued by the enigmatic black spot on the wall, the only discernible feature on my side of the abyss's entrance, I resolved to investigate it further. Sporadic bursts of plant life sprouted from the ground at random intervals, piquing my curiosity. Gathering several fist-sized rocks scattered around me, I arranged them into a small pile, marking the spot where I had ascended from the abyss in case a swift retreat became necessary. With that precaution taken, I proceeded leisurely toward the peculiar section of the wall. As I drew closer, I noticed a hole in the wall, from which water trickled in gentle waves. The entrance to the hole was obstructed by an aging metal grate, its rusted state revealing signs of decay, with fragments of the grate having crumbled away. Now, in close proximity to the opening, I discerned a cacophony of noises emanating from the other side. Peering through the grate, I observed a tunnel with another grate positioned thirty-five feet away. However, unlike the one adjacent to me, this one rested on the tunnel's ceiling.

Curiosity surged within me as I caught glimpses of movement on the other side. Testing the stability of the metal grate, I discovered that certain sections disintegrated with little pressure. With a few solid kicks, portions of the grate easily gave way, creating a passage through the decaying barrier. Clearing the path of the deteriorated grate, I carefully maneuvered through the opening. Proceeding cautiously, I reached the opposite end of the waterway, my footsteps causing slight splashes in the shallow stream that flowed beneath. Upon arriving, I noticed that light emanated from the grate above. Moreover, I found myself standing at a junction in the tunnel.

Ensuring there were no nearby zombies, I glanced in both directions before directing my gaze upward. Just above me, through a sturdier metal grate, a sight took my breath away. People could be seen walking above, surrounded by towering structures. Though lacking the branches that reached out to the rocks like the tower I had called home, they bore a resemblance to it. However, the sheer number of these structures was staggering. Carts adorned with bright lights moved autonomously, emitting a soft hum as they glided. Other lights, too intense for my eyes, illuminated almost every inch of the world above. The amalgamation of noise and light overwhelmed my senses, causing me to instinctively retreat.

A part of me yearned to approach these people and discover their identity. However, given that I had already been shot by one of my own people and Star's capture, my cautious disposition prevailed. Star had been taken by mysterious beings, and it seemed likely that these individuals employed similar metal creatures. They might even be the ones responsible for Star's disappearance. Equipped with my supplies and having a possibility of finding Star, I decided to take it slow, so I surveyed the two underground paths that stretched before me. After thinking for a moment, I chose to use them as avenues to gather more information about these people before reaching a definitive conclusion.

Chapter 22
EXPLORING
WIND: Underground Tower #4

"Hey, Elephant, I haven't seen you in a while," I said as I made my way toward the meal token booth to receive my earnings. It was stationed on the two hundredth floor and was much larger than the other floors as it had a whole two floors of head space above. It was only partially crowded.

"O, hi Wind. Yeah, I've been sick lately. Still getting over it, but I have to start pulling my shifts again, or the food will run out."

I nodded, knowing many others that were in Elephant's situation. He put himself out there twice as much to feed his new family. His wife had just given birth two months earlier.

"Well, I was actually looking for you."

Elephant's large eyebrows knitted at that. "Looking for me? Why would you be looking for me."

"Well, I need your help. You see, we are in a bit of a situation."

"What's wrong? Are you still having a hard time? About your brother, I mean."

"Let's get our food tokens first, then let's talk."

"Alright," Elephant replied, concern in his eyes. We waited in a short line to receive our pay for our jobs. As we waited, I looked around the floor and saw the food dispensary units that lay around the floor. It was where most people purchased their daily meals. Soon, we got to the front of the food token line, where we received our earned food tokens. After receiving our portions, we moved over to one of the many tables scattered throughout the large room.

"So, is this about your brother? We have all been concerned for you."

"Well, funny you should mention that. It does involve that a bit, but I think it's better for me to start at the beginning. Well, you know how everyone was talking about how Redwood and Stump were found dead. Well, it made me curious what the higher floors aren't telling us. So, I started digging."

"Digging? How would that help?"

"Not actually, but with the computer I have access to. As it turns out, accessing the upper floor files was easy."

"What!" Elephant said in a loud whisper. "You could get punished for doing that. What if someone finds out?"

"Hear me out before you freak out about the little stuff."

"Little stuff?"

"Yes, miniscule." I paused briefly, looking around to ensure there wasn't anyone close to our table. "I found proof that the higher-ups sent my brother to die."

"You did!"

"Yes, and they are going to do it again in three days."

"What!"

"So no matter what, don't go out into the tunnels."

"You found this on the computer thing?"

"Yes, and more. The upper floors, as it turns out, don't work but live off of our hard work. We struggle to live off of these measly rations while they are filling their stomachs without lifting a finger. Worst of all is that they have a contract with the Zombies."

"A contract with the Zombies. Don't be silly." Elephant laughed. "You had me going there." He stopped laughing when he saw my facial expression. "You can't be serious."

"I'm dead serious."

"What do they get out of it? It's not like the Zombies are providing them with stuff."

"That's the thing. I haven't figured that out. It just doesn't make sense. But they have a contract with the zombies on file."

Elephant sat back, thinking. "And you said they are going to send more of us to die in three days."

I nodded in the affirmative.

"We can't let anyone go then."

"Agreed, that is part of what I wanted to talk to you about. I've told fifty others. They will make sure their families

133

don't go. We have to send the people on this list." I pulled out a list with thirty names on it.

"What is this?" Elephant asked, taking the list of names.

"All the traitors in our midst."

"When you say traitor?"

"They are helping the higher-ups to gain position into the upper levels of the tower."

Elephant's eyes skimmed over the paper. He nodded at a couple of names and whistled at others.

"So?" I asked, "Can I have your help?"

"Well, you aren't leaving me with much choice. What is the plan?"

"We are going to have to disarm and then confront these people first. Then we are going to have to deal with the upper tower floors."

"How?"

"Well, in three days, they are going to want people to go out. I figured that would be a good time to hold a lower-floor meeting. I'll need someone in the crowd for each of these thirty people."

Elephant nodded. "Just tell me who my target is."

"We aren't killing them."

"If they are in on sending our boys to their deaths, then they deserve it."

"Yes, but we don't want to become the problem that others want to solve with violence."

Elephant nodded. "Alright, you have my word."

"Good, things are going to come to a head in three days.

Chapter 23
THE CHANGING
STAR: The surface
Z.O.M.B.I.E. Games: Drifting Planes

That night, my attempt to find rest was thwarted by the restless movements of those around me. The proximity of so many people was unfamiliar to me, and the events of the day weighed heavily on my mind, requiring careful processing. I lay at the base of the stairs leading up from the storage cache room, my belongings—my trusty pack and weapons—within reach, with sunglasses perched atop the pack in their protective cases. As an hour passed, the rhythmic patterns of breathing indicated that most, if not all, had succumbed to slumber. Finally, my own eyes began to drift shut, ready to embrace sleep, when a rattling noise from above shattered the silence. Instantly alert, I instinctively reached for my weapon, fixating on the entrance above, where a sliver of light seeped through the meeting point of the double doors. To my astonishment, I discerned movement and observed the surrounding light diminish dramatically as a looming figure cast its shadow over the opening. Something large loitered between the door and the specks of light in the darkened sky.

With stealth, I slipped out of my sleeping bag, arming myself fully with both gun and sword. Prepared for any confrontation, I ascended the stairs, navigating with limited visibility. Once again, the doors quivered under external pressure, their creaking hinting at an intelligent force attempting to pry them open. The proximity of the threat compelled me to position myself merely a foot away from the opening, peering through the narrow crack, striving to discern the entity beyond. The celestial light bathed the surrounding landscape, illuminating the distant tree, while the shadowy figure above me remained concealed in darkness.

All I could discern was the silhouette of a human frame. I observed as the creature eventually retreated, "Dig it out," came a raspy voice from outside. The voice sent a chill down my spine, reminding me of the Zombie creatures that had killed Rock. Its bone-chilling resonance was unmistakable.

This isn't good, I thought, realizing there was no escape within these confines. We were trapped, and I couldn't allow them to breach our sanctuary. I reassessed the secure bolting mechanism in place to fortify the doors, finding it still intact, but the scraping sounds from outside indicated that several creatures were tirelessly engaged in their efforts. The scratching grew dangerously close to a digging sound.

To glean a clearer understanding of the situation beyond, I pressed my eye closely against the door's peephole, straining to observe the events unfolding outside. As I withdrew, examining the edges of the door and searching for weak points, my gaze landed upon a sizable hole near the base—a hole that hadn't been present when I had initially secured the door. Somehow, the creatures outside had created that breach. If they could accomplish that, I dreaded to consider the extent of damage they could inflict once they uncovered the sides of the door frame. Fortunately, the structure was sunken into the ground, which had initially masked the hole's existence.

Time was running out before these creatures found their way inside. I needed to act swiftly. That's when it dawned on me—the hole was just wide enough for a bullet to pass through. Hastily, I retrieved my gun, ensuring it was loaded without causing any disturbance. Taking position, I aimed out into the open space beyond. The limited view offered little clarity; the gun barrel nearly obscured the entire hole. Employing my habitual practice of keeping both eyes open, I used the eye farthest from the gun to peer through the aperture. In contrast, the eye closest to the gun ensured I kept it directed straight through the opening. The angle was tight, but I managed to discern a figure stooping in front of the door.

Summoning my resolve, I squeezed the trigger with unwavering hands. The resulting rattling of the gunfire reverberated through the stairwell, its deafening echo permeating the room below. The air filled with screams and frantic voices. Some sought clarification, questioning the cause of the commotion, while others expressed their fear through incoherent outbursts or trembling whimpers. Their trepidation was justified, for unlike me, they were blind to the unknown lurking within the depths of the room.

Disregarding the cries of fear echoing from below, my attention remained fixated on the lifeless body sprawled before me. Loading another casing into the chamber with only sheer muscle memory, my eyes remained locked on the hole, peering into the darkened landscape beyond. Another figure bent over the fallen, prompting a second resounding blast. The sparks generated by the bullet grazing the door's edge blinded my night vision, causing me to blink rapidly while steadfastly maintaining my aim.

The chorus of terrified voices persisted from below, yet I continued to tune them out. Reloading once more, I continued blinking, willing my sight to return. Gradually, my peripheral vision regained clarity, with only the focal point remaining illuminated by the lingering afterimage of the sparks. Instead of gazing directly through the hole, I shifted my focus just to the side, utilizing my peripheral vision to detect any movement beyond. Adjusting my position, I peered out from a different angle, but still, there was no sign of anything. Only then did I respond to the voices below.

"They were digging at the entrance. I took one out, and the second is at least wounded," I shouted, my voice carrying through the tense atmosphere.

"Star, is that you?" a voice I didn't recognize called out.

"Yes, everyone needs to calm down and rest. Nothing is getting in," I reassured them, though inwardly, I doubted the truth of my words. My intention was to keep them calm and out of my way. The creatures knew our location and were far more cunning than the slow, mindless creatures I had fought throughout my life. If I didn't stop them, they would surely dig us out.

However, an unsettling sensation washed over me, originating not from outside but from within my own body. Pain surged through me, causing me to gasp and moan. A tingling sensation spread across my entire being, accompanied by sharp, biting pains. That was when I heard sounds of discomfort and pain echoing from below as fear intensified within me. The movement and groans of pain below reminded me of Rock as a zombie tore him apart. I immediately thought that they were being attacked by more zombies. That image made me dread what I might find below. My mind raced as I wondered how I missed a second entrance that allowed Zombies in. How had I overlooked another entrance when our lives depended on it? I rushed to get down and help, but my body protested as pain shot through me. Despite the agony coursing through my body, I persevered, gradually descending the stairs, inch by agonizing inch. Every step brought with it waves of pain, at times rendering me immobile, while other moments saw me propelled forward by sheer determination.

The others depended on me, and an instinctual drive compelled me to keep moving. After what felt like an eternity, I finally reached the bottom of the stairwell, peering into the room. Even with my clear eyesight, the darkness obscured distinct details, revealing only indistinguishable forms sprawled across the ground. Moans filled the air as all of those in our group writhed intermittently.

My gaze strained to pierce the darkness as my vision blurred with pain. I searched for the elusive zombies that had assaulted my comrades but couldn't make any out. Judging by the symptoms that everyone is manifesting, it seemed evident that we might have been infected. A surge of intense pain coursed through my body, leaving me sprawled on the ground. It was at that moment that I decided it no longer mattered if the zombies claimed me; I simply couldn't endure the agony any longer.

A veil of unconsciousness shrouded me, embracing me in its blackness.

I blinked awake as someone gently shook me. "What?" I startled, jolting upright.

"Wake up," Kyle said, his voice cutting through the haze. I blinked, adjusting to the brightness streaming in through the hole in the doors above. Scanning my surroundings, I located my sunglasses and placed them on my face. "What happened?" I inquired, still disoriented.

"We're trying to figure that out," Kyle replied, his voice laced with confusion as he guided me towards the exit. "We were all asleep when we heard gunshots, just before everyone...changed," he explained.

"Changed? We changed?" I questioned, still grappling with the remnants of disorientation. A sudden surge of memories flooded my mind, sending a shiver down my spine. "Where are they? What happened to the zombies?" I pondered internally, seeking answers.

"What zombies?" Kyle inquired, his brow furrowed in bewilderment.

"The ones that attacked last night," I clarified, my voice laden with a mix of concern and disbelief.

"As far as I'm aware, there were no zombies last night. We underwent a transformation, and it wasn't a pleasant experience. It seems like it affected you the most," Kyle murmured, his words carrying a tinge of sympathy for my apparent suffering.

"But there were zombies. They were trying to get in. One of them even spoke, giving orders to the others to dig," I blurted out, urgency lacing my words.

As our voices began to rouse the rest of the group, stirring them from their slumber, I glanced up the stairs and noticed sunlight seeping through. Signaling for Kyle to follow me, we ascended the stairs, both armed and ready. Unbolting the doors, we pushed them open with little effort, allowing the light to flood in and revealing the commotion below as people started comprehending the situation.

Scanning the area, I couldn't spot any bodies. "Where are they?" I questioned aloud, my confusion growing.

Kyle, too, looked around, searching for any signs of the zombies. "Look at these scrape marks in the earth," I pointed out, indicating the visible traces near our previous location.

Kyle examined the marks and nodded in agreement. "It does appear that something tried to break in," he mused, his tone filled with intrigue.

Pondering our surroundings, I realized that the zombies must have retreated after my gunfire, as there was no evidence of their presence in the waist-high grass. Determined to gather more information, I decided to scout the vicinity, and Kyle joined me.

"You mentioned that one of them spoke?" Kyle queried, his curiosity evident.

"Yes," I confirmed, sensing that Kyle possessed knowledge about these enhanced zombies. "What do you know about these zombies?" I inquired, seeking answers.

"Well, the general public sees them as mere enhancements in zombie games, believing they were artificially created and controlled. The higher-ups keep the truth tightly guarded. In reality, they are previous participants who have been transformed into zombies. Due to their preexisting enhancements, once they turn, they possess even greater capabilities. It's unusual that they can communicate, indicating a level of coordination. I haven't come across that before in my research, and I know more than anyone should," Kyle disclosed.

"It certainly makes them more dangerous," I acknowledged, silently absorbing the newfound information. As we continued our exploration in silence, a safe distance from the rest of the group, I seized the opportunity to address something that had been bothering me. "I noticed you lied last night," I whispered.

Confusion flickered across Kyle's face. "What?" he asked, taken aback.

"About the number of people who could survive until the end," I clarified, searching his eyes for an explanation.

Kyle's surprise lingered, and he met my gaze with a mixture of caution and vulnerability. "How did you...?" he began to ask, but I interrupted.

"I just could," I shrugged, indicating that the details were less important than the fact that I had uncovered the truth. "So, what does that mean for us? Is that why you wanted me to destroy the map?" I probed further, attempting to unravel his intentions.

"No," Kyle deflated slightly, his expression betraying a weighty burden. "I can't reveal too much while we're being monitored, but trust me, it will be far better if we work together until the end rather than fighting amongst ourselves now," he sighed, his voice filled with hope and weariness.

I nodded in understanding, acknowledging the importance of unity in our precarious situation. "We should head back now. I don't see any signs of their presence," I muttered, shifting my focus to the group's well-being.

However, before we could turn back, Kyle reached out to stop me, a sense of urgency in his eyes. I turned to face him, meeting his gaze, curious about what he had to say. He glanced around hesitantly before pulling me closer, his touch sending a shiver down my spine. He moved my head slightly and whispered into my ear, his voice filled with determination. "I need you to trust me. I have a plan to get all of us out of here, but it will take time," he revealed, his words resonating in the depths of my mind.

I nodded, quietly indicating that I had heard and understood his plea for trust.

"Good," Kyle continued, his voice barely above a whisper. "To cover up what I just said, I'm going to kiss you. It will help us blend in with the other participants and prevent any suspicion from the game organizers," he explained, his words causing confusion to cloud my thoughts.

"What? Wait, what?" I stammered, attempting to pull away, but it was too late.

Kyle's lips landed firmly on my cheek, leaving me startled and repulsed. Reacting quickly, I recoiled and began

141

wiping my cheek in disgust. "What the!" I exclaimed, my voice filled with a mixture of surprise and indignation.

Kyle, undeterred by my reaction, grinned mischievously. "That's how my family shows affection to friends. A big kiss on the cheek is a surefire way to know you're a Pecoraro's friend," he chuckled as if it were a lighthearted gesture.

"That's utterly disgusting," I mumbled, still repulsed as I continued to clean my face.

"I'm telling you, some countries did this as a greeting in the past," Kyle chuckled, persisting with his light-hearted demeanor.

"You're pulling my leg," I grumbled.

"I would never pull one over on a friend." he insisted, following me as we made our way back to the rest of the group.

As we rejoined the others, most of them were busy checking their gear in the warm sunlight. A quick look over them all showed that several of them were out of sorts. Gurney, with his usual grumpy tone, was the first to address us. "Where were you two, and what happened last night?" he inquired, his speech and movements strangely stiff. The curiosity of the group was evident in their turned heads as no one seemed sure of what actually transpired the night before.

I took a moment to compose myself before responding. "I shot a zombie right here last night. This morning, I searched for its remains. However, I couldn't find any signs of them, so I scouted around quickly to see if they were still in the area," I explained, laced with apprehension and determination.

"So, that was the noise we heard," remarked Trevor, a blond-haired man who was adjusting his backpack in the midst of the group. "We were wondering what was going on before the Changing began. We didn't get a chance to ask since the chaos of the Changing drowned out everything else. Did you manage to kill it? I don't see a body," he questioned, his curiosity piqued.

"I shot him in the head. He shouldn't have gotten up," I replied, my voice firm and resolute. Trevor offered his perspective, "You probably only nicked him. It's not easy to kill a zombie."

"I don't miss," I retorted, confident in my marksmanship.

Kyle chimed in, supporting my assertion. "That's true. He's a sharpshooter," he added, his tone filled with admiration for my skills.

Trevor simply shrugged, his nonchalant demeanor contrasting with the situation's intensity. My eyes narrowed, noticing he also had stiff movements with his left arm, just like Gurney. Something was off with the people around me, but none seemed to notice it in the others. Meanwhile, Kyle tugged on my arm, giving me a sly wink before expressing his doubts. "You mentioned that one of them talked? Zombies aren't supposed to talk," he muttered, his voice filled with skepticism.

Confused about Kyle's motives and the game he seemed to be playing, I decided to play along, not fully grasping his intentions. "He did talk, though. He instructed the others to dig. Look, you can see the marks they left behind," I responded, pointing towards the entrance where large gouges in the earth indicated some form of excavation, resembling the marks left by an animal's desperate claws.

The group collectively turned their attention to the entrance, contemplating the implications of talking zombies. Gurney, lost in thought, muttered with a pensive tone, "Talking zombies? That's something to consider."

"They're not just talking; they're smart too," I interjected, emphasizing the depth of their intelligence. "I've encountered something like this before. There was a creature similar to these that we had encountered in the caverns. It killed a friend of mine after swinging from a cave's roof," I shivered momentarily, the memory still vivid in my mind.

Curiosity piqued, Trevor inquired further, seeking clarification. "So, you've dealt with them before? You've killed them?" he questioned, his voice tinged with awe and concern.

"I'm not entirely certain. We set up an explosive tripwire and made our escape," I replied, recalling the risky encounter.

"Well, we better pack up and get going," Trevor said, taking charge of the group. Everyone seemed to agree, and they followed his lead. It appeared that Gurney had lost his credibility as the group's leader after failing to find the supply cache and the embarrassing incident from the previous day. I was fine with that, as Trevor was much more easy going than Gurney had ever been.

As they finished their preparations, I pulled Kyle aside. "What is wrong with everyone?"

"What do you mean?" Kyle asked, looking them over.

"I mean, look at Gurney and how stiff his speech and movements are. Trevor is favoring his right arm. That guy over there is looking out into space, and those two are looking for bugs."

"O," Kyle smiled. "It is the changing. It takes some time to get used to it. Look at Amy over there. She has enhanced agility, but it takes a day or two to get used to it. See how clumsy she is. Shawn over there is trying to filter out every noise around, and Gurney there is trying to get used to his hardened body. It will be like this for a couple of days. Don't worry, it's normal in the games. People often refer to it as the drunken stage of the games.

"Why aren't we like that?"

Kyle smiled and told me to pack up and we would talk on the road.

Over the course of a day's travel, I gradually got acquainted with the other team members. It turned out they were all already familiar with each other, having been introduced two weeks before the game. The city had organized various promotional activities for each of them, allowing them to gain favor or disfavor with the public. This gave them time to form alliances and make general plans.

It became apparent to me how much of a disadvantage I was at compared to the others. Unlike them, who had the opportunity to strategize and prepare before the games, I was thrown in at the last moment, forced to navigate the challenges on the fly. Furthermore, gathering a large following during those two weeks was in each individual's best interest. Popularity translated into points, which could be used to choose one's partner for the Killer's Gambit and also offered other benefits, such as selecting desired enhancements during the Changing.

As for myself, I had no idea what enhancements I had received from my night of pain. However, throughout the day, I learned a lot about the others in the group. Trevor, the blond man who had assumed the leadership role, had acquired a faster metabolism and hardened skin on his left arm. Gurney opted for hardened skin on his arms and legs to protect against scratches and bites, along with enhanced vision.

Nancy, who stuck close to Trevor, chose a hardened left hand and arm, along with a better metabolism. It seemed that many people opted for improved metabolic functions. I discovered that in previous games, people often perished due to the scarcity of food or weakened state caused by hunger, making them easy targets for Zombies or other competing groups. Additionally, choosing a better metabolism required fewer fame points since it was more entertaining for people to meet their demise in alternative ways.

Kyle introduced me to Ernie, Drake, and Laurel early in the day. Ernie had heightened reaction speed and a hardened left arm. Laurel had opted for speed, both mentally and physically, enabling her to move faster than an average person. Drake chose an enhancement that allowed him to control insects infected by microorganisms, gaining access to their sensory perceptions.

Later, I discovered that Jillian had also chosen a similar power. Simon, on the other hand, remained a mystery as he kept his selected enhancement a secret. Ninna went for increased muscle mass, causing her small frame to bulk up significantly in just a day. However, she had to consume more rations to sustain her growth.

Sandra and Malori focused on enhancing their appearances. Sandra, who initially had a heavier build, visibly slimmed down throughout the day, attaining a leaner physique.

145

Malori, who appeared plain before, now looked stunning, according to Kyle, who couldn't help but mention it repeatedly.

The remaining members of the group didn't deviate much from the standard enhancements. Throughout the day, I gradually got to know the entire group, which included Shawn, Dale, Mike, Alvine, Amy, Katty, Wade, Devin, Juan, and Reyn. Multiple times, people asked me what powers I had chosen, only to be disappointed by my lack of knowledge.

"You must have gotten something," Kyle persisted for the third time. "Don't you feel any different?"

I rolled my eyes, growing tired of hearing the same question. "As I've said before, I felt the pain, but I don't feel any different today compared to yesterday."

Undeterred, Kyle suggested, "Maybe you have the metabolism power. Are you feeling hungry?"

I shrugged. "Hey, I didn't receive anything. Everyone keeps talking about their different powers, but just look at Alvine over there," I muttered.

"What about him?" Kyle inquired.

"Well," I continued, "He claimed to have acquired Metabolism and reaction speed. But just look at him. There's no sign of increased reaction speed," I grinned.

"How do you know he doesn't have enhanced reaction speed?" Kyle asked curiously.

"Because he has been swiping at that bug three times already. If his reaction speed were truly faster, he would have snatched it out of the air, and from what I've seen, he would have struggled to learn how to walk again like Laurel," I muttered.

"Well," Kyle explained, "That's because he received an enhanced Metabolism last night. He won't gain the reaction speed until tonight."

"But everyone was boasting about their powers. I thought they received them all last night," I quipped.

"Oh no," Kyle laughed. "Receiving multiple enhancements all at once would likely be fatal for a person. They are given one power each night until they have received all the ones assigned to them. The maximum is four, but that's rare. Most people only have enough funds and popularity points for two. Some even need a wealthy sponsor to acquire those," Kyle said.

I nodded in understanding.

"But that's not all," Kyle continued. "There are also experimental powers."

"Experimental?" I questioned.

"Yeah, those powers start randomly appearing among everyone between day five and day ten. And if someone manages to survive until the thirtieth day, they receive a random power from the selection. Only two people get the heavy-duty item, and that's purely luck," he replied.

We walked in silence for a while, allowing me to ponder everything I had learned throughout the day. I couldn't help but wonder about the powers I had received and why the process had been so excruciatingly painful.

After a while, Kyle's voice broke the silence. "Do you think those Zombies will return tonight?" he asked, bringing me back to the conversation.

"They were searching for us," I answered.

"But there are no Zombies in the plains during the first few days," he mentioned.

"It doesn't matter how it used to be. They were there last night, and chances are they'll find us again tonight," I responded.

"So what should we do? We still need to sleep," he mused.

I gazed at the cliff edge overlooking the ocean, the path we were following. "I have an idea, but it will take some time to set up," I muttered.

"So we should start early?" Kyle asked. I nodded in agreement.

"Well, judging by the position of the sun, we have a couple of hours left in the day. Let's push a little further. The fewer days we spend out here, the better," I suggested.

Chapter 24
AN UNCOMFORTABLE NIGHT
STAR: The surface
Z.O.M.B.I.E. Games: Drifting Planes

After explaining my plan to Kyle and Trevor for setting up camp for the night, I eagerly awaited the team leader's decision to break for camp. The hours seemed to vanish as we pressed forward. The sun began its descent, but I wasn't familiar enough with its patterns to realize how late it was getting. Finally, Trevor signaled the group to stop, declaring that it was time to prepare for the night.

Without wasting a moment, I retrieved the rope, metal shafts, and a small hammer we had obtained from the last supply cache. Others also emptied their backpacks, revealing thin but strong ropes. Kyle assured us that they were sturdy enough to hold an elephant. After a brief discussion about elephants and their weight, I felt confident that the rope wouldn't snap under my own weight.

I packed all the necessary supplies for setting up camp on the cliff wall into a single pack, including the metal shafts, hammer, and as much rope as I could fit. Then, I fashioned a makeshift harness by tying a rope around my waist, arms, and legs. I handed the other end of the rope to several of the team members. "Hold on tight," I instructed.

"Don't just jump," Ninna yelped, tightening her grip on the rope with her increased strength from her transformation. I paused just before the edge of the cliff, turning back to her and the others holding the rope. I could see disbelief in her eyes as they expected me to simply leap over the edge.

"I'm not just going to jump. That would be painful. I'm going to lower myself down while you hold on," I grinned.

I tossed the remaining rope over the edge and, against my earlier words, jumped off, but I held onto the rope, allowing myself to descend only a couple of feet before coming to a stop. Using the rope as leverage, I propelled myself down the cliff, kicking off the wall to control my descent.

I managed to descend twenty feet before securing the remaining loose rope to the harness I had fashioned. With that done, I began hammering the metal shafts into the cliff wall, finding crevices that could hold them securely. I pounded them in with all my strength, ensuring they would bear even the weight of an elephant if luck was on our side. Then, I attached a rope to each metal shaft and tied the other end to my harness. I repeated the process, working swiftly along the cliff wall until all twenty-three shafts were in place with their ropes attached. I worked as fast as I could, but by the time I tied off the final rope, the sun had vanished beyond the horizon, and darkness was rapidly descending. With the task completed, I ascended the rope, still held by my teammates.

"That took longer than expected," Trevor admitted when I reached the top. "We should have started sooner. We still need to get everyone harnessed and suspended," he said.

"Well, let's get on with it," I replied, already untying the ropes attached to me. Several hands reached out to help, and soon, people were securing ropes to sleeping bags and themselves. Thankfully, there wasn't resistance to the idea of sleeping on the cliff after realizing that zombies had come for us the day before, and most people still had changes to go through that night.

"Excuse me, could you assist me?" Malori asked, extending a rope toward me.

Turning to face Malori, I couldn't help but blink in surprise. Kyle had been praising her beauty throughout the day, and although I had caught glimpses of it from afar, I hadn't been this close to her since the morning. Her presence made my heart race, pounding rapidly in my chest.

"Um, yeah, sure," I stammered, my voice betraying my nervousness. Reaching out, I grasped the rope she offered. First, I tied it securely to the sleeping bag, ensuring it wouldn't come loose. Then, I found a midpoint on the rope and tied it there as well, creating a stable connection. Finally, I fashioned

149

the end of the rope into a harness, securing it around Malori. With each step, my heart pounded faster, intensifying under the weight of our proximity. It reminded me of a similar sensation I had experienced when I was close to Wind, but this time, it felt even more amplified. The feeling made me uneasy, and I hurriedly finished securing Malori to the rope before moving on to fasten my own harness.

"Thank you," Malori said sweetly, her words causing a blush to creep onto my cheeks.

I didn't turn back to face her, instead choosing to wave my hand dismissively as I focused on adjusting my own straps.

As the others were being slowly lowered down the cliff, having taken the time to prepare their own equipment, Ninna and Gurney held onto the rope, ensuring a safe descent for each person along with their sleeping bags and gear. Meanwhile, I continued to check and adjust my own knots and equipment, focused on the task at hand. Trevor approached me, curiosity evident on his face.

"How did you come up with this plan?" he inquired.

"We endured countless days living like this, with a horde of Zombies constantly lurking above us," I replied.

"Really? That sounds like quite a story. I'd love to hear more about it sometime if we manage to survive the night," he said with a smile.

"You won't need me to; you'll get to experience it firsthand," I assured him, my gaze fixed on the vast plains.

With the sun completely gone, the stars began to twinkle in the sky, casting a faint glow over the surroundings. I removed my sunglasses and noticed that my vision seemed sharper in the darkness without them. It was an incredible feeling to be able to observe the minute details and vibrant colors of the surface world, a stark contrast to the monotonous plane walls of the tunnels I had grown accustomed to.

Gazing up at the night sky, a broad expanse unfolded before my eyes, adorned with countless shimmering stars. It was a sight that had eluded me until now, as my only prior encounter had been through the pages of articles and descriptions. Yet, at this moment, the celestial canvas revealed itself to me in all its breathtaking glory.

The stars, like celestial jewels, punctuated the darkness with their radiant presence. They seemed to dance across the vast expanse, twinkling with an ethereal brilliance that captivated my senses. Each tiny point of light held within it a story of cosmic wonder, whispered secrets of distant galaxies, and the passage of time itself.

I marveled at the intricate patterns woven by these celestial bodies, connecting them into familiar constellations from my readings. The Milky Way, a celestial river of stardust, stretched across the sky, painting a luminescent pathway amidst the sea of darkness. It was as if nature itself had become an artist, using the heavens as a canvas to depict its grandest masterpiece.

The sheer magnitude of the starry spectacle overwhelmed my senses. It was a symphony of light, a tapestry of dreams and possibilities that stretched beyond the boundaries of imagination. Each star, with its unique brilliance and position, painted a story of cosmic significance, inviting me to contemplate the mysteries of the universe.

Immersing myself in this celestial spectacle, a newfound appreciation blossomed within me. The articles I had read paled in comparison to the breathtaking reality before me. No words could capture the sheer awe-inspiring beauty that unfolded above.

Even as the last few individuals made their way down the cliff, my attention was suddenly drawn to a figure approaching us, running from a distance. Their movements were too fluid to be those of the zombies I had become familiar with, indicating that it was either an enhanced Zombie or a human. Sensing urgency, I turned to Trevor.

"We need to hurry; they're coming," I urged, pointing towards the approaching figure.

"I can't see anything in this darkness," Trevor complained.

"Just get everyone down quickly." With those words, I retrieved my rifle and aimed it toward the plains. Peering through the sights, I quickly located the figure, making her way towards us. It was a young woman, her hair billowing in the wind as she ran. There were no discernible signs of a Zombie, such as shrunken eyelids or grotesque growths resulting from excessive feeding. Her appearance and well-maintained clothes indicated that she was human. Another glance revealed a creature following closely behind her. Although its movements were less coordinated, it possessed speed and stamina. Taking a deep breath, I controlled my breathing and pulled the trigger, sending a shot through the tall grass. The bullet struck the creature square in the face, causing it to collapse onto the ground. Startled by the gunshot, the woman stumbled and fell into the grass, momentarily disappearing from my view.

During that brief moment, I observed several others moving through the plains. A group of approximately a hundred Zombies was making its way through the tall grass. I wondered where they had concealed themselves during the daytime to emerge so quickly. There seemed to be no hiding spots in the endless fields. Kyle had mentioned that zombies were usually encountered closer to the city, yet here they were. Their numbers were too overwhelming to engage in direct combat. I didn't possess enough ammunition to take on the entire group, and there wasn't time to get some from the others as many had descended down the cliff by now.

As I scanned the approaching zombies, my eyes locked onto three figures that stood out from the rest, moving with unmatched speed. Meanwhile, the woman had risen to her feet and was steadily making her way toward me.

Calculating the distance, I realized that the three swift zombies would reach her before she could reach me. With another round already loaded in my weapon, I focused my aim and regulated my breathing.

These three targets proved to be more challenging. Their movements were abrupt and erratic, surpassing the agility of any ordinary human or zombie. I took my time, adapting to their unpredictable motion, carefully judging the optimal moment to take my shot. Eventually, I squeezed the trigger, but instead of hitting the head, the bullet struck a shoulder. Nevertheless, the impact knocked the creature to the ground, causing it to lag behind the other two.

Swiftly reloading, I aimed once again, this time achieving greater success. The second shot found its mark, piercing the zombie's jaw and sending bone fragments cascading into its brain, effectively terminating it from its earthly existence.

The third shot was a disappointing miss, and it heightened the pressure I was under as the distance rapidly closed between the relentless Zombie and the determined woman. Realizing that another miss would be disastrous, I opted for a delay tactic. With precise aim, my next shot found its mark in the creature's leg, a steadier target compared to its erratic head. The impact sent the Zombie crashing into the tall grass, vanishing from sight. Meanwhile, the initial Zombie I had shot earlier resumed its relentless advance, albeit at a slightly slower pace, allowing me to deliver a well-placed headshot.

Only Trevor and I remained atop the cliff, the urgency in his voice echoing in the air. Understanding the need to act swiftly, I looked over and comprehended that Trevor required someone to secure the rope. Shouldering my gun, I hurried toward him, grasping the rope firmly from his hand. "Hurry!" I shouted, urging him on.

Trevor nodded in acknowledgment and swiftly descended, rappelling down to the metal rods below. Glancing behind me, I caught a glimpse of the woman who had sprinted toward us. With her proximity, I realized she was around the same age as Wind, her striking appearance momentarily reminding me of Malori. Her long black hair cascaded gracefully, and her features boasted a sharp elegance—a slender nose, thin eyebrows, and a well-shaped mouth. Beads of sweat adorned her forehead, with a few stray strands of hair clinging to them.

I kept my gaze fixed on her as she sprinted with unwavering determination, giving it her all. Lost in the intensity of the moment, I suddenly became aware of Trevor's absence from the rope, his weight no longer pulling at it. Startled by the abrupt shift in weight, my hands reflexively shot up, inadvertently colliding with my face. Tears welled in my eyes, blurring my vision, and I hastily wiped at my nose, hoping the girl hadn't caught sight of my brief moment of vulnerability. It dawned on me then that I had neglected to find someone to secure the rope for my own descent. Overwhelmed by the recent events, I chastised myself for failing to think clearly. Swiftly, I retrieved a rod from my pack and began hammering it into the ground. However, my progress was abruptly interrupted by an unearthly screech, a chilling reminder that time was running out.

I glanced upward, realizing I had run out of time. With urgency, I looped the rope around the pole just as the woman reached me, confusion etched across her face. "Who?" she uttered, her voice laced with uncertainty. "You're not a Scout," she observed.

"No, I'm a Star," I stated, stepping closer to her, looping a section of the rope around her waist and arms. She stepped back, fear flickering in her eyes. "Who are you?" she mumbled.

"We don't have time," I responded, stepping forward and adjusting the rope's positioning. "Hold on to me," I instructed, determination in my voice.

"What? But that's a cliff," she protested.

"Shh," I hushed her, gently pulling her toward me. "Hold on. They're almost here."

Reluctantly, she complied, grasping onto me. "No, not like that. You need a proper hold," I grumbled, assisting her in finding a secure position. "Here, around my shoulders... better... Ready?" I asked, not waiting for a response. Without hesitation, I leaped off the cliff, gripping both sides of the rope that encircled the metal stake. Grateful for our fortune, I felt the initial resistance, halting our descent several feet down. Concern had nagged at me, fearing that our combined weight might tilt or dislodge the stake from the ground. Regrettably, I hadn't managed to secure it as firmly as I would have preferred.

With swift efficiency, I began lowering the two of us down the cliff face. The woman clung to me tightly, her legs wrapped securely around my waist, while her grip around my neck felt as unyielding as steel. Despite my efforts to move with haste, time slipped away from me, and as we approached the poles, I had firmly lodged into the cliff. A sudden jolt disrupted my grip on the rope. Desperately, I reached out to reclaim it, but to my dismay, there was no resistance above, and we plummeted downward. Acting on instinct, I instinctively enfolded my arms and legs around the woman who held onto me for dear life.

Though I still clung to the rope originating from the cliff's top, my gaze fixated on the second rope, tightly knotted around the sturdy metal rods I had diligently anchored into the cliff. In that breathless moment, anticipation hung heavy in the air as I awaited the crucial instant when the second rope would go taut. It came without warning, and the sudden jerk made me regret holding my breath.

A rush of air escaped my lungs as the ropes encircling my body constricted, abruptly halting our descent. Instead, we swung forcefully toward the cliff, and the impact crushed me between the unyielding surface and the girl's weight. My grip on the loose rope weakened, but fortuitously, I had wound it securely around my wrist, preventing its loss into the depths of the vast ocean below.

The girl groaned, her arms also colliding with the unforgiving cliff surface. Determination propelled me as I brushed aside my own pain and reached upward, clutching onto the rope above. Struggling with all my might, I pulled myself and the girl upward, grappling with the challenge at hand. It wasn't until I managed to rotate my body and plant my feet firmly against the vertical wall of the cliff that progress became more feasible.

"What are you doing?" the girl inquired, positioned in a manner that essentially had her lying atop me as we ascended, my hands gripping the rope and my legs pressed against the wall.

"Almost there," I puffed out between exertions, gradually making headway until we reached the point where my sleeping bag was attached to the rope. The girl's gaze fell upon the bag, and realization dawned upon her that it was our intended destination.

"How are we both going to fit in that?" she questioned.

I lacked an answer, opting instead to continue my upward ascent until we were positioned above the sleeping bag. "Grab it," I gasped.

The woman complied, and with some awkward maneuvering, we managed to slide our feet into the bag. As I lowered us into its confines, the woman pulled it up around us. Finally, I could release my grip, my arms trembling from the strain.

"Did you secure the cords around the bag?" the girl inquired.

"Yeah, I don't trust the material to support our weight," I replied.

"It seems well done. It feels surprisingly rigid," she murmured.

"Thanks," I said, my breath still labored, my muscles quivering. I tried to hide my pain and discomfort, which wasn't easy. We were tightly squeezed within the confines of the sleeping bag, and I couldn't help but perceive the closeness between us.

My failure at hiding my pain was confirmed by the girl's inquiry, "Are you alright?"

"I hit the cliff hard. My back hurts," I added.

"So do my arms," she added, rubbing her arms that remained wrapped around my back. Her movement pressed her chest against me, and I couldn't help but blush at our closeness.

"I'm Star, by the way," I introduced myself.

"Oh, that's what you meant earlier. So you're not a celebrity?" she grinned.

"A what?" I queried.

"Never mind. Anyway, Star, that's an interesting name. I like it. Mine is Kikki," she smiled.

"Well, Kikki, could you retrieve the gun from around my shoulder? I have a feeling the night isn't over," I instructed.

"What? There's no way they'll make it down the cliff. Zombies can't do that. Besides, they despise water," Kikki responded.

"Some of them are different. Didn't you notice the three that were faster than the rest? They would have caught up to you if I hadn't shot them," I replied.

"I was a little too preoccupied with running to pay attention to what was behind me," Kikki admitted, shifting uncomfortably as she retrieved the gun from my shoulder. Once again, our movements brought us into some awkward positions not exactly deemed appropriate for first encounters.

With some effort and considerable awkwardness, I finally held the gun in my hand, pointing upward toward the cliff's surface. The piercing screeches of the approaching zombies resonated above. Memories of Reed flooded my mind as I aimed at the cliff's summit. And that's when I spotted them—two creatures descending the cliff wall like spiders, an eerie sight that sent shivers down my spine. I knew time was limited before they reached our level. Regulating my breath, I aligned my shot and fired. Despite the slight swaying of the sleeping bag and Kikki's movements, the proximity of the creatures made the shot relatively easy for someone of my skills.

The first of the creatures careened through the air, plummeting into the water below. In the urgency of the moment, I reached for the pocket where my bullets were stashed.

"Hey, what are you doing?" Kikki's voice seethed with anger, grumbling in my ear. "I don't recall giving my consent for that."

"I'm reloading," I grumbled in response, disregarding her restless movements. Extracting a bullet from my breast pocket, I deftly slid it into the chamber. "Hold still. There's one more on the cliff wall," I muttered.

I felt her tighten her grip around me upon realizing that more zombies were descending upon us. Swiftly, I loaded the bullet, taking careful aim. With the zombie merely a few feet above one of the sleeping bags, I squeezed the trigger. The bullet found its mark, and the lifeless body plunged into the depths of the ocean below.

"Did you get it?" Kikki inquired.

"What was that?" came a shout from another sleeping bag.

"Two zombies were scaling the cliff," I yelled back. "I took them out. I don't see any more of them coming down," I added.

"They can climb cliffs?" another voice exclaimed.

"Apparently," I replied.

"Will more come?" someone asked anxiously.

"He won't know that. It's not like he invited them," another voice interjected.

"What are we going to do?" a voice filled with panic echoed.

Trevor's voice cut through the rising tension. "Wade, how's your night vision now?" he asked.

"It's good. I saw the creatures coming. I was about to shoot the second one, but Star took it out before I got my shot off," Wade responded.

"Who else can see?" Trevor inquired. "I can," a voice chimed in.

"Who's that? I haven't memorized all your voices yet," Trevor queried.

"It's Juan," he replied.

"Then we'll have to take shifts," Trevor ordered.

"What about the Changing?" another voice raised a concern.

"We can only do what we can. Wade, you take the first watch. Everyone else, get some shuteye. Wake Juan up when you can't stay awake anymore, okay?" Trevor directed.

"Got it," Wade acknowledged.

"We should be better prepared tomorrow once the second wave of powers comes," Trevor reassured the group. "Get as much sleep as you can. Looks like we'll need to stay vigilant all the way to the city," he concluded.

"Which city?" someone asked.

"Does it even matter?" grumbled another voice in response.

There were murmurs of agreement and discontent, but gradually, the voices subsided. Exhaustion weighed heavily upon me after a day filled with travel, and despite the awkward position I found myself in, with Kikki pressed against me. Her warmth felt good and comforting, and I held her even as I succumbed to sleep, clouding my senses.

Chapter 25

2nd Changing

STAR: The surface
Z.O.M.B.I.E. Games: Drifting Planes

I awoke to an agonizing pain that surged through my body as if my nerves were ablaze. Unlike some of the others who screamed out in agony, I fought back the urge, my trembling body whimpering in silent torment. Kikki, still clinging to me, stirred awake, concern lacing her voice.

"What's wrong?" she asked, her worry palpable.

"A Changing," I managed to utter through clenched teeth.

"A what?" she exclaimed, her voice filled with confusion.

"A Changing," I repeated, my body convulsing with each piercing wave of pain. "It will pass. There's nothing you can do."

"But you're in pain," she insisted. Suddenly, others awoke from their slumber, their cries of anguish mingling with the air. "Is this happening to all of you? Are you infected?"

I shuddered, momentarily overwhelmed by the pain, before I responded. "It's not a Zombie thing. I can't quite explain it. It will pass. We just have to endure it."

"Are you sure there's nothing I can do?" Kikki asked, her voice filled with genuine concern.

"No," I wheezed, struggling to catch my breath.

Kikki shifted, reaching out to place her hand gently on my head. Her soft touch brought a stark contrast to the torment coursing through my body. I focused on that touch, willing myself to block out the rest of the pain. I centered my mind on the rhythmic patting, making them the sole existence in my world. Despite the lingering shudders of agony, I managed to tune out everything else.

Uncertain of what else to do, Kikki hesitated momentarily, her hand hovering. "Please don't stop," I pleaded, desperation lacing my words. "It was helping."

"Alright," Kikki whispered, resuming the gentle pats on my head.

Time blurred as the pain persisted, yet my focus remained anchored on the soothing touch upon my scalp. Eventually, my consciousness let go, and the black of sleep took me.

I awoke to discover Kikki still peacefully asleep, her hand remaining on my head due to the limited space and entanglement of the sleeping bag. Without the stress from the previous night, I became acutely aware of the contact between us. Her rhythmic breathing drew us closer together while my body protested from the uncomfortable position, prompting me to shift slightly. The movement stirred Kikki, and she yawned, retracting her hand to gaze down at me.

"Good morning," she greeted.

"Morning," I replied, observing the faint sunlight filtering through the top of the bag. We shared a brief moment of silent exchange, during which I anticipated her letting go of me. However, as the seconds passed, it became apparent that she had no intention of releasing her grip. A blush tinged my cheeks as I gathered the courage to address the situation.

"I'm going to need you to let go of me," I stammered.

"Huh?" she mumbled, clearly perplexed. "There's not much space in here. I don't really have anywhere else to go."

"No, I mean, I need you to let me out. I have to scale the cliff," I clarified, pointing upward.

"Oh," she uttered, gingerly disentangling her arms from around me. "Sure, but are you up for it? I mean, considering last night..."

"I'm fine," I assured her, locating my sunglasses and slipping them onto my face. Then, reaching for the rope that secured the sleeping bag, I added, "Once I reach the top, wake everyone else so we can start moving."

She nodded in understanding as I extricated myself from the sleeping bag, ascending the rope with a newfound ease that surprised me. The physical exertion from the previous night seemed distant as I effortlessly pulled myself up the rope. I briefly wondered why it was so easy when I remembered the Changing. But once again, something was off. I should have had to take time to get used to the power, but the ease and speed of my body's movements were undeniable. In no time, I reached the point where I had anchored the metal stakes into the cliff wall. I easily moved my grip from the rope over to the cliff's jagged surface. My fingers instinctively found holds on the rugged surface, allowing my body to ascend swiftly, scaling the cliff face with remarkable agility until I emerged at the pinnacle. Swiftly uncoiling the rope secured around my arm, I anchored one end, flinging the other off the cliff's edge. The rope's length proved sufficient to reach the bags below, and one by one, people began hauling themselves up.

Soon, several sturdy individuals stood atop the cliff, working in tandem to assist those lacking the confidence to ascend using the rope. Some were due to their newly found powers they awoke with, while others needed help simply because they didn't have the strength. Kikki was among the first to reach the summit, stretching her limbs beside me as I surveyed the surrounding plains.

"So, where are you from?" she inquired.

"We'd like to know that about you," Trevor interjected, approaching us.

Kikki shied away from Trevor, inching closer to me before responding, "I'm from the City of Hope."

Trevor appeared puzzled by her answer. "You mean you're not from the City?"

"I am. The City of Hope," she replied, her confusion evident.

"No, I mean 'The City,'" he clarified.

"Their city is called 'The City,'" I interjected.

Kikki chuckled, finding the nomenclature amusing. "No, I'm from a city four hundred miles south of here."

"There are other cities?" Trevor pondered aloud.

"Yes, several. We've been exploring and have come across several settlements. However, they are all located to the south. Yours is the first we've encountered north of the City of Hope," Kikki elaborated.

"This is groundbreaking news," Trevor exclaimed. "I wonder if the royals are aware of it."

"Royals?" Kikki questioned. "You have a monarchy?"

"A what?" Trevor queried.

"Are you governed by a king or queen?" I clarified.

Trevor replied, "A King."

Kikki was astonished, saying, "Wow, now that's crazy."

By then, Kyle had approached us after being hauled up and immediately inquired about Kikki. I quickly filled him in on the situation, prompting Kyle to swiftly pull Trevor closer. "We can't let the others know," he whispered.

"Why not?" Trevor questioned.

"Did you ever wonder why I was chosen for the games?" Kyle posed the question.

"Well, yeah, we all wondered why a royal would be placed in the games. What did you do for them to send you here?" Trevor inquired, his curiosity evident.

"I uncovered information that others were desperately trying to conceal. I was attempting to share that knowledge when they caught up with me. One of those revelations involves her," Kyle explained, nodding towards Kikki.

Curiosity growing, Trevor pressed further. "What did you find out?"

"I can't reveal it here. But you've just discovered part of it," Kyle replied, gesturing towards Kikki. "We shouldn't discuss it any further where they are listening."

"So, they do know," Trevor pondered.

"And if they know that we know and suspect we might expose the truth, they won't let us return to the city," Kyle cautioned. "We need to act as if she's merely a wandering nomad who made it here. We haven't had one in a hundred years, but we can play it out that way. It will ensure our survival."

163

Understanding the gravity of Kyle's words, Trevor nodded. "Agreed." He then turned to Kikki and me. "You get that?" he asked.

"I understand the general idea, although I don't fully grasp what you're saying," Kikki admitted.

"Just pretend you've been hiding and wandering your whole life," Kyle advised. "It's the only way."

Kikki frowned, initially hesitant, but eventually nodded in agreement.

"Good. Now, let's go introduce you to everyone else," Trevor declared, leading them towards the group.

I chose not to join them and instead descended the cliff to retrieve the remaining equipment. Methodically, I extracted the stakes from the rock's face, sliding them into my pack for future use. Once I ascended again, the group began to move, aiming to cover as much ground as possible while basking in the safety of the sunlight.

Throughout the day, everyone seemed captivated by Kikki's presence, leaving me in solitude. As we journeyed, I marveled at the vast world unfolding before my eyes. My entire life had been confined to tunnels and the tower, but now, the world had expanded exponentially. The abyss had felt like an entirely different realm, on the fringes of familiarity. With the open sky above, the vast ocean to my right, and the plains to my left, I felt transported to a new world—a world abundant with space and unfamiliar scents. At times, I would pause just to observe my surroundings.

On that particular day, the sky was distinct from the previous days. A blanket of clouds stretched across the ocean. Curiosity led me to ask Kyle about them, and his explanation of the water cycle was more than I anticipated.

As we continued along the path, the plains to our right gradually revealed the remnants of a barbed wire fence. Kyle mentioned that there were numerous fences in the past, but now only those made with metal posts remained. These fences served as a deterrent for the less intelligent zombies, as they would become entangled and tear themselves apart. Staying on the path was essential due to the hazards that awaited those who ventured into the plains, such as pits or sporadically placed wire.

Throughout the day, I noticed Kyle's physical transformation. His once bulky form visibly slimmed down. While he remained large, it was clear that he was not as massive as before. When I inquired about it, Kyle explained that he had selected the option to develop a toned body, causing his excess fat to convert into muscle. It didn't happen all at once, but as the daylight hours passed, it was noticeable. I was astonished to witness the gradual change as his body size diminished, with the newly formed muscle hidden beneath a layer of fat.

Even as the day progressed, the clouds also thickened, threatening to blanket the sky. Sensing the approaching cover, Trevor halted the group and instructed us to set up camp. Similar to before, I took on most of the strenuous tasks but pre-prepared the metal stake to avoid the mistakes from the previous day during my descent. While I worked, I observed the growing size of the waves below. I wondered if they would continue to escalate until they crashed over the cliff, prompting me to inquire upon returning to the surface.

"Will those waves reach us?" I asked Kyle, pointing toward the swelling masses. "They seem to be getting larger."

"No, they shouldn't grow much bigger than that, but we might experience some turbulence if we hang as we did last night," he responded.

"In that case, we should secure our sleeping bags and anchor them along with the rope anchors we had last night," I suggested.

"How much extra rope do we have?" Kyle inquired.

"I'm not sure. I've already used up most of what I had yesterday. Trevor has been keeping track of our gear, though," I replied.

Kyle nodded. "I'll go ask him and see what we have."

"It would be better if we had more metal stakes," I voiced my thoughts. "Just something we can loop the hanging lines down where we're positioned."

"I'll go check what we have," Kyle muttered.

I nodded as I settled down to rest after the strenuous task of setting up the lines along the cliff's edge. Whatever change my body had experienced had made it easier than the day before, though. Kikki made her way over to me and sat down.

"You seem different from the others," she observed, taking off her own pack.

"What do you mean?" I inquired.

"You carry yourself like a fighter, for starters. None of the others appear to have been in a fight in their lives. But it's more than that. It's the way you observe things... It's as if you're seeing the world for the first time," she said.

"You mean all of this?" I waved my hand toward the vast expanse of the plains and ocean. "It is my first time. I don't come from the same place as them. This is all new to me," I added.

"You mean you're not from The City? Is there another settlement nearby?" Kikki asked, her astonishment evident.

I shook my head. "Kyle knows more about it than I do, but I come from the tower. Well, apparently, there are multiple underground structures called towers, but I've only known mine as the tower. I've spent my entire life in the tunnels," I explained.

Kikki's eyes widened. "How is that possible? That's where most of the zombies went. How did you survive down there?" she asked.

"We constantly fought them. I've been fighting them since I was twelve," I answered.

"And how did you end up here?" she inquired further.

I shrugged. "I was sent to die, but I didn't. When my friend and I returned to the tower, they tried to kill us. So we left and lived in the tunnels. Then, one day, we were attacked by flying metal bugs, and I found myself up here. Kyle seems to understand more about what happened. He mentioned that there is more than one tower." I shrugged again.

"Sounds like you've had it rough," Kikki commented.

"I assume it's no rougher than your situation. Otherwise, how would you be out here alone?" I said with a smile.

Kikki's face darkened, but she smiled back. "Yeah, I guess."

We fell into silence, which was broken by Kyle's arrival.

"Trevor didn't find anything useful in the supplies," he said.

"What are you looking for?" Kikki asked.

I was the one who answered. "We need something to anchor ourselves to the cliff so we won't be tossed around by the wind. Otherwise, we'll end up covered in bruises or worse by morning," I replied.

"What about the barbed wire fence posts? There were several of them close to the path about half a mile back," Kikki suggested.

I grunted, getting to my feet. "That would work," I grinned.

"Where are you going?" Kikki and Kyle asked in unison.

"To fetch the posts," I replied.

"No," Kyle intervened, stopping me. "You've already been doing more than your share. I'll talk to Trevor and have a couple of people go get what we need," he said.

Trevor eventually assembled a diverse group to retrieve the posts. He ensured that at least one person with enhanced senses and abilities accompanied them, but the majority consisted of the stronger members of our group. I settled back to rest next to Kikki, feeling the weariness seep into my bones.

"Did you manage to find someone willing to share a sleeping bag with you? We still have only twenty -three bags," I asked her, concerned about her sleeping arrangements.

"I couldn't find anyone suitable," Kikki replied, her tone tinged with disappointment.

I sat back up, a sense of urgency creeping into my voice. "What? Seriously?"

"Well, there weren't many options to begin with," Kikki explained. "Most of them are much larger than you, so there's no way I would fit comfortably. I don't want to share with a man, either. Out of the eight women, only Nancy, Katty, Sandra, Malori, and Jillian are small enough. Jillian's a bit peculiar with those bugs always around her. Katty, Nancy, and Sandra all give me strange looks. And Malori seems more interested in seeking attention from every guy around. So, unfortunately, I don't have any suitable options," she concluded with a hint of resignation in her voice.

"So what does that mean?" I asked, my voice tinged with uncertainty.

"Well, it means we will have to share," Kikki smiled.

"You just said you didn't want to share it with a man, though. Doesn't that make you uncomfortable? Being so close, I mean," I stammered, my cheeks blushing as I recalled the intimacy of the previous night.

"Well, it's far from ideal, but considering the circumstances, you're my best option," she reassured me.

"But there are eight other women; surely one of them would be better suited," I suggested, hoping to divert her choice away from me.

"They might be smaller than the men, but they're all bigger than you. And I've already explained why none of them work. Besides, you're the smallest one here," she responded, her voice gentle.

"But I'm a man," I protested, feeling a twinge of self-consciousness.

"Mmm, more like a boy. And anyway, out of all these people, I trust you the most," she said softly, her words making my heart skip a beat. Still, I bristled at being called a boy, but I let it slide. I was accustomed to being treated as younger due to my size.

Trying to shift the conversation, I pressed further. "You've been talking with them all day, though," I pointed out.

168

"You risked yourself to save me. None of them did that. And from what I hear, you've been doing your best to help everyone survive, not just yourself. So you're my best option," she said, her grin reassuring.

Feeling a mix of frustration and resignation, I finally gave up. "Fine," I sighed, leaning back and gazing up at the darkening sky. A thought crossed my mind, diverting the topic. "Do the zombies come out if the clouds cover the sun?" I asked, peering at the approaching darkness.

"It depends. If it's a fully overcast day, they might not emerge. But with those dark clouds coming, it's almost guaranteed that they'll be out," Kikki explained, her tone filled with caution.

Curiosity piqued, I looked out over the plains, wondering where the zombies disappeared during the day. "Where do they hide during the day? And what happens to them if they're left out in the sun with nowhere to hide?" I inquired.

Kikki paused for a moment before responding. "They don't like the sun, but it doesn't harm them much. It blinds them and puts them in a hibernation-like state. They tend to seek shelter in places like tunnels where they don't have to deal with the sunlight. However, not every place has such hiding spots, so most of them simply drop where they stood during the day and rise again at night," she explained.

"So, those grasses could be concealing a multitude of zombies?" I murmured, pointing towards the fields as I noticed the returning group that went to fetch the fence posts.

"Yes, it's possible," she confirmed. Suddenly, my attention was diverted as I caught sight of movement in the distance.

"What's wrong?" Kikki asked, standing beside me as we peered into the grassy expanse.

"I think I saw something unusual," I replied, my voice filled with concern. Pointing towards the tall grasses, I observed several lines appearing and moving toward the returning group.

"Not good," Kikki whispered, her voice laced with worry.

I let out a piercing yell, my voice carrying the situation's urgency. Sandra, the member of the post-gathering group with enhanced hearing, paused and turned her attention towards me. I repeated the warning, my voice echoing through the air. Sandra swiftly relayed the message to the rest of the group, prompting them to pick up the pace back to us. Their path was encased on either side by tall grass most of the way between us. Kikki and I rushed to warn the remaining members who were already positioned on the cliff, ready to face the imminent threat. In no time, everyone was on their feet, weapons drawn, preparing for the impending battle.

Above us, the ever-darkening clouds seemed to gather momentum, swiftly moving across the sky as the rain began to pour down. The atmosphere was tense, charged with both anticipation and fear.

My gaze fixed upon the grassy expanse, and my heart skipped a beat as seven menacing figures emerged from the sea of green. The group sprang into action, opening fire as bullets tore through the air. Four zombies stumbled backward, their bodies riddled with the impact of multiple shots. A swarm of bugs suddenly took flight from the grass, attacking one of the zombies with ferocity. Seizing the opportunity, I aimed my weapon and fired, swiftly taking down another undead creature. However, more zombies emerged from the tall grass, forming a deadly barrier between the group returning with the fence stakes and my position on the cliff's edge.

Reloading my weapon with practiced efficiency, I continued to fire, my movements precise and calculated. One after another, the zombies fell to the power of my bullets. Yet, despite my efforts, the horde seemed to multiply before my eyes. Soon, a staggering number of forty zombies stood between us and the approaching group, a daunting obstacle that threatened to engulf us in a wave of danger.

"Do you have any experience with guns?" I asked Kikki, who stood beside me, her knife poised and ready.

"I do, but I lost mine about a week ago," she replied.

"Here, take mine," I said, thrusting my gun into her hands along with a handful of bullets. In my haste, some of the bullets slipped from my grasp and fell to the ground. Nevertheless, I wasted no time and swiftly moved toward the advancing zombies, drawing the swords hanging from my belt. Though intermittent gunfire still rang out, the initial barrage had subsided as those with machine guns had to pause to reload. I charged forward, finding myself quickly immersed in the midst of the fray. My blades flickered and danced from one zombie to another as I skillfully cut through limbs and ligaments. It felt strangely easier than I remembered, as if the zombies' movements were sluggish, reminiscent of the chilling encounters within the tunnels.

As I fought my way through, a sudden burst of light illuminated the sky, causing the zombies to shriek and recoil. Startled, I also took a step back, putting some distance between myself and the undead horde. The group that had ventured to retrieve the stakes rushed past me, joining the main group. Then, a deep rumbling filled the sky, carrying a sense of anger. Fear gripped me, and I instinctively ran after the group. The bursts of light recurred, accompanied by the rumbling of the sky.

With the arrival of the lightning, the zombies retreated into the grass, attempting to conceal themselves from the unexpected illumination. This respite allowed our group to regroup and descend to the safety of our sleeping bags below. It took a collective effort to secure everyone against the cliff wall, but once accomplished, we were shielded from the rain that now poured down upon us.

Once again, I found myself cramped with Kikki inside my sleeping bag. I had loosened some of the cords that suspended it, providing a bit more room, but we were still tightly pressed against each other. Fortunately, the sleeping bags proved to be dry despite the rain. Their waterproof outer layer proved invaluable, as only the water that had soaked our clothes managed to seep in.

Another rumble reverberated through the sky, causing me to shiver involuntarily. "Are you alright?" Kikki asked softly in my ear.

"What's wrong?" I inquired, still trembling slightly.

"What do you mean?" she replied.

"Why is the sky so angry?" I explained, seeking an understanding.

"You mean the thunder?" she responded.

"Thunder?" I repeated, seeking clarification.

"Yes, that sound," she answered patiently.

"So, that's thunder? Why does it growl at us?" I asked, continuing my line of questioning.

Kikki giggled softly. "It's not growling at us. That's just what it does," she explained.

"I don't like it," I replied, feeling a sense of unease. "It feels unnatural."

"Well, I think you'll find it's quite natural. It's simply air being displaced rapidly when lightning strikes," she muttered reassuringly.

"Is that the flashing?" I asked, trying to grasp the concept.

"Yes, the flashing. It's a form of electricity," she responded, her patience evident.

Another thunderclap echoed through the air, this one closer and more powerful than before. Overwhelmed by fear, I clung tightly to Kikki, feeling utterly defenseless. It was a sensation I disliked, reminiscent of the few times I had experienced such vulnerability within the tunnels.

At least there, I had the means to fight back. On the exposed cliffside during a storm, I was entirely at the mercy of the elements, devoid of any control.

"It's going to be alright," Kikki reassured me, gently patting my head. "You're not alone."

"Is it silly to be scared of thunder?" I asked, still embraced by fear and trembling.

"No, it's quite common among kids," Kikki explained. The way she emphasized 'kids' didn't offer much solace;

instead, it served as a reminder of how she had referred to me as a boy just a little while ago. Nevertheless, I clung to her as if she could shield me from the noise.

Another thunderclap echoed through the air, causing my muscles to tense up. Trying to divert my attention, Kikki interjected, "Did your parents have an affinity for the night sky?"

"What?" I asked, confused by the sudden topic.

"You know, because of your name," she clarified.

"No, they never had the chance to see it. I've spent my entire life underground. Except for the past couple of days," I muttered.

"Oh, right," Kikki pondered. "I momentarily forgot about that... The tunnels, huh?" she quipped, acknowledging the irony.

"Yeah," I replied, my grip on her loosening slightly. The conversation had managed to draw me away from the grip of my fear, if only for a moment.

"How did you manage to survive down there?" Kikki inquired, her curiosity piqued.

We spent a good half an hour conversing, delving into the depths of our respective experiences, before I finally started to relax enough to drift off to sleep.

Thankfully, no zombies ventured near our location that night, wisely avoiding the treacherous cliffs. I managed to sleep for a short while, but my respite was short-lived. In the middle of the night, a searing fire tore through my muscles, jolting me awake. The spasms were so intense that they also roused Kikki from her slumber.

Recognizing the familiar symptoms from the previous night and having them explained to her by the others during the day, she asked, "Are you going through another Changing?"

Unable to form a coherent response, I simply gritted my teeth and braced myself, enduring the relentless waves of pain that washed over me throughout the night.

Chapter 26
ENCOUNTER

REED: Earth's surface: THE CITY

A.K.A

Last City on Earth

A week had gone by, and I had managed to learn a lot about the people living above. One of the most useful things I discovered was sunglasses. It was incredible how they protected my eyes when I put them on. Unfortunately, to acquire them I had to steal them. With the sunglasses, I could explore during both the day and night. The sun's burning sensation on my skin was still unpleasant, but I could bear it.

The most crucial information I gathered was Star's whereabouts. They had imprisoned him in a brutal game called the Z.O.M.B.I.E. Games, which the majority of the population watched through street streams. My challenge now was to figure out Star's exact location and anticipate where he would be next.

Over the past week, Star's group had made steady progress and was currently outside a city known as the Lost City. During storms and each night, they found shelter by hanging off a cliff, just as Star and I had before in the abyss. Two times, zombies attempted to ambush them in the dark, but the group's heightened senses made it difficult for the zombies to catch them off guard. On both occasions, the zombies, capable of climbing walls, fell to their demise, disappearing into the dark waters below. I watched these moments with tense muscles, fearing I might be too late to save my dear friend.

Aside from the updates on Star, the week proved to be productive in other ways. I discovered a talent for scavenging items. Security was less stringent outside the central city, allowing me to pick locks at night and acquire food and supplies. I stored these items in my underground den beneath the bustling city. The close confines of the tunnels reminded me of home, although they were not as spacious as the tunnels back at the tower. However, something was missing—I longed for my sister and my best friend. I thought about Wind from time to time, but my focus was primarily on finding ways to locate Star. I noticed that some people possessed handheld devices that displayed the Z.O.M.B.I.E. Games. Additionally, I overheard conversations about newly developed batteries available on the market. Hence, my mission for the night was to acquire two devices and as many batteries as possible.

Before setting out, I double-checked my equipment to ensure everything was in place. Three small metal pins were securely stored in my belt, and three small knives were tucked along the back of it. I also had a fourth knife attached to my leg. I had obtained these weapons just the night before, along with their sheaths, which I concealed under my military-style overcoat. A new flashlight was in my pants pocket. Satisfied that everything was in order, I decided to leave my bulky guns behind. Carrying a gun would make me stand out too much since no one aboveground carried them. My goal was to complete the mission quickly, being seen by as few people as possible. With that in mind, I climbed out of a sewer grate in a deserted alley, knowing that although I disliked being without a gun, it was necessary for the task at hand.

I made my way down the street, lined with tall buildings ranging from six to seven stories to towering structures that seemed to reach a hundred stories high. Many of the windows were illuminated, reminiscent of the tower I once called home. Most of the ground level was occupied by shops, and I stopped in front of one called PINEAPPLE. It struck me as odd that a store would bear my uncle's name, but I took it as a positive sign. My uncle had passed away, and I figured he wouldn't mind if I procured some goods from a store that shared his name.

With swift movements, I positioned myself in front of the door and pulled out one of the lockpicks. The lock wasn't overly complex, and it took me only a minute to hear the satisfying click and test the door handle. With a grin, I stepped inside and closed the door behind me. Once again, I thanked Star for teaching me how to sneak into unoccupied rooms back in the tower when we were young. I navigated through the store, which was filled with small computers and tablets displaying default screensavers, until I reached the desired displays. Crouching down, I began working on the lock. My hands slipped twice, but eventually, the lock yielded, allowing me to grab two PINEAPPLE phones from the cabinet.

As I moved to find the portable batteries, the door suddenly swung open, and six men barged into the room. "Freeze!" one of them yelled, shining a flashlight in my eyes. Thinking quickly, I spun around and dashed toward the back of the building, evading the men.

"He's going around the back!" I heard someone shout as I made my way to the bathroom. Having scouted the outside of the building beforehand, I knew the bathroom window was open but covered by a screen. The back door was locked, and I assumed it would be locked from the inside as well, so I disregarded it as a possible escape route.

Upon finding the bathroom, I was relieved to see a lock on the door. I swiftly slid behind it, seeking refuge in the cramped space. With a flick of my wrist, I locked the door and then made my way over to the window. I began cutting away at the screen, halfway through the process, when banging erupted on the other side of the door.

"You have no way out!" a voice shouted. "Come out, and we'll go easy on you."

"Yeah," another voice chimed in. "If you cooperate, maybe we won't send you into the Z.O.M.B.I.E. Games."

I didn't stick around to hear more because I was already pulling myself through the window and onto the back alley street. I grunted as I landed awkwardly on the ground, rolling slightly to lessen the impact.

"Hey, you!" a voice called from down the street.

I cursed my luck that they had stationed men at the back. I quickly scrambled to my feet and started running. Knowing that I couldn't make my way out through the back, where I heard more men, I charged at the lone guard blocking my path to the main road. Taking short, swift steps, I surged forward. The man obstructing my way was at least twice my size, but I had grown up fighting. I may not have been as skilled as Star with a blade, but I was no stranger to brawling. I knew how to incapacitate a man swiftly. A rapid strike to his groin, followed by an uppercut to his face as he bent over, cleared my path to the street, and hastened away from the crime scene.

"He's over there!" a voice yelled from behind. Without wasting a moment to look back, I sprinted forward. I took a right turn at the next street and quickly followed it with a left, hoping to shake off my pursuers.

Unfortunately, my maneuver didn't throw them off my trail, and I had no choice but to keep running instead of returning to my hideout. No matter what I tried, I couldn't seem to create enough distance between us to slip away unnoticed. I was starting to lose hope when I spotted a vibrant sign-up ahead. It displayed the number 0288 REV, accompanied by the sound of music emanating from the inside. Two large men stood guard outside.

A group of people around my age was approaching the guards, presenting me with a moment of opportunity. They were dressed in attire similar to my military outfit, with slight variations. I figured I could blend in with them. Slowing my steps, I slipped in behind the group, and the guards barely spared me a second glance as I entered the building.

The music's volume escalated dramatically upon stepping inside, assaulting my senses. People were energetically jumping up and down in the middle of the floor while others were getting drinks from the side. I navigated through the crowd, attempting to make my way to the other side in search of an exit.

In my haste, I accidentally bumped into a young man, causing his drink to spill on both of us. I quickly murmured an apology and continued moving past him. However, he raised his voice, commanding the attention of everyone nearby. The music softened, and people pulled away, creating a barrier between us and the exits.

Frustrated, I turned toward the man. He was tall, in his early twenties, and wore cleaner clothes compared to mine, as I hadn't thoroughly washed mine since Star was taken. With short blond hair and a winning smile, his eyes had a coldness to them.

"What's the hurry, runt?" he said, approaching me. "You spill my drink and think a simple sorry will do?"

My eyes darted towards the door, where voices could be heard demanding entry. The man in front of me noticed my glance and followed my gaze. "Ahh, it seems you've caught someone else's attention tonight. I wonder who else is looking for you," he grinned.

As he spoke, a voice shouted from near the entrance, and several other men moved from their positions around the room toward the door. These men had communication devices in their ears. One of them approached our circle. "The King's men are outside," he muttered.

"The King's men?" the tall young man whistled in surprise. He then looked back at me, his expression now filled with respect. "I wasn't expecting that kind of trouble. Who are you to attract the King's men?" he asked.

When I remained silent, the man took a step closer, studying me with newfound curiosity. Suddenly, something seemed to click in his mind, and he stepped back.

"It can't be," his eyes widened.

"What can't be?" I growled, my hand instinctively reaching for one of my knives.

"Reed?" the man gasped.

I blinked in surprise, my body tensing. I pulled out two knives as I asked, "How do you know my name?"

"You're Star's friend. How did you end up here? I mean, you're in the city... in my club," he stammered.

"Get out of my way, or I'll carve my way through," I threatened, my instincts urging me to escape.

"Whoah, now," the man said, lifting his hands in a gesture of peace. "We're on the same side," he grinned.

"I don't know you," I replied, eyes filled with murderous intent.

"But I know you. Put those knives down, and let me explain," he pleaded. A commotion outside caught his attention, and he turned to face that direction while continuing to speak. "On second thought, let's get you out of here first, and then we can talk," he suggested.

The crowd dispersed, leaving me utterly bewildered. The man walked past me and headed down a hallway. "Keep up. They'll be in the building soon," he urged.

With only a moment's hesitation, I made up my mind. It was best to seize the opportunity and escape while I still had the chance. Thus, I followed the enigmatic man who seemed to know who I was. Part of me was also intrigued to discover how he had acquired such knowledge.

Chapter 27
POWERS
STAR: The surface
Z.O.M.B.I.E. Games: Drifting Planes

When I awoke, I was startled at how loud the world was around me. I was surprised that I could sleep through the cacophony. At first, I thought the storm was continuing, but then I heard the pounding. It was loud and came in a pattern. No, there were two of them. One was slow, while the other started to increase in pace.

Thump thump…thump thump… thump thump

I was starting to panic when Kikki stirred.

"What is it!" she bellowed in my ear.

"Ahh, not so loud!" I exclaimed back, the volume of my voice making my head hurt. "Why is everything so loud?"

"What is it?" Kikki sounded panicked, but I was starting to piece together what had happened—the changing. As soon as I realized that, I focused on the sounds around me. "Star?"

"Quiet," I said, losing my focus and getting bombarded once again with the noise of waves, heartbeats, and animals in the sky. I struggled once again to sort through the noises. I tried to focus on just one of the noises. The sound of the heartbeats was the most distinguished, rhythmic sound around, and I clung to it. I let my mind just focus on the one noise. Soon, all I could hear was the rhythm of Kikki's and my heartbeats. Slowly, I let other noises back in, one at a time. It was slow progress, and I could hear others calling out from their sleeping bags, wondering why no one had climbed the cliff yet. I heard them, but I didn't. It was background noise and wasn't important yet. No, just the heartbeats, waves, and creaks of the ropes for now. I would add people's voices when I was ready.

The struggle continued, but Kikki stayed quiet until I opened my eyes.

"Is everything alright?" she whispered softly.

"I think so. My hearing improved last night during the Changing. It took some time to get it under control."

"It sounds horrible," Kikki replied.

I nodded, not wanting to elaborate. Our proximity was already getting to me. "Help me out,"

Kikki obliged, and I soon found myself flying up the cliff face. I didn't climb as fast as I did the previous night. Noise crashed into my head twice as I made the accent, and I had to stop both times to get ahold of myself. Thankfully, my climbing skills had improved with my enhanced dexterity and speed the day before. When I got to the top, I surveyed the land around me, looking for any signs of the zombies from the night before. Again, there was no sound from them, and I knew they didn't have a beating heart, so I couldn't locate them from a heartbeat. I sighed and went to work, pulling up Kikki and the others.

Kyle was surprised at how fast I got used to the new powers when I told him about the hearing. He said it was abnormal for someone to get used to them in less than twelve hours. My first didn't even pose a challenge, and the hearing only took me an hour to master completely.

"Well, it's too bad you probably won't get any more powers. That skill in adapting to them is amazing." Kyle mused, a smirk on his face. The way he was looking at me made me feel like it was a funny joke, but it was going over my head.

"What?" I asked.

"O, nothing," Kyle said as his eyes returned to Malori.

"In the towers, it wasn't polite to stare." I quipped

"Huh, what?" Kyle replied, not shifting his eyes. I just shook my head and continued forward. It unnerved me how we had changed over the last two days. The Changing affecting our minds and bodies. Part of me wondered if I would still be the same person at the end of this; probably not.

Chapter 28
Floor Meeting
Wind: Underground Tower #4

I woke up a little on edge. Today was going to be a big day. It was the day that the entire lower levels learned the truth. The truth about how we had been relying on people that didn't have our best interests at heart. That the upper tower wasn't a group working to save us but was a group living fat off our blood and sweet. I quickly got dressed and ate a meager breakfast before heading to the door. I headed to the elevator and made my way down to the first floor. It didn't take me long to make my way out of the building onto the ground. It always felt strange when I walked out of the tower, as most of my life was spent inside. Military training, which all lower-level citizens had to take, was held in the building. Still, some enclosed tunnels on the thirtieth floor were also included, which made a loop. Here, though, was the largest open space I had access to, and it felt so big. Looking up at the tower, which had gone off into space for what seemed like forever, I looked up to see the support beams shoot off from the building and off into the cave walls that surrounded the tower. It was crazy that people built all of this. People were capable of so much, and yet we were stuck in a tower fending off a zombie hoard that never seemed to deplete.

"I wonder what other secrets the upper tower has been keeping from us," I whispered as my eyes dropped to the people already milling about. To my surprise, there were already a lot of people milling about besides the normal people who occupied the space around the tower. A portion of them had been cleared out for the lower tower meeting. Their things piled to the side of the cavern.

I was surprised at the number of people gathering to get a place, but it was still half an hour before the meeting started. There wasn't room for seats, so everyone was standing around. Many wore their military equipment and weapons, while others donned their job uniforms. There were quite a few maintenance crews to take care of the tower's structural integrity.

My eyes were scanning for two categories of people. The first were those people I needed to be wary of, the people on the payroll of the upper floors. Second was the team I had put together. I noticed many of both groups. I noticed that both categories had come fully armed. I noticed Elephant in the gathering crowd standing a few people away from the target I had given him, a strong man named Fossil.

Let's just hope that this doesn't turn into a bloodbath, I thought as I centered myself in the grouping. I continued to watch the crowd as more people gathered in. Soon, over a thousand people were milling around the makeshift stand that overhung the group. It was amazing how many people the area could hold. More continued to show up, and I watched as my team repositioned themselves for the right time.

My nerves grew as the time passed. Finally, the doors opened to the tower, and an elderly man from the upper floors stepped out. He was dressed all in white and slowly made his way toward the stand. The crowd moved aside, making an aisle for the man to walk through. As he passed, the aisle moved in. I took the chance, as I had been in the middle, on the edge of the aisle, to slide in behind the old man and moved forward with him like some did to get a closer view. It was frowned upon to skip forward like that, but I needed to be closer to the front for this. I realized just how slow the man walked as I tried to slow my racing heart. Finally, we made it to the podium, and I allowed the man to go up by himself as I stood below. I watched the man make his way up to the top of the stage. He pulled out a megaphone and switched it on. As he did, people moved forward, which was the norm. We had to, so that everyone would be able to hear the announcements. Soon, we were cramped together, which initialized the plan. I noticed Elephant move in on Fossil a little to my left before the gaps between us close up.

183

I felt a hand on my shoulder and jumped, turning quickly.

"You ready?" Mountain whispered into my ear. I reddened visibly at how close he was. My heart was already beating fast from my nerves.

"I thought it was going to be Microwave that helped me."

Mountain smiled at that. "I switched roles with him. He knew you had told me."

"Oh," I said nervously, still feeling his body pressed against mine.

"Thank you all for coming here," the older man from the higher floors had started to welcome us like they always did prior to requiring something special from us or the annual meetings to describe how our resources were doing. We had always paid close attention to the speeches in the past because we cared about helping others. That is why we fought on the front lines. That's how we were raised. Now, it has been revealed to me as a blatant lie.

I looked over at Mountain, who nodded back at me. It was time that I showed everyone what they were. That and time to get some real answers.

Quickly, with the speed of a trained soldier, Mountain jumped up the stairs with me right behind him. The old man didn't even see it coming. One moment, he was delivering his speech, and the next, Mountain was standing over him, pinning him to the ground. I grabbed for the megaphone, lifting it to my lips. As I did, there were several cries from the crowd, and people began to cry out. They had nowhere to go through as they were all packed in.

"People from the lower tower, silence!" I proclaimed. Most people quickly fell silent, but a few cried out.

"I said silence!" I yelled once more into the megaphone.

This caused those around the louder people to shush at them. They went silent under the onslaught. They didn't have much else of a choice as they couldn't move due to the packed crowd. As things went silent, I felt like the crowd leaned forward to hear what I had to say.

"Thank you," I continued. "Now, I know many of you are confused right now. I am afraid I have some bad news. We have traitors in our midst."

A roar of whispers swept through the crowd at my words, only to be silenced by my next words. "Men, bring forward the traitors."

At that, people looked around, and slowly, pockets of people began to move. Space opened up in the crowd, and one after another, men that I had spoken to carried unconscious bodies forward.

"As many of you know." I continued. "I work with the screening team, one of the few groups with access to one computer. I followed protocol, performing my duties for a couple of months, but then I lost my brother. It was hard on me like it has been on all of us. We all have lost people. But my brother's death was strange. It happened at the same time that Stump and Redwood were killed. That and every single team that went out did not come back. So I thought it was strange. I felt like we were not getting the whole truth."

The entire crowd was quiet as all the men I had entrusted with the truth finished making their way forward, dumping unconscious bodies at the front and stripping them of their weapons.

"I went searching for the truth in a manner that most of us do not have access to. I went to the computer. On the computer, I found files from the tower's upper levels. These files explain how the people in the upper tower sent our people out as sacrifices to the Zombies. They have some sort of agreement to benefit from our deaths."

The rumble of whispers came again, but it was louder this time and gradually grew.

"That is not all!" I proclaimed, instantly silencing the crowd. "This man was going to send more of our boys to their deaths. They plotted to send a second sacrifice to the zombies. They do this to us, and yet they don't even work. They sit around idly growing fat off of our hard labor. All the food that is produced by our hard work and, they say, is needed for storage

185

to put against harder times only goes in their bellies. They starve us while they throw food away. I found this all in the files. They are using us and throwing us away."

"How do we know you are speaking the truth!" someone closer to the front of the crowd yelled.

"I can show it to you," I replied. I can show you all the truth. These men here were helping the upper tower. Their names are on a list of possible advancements for special services, services that were against us. Stump and Redwood weren't out there for fun; they were out there making sure no one came back alive. It said so in the file."

"If what you say is true," another person yelled, "We won't stand for it."

"Zombie food." Another yelled out.

This time, the crowd erupted, and even my yelling with the megaphone didn't help. The crowd was getting riled up, and it almost looked like some were about to storm the tower.

"Silence!" I screamed, trying to get them under control again. I knew a mob wouldn't do us any good. Killing wasn't the answer. We needed the truth and to fix the system. Still, we were so limited in the tower and needed the information that the upper tower had.

Gunshots rang through the cavern, and people screamed. I covered my ears as well, dropping the megaphone. Mountain, who had been the one shooting, picked up the megaphone. A gun in one hand and a megaphone in another made quite the view. "You will listen in silence for the rest of what Wind has to say. She is the one who found the information. She is the one who has brought you the truth. You owe her respect."

When he finished, the entire cavern was completely silent. There wasn't even the normal background noise of shuffling feet. Mountain handed me the megaphone again, and I thanked him before bringing it to my lips.

"We can not just go and attack the upper tower. They have the information that we need. We have been kept in the dark about a lot of stuff. So first, I will show you the evidence I

186

have. At the same time I do that, those I have preselected will interrogate this man and his traitors for information. We don't know how many floors there are. We don't know what they have for weapons or armed troops. We need to find this out fast before they descend on us. So, I need people to get organized. I need leaders to lead and soldiers to fight. This is going to be like a zombie horde attack. We need unity. So let's plan and come together. We need to do this smart. I don't want any more of you to die from a stupid mistake. Who is with me!"

This time, people cheered.

When the cheer died, I continued. "Now, I will go over to the screening area, and we will have a line. Anyone who wants to see the evidence for themselves, form a line, and I will show each of you. Those of you who want to help, go find Elephant. He will start organizing our war party to infiltrate the upper tower. We are not killing; we are infiltrating. They are not zombies but people up there. Bad people, but still people. Let's not become them in the process. Now follow me."

Chapter 29
POWERS
STAR: The surface
Z.O.M.B.I.E. Games: The Lost City

I stood alongside Gurney at the crossroads, facing a crumbling archway that served as the entrance to the lost city, tempting me with its unknown possibilities. To the left, a roughly paved road veered around the city. The path that we had discussed would be the best route. Yet, my gaze was drawn to the archway, its dilapidated buildings beckoning me inside. Some structures reached for the sky, while others lay in ruins or leaned on their neighbors for support. Nature, relentless in its pursuit, had claimed the ground and buildings alike as if reclaiming what was rightfully its own.

"Why are we taking the long way around the city again?" I inquired, my curiosity yearning to explore its hidden depths and winding tunnels. The open expanse behind us seemed less enticing in comparison.

"It's a death trap," Gurney grumbled, weariness etched on his face. "Most of the Zombies in the area reside there."

"How long would it take to go through?" I asked, my desire for adventure getting the best of me.

"I've never seen a group make it through in a day. Those who attempt the city route usually end up fighting their way through the last few hours before finally reaching the other side. Some make it halfway and set up camp in a cleared-out building, attempting to survive the night before completing the journey," he replied.

"How successful are they?" I pressed for more information.

"Not very often," Gurney mused. "But then again, they're usually smaller groups. I've never seen a group stick together like ours," he added.

"Why is that?" I probed further, eager to understand the dynamics at play.

"Well, part of it is human greed. The fewer people who make it, the larger the reward for each individual. Plus, there's the widely known rumor that only three people can make it through. We all believed it until Kyle set us straight. But I think there's another factor: trust. Most people thrown into the Games are criminals. Lately, however, city officials have been sending less severe cases. People don't trust murderers and rapists, and they have good reason not to. Now, they're sending petty thieves. I even heard Laurel was put in here for jaywalking," Gurney explained, his frustration evident.

"Jaywalking? What's that?" I inquired, realizing my lack of familiarity with the concept.

"Ah, right. I forgot you probably don't have cars down in the towers. Let's just say she was walking where she shouldn't have been," he replied, his patience wearing thin.

"So, what did you do?" I pressed further.

Gurney's face darkened, and he responded, "Tax fraud."

"A what?" I asked, puzzled by the unfamiliar term.

"I tried to cheat the king out of his dues," Gurney tried to explain, but my confusion persisted. Giving up, he said, "It doesn't matter. The point is our group doesn't have the same dynamics as those in the past. Half of us were picked up by the enforcers because a family member was found opposing the king."

"That sounds unfair," I mused, sympathizing with the plight of the people in the City.

"When is anything ever fair? The City's residents have been oppressed for a long time now. Those who dare to stand up against it are swiftly punished. It's becoming a powder keg, and this is the royals' way of suppressing dissent by eliminating family members as a warning to the general populace," Gurney added.

I didn't fully grasp everything Gurney was saying, but it didn't matter at that moment. Survival was my primary focus so I could find Reed. "Well, luckily, we have enough food for the long journey around. Although I'm not sure how I feel about traveling at night," I remarked, expressing my reservations.

"It's the safest way to navigate the path," Gurney explained. "If people are asleep and a Zombie manages to enter, the entire group could be wiped out. Often, a group has been doomed because the person on watch fell asleep." He shook his head, emphasizing the risks involved.

"If we're going to transition, we should return to the group and get some rest before we set out tonight," I suggested, aware of the importance of being well-rested.

"Agreed… And Star," Gurney grinned, catching my attention.

I turned to face him, waiting for his words. "Yeah?" I replied.

"Just...umm, thanks," Gurney paused, searching for the right words. Finally, he managed to convey his gratitude: "I don't think we could have made it this far without you. The whole group agrees. I'm sorry for doubting you in the beginning," he muttered, his gaze fixed on the ground.

"Hey, it's understandable. I mean, I emerged from that clearing with gear indicating that I had killed someone. Now that I know most of you aren't actually criminals, I can comprehend your skepticism. I would have felt the same way. I'm just glad we reached a point of understanding through conversation. The person you should really be thanking is Kyle. If it weren't for him, I would have left you all behind," I reassured him, placing my hand on his shoulder.

"I'll be sure to do that later," Gurney grinned. We stood in silence for a while until he asked another question. "Have they stopped yet?"

I understood what he was referring to. The rest of the team had received their initial powers through fame points and sponsorships. Then, on the sixth day, they all acquired a new power. It wasn't particularly extraordinary, allowing their eyes to emit light that could be switched on and off at will. It was useful, rendering flashlights unnecessary, but it also attracted the attention of nearby Zombies when used at night. Furthermore, the emitted light wasn't strong enough to repel the zombies.

On the contrary, I found myself constantly receiving new powers without any respite. The true nature of my first power remained a mystery. Still, the second one had undeniably heightened my reflexes and speed. It was as if the world around me slowed down when facing the zombies, allowing me to effortlessly dispatch them with my swords, their movements appearing sluggish and feeble in comparison.

On the sixth day, I also gained glowing eyes, but on the days in between, I acquired enhanced hearing, smell, metabolism, and good looks. These powers continued to add up each time I attempted to sleep.

"No, they just keep coming," I replied to Gurney's astonishment.

"That's insane. They told us the maximum we could purchase was four," Gurney muttered in disbelief.

"Well, I was thrown into this without any choices. I never got to make decisions. I still don't know what the Changing on the first day did to me," I murmured, reflecting on the mystery of my initial power.

"It must be challenging to adapt to them," Gurney mused. "I opted for increased vision and the ability to harden the skin on my arms and legs. Just those two changes have required a lot of effort for me to get used to. I can't imagine having to adjust to a new ability every day," he commented matter-of-factly.

"It definitely hasn't always been easy," I sighed.

"Especially when it comes to mastering the power to harden my skin. At first, I had no control over it, and my arms and legs would turn solid as steel at the most inconvenient times. It was like living with immovable limbs. I couldn't even hold a weapon properly."

I nodded sympathetically. "I can imagine how frustrating that must have been. But I guess it's a matter of practice and learning to regulate the power," I said.

He chuckled ruefully. "You're right about that. It took a lot of trial and error, but eventually, I managed to find a balance. And let me tell you, it saved my life more than once."

Curiosity flickered in my eyes. "How so?" I asked.

Gurney took a deep breath, recounting a harrowing encounter in vivid detail. "There was this one time when we were in that grassland when a particularly vicious zombie lunged at me. I thought I was a goner, but as it sunk its teeth into my arm, I realized something extraordinary. The arm it bit into had hardened to the consistency of solid rock. I could barely feel a thing. At that moment, instinct took over, and I unleashed a powerful punch with my hardened fist, shattering the zombie's skull with a single blow."

My eyes widened in astonishment. "That's incredible! So your ability not only offers defense but also enhances your offensive capabilities," I smiled.

He nodded, a mixture of pride swelling within him. "Exactly. It's a game-changer, allowing me to face the undead with newfound confidence. I still have a lot to learn about my power, but this one has undoubtedly been a valuable asset in our fight for survival."

"Well, thankfully, I didn't have to deal with anything regarding the metabolism power. Surprisingly, the hardest one to handle was the power of good looks," I revealed.

"Oh, really? Why was that?" Gurney inquired.

"It felt like I was constantly sweating when I first acquired it, and the girls in the group couldn't keep their eyes off me. It took me until the second day to realize that it was some sort of attraction ability specifically designed to appeal to the opposite sex. Once I figured out how to control it and turn it off, things got better. Kikki even mentioned that I looked older and generally more attractive now. But those first two days..." I trailed off, recalling the uncomfortable experience.

"Yeah, we all had to endure it, too, with Malori. It wasn't any different when she obtained that power on the first night. All the guys couldn't take their eyes off her until she gained control over it. Although I must warn you, she still enjoys using it occasionally, so be cautious around her," Gurney cautioned.

"At least you were aware of the effects beforehand. I thought there was something wrong with me every time I got close to Malori. I mean, she's like twice my age," I muttered, expressing my confusion.

"Well, when a woman is attractive, age doesn't really matter," Gurney grinned mischievously. "By the way, it makes me wonder. You were sharing a sleeping bag with Kikki the whole time. How did she react to your... ahem, charm effect?" He couldn't hide his amusement.

I looked at Gurney, who was sporting a big grin. I shook my head, choosing to ignore the question entirely. "We should head back now," I deflected.

Gurney chuckled at my blatant attempt to change the topic but fell into step beside me. Together, we made our way back to the group, where most of them were trying to rest as much as possible on the solid ground before nightfall.

Chapter 30
GOING AROUND

Reed: Earth's surface: THE CITY

A.K.A

Last City on Earth

"Reed, have a seat," Somner, the man I had followed out of the club, said. He had introduced himself as such on our quick evacuation of the building. Now, he was signaling to several lazy-boy chairs which were scattered around the room of the new building we had entered.

I looked between Somner and the five guards that stood close at hand.

"No, I'll stay standing."

After taking a seat himself, the man smiled at me, "You don't disappoint, so tell me, how did a dead man find his way to my club with an army of city enforcers behind him?"

"So we lost them?" I said, looking at the door and then the men guarding it. I didn't see guns on them, and I thought I might be able to take them even with the numbers.

"We have, but I can always send for them if you want," the man threatened, seeing the thoughts that flew through my mind. He could tell I was in fight-or-flight mode.

"How do you know me?"

"You're famous, you and Star. Star's appearance in the Z.O.M.B.I.E Games got people looking into his background, and there was a lot of footage surrounding you and Wind. You are the one who went missing with Star, and then he appeared in the games. Everyone thinks you are dead since you always appear together."

At the look of confusion that must have been apparent on my face, the man pulled out one of the devices that I had been trying to steal and began to press the face of it with his thumbs. He then handed it over to me. On it was a video of Star, Wind, and me eating dinner.

"How?" I exclaimed, anger in my eyes as I looked up at Somner.

"It's the spiders. They are The City's spies in the towers and tunnels. There was never enough food in the towers to feed real spiders. They were originally installed into the facilities to ensure the towers didn't rebel against The City. Still, then the Royals had the idea of broadcasting the footage to show the people that others had it worse."

I felt violated as Somner spoke, "So I've been watched my entire life?"

"Yes and no. The footage became dull and repetitive, and people stopped watching it decades ago. It wasn't until recent promotions that interest was returned. It was around the same time you and Star went missing. You were one of the highlights of some of the footage. That was months ago, though. Both of you just disappeared, so you can imagine our shock when Star appeared in the games. After that, everyone started to binge-watch his life, including you. I'm personally a big fan of yours. You guys are tough. We need men like you."

"I have my own things to take care of," I replied, looking at the door again.

"Yes, what is that?"

"I'm going to save my friend."

Somner smiled back, "I have some friends that I want you to meet. I think you'll find that your objectives are the same."

"My only objective is Star."

"But you are a one-man army; it would be easier with help."

I looked at the man, who was smiling all relaxed back at me. It was unsettling. Just the fact that we had talked so much was unnerving. It had been so long since I talked with anyone other than Star. Still, he was right. It would be a lot easier to get to Star if I had help. But I couldn't trust anyone. I knew that ever since I got shot. Trust wasn't something I was going to give out easily.

"I'll be a two-man army when I get Star back."

"Then what?" Somner continued to smile. "I can't imagine life has been relaxing on your own."

"You would be surprised. It was fine before your people took him."

"Yes, I want to know about that. The government hasn't provided any information on how Star was found." When I didn't answer, he shrugged. "Doesn't matter; what matters is that they found you. I can help it so they don't." Somner stood up and took a step toward me. "Tell you what, it's pretty clear you don't trust me, which I can understand. How can I earn your trust?"

"I need one of those with the energy packs so I can get my friend."

"Landry, give him your phone."

The guard Landry stiffened but then obliged after Somner gave him a look. I took the device cautiously, along with an energy pack.

"Anything else?" Somner asked.

"No, I'll be going now."

"All right, but if you stay, you'll reach your friend faster."

"How so?" I said, raising an eyebrow.

"Well, we were going to take a helicopter and fly over the zombie hordes to pick him up. It would only take about thirty minutes to reach him."

I froze at the thought of seeing my friend in less than an hour. I knew that it was already going to be hard to get to Star all by myself, but if what he said was true, then I could go get him right now. "Show me this helicopter."

"Well, that's the thing. It isn't quite in our possession. That is why I said we could use a man like you. We need to steal it."

"And you want my help to get it?"

"You are a sharpshooter; we could use a man like you."

I knew I had to make a decision, and the final factor was what was best for Star. I knew he would be safer if this panned out than if it didn't. It didn't matter if I had to trust someone if it was for Star. For him, I would do this.

"Let's go get this hellcopter."

"Helicopter but sweet. Let's get you to the others. Things have been a mess ever since they took our leader and put him in the Z.O.M.B.I.E. Games."

"Leader?"

"Yeah, we rebels have been riding leaderless, which has made things hard to get done. With your help, though, we should be able to convince the others."

"You're part of the Rebels?"

"Well, yes, what do you think we have been talking about?"

I nodded, remembering what I had heard during my spying. The rebels would be on Star and my side. Maybe Somner could be trusted. But if they didn't have a leader, it would take forever to get things done. "We should just do it ourselves. Why get other people involved?"

"No, we should get them involved; that way, we can get some leadership."

"What do you mean?"

"Well, I just figured that Star was in the games with our leader, and you are here, Star's friend; it just might help sway decision-making."

"I know what will, if that doesn't work," I replied.

"O, man, that sent chills down my spine. Dude, you are so cool."

"Let's get going. I want to save my friend."

"Yes, alright. Give me a second to call ahead." Somner started to use the device in his hand again. "I still can't get over the fact that Reed himself just appeared in my club," he giggled before lifting the device to his ear.

Chapter 31
EXPLORING

Reed: Earth's surface: THE CITY

A.K.A

Last City on Earth

"Why did you call this meeting, Somner?" A voice called out as the room filled up with people.

"Because someone had to Merlin," Somner replied, exasperated.

"I thought we agreed to keep low for the time being," Merlin argued back.

"No, the scared people in the room said that last meeting. We disagreed on it."

"We aren't scared," a woman put in. "We are just being cautious."

"If K was here, you wouldn't be scared."

"But K got himself captured."

"He also devised a plan for us to save him and the others. Yet what have we done to progress that? Nothing, while every day could be their last. It only takes one day for every single one of our people out there to die." Somner argued back.

"We still agreed to wait last time. It's too dangerous to act now." the woman replied. "If this is what we came to talk about today, I am leaving."

I could see the people in the room were disgruntled and scared. Not one had noticed me in the dark corner next to the door they had walked in through, though. But I needed to end this argument if I wanted these people to help save Star. It wasn't going to save my friend. I knew what I had to do even though I was scared to do it. I had been in isolation for so long that being around all these people made me uncomfortable, but I had to bear it for Star.

I took one last deep breath and cleared my mind as best I could before bellowing in as deep a voice as I could muster, "You call yourselves rebels?"

At my words, the whole room jumped, and heads turned and looked at me. I was already standing and moving forward. I used the momentum to keep my mind off of the number of eyes that were on me. Exclamations of disbelief sounded through the room. Sooner then, I wished I had made it to the front and turned to face the room. Unfortunately, all the things I wanted to say disappeared when facing the group.

"Who invited a new person?" Someone called out.

"What, you don't recognize him?" their neighbor asked. "That is Reed, Star's friend from the tower."

Other mutterings filled the silence as I tried to pull thoughts and words back into my mind. Finally, I was slowly able to break through the stage fright and was able to regain some of my composure. Somner had coached me a little on approaches I could take. The most direct one was the one I liked the most.

"Quiet, how do you get anything done?" The room immediately went quiet. "There, much better. Now, I'm not a people person. I've only encountered a few over the last several months. So, I'm going to get right down to the point. Your leader, K, left me in charge of ensuring his missions were fulfilled. So why hasn't anyone tried to even prep to go and rescue our people?"

The room remained quiet as I looked around. Finally, someone called out, "Why would he leave you in charge?"

"He took one of us with him to keep the contestants safe, and he left one of us here to keep you in line," I replied, using the words Somner had provided me. I looked over the room as people thought about it. One man dressed in a uniform smirked at me. I could tell he knew I was lying just from his face.

"That's not proof," someone called out.

I was about to reply when the man who was still smirking stood up. "How do you think that Star entered the games? You think that was the Royals doing? No, that was us. I escorted Star myself to Alejandro to be placed in the games. Reed here is telling the truth, and I will follow his lead."

199

More muttering went around the room, but the man who had stood seemed to be well respected since no one had questioned him.

Somner took the chance to speak up. "Right, so Reed, what is the first step?"

"We need to get our hands on the Hellcopter."

"Right, so let's go get that Helicopter." Somner said, "It should be a cinch with Reed's skill set."

I sat back as Somner and the other man took charge of organizing what needed to be done. I watched, and just my presence eliminated any questions. People took their orders, and slowly, the room emptied as people went to perform their assigned tasks.

Eventually, only Somner, the man I learned was Burt, and myself were in the room.

"So," Burt smiled at me. "How do I have the pleasure of finding you here at this meeting?"

"He showed up in my club with an army of enforcers behind him," Somner answered for me.

"Did he now?"

"Is it true that you put my friend in the games?" I whispered danger in my voice.

"Yes and no. Others found him. I simply pulled some strings to get him out of the hands of those who would do him harm and help our own people. I think all of our people would have died the first night without him."

"So you're telling me you did him a favor."

Burt sighed. "Reed, I am trying to fight for those you can't. I'm sure that is something you can relate to. You've been doing it for your whole life.

"Yes, until those people abandoned me and my friend."

"And our leaders have abandoned us as well. They use us as slaves and experiments. They don't use what they have to help mankind at all."

"But you put my friend out there." I pointed.

"Yes, but we were always going to bring him back and give him a home with us. We still will."

"You should have asked," I grumbled.

"If I could have, I would, but unfortunately, life isn't fair. We only have power over what we are given and have what we take ourselves. You, of all people, know how unfair it is."

I nodded at that.

"Good, now let's get you armed. I want you ready to deploy with my men so you can save your friend firsthand.

"I wouldn't have it any other way," I replied, getting up and moving toward the door before realizing I had no idea where I was going. I turned to Burt and Somner, "I think you should lead the way."

Burt smiled back at me. "It's good to have you."

Chapter 32
EXPLORING
WIND: Underground Tower #4

It took a while to show evidence to all those who wanted it. About a tenth of the lower tower, a total of about six hundred people wanted to see it. Those who didn't look took the word of all those others who went and saw. I was able to do it in groups of fifteen, and it took fifteen minutes a piece for me to show the highlights of what I found. By the time I finished, a whole day had passed. I hadn't even taken a food break. My stomach was growling furiously as I slowly exited the screening room out into the cavern that held my entire universe. I was surprised to see the grounds still bustling. People moved around while others barked orders. What used to be the outcast living quarters, those that didn't earn their right to live in the tower, now a military camp. People moved around, and supplies were gathered from the upper floors and stockpiled below. The outcast had been moved into quarters in the tower.

I stopped and stared in confusion until I felt a presence next to me. I turned to see Mountain standing next to me, a bowl with a spoon in his hand.

"Here, you must be hungry," Mountain said, handing the bowl over to me.

"Starving," I said, grabbing the bowl and unceremoniously began to dig in. "What have I missed?"

"Well, before we could send a group up to investigate the upper tower, they shut down the elevators that lift past the two hundred and fiftieth floor. They cut us off."

"Are they preparing to come down?"

"We don't know. We just don't know what they are capable of. We have guards watching the elevators that go up and are removing any supplies from the upper floors and moving them down here."

"Who is in charge right now?"

"Funny enough, Elephant is. You put him in charge, and everyone followed suit. That is until you were done with your sideshow. Everyone is kind of waiting for you."

"Me?"

"Yes, you. Like it or not, you earned everyone's loyalty. I don't think anyone would go against your word right now."

I looked at Mountain in shock, food unchewed in my open mouth. He laughed at my expression and then took a closer look at me. "You must be exhausted. Come take a quick nap. We can handle things until you wake up."

I nodded and let myself be led over to a tent in the open space where a cot was made. Mountain made sure I had everything I needed and then went out to let me sleep. I fell asleep quickly, even though my mind was reeling. Foggy and reeling—not a good mix.

Sleep really did me good because the pain in the back of my head had disappeared when I woke up. I opened the flap of the tent and found Mountain sitting out front, along with Bomb and Turtle.

"You're up?" Bomb said as Mountain quickly got to his feet. The other two were a little slower at it.

"Yes, how long did I sleep?"

"Only a couple hours."

I nodded at that, looking at the still-busy floor.

"We were to bring you to the commander's tent when you woke up." Bomb continued, clearly taking control of his squad.

"Commander's tent?"

"Yeah, it turns out some of us were promoted while you slept," Mountain replied.

Bomb stuck out his chest at that, "Yes, we are now the Commander's guard."

I wrinkled my eyebrows at that. "So, shouldn't you be guarding the Commander?"

The boys all gave each other looks with smirks. Mountain was the one that spoke up first. "Remember what I was saying before you went to bed."

203

I thought back, and then the pieces started to fit together. "Me? I'm the commander?"

"Everyone agreed it was you."

"But I'm not a strategist."

"No, but you have everyone's trust. They know you'll pick the best people for the job," Mountain replied.

Turtle nodded, and Bomb piped in, "And they picked the best people to protect you."

I nodded at that. "Thanks, but why do I need protection?"

"Well, we are at war arn't we?" Bomb continued. "It's us against the upper tower."

I rubbed at my head before just shaking it. "Well, lead the way then. Let's see what kind of trouble I put myself into."

As it turned out, we didn't have to walk very far to get to the Commander's tent *or my tent, I guess*. It was much bigger than the one I had taken a nap in. Inside, I found Elephant and Zebra talking with Ant. They all fell silent when I walked in.

Elephant was the first to greet me. "Finally, you're up."

"Yes, what is this I hear about being made Commander?"

"Well, people wanted to know who was in charge now that we don't trust the upper tower as they were in charge. So there was a quick pole, and everyone agreed that it should be you."

"Didn't anyone think someone else might be better at this than me?"

"We didn't say you were alone," Elephant smiled. "Everyone trusts you after that stunt you pulled and how you showed everyone the facts yourself afterward. There really wasn't another choice."

"Fine, so I'm in charge? What do I have to do?"

"Well, we were just discussing how we should get into the upper tower."

Ant nodded and added, "We were thinking of cutting our way up or blasting."

I shook my head at that. "That would draw all their attention and create a kill zone."

"That's what I said," Zebra nodded.

"Can't we just scale the outside?" I replied.

"Again, we would be easy targets. They are sure to be watching for breaches from the window."

"Yes, but they would only be doing that for the 250th floor and maybe the 251st floor. If we found a blind spot and made our way up five floors from the outside, then made our way in, we could establish a base and figure out what we were up against."

The three men smiled at me.

"See," Elephant clapped me on my back. "You're going to make a great commander.

Chapter 33
EXPLORING

Alejandro: Earth's surface: THE CITY

A.K.A

Last City on Earth

"Why are they not splitting up?" King Palumbus asked me as he looked out the window in his personal room.

"I'm not sure… this has never happened before," I muttered before recognizing my error and quickly continued to make up for my mistake. "It might have something to do with Kyle Pecoraro, though. I've overheard some of them talking about him. He seems to be trying really hard to keep the group together."

"A Pecoraro, huh." the king said with a snicker. "They always have caused problems. I should have done away with that line long ago."

"My lord?"

"So what are you going to do about this, Alejandro?" I noticed the emphasis on my name.

"I could reinforce the rumor that only three people make it out alive."

The king turned, and his features seemed predatorial. "That might be in your best interest."

A shiver went down my spine as I looked into the eyes of a real-life devil. "I'll fix this."

"You've had to fix a lot," the king muttered. "I am losing my patience."

"Yes, my lord." I nodded vigorously.

"We need the rebels to know what will happen to them if they continue. We need a show. Do I make myself clear?"

"Yes," I replied as my mind raced.

It was very clear to me how the conversation had ended. He wanted me to show the people in the game suffering and dying for the whole city to see. What he didn't want was to show the city that if you work together, you can get through hard things. That would only promote the rebel movement. And it was all being placed on my shoulders. I was relieved when he waved his hand in dismissal and allowed me to leave. I quickly made my way to the elevator and started to head down.

I would have been better off in the games. I thought to myself as the floor number displayed on the screen descended. Once the elevator reached the bottom floor, I quickly exited and started to make my way across the large floor when I heard a group of people talking as they walked by.

"It wasn't just any helicopter that they took. It was one of the king's combat helicopters. It just took off and flew away."

I didn't catch more in the conversation, but that didn't bode well. For me, specifically, it meant that I had better do a good job with the games, or I would be a goner. The King wanted results, and he wanted them now.

As soon as I got out of the building, I made a couple of calls. I explained what I wanted, and there was only a little pushback until I cleared my throat: "Send in a drone. We need to break them up today, or it will be all our necks."

As soon as I returned to the Zombie games control center, the drone was almost to the group. I sat down and watched the feed as the drone moved closer to the group to deliver the message that, truly, only three people were going to make it out. The rest would be thrown back into the lost city.

The drone approached the group and slowed down. Immediately, though, a gunshot rang out, and the drone's screen went dark.

"What just happened?" I yelled to the dozens of people in the room.

"One second, sir, I'll send you the feed of one of the bug drones." He was referring to our eyes and ears that watched the group. Unfortunately, they were only designed to do those two functions and wouldn't let me deliver a message to the group.

I grabbed a keyboard and mouse and quickly pulled up the feeds that were sent my way. I rolled back the time a bit and watched as my drone approached. It wasn't until it was right in front of them that Kyle Pecoraro lifted a gun and shot the drone down.

"What was that for?" Ernie yelled, followed by agreement from some of the others.

"It was a drone," Kyle replied as if that explained everything.

"Yes, but it could have been sent here to help us." another replied.

"More likely sent to cause us problems," Kyle responded. We can't trust anything the game leaders send our way. They are out to get a good show. If another one comes, take it out before it can sow discord amongst us."

There was a murmur of agreement from the others present.

"Crap," I yelled at the screen. "This is total crap!"

"Sir?" one of my assistants asked.

"Find another way to deliver a message."

"Yes, sir."

We tried three times in total to deliver a message, but each time, Kyle convinced the group to ignore even looking at the information we sent. I was getting frustrated until someone came up to me.

"Sir, do we have to split them up or just put on a good show?"

"What do you mean?"

"Well, I've made contact with a couple of the enhanced zombies, and they are smart. I could suggest to them that we lay a trap for the group."

My eyes widened at that. "I guess we could try a different approach. We need something to work or we are in trouble. Set up communications with them and bring in anyone who you think will help convince the Zombies to do as we want. I want results."

"Yes, sir."

Chapter 34
GOING AROUND
STAR: The surface
Z.O.M.B.I.E. Games: The Lost City

I was roused from my slumber by a gentle shake on my shoulder and a soft voice calling out, "Wake up." Startled, I instinctively reached for my sword, but my hand froze in mid-motion as I recognized Kikki crouching beside me.

"What's going on?" I asked, rubbing the sleep from my eyes.

She informed me, "We're an hour away from sunset, and Trevor said it's time to get moving."

"Alright," I replied, rolling out of my sleeping bag. The nap had been refreshing, a welcome change from the uncomfortable sleep I had endured while dangling on the cliff. It was also more spacious now that I didn't have to share the sleeping bag with another person. Kikki still had her pack, which contained a blanket she used for her own nap. Over the past week, we had grown closer, building trust and looking out for each other instead of solely focusing on ourselves. Our bond had deepened, and I couldn't help but appreciate the warmth she brought into my life, figuratively and literally. I swiftly packed my bag and checked my gun. Kikki had one of the other guns, which she had proven capable of. I also felt more comfortable with it being in her possession.

As a group, we experienced a turning point two days earlier when Malori had a breakdown in front of everyone. We had stumbled upon a small cache of supplies, including additional bullets and three more guns. Although part of me wished there had been another sleeping bag among the items, we had spent the night in an underground bunker I had cleared out. Like every night, a horde of zombies had descended upon us, relentlessly pounding at the door and emitting spine-chilling screeches as they attempted to unearth our group.

Malori's emotions became overwhelming, and it took the combined efforts of three people to calm her down. Meanwhile, a few of us realized that action was necessary before the zombies breached our defenses. We swiftly engaged in a fierce battle, utilizing a significant portion of our ammunition, but emerged unscathed. Opening the door, we unleashed a barrage of bullets, decimating a sizable portion of the undead menace before sealing ourselves back inside and securing the entrance. This process was repeated over and over again until the zombies finally relented for the night.

After the second encounter, we bolted the door behind us and waited for another half-hour before attempting to rest. Everyone stayed awake, providing comfort and support to Malori, whose distress had shattered the tranquility of the night. Amidst her intermittent sobs, she revealed her story, sharing how she had been unjustly accused of theft and assault against a member of the King's court. Malori let out a disheartened chuckle as the room fell silent, acknowledging the lingering skepticism.

"You probably don't believe me, though. It sounds crazy, right? That they would just pluck someone from their life and send them here," she confessed.

"No, it's not," Shawn interjected from his corner of the room. "I was snatched from my own condo. I didn't even learn about the charges against me until the second day of the promotional games."

Stories then began to unfold, and it became apparent that most of the group had been plucked from their ordinary lives, with fourteen seemingly snatched off the streets. Another four admitted to minor offenses that warranted only a short stint in jail. The exceptions were Trevor, Dale, Kyle, Gurney, and myself, who hadn't revealed any details about our past. Yet, the group remained oblivious to this fact. It seemed that a shared sense of injustice had forged a bond among them, uniting them in their quest for survival.

The group's unity was evident as everyone shared equipment and ensured that each member was prepared for the journey ahead. Together, we moved towards the crossroads in front of the Lost City. I wandered to the right side for a second time before following the others in the group to the left, moving towards the hills that stretched inland from the Lost City.

As we walked for an hour, the crumbling walls of the Lost City receded into the distance. The broken road meandered through the open plains, leading us closer to the hills that skirted the city. The once-imposing city wall, standing forty feet tall in its intact sections, now exhibited signs of decay and collapse due to years of neglect.

Occasional trees dotted the landscape between the road and the city wall. In contrast, a line of trees stretched ahead of us, covering several miles before the ascent into the hills. Lost in awe of the surroundings, I was interrupted by Kikki's voice to my left.

"What's on your mind?" she inquired. I had been gazing into the distance, marveling at the sights. However, an underlying feeling of insignificance still lingered at the edge of my thoughts.

"Those trees," I began, "can you eat them?"

Kikki chuckled in response. "Eat the trees? Where did you get that idea?"

I shrugged. "I don't know. I only saw them for the first time a few days ago. It felt hard on the outside when I touched one, but the green parts above seemed soft. They swayed with the wind. I just thought maybe you could eat them. They reminded me a little of the mushrooms Reed and I survived on before I was brought here."

"Well, you can't eat the trees themselves, but some trees bear fruit that is edible," Kikki explained.

"Fruit?" I repeated, unfamiliar with the concept.

"You've never had fruit before?" she asked, tilting her head.

"We didn't have many options for food in the tower," I replied. "We relied on mushrooms because they grew well. There was this dense, chewy substance that I never figured out

211

what it was. And we had these special vitamins that everyone took daily. Bread and cheese were common, but on Sundays, we would get supplied with burger meat. I always looked forward to burger night."

"Did you have cows underground?" Kikki inquired, curious about our provisions.

"Cows?" I inquired, genuinely puzzled.

"You know, the source of your meat and cheese," she replied with a hint of disbelief.

"Well, those come from different places," I explained, confused. "The milk comes from the female cockroaches in the cockroach farm on level 488. As for the meat, it's a variety of bugs that they grind up to make it. Do you call that mixture cows?" I asked curiously.

Kikki stopped abruptly, staring at me incredulously. "You must be kidding me," she muttered, her jaw dropping.

"I'm not lying," I muttered defensively.

"You love eating bugs? I've been sharing a sleeping bag with a bug burger boy," she muttered.

"You don't like burgers?" I asked, taken aback.

"No... Burgers are delicious, but you're supposed to use proper civilized meat, like cow," Kikki explained.

"And what is a cow?" I asked, genuinely curious.

We continued walking slightly behind the rest of the group as Kikki enlightened me about what a proper burger consisted of and introduced me to the concept of cows. It turned out she believed I needed a major education, and she proceeded to explain which animals were worth eating and which ones were not.

As the radiant sun descended beyond the horizon, casting a dim glow over the landscape, we pressed on along the path bathed in the light of the moon. The transition from day to night brought about a palpable shift in our group's demeanor, a heightened sense of alertness gripping us all in the absence of the sun's protective embrace.

At that moment, I instinctively found myself gravitating toward the front, my heart pounding with anticipation. A tingling excitement coursed through my veins as I used the new powers given to me – the power of enhanced hearing and night vision. It was as if a dormant part of my being had awakened, granting me an advantage in this game of survival.

Every sound became magnified, resonating with an exquisite clarity that surpassed the limitations of mere mortal senses. The rustling of leaves underfoot, the distant hoot of night creatures, the soft whispers of my companions – they all reached my ears with a newfound intensity, guiding us through the darkness with uncanny precision.

But it was my night vision that truly left me in awe. As the world around me cloaked itself in shadow, I witnessed a mesmerizing transformation. The once-obscured details emerged from the abyss above, revealing a hidden tapestry of shapes and hues. Shadows took on a life of their own, dancing in an intricate choreography as I navigated the path ahead. The moon's gentle radiance, though only a fraction of its full glory, illuminated the terrain with a glow, guiding my every step.

Jillian and Drake, their loyal companions of controlled infected bugs, also proved to be invaluable allies. With their assistance, our vigilance expanded beyond the limitations of our mortal senses. The insects, ever obedient to their masters, scouted the surroundings with unparalleled efficiency, their keen perception and nimble movements providing an invaluable layer of protection.

We encountered only four wandering zombies throughout the night on the plains before reaching the tree line, and I dispatched them silently by cutting their heads off in the blink of an eye before scrambling their brains. The trek took most of the night, leaving us with only an hour of darkness remaining to traverse through the woods. We halted and began setting up camp, fatigued from the day's arduous journey.

As we organized our camp, Kyle approached me. "Hey buddy," he greeted.

I looked at Kyle, noticing his leaner and more toned physique, sensing that something troubled him. "What's wrong?" I asked, concerned.

213

"Something doesn't feel right. I didn't want to alarm the others, but I'm sure some of them have already noticed," he whispered.

"What is it?" I inquired, my anxiety heightening.

"We only encountered four zombies the entire night," he responded.

"And that's not a good thing?" I asked, seeking clarification.

"Maybe not. We should have come across larger groups more frequently. Considering the history of the Zombie games, it's abnormal to have such a peaceful night. Moreover, we've been relentlessly pursued by zombies every night since we arrived... until last night," Kyle explained.

"So, what are you suggesting?" I probed, feeling the tension mounting.

"I don't know. It just feels strange and makes me uneasy," he replied.

"Well," I began, "if there's nothing we can do to change our circumstances, we'll have to adapt. It's better than resisting the unknown." Kyle nodded, but he continued to ponder the situation. Sensing his restlessness, I asked, "I've been thinking about something lately. It has to do with you recognizing who I am."

"And?" he prompted.

"Well, there have always been unanswered questions about the tower. I wondered if you might have some insight since you recognized me," I said, inviting him to share any knowledge he might possess. Kyle nodded, signaling for me to continue. "You see, I've always wondered what transpired on the upper floors of the tower. And I'm curious about why Redwood and Stump shot Reed upon our return. Furthermore, the zombies seemed to anticipate our arrival.

Kyle nodded once again, his understanding evident. "I see. You wouldn't know most of that since you were from the lower floors," he muttered. "Let's just say there were a lot of political games being played to maintain or gain power. Up there, on the upper floors, there was another exit that led to the tunnels. As the population grew on those upper floors, they would kick people out into the tunnels to reduce numbers and ensure there was enough food to go around. People lived in constant fear of being thrown into the tunnels, so they lived each day as if it were their last. Their lives were filled with luxuries compared to the hardships you faced in the lower tunnels. Sadly, some of the zombies you encountered were those who had been cast out from the upper tower," Kyle explained, giving me a glimpse into the grim reality.

"In short, the upper towers were corrupt, and good people didn't last long. But it attracted viewership. Over time, however, it became repetitive, and people started focusing on their own problems instead. So, about half a year ago, in an attempt to reinvigorate the interest of The City's inhabitants in the towers, the royals made contact with the leaders of each tower, offering assistance. But it came with conditions—they had to keep The City's existence a secret and fulfill certain tasks. They thought it would be entertaining to watch a tower make a treaty with zombies, never imagining it would actually happen. But somehow, your tower accomplished it and offered you up," Kyle finished, his voice tinged with sadness.

I stood there in silence, anger bubbling beneath the surface. "So it was all for the entertainment of others," I said through gritted teeth, struggling to contain my frustration.

Kyle nodded, his expression reflecting the weight of the situation. "The world is a bit messed up right now. But there are those trying to fix it," he said, his words carrying a glimmer of hope.

His gentle words managed to soothe some of the anger within me, leaving behind a weariness. I wished I hadn't learned the truth.

Kyle patted me on the back and left me to process the information. I took a few moments to let it all sink in. However, my thoughts were interrupted as Kikki approached me and asked what I was doing.

"I was contemplating what I should eat today," I replied with a smile, attempting to shift my focus. I then made my way

215

towards Simon, who was preparing a rabbit that Drake had found with the help of his bugs and shot down. "What's on the menu today?" I inquired.

"Rabbit," Simon replied as he began skinning the animal.

I observed with fascination, eager to learn more about rabbits. Turning to Kikki, I asked, "Is rabbit considered edible?"

Several members of the group chuckled, having overheard our previous conversation about my affinity for bug burgers.

Chapter 35
THE LOST CITY
STAR: The surface
Z.O.M.B.I.E. Games: Woods Around The Lost City

We embarked on our journey early that morning, driven by the relentless pursuit of reaching our destination. To my surprise, it was the first night in what felt like an eternity that I had been spared from the agonizing pain that usually jolted through my body. In an attempt to shield myself from the blinding sunlight that threatened to rob me of my precious sleep, I resorted to wearing sunglasses and draping a cloth over my head. It was a makeshift defense against the relentless brightness that tried to pry my eyes open. The others took turns keeping watch throughout the night, but due to my transformations, they had spared me from the watch shifts.

Fortunately, our group boasted enough members to ensure that the shifts were short, granting everyone ample time to find respite in the embrace of slumber. As I awoke, an unfamiliar sensation washed over me—I felt rested, a welcome relief from the exhaustion the constant transformations inflicted upon me. The struggle to control my newfound powers during waking hours. The initial ease of controlling the powers slowly waned as more and more showed themselves. As it became harder, I became determined to master them quickly to both maintain my pride and stay safe. I didn't need to lose control of my body in a fight.

Kikki, having stirred from her sleep as well, joined me as we shared a modest meal of hardtacks salvaged from the supply caches. "How many more days until we reach The City?" she inquired, her voice laced with a blend of curiosity and anticipation.

I pondered the map I had once possessed and committed into memory, now lost to the ocean after Kyle had meaningfully discarded it. I engaged in a rough estimation and prayed that the map had been drawn to scale; I responded,

217

"Ten days in total. Six to navigate around the lost city, three to reach the gorge, and another day to ascend to the overpass before finally entering the forest outside The City."

"I wonder what The City is like," Kikki mused, her imagination painting vibrant pictures of a world unseen.

I shrugged, my voice tinged with a hint of wistfulness. "I wouldn't know. The tower was the only place I've ever known. The lost city we left behind was my sole reference point to the concept of a bustling metropolis that Kyle spoke of."

"I can't wait to show you around the City of Hope," Kikki exclaimed, her enthusiasm contagious.

A small smile curved my lips. "Well, there's still much that needs to transpire before we can even think of that," I muttered, acknowledging the arduous path that lay ahead.

"I know," Kikki whispered, her voice filled with unwavering determination. "But once we reach Kyle's city, we can then make our way to mine. You'll come with me, right?" Her question carried a note of vulnerability, seeking reassurance.

"I need to find my friend first," I replied, gathering my belongings and preparing for the day's journey. "Once I've located him, we'll find our way to your city together."

"How long do you think it will take to find your friend?" Kikki inquired, her genuine concern evident.

I sighed, my voice tinged with uncertainty. "I don't know. I don't even know if he's still alive," I admitted, grappling with the possibility of a grim outcome.

"Well, I'll help you search for him. And then, we can head back together," Kikki declared matter-of-factly.

A sense of gratitude warmed my heart as I met her gaze. "I'd appreciate that," I said, sincerity resonating in my words.

The rest of our group busied themselves with packing up while Kikki continued to share stories of the City of Hope and all the places she wanted to show me when we got there. I listened and asked questions when I didn't understand a term.

For two consecutive nights, our journey remained relatively uneventful, with only a handful of zombies crossing our path. These zombies differed greatly from the sluggish ones I had grown accustomed to encountering in the tunnels. They possessed the agility of a normal human yet lacked the ability to run. Although they could lunge short distances, their overall pace remained unremarkable.

With the scarcity of immediate threats, some members of our group saw this as an opportune moment to hone their unique powers and push the boundaries of their abilities. Reyn and Gurney, in particular, took advantage of the situation to refine their skills in dispatching the undead.

Reyn's advanced hardening powers allowed him to move rocks along his body, demonstrating remarkable mastery over his abilities. He transformed his entire body into an impenetrable rock-like state, leaving only his head vulnerable. He engaged two zombies simultaneously with unwavering precision, effortlessly shattering their feeble attacks against his unyielding form.

Gurney, on the other hand, had developed a new technique utilizing the hardened tip of his arm as a lethal weapon. Like a swift and deadly sword, he plunged it into a zombie's skull, swiftly ending its existence. His proficiency in this newfound method was evident as he executed the maneuver with unwavering accuracy.

Jillian and Drake, having already attained mastery over their power to control insects, showcased the devastating potential of their abilities. In a chilling display of teamwork, they commanded their swarm of insects to engulf the zombies, infiltrating their orifices until their heads were buzzing. The little creatures would eat their way through the brain before rupturing in a gruesome manner back out the way they had come. The sight of the insects emerging from the decimated craniums was a testament to their control over these tiny creatures.

Recognizing the need to augment his leadership with enhanced combat skills, Trevor approached me, seeking guidance in swordsmanship to complement his exceptional speed powers. Spotting a lone zombie, we seized the opportunity to engage in practical training. I instructed Trevor on the art of precise strikes, emphasizing the importance of severing the joints and ligaments before delivering a fatal blow through the eye to scramble the brains within.

Together, we executed a methodical dance with blades and zombies. With each well-placed slice, we disabled the creature's ability to move, rendering it helpless before delivering the final strike to ensure its demise. Trevor's progress was evident as his movements became more fluid and calculated, displaying a growing prowess with the sword.

Engaging in battles against the undead, I grew more adept at utilizing my newfound powers. I took charge of most of the encounters, employing my swords to conserve precious ammunition. With the heightened speed bestowed upon me, the zombies posed little threat, swiftly falling under my blade.

On the fourth night, as we traversed around the lost city, I found myself once again at the forefront, vigilant and watchful amidst the dense woods that enveloped our path. Kikki trailed closely behind, with Kyle not too far off. The night had been tranquil thus far until a peculiar scent wafted through the air, carried by a gentle breeze originating from the direction we had just come. It struck me suddenly, causing me to halt in my tracks, my senses on high alert as I scoured the surroundings for any signs of the undead.

"Is something wrong?" Kikki's voice broke the silence, her tone filled with concern.

"I smell zombies," I responded, my senses heightened.

As soon as the words left my mouth, the rest of the group, not far behind, came to a sudden halt, scanning their surroundings. It was at that moment that a sharp snapping sound echoed through the air, jolting me with surprise. Instinctively, I rolled away swiftly, narrowly evading the zombie that had dropped from the tree above. Rising to my feet, swords drawn, I relied on my newfound agility and strength.

With precise movements, I swiftly ended the undead's existence, plunging my blade into its eye socket.

Yet, there was no time to revel in my victory. My heightened senses picked up on the cries and shouts of my companions. Two creatures were viciously tearing at an unmoving figure. Meanwhile, another one of my companions grappled with a third zombie on the ground. Gunshots reverberated in every direction as more zombies descended from the trees, enveloping our group. Amidst the chaos, beams of light pierced the darkness as my companions activated their eyes, creating a disorienting strobe effect. Swarms of bugs came in from all directions, latching on to a few zombies that had fallen.

Though I wanted to focus entirely on the group's predicament, my attention was pulled toward the zombies that were blocking our path and closing in on us. With lightning speed and graceful precision, I propelled myself forward, using my speed to cut through the approaching horde. Kikki remained close behind, her bullets finding their mark amidst the mayhem. Kyle, less nimble, positioned himself just behind Kikki, his shots occasionally missing their targets.

"What do we do now?" Kyle's voice trembled with panic. "There are more ahead than behind us," Kikki replied, her voice laced with urgency, as I continued my onslaught against the relentless zombies. "We need to go back," she added.

In the midst of firing their weapons at the encroaching undead, my comrades had regrouped, defending themselves against any zombies that dared to draw near. As I cleared a path through the relentless horde, I swiftly caught up with Kikki and Kyle, who were making their way back to the rest of our group. Sheathing my swords, I unslung my rifle from my back. Taking aim with precision, I dispatched a few zombies from a distance before reaching Kikki and Kyle.

Pointing back to the direction I had just fought through, I urgently conveyed, "There's a massive horde approaching from ahead."

Kikki's gaze followed my outstretched arm, and she cursed under her breath. "We're being swarmed," she exclaimed.

"We need to move now!" Kyle's voice boomed with urgency as he led the way, retracing our steps.

"I agree," Kikki chimed in, her voice resolute as she followed closely behind me.

Turning to face our companions, I realized that their focus was solely on dispatching the immediate threat of zombies. Fists, guns, bugs, and flashing lights made the scene look chaotic, and I could tell no one had yet considered our next move as they were just trying to survive. They weren't fighters but were only starting to learn how to fight.

"Everyone!" I shouted with all my might, my voice cutting through the chaos. "We need to move NOW! Follow Kikki and Kyle!" Pointing in the direction they had begun moving, I swiftly fired another shot, ensuring a zombie kept its distance.

At my urgent call, the others swiftly turned their attention to me and the realization of the urgency at hand. They started to regroup and follow Kikki and Kyle, who had already taken the lead. I allowed them some space, moving at a slower pace to ensure their safety.

However, before catching up, I took a moment to pay my respects to the fallen bodies of Jillian and Trevor, lying lifeless on the ground. With a whisper, I solemnly uttered, "Rest well, and may your bones never rise again." Drawing a sword from its sheath, I performed the last rites, a necessary action to ensure their bodies wouldn't rise to harm others before moving to catch up with the rest. Unfortunately, the last rites didn't prevent other zombies from consuming them as spare parts for their own repairs.

Just as I was closing the gap between my companions and me, a peculiar noise reached my ears, growing louder with each passing moment. Its irregular rhythm caught my attention, emanating from the trees ahead. Before I could raise the alarm,

Sandra's voice pierced through the chaotic atmosphere, shouting, "Something's coming from the trees!"

That's when I saw them. Four zombies swung through the trees with unexpected agility and grace, defying all logic. They moved in near silence, and only the creaking of the branches gave them away. Gunfire erupted to the treetops, scattering flickering lights and casting an eerie glow on the surroundings.

Amidst the gunfire and the disorienting glow of activated eyes, my attention almost eluded the six zombies approaching from the left. The cacophony of noise masked my warning shouts, so I swiftly propelled myself forward, determined to intercept the creatures before they reached my friends. I managed to squeeze off two shots, but one zombie evaded the bullet with supernatural reflexes, merely grazing its head. The second shot only succeeded in knocking a zombie's head back, momentarily halting its progress before it regained its footing and continued its lumbering advance. It was at that moment that I realized something was dreadfully amiss. These were not ordinary zombies; they resembled the talking zombies that Reed and I encountered in the tunnels. Two of the creatures displayed heightened reflexes, prowling toward me, while the remaining four were similar to the one I had managed to momentarily delay with the bullet. And in the recesses of my mind, I couldn't forget about the four swinging zombies in the trees.

In a split second, I managed to fire off one last shot, striking the shoulder of a faster zombie, causing its arm to be blown clear off, tumbling to the ground. Swiftly, I holstered my gun and retrieved my two trusty swords. It was a narrow escape, but a barrage of bullets ripped through the approaching creatures, tearing apart the second zombie with its heightened reflexes. Another slower zombie crumpled to the ground, lifeless. However, the remaining four pressed forward, seemingly unfazed by the hail of bullets. Thankfully, the shooter ceased firing as the creatures drew near, allowing me to lunge forward with deft movements. I strategically targeted their

223

joints, evading their clumsy lunges with my remarkable speed and heightened reflexes. Yet, a chilling realization gripped me as I noticed my sword making no impact against the creatures' unyielding bodies. I found myself surrounded, dancing, and swinging my blades, struggling to keep track of all the adversaries closing in. In a moment of distraction, I lost sight of one of them. In my panic, I made a fatal error, stepping directly into the grasp of a zombie reaching out for me.

Suddenly, a rocky fist collided with the creature's face, sending it staggering backward. I turned to see Reyn, covered in stones except for his head.

"Thanks," I acknowledged, gratitude evident in my voice.

"It's getting back up," Reyn warned.

Instantly, a spray of bullets pierced the air, striking the farthest zombie. I watched as one bullet found its mark, penetrating the creature's eye socket. The impact caused its body to jerk momentarily before collapsing motionless to the ground.

The sight of the fallen zombie triggered a realization within me. I cursed myself for not attempting it sooner, as it had been a reliable tactic against the slower zombies in the tunnels. With my heightened reflexes, it shouldn't be much different. Determination surged through me as I lunged forward, using one sword to parry an oncoming arm while thrusting the other directly into the zombie's eye socket, executing a spinning motion to scramble the brains within. With Reyn's assistance, skillfully deflecting and obstructing the zombies' attacks, dispatching the remaining three became a swift endeavor.

However, as we triumphed over the immediate threat, my attention shifted to my companions behind me, only to discover another fallen comrade. Alvine, who had been standing just behind where one of the tree-swinging zombies landed, had suffered a fatal injury as a stray bullet pierced his neck. Blood pooled around him, and a few members of the group stood frozen in shock. My gaze fixated on Shawn's lower right arm, wincing inwardly at the deep gash. The rest of the group surveyed the encroaching horde, a sense of urgency settling upon them.

"We need to move!" Kyle's voice pierced through the chaos, capturing everyone's attention. Kikki wasted no time in urging Katty and Malori, who stood near Alvine's lifeless body, forward with forceful shoves. Drake and Nancy assumed their positions at the front, again taking the lead. At the same time, I lingered behind, solemnly performing the last rites on the deceased.

Amidst the hurried escape, I kept a watchful eye on Shawn as he maneuvered through the turmoil. The man, in his late forties, appeared emaciated and filled with fear. I approached him swiftly, matching his pace. "Shawn," I called out.

He gasped for breath, responding, "Yes?"

"How did you get that gash on your arm?" I inquired, concern etched on my face.

Shawn glanced down at his bleeding arm, then back at me. His eyes pleaded for reassurance. "It's just a scratch, right? It wouldn't be enough to infect me, would it?" His voice held a mixture of desperation and denial, tugging at my heartstrings.

"I'm afraid it doesn't work that way," I murmured, my voice laden with regret.

Shawn's shoulders slumped, and he spoke softly, "I hardened my left arm as an enhancement. If only I had chosen the right arm instead, I wouldn't be condemned to this walking death."

"Come over here," I directed, leading him towards a prominent rock jutting out of the ground. A sizable crack ran across its surface as a determined sapling struggled to emerge from the earth below. Shawn followed hesitantly, his fear palpable. I wished I didn't have to be the one to do this, but with a swift motion, I seized his arm and positioned it on the rock. My other hand unsheathed my blade, and in one fluid motion, I brought it down with all my might, severing the limb and causing blood to spurt from the stump.

225

Shawn cried out in agony as I retrieved a length of rope from his pant leg pocket, tightly binding it around his arm to stem the flow of blood. The others had moved ahead, leaving Shawn and me alone at that moment. I diligently wrapped his now-amputated limb, working swiftly with my nimble hands.

"I'm sorry, but it was necessary," I apologized.

Shawn managed to muster a feeble word, "Star?"

"Yeah," I responded, still focused on expertly bandaging his wound.

"Why... why take... my arm? I'm going to turn anyway. Just kill me," he pleaded, his voice filled with despair.

"No," I growled, the determination evident in my tone. "You were infected, but I acted swiftly and eradicated the infection completely. You're no longer infected. I'm going to bring you home to your family." With those words, I grasped Shawn's arm, helping him to his feet. "Now, I need you to run. I know it will be painful, but you must run!" I urged as the horde of zombies came into view behind us.

Shawn required no further encouragement. Despite the discomfort, he ran, awkwardly cradling his amputated arm close to his chest, his remaining hand exerting pressure to staunch the bleeding. In life-or-death situations, the human spirit finds the strength to endure. As I followed closely behind him, I couldn't help but ponder Shawn's belief that he was already condemned to death.

We pushed ourselves to the limits, running throughout the night, desperately trying to outpace the relentless horde chasing us. We found respite only when the first rays of sunlight pierced through the horizon. Collapsing in a small clearing within the woods, we were physically spent, our muscles throbbing from the relentless pace we had maintained to stay ahead of the pursuing zombies. Thankfully, it had been a downhill stretch. As we came to a halt, everyone crumpled to the ground, seeking reprieve from the exhaustion. The exception was Katty, who approached Shawn with purpose.

I observed with astonishment as she carefully unwrapped Shawn's bandages, then retrieved a knife and pricked her thumb. A few drops of her blood fell onto Shawn's open wound. At first, nothing seemed to occur, but gradually, a thin layer of film began to form around the wound, creating a protective barrier.

"Let it work for a couple of hours, and then you can scrape off the film," Katty instructed.

I couldn't contain my surprise as I blurted out, "What is that?"

Katty paused, then proceeded to explain, "I chose a rare ability in the Zombie games. It's called Healer's Blood. It enables my blood to heal others. My daughter is gravely ill, and I couldn't afford the treatments provided by doctors. So, if I made it back, it wouldn't matter unless I could save her. I used my sponsorship to obtain this power."

"That's truly incredible," I exclaimed, admiration evident in my voice. "If my friend Reed and I had you with us in the tunnels, we wouldn't have endured such hardships," I added, a smile gracing my face at the thought.

"Your friend?" Katty inquired, curiosity sparking in her eyes.

"Yeah, his name is Reed. He was shot right here," I gestured to a spot on my own chest. "Took ages to heal. But with your abilities, it would have been a breeze."

"Well, it won't make a difference if none of us make it out of this alive," Katty remarked somberly, her spirits momentarily dampening.

I shrugged nonchalantly. "I should have met my demise long ago. But there's always a chance," I muttered, a flicker of determination in my words.

Katty nodded in understanding and then retreated, collapsing onto the ground to allow her body the rest it desperately needed after the grueling events of the day.

Chapter 36
BIG BUG
STAR: The surface
Z.O.M.B.I.E. Games: Woods Around The Lost City

After a mere six hours of respite, Kyle roused us from our slumber, urgency etched in his voice. "To stay ahead of the horde, we must move immediately," he declared.

Agreeing in unison, we set off, retracing our steps back the way we had come. With every stride, we pushed ourselves to create a substantial gap between us and the relentless horde before nightfall descended upon us once again. As darkness cloaked the land, we remained vigilant, our senses attuned to any lurking danger. Night fell, and we continued pushing. Throughout our journey, we encountered only three fleeting skirmishes with the undead, dispatching them swiftly without a concrete plan in mind. Our sole objective was to maintain distance and outpace the zombies' relentless pursuit.

We stopped for small breaks to both relieve ourselves and eat from our meager supplies. Kyle got snapped at by Ninna when he complained that the women were taking too long. I could have told him that wasn't a wise decision as everyone was tired, angry, and fatigued. Just one of those was reason enough to give a female some space. I remembered when Wind had rough days. Reed and I spent a lot of time at my place during that time. Even then, we got a talking too for avoiding her. There just isn't any winning sometimes.

Descending the hill with increased speed, we found ourselves traversing an open plain as the sun began its ascent into the sky. Fatigue engulfed our weary bodies, prompting our group to collapse in exhaustion, succumbing to the beckoning embrace of sleep. Amidst the collective weariness, I approached Kyle, who had unceremoniously collapsed when the decision to rest was made.

"Kyle, we can't afford to linger," I whispered urgently, my voice tinged with concern.

Lifting his heavy head, Kyle met my gaze, his weariness evident. "What do you mean?" he inquired, seeking clarification.

"We can't risk spending too much time here," I reiterated, reminding him of the impending danger. "Navigating the lost city will take a full day, and with the horde closing in, we must time our passage carefully."

Comprehension flickered in Kyle's eyes as he reluctantly nodded. "Fine," he muttered wearily. "Just two hours."

Aware of the fleeting nature of our respite, I took up the responsibility of keeping watch as the rest of our group succumbed to sleep. My gaze scanned the vast expanse of the plains, aided by the clarity afforded by my sunglasses. As the hour wore on, exhaustion threatened to overcome me, and I resorted to a sharp slap across my own face to jolt my senses awake. Vigilant once more, I rose to my feet, surveying our surroundings to fend off the encroaching drowsiness.

Having endured the arduous task of carrying Reed through treacherous tunnels, I understood the danger of succumbing to fatigue. The key was to keep moving, to resist the temptation of rest. Ceasing one's momentum was an invitation for weariness to consume the body. One could extend their endurance by relentlessly forging ahead, staving off the inevitable crash. Lost in contemplation, I was stretching my fatigued muscles when my eyes caught sight of a group of zombies emerging from the tree line several miles distant. A shiver ran down my spine as I observed their peculiar behavior—a semblance of intelligence displayed through their eerie communication.

Reacting swiftly, I roused the rest of our group from their slumber, their groggy responses reflecting their struggle to awaken. Laurel and Malori stirred reluctantly while Shawn, in a moment of disorientation, almost launched an attack before recognizing me. Nancy's voice pierced through the tension, questioning the nature of these new foes. "Are they human?" she pondered aloud, seeking reassurance.

229

Wade's response quivered with unease, his fear-laden voice breaking the tense silence. "They are basking in the sunlight," he uttered, his words carrying an underlying sense of dread.

Devin interjected, his uncertainty palpable. "Are we certain they are not human?" he questioned, his tone tinged with a glimmer of hope.

Wade and Amy, possessing heightened visual acuity, spoke in unison, their voices resolute and devoid of doubt. "Definitely not human," they declared, their discerning eyes piercing through the distance and capturing the grotesque reality of the creatures.

Ernie, grasping for reassurance, voiced the question on everyone's mind. "Do you believe we can eliminate them?" he inquired, his words tinged with trepidation.

My hand delved into my pocket, fingers closing around the remaining ammunition, a stark reminder of our dwindling resources. Counting the rounds, I realized with a sinking feeling that I possessed a mere twenty shots. Knowing the importance of our collective firepower, I voiced the question. "How much ammunition do the others still have?" I asked, the gravity of our situation weighing heavily upon me.

My comrades exchanged glances, their expressions sour with the realization that our ammunition supply had been significantly depleted. The swift consumption of bullets during the previous two nights' encounters had left us in a dire predicament. Automatic weapons had been our primary choice, resulting in a rapid expenditure of ammunition. Only three rifles remained, and I had initially claimed the majority of the ammo for myself, the others allowing it in acknowledgment of my superior marksmanship.

It didn't take long for the truth to surface—a mere two clips for the automatics and a mere twenty-five bullets for the rifles remained. The collective realization that our bullet reserves were running critically low only served to deepen our sense of discouragement. While a few members of our group possessed unique abilities that could fend off individual zombies without significant risk, none among them were seasoned fighters.

"We must press on," I asserted to my weary companions, my voice tinged with determination. "We need to reach a cache within the city."

Devin, seeking clarity, voiced his concerns. "But how will we locate supplies within the city?" he questioned, his tone laced with genuine curiosity.

With a sense of purpose, I responded, revealing a piece of information I had kept to myself until now. "I possess a map I obtained from the Killer's Gambit," I explained, acknowledging the astonishment in Gurney's voice. "I know the whereabouts of another cache, a little over three-fourths of the way through the city."

Nancy, frustrated by the lack of information sharing, expressed her discontent. "You had a map all along, and you didn't think it was necessary to share it?" she retorted, her voice betraying a mixture of annoyance and disappointment.

"We don't have time to dwell on that now," Kyle interjected, assuming a leadership role following Trevor's demise. "Pack up and prepare to move. Star, lead us to the cache."

Thankfully, the others needed no further urging. In swift succession, everyone gathered their belongings, and we set forth toward the lost city. Instead of retracing our steps to the front gate, we opted for one of the breaches in the city's wall closer to the tree line. The tall grass impeded our progress slightly, but Drake led the way, utilizing his control over insects to scout the area for potential traps. It would have been advantageous to have a second person assisting in scouting, but Jillian's absence meant we had to proceed in a single file, following Drake's lead.

Navigating through the random wire fences, pit holes, and occasional clusters of zombies, dormant during the sunlit hours, proved to be a slow and arduous process. It took us two painstaking hours to reach the city wall and an additional half-hour to guide everyone through the maze-like gaps in the

231

decaying barrier and into the city's heart. As I leaped down onto the other side of the wall, I noticed the ground was covered in a layer of moss, yielding beneath my feet with each step. It was an unfamiliar sensation, unlike the solid ground I had grown accustomed to in the corridors of the tunnels.

The remainder of our group joined me, forming a unified front as Drake continued leading the way, his bugs scouting ahead diligently. After the unsettling incident in the trees, he made sure to have them inspect both high and low areas for any potential threats. We maintained a brisk pace, propelled by a sense of urgency, yet the sheer magnitude of the Lost City overwhelmed our senses. Towering trees sprouted from within and outside colossal structures, casting a surreal spectacle upon our vision. We maneuvered around and beneath tilting buildings, leaning precariously against their still-standing counterparts. Mindful of the shadows that concealed lurking dangers, we steadfastly sought refuge in the sunlight.

Amidst our progress, the shuffling sound of zombie footsteps emanated from the buildings surrounding us, while it seemed like a multitude of eyes fixated upon our every move. Zombies occupied various levels of the structures, a constant reminder of the imminent peril that loomed over us. Although we pressed on with determination, the day's weariness and lack of sleep eventually began to take its toll. Our pace slackened, and the fear of being trapped within the city after nightfall without the hidden cache served as our sole motivation to keep moving. Well past noon, we arrived at a sizable bridge, partially collapsed and submerged in the river below. The sturdy support pillars remained intact, with wires stretching between them, forming a makeshift crossing for the cautious. Ascending the wire ropes of the initial support tower, we cautiously advanced toward the substantial cables spanning the wide and deep river beneath.

At this moment, despair began to seep into the hearts of my companions. From our elevated vantage point, it became apparent that we had only crossed half the city. With a mere three hours of sunlight remaining, the entire metropolis would soon be inundated with hordes of zombies seeking refuge within its structures during the day. There was no chance that we were going to be able to reach and locate the cache in time. Exhaustion had taken its toll on us all, leaving us feeling dejected and defeated.

I rallied my weary comrades, urging them to persist despite the overwhelming odds. Though some of the group harbored a grim understanding of what the night would entail, others clung to a flicker of denial. However, as we reached the bridge's other side, our situation turned for the worse. Leading the way, I descended down the cord bridge when my heart sank. Looking to the other side of the cord bridge, I could see approximately twenty zombies roaming about under the unforgiving sun on the ground below. I quickly realized they were among the group that had emerged from the forest earlier. Momentarily perplexed by their sudden appearance and pondering how they had managed to outpace us, another disquieting thought struck me—where had the remaining dozen or so zombies disappeared to?

Frozen in my tracks, I surveyed the path we had traversed, only to discern the ominous truth. The other zombies had set their sights on encroaching upon the rear of our group. Reacting swiftly, I swung around, rifle in hand, and dispatched one of the zombies teetering on the makeshift wire bridge. The sudden crack of gunfire shattered the concentration of those desperately clinging to the cords with exhausted limbs, their gaze fixed on their hands and feet to avoid plummeting. Surprised cries were swiftly replaced by panicked screams as my companions comprehended the dire circumstances we found ourselves in. Reloading my rifle, I took aim and eliminated another zombie advancing from the rear. At the same time, Gurney unleashed a barrage of bullets from one of the remaining machine gun clips, toppling an additional eight zombies from their tenuous perch on the ropes.

With my attention fixed on the zombies below, I unleashed a barrage of bullets, one after another, aiming to suppress their advance. However, just as I reached for the
233

fourth bullet to reload, a fierce gust of wind suddenly assailed the bridge, threatening to hurl me off the precarious support cord. Reacting instinctively, my hand shot out, seeking the thinner cord that had aided our ascent. In the chaotic motion, my flailing hand inadvertently tore through the stitching of my bullet pocket, causing its contents to cascade down into the river below.

After regaining my balance, I fumbled to retrieve another bullet to reload, only to be met with dismay as I discovered the hole in my pocket. One of the bullets had caught on the side, and I swiftly salvaged it, loading it into the chamber of my gun with a frustrated curse. Just a single round remained in my possession, while more than twenty enhanced zombies still lurked below. Desperation compelled me to assess my surroundings, searching for any glimmer of a solution. It was then that a peculiar sight caught my attention—an immense insect hovering in the sky. Initially dismissing it as inconsequential, I pressed on toward the encroaching zombies, realizing that I had to make an attempt. If I couldn't eliminate them or most of them, the others stood little chance, especially given our precarious footing on the bridge.

Drawing closer to the approaching horde, I seized an opportune moment, firing off a shot when I was a mere twenty feet away, sending one more zombie into its eternal slumber. Exhausting my last bullet, I suddenly became aware of the escalating buzz emanating from the insect in the sky. Its proximity intensified, accompanied by a resounding thud. Then, a sharp zipping sound pierced the air, and the earth directly in front of my impending landing spot erupted violently, engulfing my surroundings in a cloud of dust.

Disoriented and robbed of my footing, I struggled to locate the steadying cord, my hands grasping at the empty air as my body tilted. A pang of disappointment mingled with a tinge of fear coursed through me as I plummeted downward, hurtling toward the water's surface. The impact created a splash that was swallowed by the cacophony above. Helpless against the force of the current, my body was swiftly carried away, colliding against a merciless rock. Darkness enveloped my senses as I drifted downstream, carried away by the relentless flow of the river.

Chapter 37
Where is Star!
Reed: Earth's surface: THE CITY
A.K.A
Last City on Earth

I was so close, Star was so close, but as the attack hellcopter sent out a blast of bullets into the Zombies below, I feared that Star was too close. My job was to take out the Zombies that were making their path along the makeshift wire bridge above. I took aim and quickly sprayed a line of bullets that sliced through the line of zombies. My aim was true, as always, and I easily took out the remaining zombies.

I turned my attention back to my friend only to realize that my fears were justified. The wire where Star had been standing was engulfed in dust. I watched as the dust dispersed due to the breeze from the hellcopter propellers. As it did, my stomach dropped. Star was nowhere to be seen.

The pilot landed the hellcopter, and I jumped out with several others. They secured a perimeter while I moved over to the river and looked down. That was the only place that Star could have gone. There wasn't anything there—not a single sign of my friend in its currents.

"Star!" I yelled. But it was no use. The other contestants were making their way to us. I looked back downriver and knew I needed to convince the others to follow it to find my friend. There was no way he would die so easily after we had gone through so much. There was no way he would leave me behind. We were brothers, after all, family.

I moved back and quickly helped the others onto the helicopter. I reported Star missing but was told it was too late as the hellcopter's invisible wings beat faster, lifting us up into the sky. I was so close, but I was too slow. I had failed my friend.

Chapter 38
WHAT IS THAT SMELL?
STAR: The surface
The Lost City

I regained consciousness, my body drenched and the cold ground chilling my face. Every fiber of my being ached, but the chilling, shuffling sounds surrounding me sent a deeper chill down my spine than the freezing water. Instinctively, I kept still, fear paralyzing me as I surveyed my surroundings with wide eyes. A voice pierced through the eerie silence, sending shivers through my core.

"Why wait for-er?" a raspy voice uttered, struggling to articulate the words correctly. "We ould ish have a porsh'n now."

"No," a clearer yet gurgled voice replied. "We wait."

"Bu-i smellso goond. Ush one bie won hur," the first voice persisted.

"The queens said to wait. If we don't, you'll be thrown in where he was found."

"Fin," the first voice gurgled reluctantly.

My mind raced, grappling with the realization that I was not surrounded by the ordinary Greed Zombies I had grown up fighting, but rather the intelligent and specialized zombies we had been combating in this sick game—and the ones that had killed Rock in the tunnels. A shudder coursed through me as I contemplated why I was still alive. It seemed that something wanted to keep me alive, at least for the time being. However, the prospect filled me with unease. Before long, heavy footsteps reverberated through the hallway.

"Where is he?" a feminine voice demanded.

"Here, my queen," the more eloquent of the two speakers responded.

"Do we know his capabilities yet?" she inquired.

"No," came the response.

"Well, we should test him first before distributing him. I want the best for infiltrating the city. We're so close to finally satisfying our hunger," she stated.

"Yes, my Queen."

"How is the tunnel progressing?" the feminine voice continued.

"Shoul be wone o wo diys," the less articulate creature replied.

"Ugh, your speech is deteriorating. Next time we have a human in the tunnels, make sure you have a portion. I can't bear being spoken to by it," the female voice expressed her disdain.

"I'll take care of it," the other creature assured before his less articulate companion could.

"Good. Well, I'm off to assess our losses and see if it will impact our numbers for the city breakthrough," she announced.

My mind reeled, struggling to process the information I was hearing. These zombies seemed more human than the mindless creatures I had encountered before. They conversed, possessed a hierarchy, and devised war plans.

As I strained to listen, footsteps receded, and the creatures in the room began to approach me. However, their advance halted abruptly when the disconcerting noise I had heard earlier returned. Suddenly, an explosion rocked the ground, and a light beam pierced into the room. Though not sunlight, it was a powerful ray that bathed the zombies in its glow, eliciting agonized screeches from the exposed creatures.

I sprang to my feet and dashed toward the newly formed hole in the room. With a leap, I hurled myself out of the opening, descending a few feet to land on the soft grass below. Standing before me was that peculiar bug again, the same one I had glimpsed in the sky just before plummeting into the river.

Only now did it loom large enough to devour me in a single gulp. A mesmerizing whir emanated from its spinning top, and its wings were a blur of motion, forming a hypnotic circular pattern.

The air reverberated with the sharp sound of gunshots as individuals emerged from the bug's interior, leaping onto the grass. They swiftly approached, racing past me and disappearing into the hole. Suddenly, a searing pain jolted through my leg, and I glanced down to find a fuzzy bug attached to it. Without hesitation, I snatched the insect, forcefully detaching it from my flesh. The bug's body felt rigid, except for its slightly fluffy top. Yet, as soon as I removed it, the world began to spin uncontrollably. A figure rushed toward me, catching me before I could collapse onto the ground. Darkness engulfed me again, my weight supported by a pair of strong hands.

I found myself once again within the labyrinthine of tunnels surrounding my tower, enveloped by an impenetrable mist. Utter solitude engulfed me, but amidst the eerie silence, whispers reached my ears. Reed's voice, followed by Rock's and Wind's. "Reed? Wind? Is that you?" I called out, my voice reverberating into the void, but no response met my desperate pleas. Then, Rock's voice emerged from a distance, and I sprinted towards it, hoping for some semblance of familiarity.

"Star, it's your fault I'm dead. You abandoned me," his accusing tone pierced through the mist. "No, Rock, I tried to reach you, but the horde of zombies overwhelmed us," I implored, my voice filled with anguish. "No! You're to blame for what I've become!" he bellowed, his decaying face emerging from the mist, riddled with wounds, transformed into a zombie. Consumed by anger and blame, he lunged at me, his intentions clear. I stumbled backward, my retreat interrupted by an unforeseen presence. I turned, and there stood Reed, his features now distorted by the curse of the undead. Beside him, Wind, too, bore the markings of a zombie.

"You abandoned us, Star! What kind of a friend are you?!" Reed said. They seized me, forcing me to the ground, and in my terror, I unleashed a piercing scream. "I'm sorry! I tried to save you! Please, I'm so sorry!" my cries echoed through the desolate tunnels, a desperate plea for forgiveness and understanding.

Even as my cries echoed through the desolate tunnels, a flicker of recognition passed through Reed's clouded eyes. His grip on me momentarily loosened, but the torment within him was far from subsiding. "Sorry won't bring us back, Star," he growled, his voice a hollow echo of his former self. Wind, her once vibrant spirit extinguished, maintained a stoic silence, her eyes fixated on me with an unsettling intensity. The weight of their accusations pressed upon my shoulders, and I struggled to find words that could bridge the chasm between us. "I did everything I could," I pleaded, my voice trembling with a mix of fear and despair.

"The odds were stacked against us, and I fought to protect you, to keep us together." Reed's expression hardened, his gaze piercing through my defenses. "Foolish Star, you were the one who led us into this nightmare. You believed you could save us, but instead, you led us to our doom." The words struck me like a blade, each syllable dripping with resentment. The bond we once shared, forged through countless trials, now lay shattered. I closed my eyes, tears welling up, and searched for a glimmer of the friendship we had cherished. "Please, Reed, Wind... There must be a way to undo this curse. We can find a way to bring you back," I implored, my voice filled with desperate hope. Wind's icy gaze softened momentarily, a flicker of the person she once was breaking through the veil of darkness. Reed, however, remained unyielding, his bitterness etched deep within his undead heart. "There is no going back, Star," he sneered, his voice laced with scorn. "We are lost, forever trapped in this wretched existence. And you, dear friend, will bear the burden of our demise."

As Reed's bitter words hung in the air, a chilling silence descended upon us, suffocating any flicker of hope that remained. Suddenly, an eerie stillness enveloped the tunnels as if the very darkness itself held its breath. And then, without warning, Reed's hands shot out, seizing my throat with a bone-chilling grip. Panic surged through me as his fingers constricted, closing off my airway and stealing the precious breath from my lungs. I thrashed and fought against his relentless hold, desperate for even a gasp of air. But the more I struggled, the tighter his grip became, his rotten nails digging into my flesh. Darkness swirled around me, the world spinning into a dizzying blur as oxygen became an elusive commodity. The tunnel walls warped and twisted, mocking my futile attempts to escape Reed's suffocating grasp. In that harrowing moment, it felt as though I was drowning in the very abyss that had claimed my friends. The veil of darkness closed in, smothering my senses as if eager to consume me whole. Time seemed to stand still, and the weight of my failures bore down upon me with unbearable intensity. I could hear Reed's haunting laughter echoing in the void, mingling with my tortured gasps. As consciousness slipped further away, surrendering to the relentless pull of the darkness,

Chapter 39
EXPLORING

Alejandro: Earth's surface: THE CITY
A.K.A
Last City on Earth

After reviewing the available feed, I didn't even bother waiting to make suggestions for the edited public copy. Instead, I grabbed anything I could of value, small enough to fit in my pockets, and ran. First, I walked through the building, telling anyone who approached me that this wasn't a good time and that they should catch me later. Then, I made my way through a back exit to the building and walked purposefully for a block. Then, after a quick look over my shoulder, I ran.

I moved in and out of alleyways that I didn't even know existed. I didn't really have a place in mind, but I knew I had to disappear, or the king's men would find me, which I knew I didn't want to happen. If they did find me, the punishment I would receive for failing the king would be very unpleasant.

Ultimately, I made my way through the city for a while before stopping to catch my breath. My eyes scanned my surroundings for anything that could help me escape or hide. Ultimately, they landed on a manhole cover, which led down into the facility tunnels. I couldn't think of a better option, so I carefully lifted it up and made my way in. It was surprising how heavy the manhole cover was, but I slowly was able to shift it back over the hole. Underneath, there wasn't much for lighting, but as I just breathed, my eyes slowly adjusted.

"I can't believe this is what my life has become," I muttered as I lowered myself to the bottom of the tunnel's floor. It was eerie down here, but it felt a whole lot safer than being above ground, where the king's men were sure to be looking for me by now.

There were four tunnels branching off from where I had landed in the underground system, and I picked one at random and began to walk down it. I had picked the darkest one as I figured that if anyone did follow me, would think that it was the least likely one that I would venture down. I moved slowly in the dim lighting, keeping a hand on the wall. I walked for about twenty minutes and was thinking about hunkering down for the night when I tripped over something. I fell to the ground, and a clattering noise sounded near me. I reached out to feel what I had tripped on and found a large bag full to the brim. I fiddled around and was surprised to find several flashlights. I flick one on and used it to inspect my surroundings. Its light was very dim, and I wondered why a flashlight would ever be made so dim. I used the dim flashlight to inspect my surroundings. To my surprise, there was a whole bunch of stuff here. It looked like someone had made camp and was collecting supplies from above.

Looks like I have a fellow escapee down here. Maybe he can help me.

I inspected the other items that lay around. To my surprise, there were guns and ammunition close by, along with swords. They looked familiar, but I couldn't place where I had seen things like this before. I was too tired, though, and figured I would test my luck with the owner of this stuff. I hunkered down next to the machine gun. I pulled a blanket, or what was left of one, out of the pack and curled up using a bundle of cloth for a pillow. It smelled, but it was more than I thought I would have to spend the night with when I ran. With that, I fell asleep with the hope that someone would be there when I woke up.

My wish came true, though it wasn't what I had hoped for.

"Grab him," a rough voice called out, waking me from my slumber.

"Wha? What's going on?" I called out as solid arms grabbed ahold of me and pulled me to my feet.

"Alejandro, I finally get to meet you in person," someone said behind a bright flashlight that was showing on my face. "And to think I was hoping to get an autograph for my kid

243

someday from a game coordinator. Looks like I will get my chance today even though it won't be for my kids."

"Let go of me," I yelled, struggling to break free before a fist came out and clocked me in the side of my head, making me see stars.

"Letting go would defeat the purpose. I'm to lock you up until the King has time for you."

That is when I realized who had me. It wasn't the owner of the items I had borrowed. The person I had hoped would save me. Somehow, the king had tracked me through the city and undercity. I wasn't going to be saved. No, I was going to be tortured and killed brutally. My head slumped down in defeat as the men holding me began to drag my body away.

"Look at all this stuff. He was really prepared to run, it looks like." One of the men said.

"Run? Where could anyone go? The city is the only safe place to live." Another laughed back.

"But what about the girl in the games? Kiki, she lived out there."

"I guess some can. Still, that isn't living. But it might have been preferable to what is in it for this tractor." I received a kick to my side at those words, making me groan.

Well, this is not how I saw my life going, and to think I wasn't supposed to have had the job in the first place. I thought to myself before my mind focused more fully on the pain in my side and head.

Chapter 40
REED'S KINGDOM
STAR: Earth's surface: THE CITY
A.K.A
Last City on Earth

I awoke abruptly, my heart pounding in my chest. But this time, as my eyes adjusted to the surroundings, I realized that I had emerged from the realm of nightmares into a much more pleasant reality. The absence of zombies alone was enough to lift my spirits. Still, the sight of a soft pillow beneath my head and warm blankets draped over me were welcome luxuries. And there, standing by the side of the bed, was Kikki, looking down at me with a mixture of relief and affection.

"Am I dead?" I blurted out, my mind still grappling with the remnants of the nightmarish visions.

"Nope," came a voice that I recognized all too well yet found out of place in this setting. "You're too stubborn to die. I can vouch for that," replied the familiar voice.

In disbelief, I turned my gaze sharply to the other side of the bed, only to come face to face with my friend Reed. "Reed?" I stammered.

"In the flesh," Reed grinned, his presence a reassuring presence in this bewildering moment. "Where? How?" I managed to sputter, my curiosity piqued.

"Well, after you decided to get yourself captured, I made my way to the top of the abyss, only to discover this hidden city nestled beside it. I sneaked in and learned that you were still fighting against all odds. Let me tell you, the townsfolk were captivated by your struggle. It was quite the spectacle. Even some members of the resistance said it was a shame to cut the games short. They were eager to witness what you could do," he explained with a mischievous glint in his eyes.

"But how did I end up here?" I questioned.

"Ah, right before you interrupted me," Reed continued, his grin widening. "The resistance wasn't too thrilled about their leader being captured and thrown into those wretched games. Ever since they've been working tirelessly to get him back. I stumbled upon them by chance, and when they discovered who I was, they invited me to join their cause. I was already gearing up to come to your rescue, so it fit my plans perfectly. However, you had to go and take an unexpected plunge into the river when we arrived. We managed to save everyone else, but you were long gone. The group we rescued from the zombie games convinced the resistance leader to mount a rescue mission for you. Drake used his insects to search for your location, while Shawn utilized his keen sense of hearing to detect any signs of your presence. It was Drake who ultimately found you. They swiftly retrieved you but were unsure if you had been infected, so they tranked and scanned you before allowing you to wake up," Reed elaborated.

"Tranked?" I inquired, still trying to process the whirlwind of events.

"Sleeping liquid, they injected into you," Reed clarified. "Fascinating stuff, really. You should see some of the advanced equipment they have. If we had access to it back at the tower, we would have easily dealt with the zombies. Well, at least the old ones."

Reed's mention of the "old ones" stirred a sense of urgency within me, prompting me to grasp his arm firmly. "Reed, we need to get out of the city. The zombies are approaching. How long have I been asleep?" I pressed, anxiety lacing my words.

"Only five hours," Reed replied, his eyes narrowing as he absorbed the gravity of the situation.

"That means we have, at most, a day and a half. The zombies are being led by a queen or something resembling one. There may be more than one, but there's definitely at least one. She, uh, it... Whatever it is, they claimed they were tunneling up to the city. They expect to breach it within one to two days," I murmured.

Reed's gaze sharpened, determination etched across his features. "I'll inform the others," he declared, swiftly leaving me in bed with Kikki still by my side, her hand clasping his.

Observing the confused expression on her face, I couldn't help but inquire, "Are you alright?"

Kikki glanced down at our entwined hands, before quickly letting go. "Yeah, I'm fine. It's just..." she trailed off, her voice barely audible.

"Just what?" I probed gently, sensing her inner turmoil.

"It's just... You scared me. When you fell into the river, it reminded me of my exploration group all over again," she confessed, a visible shiver running down her spine. "Please, don't put yourself in danger like that again," she pleaded, tears welling in her eyes.

Having grown up surrounded by constant loss and death, I understood the weight of her words. But for me, it had become a way of life. Nevertheless, I recognized the turmoil swirling in her mind, prompting me to reach out and reclaim her hand in mine. "It's okay. I promise I'll try my best to avoid such risks," I reassured her, offering a comforting smile.

Kikki leaned closer, drawing me into an embrace, and I hugged her back, holding her tightly. We remained locked in that tender moment, perhaps a little longer than we should have, as a throat clearing interrupted us. Kikki quickly released me, her face flushing with embarrassment. I turned my gaze towards the door, where Kyle stood with a mischievous grin.

"I hope I'm not interrupting," he chimed in, unable to contain his amusement.

"You know you were," I replied bluntly, not mincing my words.

"Well, anyway," Kyle interjected, walking towards us. "I just received news about the impending zombie attack. Time is running out, so I'm not sorry for interrupting. I need your help," he muttered urgently.

Curiosity piqued, I inquired, "What is it?"

"The resistance is making preparations to evacuate everyone from the city. They've been planning it for a while now, but their efforts are focused on our people within the city limits. We want to give everyone a fighting chance, including those in the underground towers like where you're from. To reach everyone, we need to broadcast the evacuation instructions. I need your help to reach the broadcast station," he explained.

"Well, I'll need to get dressed before I can do anything else," I remarked, lifting the blanket slightly to realize that I was wearing nothing. "Seems like someone stripped me," I muttered.

"They had to scan you," Kyle clarified.

Kikki got up and retrieved a stack of clothes that had been placed nearby, handing them to me. "Here, I got you new clothes. I'll leave them here," she offered before excusing herself along with Kyle, leaving me to dress.

Once I had fully dressed, I stepped out of the room into a long hallway reminiscent of the one in the tower where I grew up. Kyle and Kikki were waiting for me outside.

"What do you need me to do?" I asked, ready to contribute.

"With the limited time we have, I'll explain the plan on the way," Kyle began, his words rapid and detailed. As we walked, he delved into the intricacies of infiltrating the inner city and reaching the broadcasting room. While Kyle's explanations encompassed broadcasting rooms, the inner city, and instant messaging, I found myself grasping only fragments of the plan. Terms like "Digi-Key" and "encrypted ghost key" whizzed past me, but the essence of the plan was clear. Disguise ourselves as captives, get captured, and then free ourselves, gain access using the magic key, sabotage door locks with Simon's electrical powers, which apparently he had, and persuade the individuals in the control room to send out a broadcast. Anyone who posed a threat would be neutralized with sleeping bullets. We would hold the doors while Kyle completed his task of transmitting messages to the towers and the people. Then, make our escape.

I did raise an eyebrow at the part about Simon electrocuting the doors.

"Oh, that's the power our boss man chose in the games," Kyle explained casually.

"Bossman?" I echoed, surprised.

"Yeah, the leader of the resistance. Bet you didn't guess it was him all along. You probably thought it was someone as handsome as me, right?" he grinned, playfully slapping me on the back with his toned arm.

As Kyle continued his explanation, a smile still lingering on his face, I shook my head in disbelief. However, our conversation was abruptly interrupted as we pushed open two large doors, revealing a bustling room filled with people and boxes. Familiar faces swarmed around me the moment I stepped inside. Shawn and Malori were the first to greet me. I couldn't help but blush as Malori, even more stunning than before, embraced me for a longer moment than I had anticipated. In the midst of my own physical transformation, I had forgotten the effect it had on others. Realizing I had the attraction power running, I quickly turned it off, not that simply turning off the power would help for a bit. Shawn simply gave me a friendly pat on the shoulder with his remaining hand and smiled.

"You did it," he said, while Malori expressed her gratitude as well. Soon, others joined in the swarm.

"We wouldn't have made it without you" and "Thought you were a goner" were repeated amidst the cacophony of voices competing for attention. I was relieved to see that the rest of the group had made it back safely. They were now considered fugitives, having been rescued by the resistance and offering their help in any way possible.

Amidst the crowd, Reyn pushed his way forward until he stood directly in front of me. "Is it true that the zombies are attacking tomorrow?" he inquired anxiously.

"That's what I overheard," I replied. "I can't guarantee the accuracy of the information, but it sounded legitimate."

249

The group murmured in response, and Kyle stepped in to address the situation. "That's why it's crucial for all of us to complete the tasks assigned to us. We have a lot to accomplish between now and then," he announced.

The group agreed, and everyone dispersed, leaving me alone with Kyle and Kikki.

"It does seem like we're not quite ready for this yet," I remarked, voicing my concern.

"We're not. We won't be until tomorrow morning," Kyle admitted with a hint of frustration. "But the zombies made it clear they would arrive tomorrow," I protested.

"I know," Kyle grumbled. "The timing is far from ideal, but it's the hand we've been dealt. It's either that or abandoning everyone to their fate and allowing many to perish, ultimately bolstering our enemy."

"Well, let's make the best of what we have," Kikki chimed in optimistically.

I nodded in agreement. "So, what can I do right now to contribute and help?" I asked, eager to play my part.

Chapter 41
EXPLORING
WIND: Underground Tower #4

"Knock it off, Bomb," I yelled across the tent. "I'm serious."

"I'm serious too," Bomb shot back, "If it's the end of the world, I should go for it, right? I mean, Flower is so pretty, and I really think I have a shot."

Mountain and Turtle rolled their eyes.

"If I were you, I would just pick Bridge. She has had a crush on you forever. You don't have a shot with Flower. She is more into Turtle." I said, trying to stem the conversation before they could get into it. I had much more pressing matters. We had held off breaching the higher floors, double and triple-checking our route up. There were two perfect support columns, one right above the other, to which we attached the rope. Once on the lower part, we could scale the higher columns up to the tower's higher floors. It was a clear shot to the 273 floor. It was higher than my initial suggestion, but the higher up we could get, the better.

"Flower is interested in me?" Turtle mumbled, stunned.

"That's not fair! It was supposed to be me!" Bomb said. "What does Turtle have that I don't."

"Flower likes calmer people," I shrugged, "like Turtle and Mountain, but she likes Turtle's eyes for some reason. She says they sparkle. Just stick with Bridge. She will keep you on your toes. Now enough of that, let's go."

What a bunch of gossiping girls, I thought to myself, shaking my head at how similar their conversations were to those of the Flower and Bridges group.

"But you told Bomb and me who to date, so what about Mountain here? It's not fair to leave him hanging alone." Turtle replied.

"I like Mountain, okay? No one else can have him." I replied before I remembered that I wasn't talking to a bunch of girls, and Mountain was right there. I reddened as I looked up at the stunned group of personal guards. They were not the best at guarding, but still, they were mine.

"You?" Bomb replied.

"Me?" Mountain stammered.

At this point, I was flustered, frustrated, and just ready to blow. "Yes, you. Men are so clueless. Now, let's go. It's about time to start infiltrating the higher floors."

"Why do we have to be there?" Bomb grumbled.

"Everyone is counting on me to help them." I snapped back. "This can't go wrong, or we are all dead."

"Fine, fine," Bomb backed off.

"She likes me?" Mountain was still lost in his own thoughts.

I huffed and left the tent, heading to the tower. I didn't bother to look to see if my supposed bodyguards were following.

It didn't take me long to get up to the 247th floor, where the work had been ongoing to get a line out to the support pillar and then up to the second pillar. I was told that they had succeeded an hour ago and that they were working on setting up the makeshift bridge and ladder we had cobbled together. The first was a horizontal run to the first pillar across from our floor. I had seen that one, but I hadn't seen how they were planning on making the ladder. A second-styled bridge was made to go up the support pillar and provide hand and foot grips so that as people made their way up, they wouldn't fall to their deaths. It was slow going, and we constantly checked to ensure that the upper tower people weren't spying down on us. We did have decoy groups out on other support beams as a decoy that would lead to the 251 floor. They were much more visible and weren't hiding. We also had a crew on the 249th floor making noises as if we were breaking through. These were all ideas that Elephant had had to draw attention away from our real plan. Whether we were entirely successful wouldn't be known until we went up.

Elephant was standing next to a breach in the wall where the first bridge was hooked up to. "Come to inspect the progress?" Elephant asked me.

"Yes, it looks impressive."

"Yes, it does. We've tested it out, and it will hold up to four people at a time, at least. We aren't going to push it, though, so we will be spaced apart a bit, making our way up."

"When will we be ready to go?"

"Another hour, maybe two. Rat is getting the troops ready right now."

"Good, the faster we do this, the better."

"I think we all understand that one." Elephant nodded. "You look geared up. Are you coming too?"

I nodded in the affirmative.

"Well, I'm not sending you up until we have established a base up there, so don't think you are leading this operation."

"Agreed."

"Good," Elephant turned back to his men, who were moving back and forth on the bridge, bringing supplies up.

"Is there anything I can help with while we wait?" I asked.

"To tell you the truth," Elephant turned back to me. "I feel like I'm in the way. You would only be worse. Just sit back and enjoy a moment before we crack open this sewer pipe."

"Fine," I replied, moving back to a wall and sitting down. My guards, who had been there the whole time, moved over with me.

"So, you like Mountain?" Bomb broke the silence that was starting to grow thick, only to replace it with awkwardness.

I rolled my eyes realizing I wasn't going to get much relaxation in.

Chapter 42
THE INNER CITY

STAR: Earth's surface: THE CITY

A.K.A

Last City on Earth

The remaining hours of the day were consumed with organizing every aspect of the operation. Thankfully, that meant some downtime for me. I spent the time reviewing the plan and reviewing building schematics. It took a lot of brain power to understand what I was even looking at, as I had never seen a building layout drawn out on a piece of paper before. Schematics, weapon and gear training, and a thousand introductions. By the time nightfall arrived, exhaustion had settled upon me, and I eagerly sought a good night's sleep. However, my slumber was abruptly interrupted by a blaring alarm, which took me a frustratingly long time to figure out how to silence. There were way too many buttons and levers on the device, unlike the simple version we had in the tower. Grumbling to myself, I dressed in the janitor outfit that had been prepared for me, simultaneously cursing Kyle for his meticulous planning yet forgetting to inform me about disabling the darn alarm. A flawlessly executed operation should begin with precision, not with a loud and annoying wake-up call.

Nevertheless, my focus lay more on the weight of the day's significance. Lives depended on the outcome, and the responsibility weighed heavily upon all of us. While battling zombies in the tunnels had always carried its own gravity, this endeavor felt grander. Like it affected the whole world and not just a small group of people. Moreover, the foreignness of the city and the unfamiliar technology further added to my apprehension, though I took solace in the familiarity of the tower's structures, which resembled the buildings here.

Arriving at the building's cafeteria, I discovered Kyle, Kikki, Reed, Simon, Katty, Reyn, and three other men I had met the previous day—John, Izaak, and Kevin—gathered around a table filled with food. I took my seat next to Kikki at the end.

"You had me worried there," Kyle commented. "I thought you overslept. I was just about to send someone to find you."

"You never told me how to turn off that darn alarm, so it took me an extra minute to silence the thing," I grumbled in response. "By the way, how are you supposed to do it anyway?" I asked, genuinely curious.

"You simply hold down the top button for a second," Kyle replied. Then, he furrowed his brow. "Wait a minute, I thought you said you turned it off?" he inquired.

"I did. A swift introduction to the wall did the trick," I nodded back.

Izaak, who happened to be taking a sip of water at that moment, nearly choked on it while the others at the table stared at me in disbelief. Reed was the first to break the silence. "I thought you enjoyed tinkering with things. Even I managed to figure out the alarm clocks here within a minute," he said with a smile.

I simply shrugged and began to eat, recognizing the importance of fueling myself for the challenges ahead. Once we finished our meal, we made our way to the bottom floor of the building, where Kyle, Kikki, Simon, Katty, Reyn, and I donned prisoner jumpsuits over our janitor uniforms. Reed and the three other men transformed into guards, armed with radios, tasers, and holstered pistols—typical attire for inner-city peacemakers when venturing into the outer city.

Handcuffed and under their watchful eyes, we were ushered into an armored van, the same vehicle frequently used by city patrols to transport prisoners, as was explained to me the previous day. Reed and Kevin, sporting their much cooler outfits, joined us in the back while John and Izaak took the front seats to drive. We awaited the signal before proceeding. Many other pieces were already set in motion, with Malori utilizing her beauty to charm one of the police chiefs from the inner city. This encounter had occurred the previous night at a bar. Wade and Shawn operated in a different part of the city, creating a diversion. Drake, having infected several beehives, deployed the swarming creatures to sow chaos within the inner city and gather intelligence. Everyone played their part in facilitating the city's evacuation and getting the broadcast to the towers.

The anticipation was agonizing, reminiscent of those times back in the tunnels when I could see the zombies drawing nearer. Yet, we had to wait for the perfect moment to take a shot. Luckily, the wait was short-lived as the radio signal came through, and the van roared to life, setting our journey in motion. Being awake in a moving vehicle was an entirely new experience for me, as my body jerked unpredictably in different directions. In my initial reflex, I overcorrected and fell right into Kikki's lap.

"Really?" Reed quipped. "Now's not the time for that."

I quickly composed myself, apologizing to Kikki, who returned a reassuring smile. There was a twinkle in her eye that caught my attention, causing me to blush slightly. I turned my focus back to Reed.

"Not cool. You've had a crush on my sister for years. But the moment another cute girl comes along, you move on," Reed remarked.

"No, I... Wait, how did you know I had a crush on her?" I asked, my mouth agape.

"It was obvious," Reed snorted.

"Is this the right time for this?" Reyn interjected with his deep voice.

"Well, we might be dead in the next few hours, so it's a good time for anything," Kyle pondered.

"Dying wasn't part of the plan," I panicked, more due to Reed's comment than Kyle's words.

"We have a zombie horde approaching," Kyle said solemnly before flashing a smile. "Of course, dying isn't part of the plan, but plans can change."

"Well, let's not change the 'not dying' part of the plan," I replied.

There was silence for a moment before Kikki turned to Reed, "So you think I'm cute?"

Reed went a little red at realizing what he had said earlier. I latched onto it and began to tease him when I was cut off as the window that led to the front of the van opened.

"We're approaching a checkpoint," Kevin informed us from the front of the van. "Let's save the chit-chat until we're through."

We all nodded in agreement as Reed and I gave each other stink eyes. We quickly gave each other a smile, indicating that we were dropping the jibs, and waited for the van to come to a halt. The sudden jolt caused me to lean closer to Kikki once again, only to jerk away when the van stopped completely. Voices from the outside became audible, and then the driver's door slammed shut. The voices continued until they reached the rear of the van. The doors swung open, revealing a man peering inside.

"That's quite a catch," the guard grinned, casting his eyes on Izaak, who was displaying what they had caught. "You won't forget me when the bonuses come around. You should make a pretty penny for bringing in this lot."

Izaak smiled, patting the man on the back. "I won't forget my friends," he replied.

The two shared a laugh, and the doors were shut again. I could hear their continued conversation, something about staying dry as rain was in the forecast. Thankfully, the van resumed its journey shortly. Another twenty minutes passed before it came to another stop, and this time, Izaak and John were accompanied by four other men when the doors opened.

"You weren't lying," the eldest among them grinned broadly. "How did you manage it?" he inquired.

"It's a bit of a long story," Izaak responded. "But I'll write up a detailed report and have it on your desk by the end of the day."

"I look forward to reading it," the man grinned. "Alright, men, bring them in," he ordered.

At the command, the three remaining men began pulling us out of the van. Reed and Kevin exited last, assisting in guiding us toward the colossal building that loomed before us. I craned my neck, gazing upward, only to find the structure stretching endlessly, seemingly touching the dark clouds above. Its expanse was vast, adorned with majestic beams extending from halfway up to the ground in all directions. It bore a striking resemblance to the tower of my childhood, albeit on a much grander scale, dwarfing the view of the underground tower from the ground floor. I couldn't tell which was bigger since I never knew how big the tower had been. The only difference was the absence of cavern walls to support it, as the beams extended all the way down to the ground surrounding it.

After we were all off the van, Izaak and John excused themselves, leaving us in the company of the elderly man in charge. Reed and Kevin stayed with us, ensuring an equal number of guards to prisoners, with the elderly guard being the odd one out.

I marveled at the interior of the building; it was unlike anything I had ever witnessed. Everything appeared vast and pristine. Marble adorned every surface, and at the center of the room stood a fountain with a statue of a woman, or was it a fish. She had the upper body of a human, anyway, with a fishtail. Water sprouted up from the tank basin and also cascaded from her fishtail and outstretched hand.

The people around us had a clean and sharp appearance. Some paused to gawk as we made our way through the building. As we moved, I allowed my beauty power to seep out of me, turning the women's heads in all directions and causing a little extra chaos to exist. None ran over, but it was definitely a show as some dropped the contents of their hands, and others bumped into people and walls. The guards asked each other what was going on as they were unaffected as they were men. It took them a minute before one member connected the dots, remembering that I had received the power in the games. There wasn't anything the guards could do about it, so they prodded us on at a quicker pace.

Eventually, we reached an elevator spacious enough to accommodate the earlier van, and we were ushered inside. As I stepped in, I heard a buzzing noise, leaving me curious about the peculiar sound an elevator could make. The tension heightened as the doors began to close. This was when things would take a perilous turn.

With a click, the doors sealed shut, and I felt the handcuffs on my wrists release. Reed had brought a magnetic key close enough to unlock the specially designed restraints. Kevin released Reyn's handcuffs as well. Seizing the opportunity, I swiftly struck the guard beside me, delivering a precise blow to his throat, causing him to collapse. Reyn, his fists transformed into solid rock with the rocks he had hidden in his clothing, delivered a powerful punch to another guard's jaw, resulting in blood splattering everywhere. Reed swiftly incapacitated a third guard while I advanced toward the lead guard, who reached for his gun as his other hand pressed the radio call button. Before he could utter a word, Simon leaned in, surging an electric shock through him, frying the radio and any other electrical equipment on the man's person. However, the man's body suffered the consequences, emitting smoke from a few areas before he crumpled to the ground.

"Did you get the camera in time?" I asked Simon.

"Fried it when you first struck. Let's hope that one of the diversions was enough to have kept the guards watching the feed from seeing us."

"Good work," Kyle commended. "I'm sure they were overwhelmed with the other things that were going on. Now, get me out of these." He gestured to his handcuffs, the motion prompting Kevin to move forward with a magnetic key. Soon, Kyle, Katty, and Kikki were all released from their restraints. I grabbed the guards and dragged them to the side of the elevator, where Katty joined me. She carefully examined the men, cutting her finger to apply her healing blood to their wounds. Though they served the royals, they did not deserve to be left to the mercy of the approaching zombie horde. We understood that as many fighters as possible would be needed

259

when the time came. However, we couldn't allow the men to hinder our progress, so we bound and secured them. Once that was done, everyone discarded their jumpsuits, stuffing them into a hidden bag that Simon had prepared.

Kyle approached the elevator's control panel and proudly pulled out the Unikey, pressing it against the wall. "Access denied," a voice echoed throughout the room.

Kyle cursed and made another attempt. "Access denied," came the frustrating response.

"What's wrong?" I inquired, joining them.

"I don't know. This should work," Kyle grumbled in frustration.

"Let me try," Simon muttered, taking the Unikey from him and attempting to use it himself. "Access denied."

"Oh, come on!" Simon growled in annoyance.

I walked over to them, concerned. "What's wrong? Why isn't it working?" I asked.

"I don't know," Kyle replied. "I tested it before, and it worked."

"Well, what's different now compared to before?" I questioned.

"Nothing has changed," Kyle responded with exasperation as Simon made a fourth unsuccessful attempt. "Maybe they've locked down the elevator."

"I could try smashing it," Reyn suggested, contemplating a more forceful approach.

"Or perhaps a shock to reset the system," Simon added, raising his hand.

Suddenly, the elevator started moving upward, the low buzzing noise that I had heard earlier replaced with gears and displaced wind. "I think it's working," I commented, hopeful.

"But we didn't do anything," Kyle said, his tone laced with fear.

Simon examined the control panel and said, "We're ascending. At least it's the right direction."

"But we don't know who's waiting on the other end or which floor it will stop at," Kyle fretted, growing more agitated.

"Well, we'll have to improvise," I declared, positioning myself near the door, ready to be one of the first to step out. "We'll find a stairwell to get where we need to go," I added, formulating a plan.

The rest of the group fell into a tense silence as the elevator halted on the 132nd floor, one floor above our intended destination. As the doors slid open, they revealed a group of thirty people frozen in surprise at the unexpected scene before them.

That's when the buzzing noise resumed, only this time it seemed much louder than before.

It was at that moment that I recognized the sound and knew how to handle the situation. "Sorry, everyone, this elevator is out of service," I smiled at them, exuding confidence and my charm.

"Why? What happened to those men?" a voice in the crowd questioned, pointing at the incapacitated guards on the floor.

"They had an unfortunate encounter with bees," I casually explained, and as I uttered the word "bees," a swarm of the insects emerged from a vent and flooded into the room. Panic ensued, people screamed, and they fled from the elevator entrance, desperate to escape the angry swarm. The bees paid us no attention, but we utilized the chaos to blend in with the others, following them toward the stairwell. Some of the people headed for the stairs, while others scurried back to their work areas, attempting to distance themselves from the furious swarm.

We swiftly entered the stairwell and hurriedly descended to the next floor. Someone ahead of us had already swiped their access card to open the door, and we slipped inside before it closed. Breathing heavily, we shut the door behind us and turned to the man who stood there, panting and sporting sizable welts on his exposed arms and face.

"Whew, that was a close call," Kyle remarked to the panting man.

261

"What was that?" the man gasped, still catching his breath.

"Looked like an angry hive to me," Kyle replied. "Simon, could you check the man's stings? We don't want any stingers left behind."

Simon nodded and approached the man. He sent a mild electric shock through his body, causing him to spasm on the floor. Kikki stepped in, strategically hitting one of the man's pressure points, rendering him unconscious.

"What was that?" I asked, perplexed.

"Just a little trick we learned in scouting classes," Kikki explained, grinning mischievously.

"We need to keep moving," Kyle reminded us, urging us to continue down the hallway. Our first stop was the women's bathroom, where we discreetly emptied the trash can. Beneath the surface layer of paper towels, we uncovered two large duffle bags. It took us a couple of minutes to unpack the dart guns loaded with tranquilizers and the pistols armed with live ammunition.

Once armed, we followed Kyle as he led us down the hallway. We didn't take long to locate the correct set of doors. The hallway was deserted, and we prepared ourselves before nodding to Simon, who positioned his hands on the doors. A tingling sensation coursed through my body, and the scent of ozone hung heavily in the air as a zapping noise emanated from the doors. With a mechanical click, the doors swung open.

Inside the room, we found twenty individuals. Five of them held weapons, while the remaining fifteen were gathered around screens. The guards turned their attention curiously toward the door, completely unsuspecting of an organized team making their way in. Before they could react effectively, all five guards had tranquilizer darts embedded in their bodies. The tranquilizers took effect swiftly, and the men crumpled to the floor with little grace.

"Nobody move!" Kyle yelled, capturing everyone's attention in the room. A mischievous grin spread across his face as he concluded, "This is a hold-up."

Chapter 43
Prison
Alejandro: Earth's surface: THE CITY
A.K.A
Last City on Earth

The king's men had brought me to a holding cell. I could tell instantly it wasn't a normal holding cell. I had been around enough of those looking for contestants to play in the Zombie games. No, this one was different. The cell bars were much thicker, and the guards carried large caliber weapons. The cells were half full of people, each in their own personal cage.

"What is this place?" I asked one of the guards that carried me to my cell.

"Ever wonder how they develop the amazing abilities on your show?" the guard responded with an evil grin.

Fear took me as I pictured myself being experimented on over and over again. It sent a shiver through my body, which made the men escorting me laugh. When we reached an open cage, he put his hand on my shoulder and unceremoniously shoved me into the cell before locking it behind me.

"Enjoy our top tier service," the man laughed as he checked the door was firmly locked. That done he shook his head one last time and left.

With the weight of my circumstances crashing down on me, I crumpled to the ground, where I curled myself up in the back of the cage and waited for my doom to arrive.

Throughout the day, I switched between sleeping and watching the other cages. Some had clearly already been subjects of experiments, while others seemed perfectly normal. Some bodies, though, didn't move. At first, I thought they were sleeping, but as time passed, I realized that they had died and no one had bothered to move their bodies yet. It was eerie as no one talked to one another. There wasn't anything to say to each other. We all knew what lay ahead of us. We were just waiting to become one of those motionless corpses scattered around the room.

Even with that knowledge, my eyes kept moving to the motionless bodies and thinking, *That will be me soon enough.*

This thought continued to repeat over and over in my head, that was until something caught my attention. It was a familiar noise but was out of place in this setting, and it took me a second to believe my ears. There were gunshots in the distance. The single guard that passed up and down the corridor between the cages on occasion or sat in the corner lifted his gun to his shoulder and walked carefully to the door. Before he got there, the door blew off its hinges and smashed into him. Five men stepped in with guns raised. Three stayed put, standing guard as two moved into the room. It was strange because the two that moved into the room weren't normal. One moved fast, practically flying through the room, while the other moved like water. His movements were so smooth and deliberate. They both placed small red flashing devices in the cages' locks. It only took the two of them two minutes to place devices on all hundred cages. Some occupants tried to talk to them, but they ignored them and focused on their tasks.

When they were done, one called out, "Stay away from the bars."

There was some shuffling, including myself, as we stood back. That was when the devices all went off at the same time. Small explosions like firecrackers swept the room. With the blast came the creaking of hinges as the cage doors swung open. The two men then started guiding us to the exit.

"Those who can grab anyone that is unable to move." They called out.

I realized at that moment that these must be the rebels, and if they were what I thought they were, which I knew they were, I was in trouble. They might leave me once they found out who I was. I needed to act quickly to not have that happen. I noticed the man in the cage next to me try to hobble towards the door. His legs were covered in thick hair, causing his movement to be stiff and slow. Whatever the experiment was, it wasn't functioning correctly. I saw my opportunity and rushed over, lending the man my shoulder.

"Thanks," he said as I helped him out the door.

"No problem," I replied. "I'm just happy we are being saved."

"They are bolder than they used to be." The man replied as we moved past some of the rebels.

"Is that everyone, Wade?" A guard called out, drawing my attention. I recognize that name. I didn't look, but my mind was putting two and two together with the movement of the men.

"That's everyone." A man replied. His voice confirmed it. He was someone I knew very well. It was Wade… the Wade. The one from the games. My eyes drifted to another man, and I realized Shawn was there as well. My blood ran cold, knowing that these men could easily identify me. I tucked my head closer to the man I was helping and prayed they hadn't seen me yet. I kept my gaze low as we were guided out of the building and did everything in my power not to attract attention.

Bodies lay on the floor, and I averted my eyes as we moved past them. Men from both sides had died in this hallway. We continued out and found ourselves outside, where an overcast sky darkened the ground around us. Several large vans were out front, and we were ushered in. It didn't take long for the doors to shut behind us and for the vehicles to speed off. The drivers picked up speed quickly, moving us away from the scene of the crime. I looked out the window and watched the buildings zip by. I kept an eye out to see if anyone was following us, but to my surprise, the road stayed clear of the king's forces. It took another five minutes for us to get onto one of the more busier roads. We merged into the flow of traffic, blending in as best as I could tell with the normal operations of the city.

Chapter 44
THE UPLOAD
REED: Earth's surface: THE CITY
A.K.A
Last City on Earth

As it turned out, the people in the broadcast room were just ordinary individuals trying to perform their jobs. I couldn't help but feel a twinge of guilt for terrorizing them. However, my remorse was fleeting, overshadowed by the memories of everything I had been through. Being a sacrifice for their show and entertainment, being shot by my own people. Additionally, the knowledge that we were fighting to save Wind from the clutches of both the zombies and the royals gave purpose to these violent actions. Nonetheless, violence against fellow humans had always felt inherently wrong to me. Shaking off these thoughts, I entered the room alongside the others.

With our guns trained on them, the workers in the broadcast room quickly complied with our orders. They distanced themselves from their computers and gathered in a corner, where Kyle and Simon went to explain the situation to them. I stood guard near the door, accompanied by Kikki and Katty. Star and Reyn worked together to rearrange the fallen guards against a wall. It didn't take long before Kyle returned, accompanied by four of the workers.

"Are you ready, Reed?" Kyle asked. "These fine gentlemen have agreed to assist with our broadcast," he continued.

I was confused. "Ready for what? Aren't you the one doing the broadcast?" I asked.

"I'll be doing one of them," Kyle affirmed. "However, I don't think like someone from the towers. It would be more effective coming from you, considering you lived there. You need to do it. They'll receive my feed as well, and I'll fill in some of the gaps. But I need you to capture their attention and make them listen."

"But..." I stammered, only to be interrupted.

"We don't have time for hesitation. Come over here, and when these two give you the signal, speak as if you're addressing your tower and the other towers out there," Kyle said.

Reluctantly, I complied and moved toward a stool accompanied by two of the men. One started operating a video camera, while the other worked on the computer. It didn't take long for a red light to appear on the camera, and the man gave me a thumbs-up, signaling to start.

"Um," I started, clearing my throat. "Hello, my name is Reed, and I come from a tower just like the one you live in. Those from my own tower might even know who I am. I used to be a scout, venturing into the tunnels and eliminating zombie hordes. Yes, I was a member of the lower tower, living there with my sister Wind and my friend Star. I was a loyal scout and fairly skilled at what I did. Perhaps not as exceptional as some, but I rarely missed a shot. However, we were betrayed by our own tower and sent out to die. But it wasn't merely a death sentence; it was intended for us to become food for the zombies."

"I've been informed that all tower leadership is essentially the same: corrupt and worthless. And I must agree with that assessment, given that cameras are placed throughout all the towers. I've been observing your acts of both good and evil. I personally experienced the evil. Stump and Redwood tried to kill me on my return from a mission because I had been sent to die. I have the bullet wound to prove it." I showed the wound. "I was supposed to die because of the corruption of the leadership. They don't care about you. Your leaders bicker amongst themselves and send people out to become zombies simply because they don't align with their own ideologies. Those of you from the upper floors who are listening know it. Of course, those who remain unaware of this are the ones battling the zombies on the lower levels. Yes, you heard me correctly: the tower leaderships are dishonorable and should not be blindly followed, as I did for so many years. But

267

do not despair, my friends in the lower tower. Only you possess the knowledge of how to fight and survive in the tunnels. You are the ones who hold hope. The upper tower can not survive without you," I paused and cleared my throat.

I then continued, "I am currently speaking to you from the surface of the Earth, where light fills the days from the sun. It is a place where zombies only emerge during the night, unlike the relentless onslaught in the tunnels. These people, on the surface, have developed a cure. They claim to possess other resources that would aid in the fight against the zombies. However, this city, much like the towers, has been corrupted by its leadership, who believe themselves invincible. They toy with human lives for their own amusement. Now, their gaze has turned toward the towers once again, seeing them as mere playthings. Although they may have promised cures and supplies, they will no longer be able to fulfill those promises.

"Today, they will be overrun by zombies due to their incompetence. Those of us on the surface have one hope: to journey south to the City of Hope. This means you will be left to fend for yourselves without further assistance from the capital. You must come together and make your way to the City of Hope. Detailed maps have been sent to your towers, outlining tunnel routes that will lead you to the surface and then to the City of Hope. Your leadership may claim they don't possess such maps, but they do. Retrieve them by any means necessary if you have to. Leaders of the towers, it's time to rectify your ways and cooperate with the people of the lower tower. Only by working together can you survive.

"I implore you to listen, for otherwise, you will starve and perish without the support you've received from the city above. Help those around you. Unite as one and fight for each other."

With those words, I bowed, directing my gaze toward the man filming.

The man nodded, and the red light on the camera turned off. It was then that gunshots echoed through the hallway, prompting Kikki and Star to respond with a barrage of dart fire.

"Hurry, upload those videos!" Kyle yelled, concluding his own broadcast. With a few keystrokes, everyone knew that it had been successful. Kyle's voice resonated through the building's speaker system while his face appeared on every available screen. Phones chimed as messages flooded in, delivering maps and videos. With the task accomplished, Kyle turned to the individuals gathered in the corner.

"Every word I spoke is true. Go home and evacuate your families once we've cleared the area. Good luck to all of you," Kyle declared.

I had already reached the door where Star had ceased firing. "Three down," he reported. "The hallway is clear."

I nodded, and with the rest of the team following closely, we proceeded down the hallway. Kyle's voice echoed from the screens, recounting the corruption and greed of the royals. He likened them to zombies, stripped of their humanity due to years of experiments. Kyle also revealed the existence of a Zombie horde with unique abilities, including the power to walk in sunlight, collaborate, and even speak. He described their underground digging efforts and their imminent resurfacing. "Pack your belongings swiftly and follow the instructions you've received," Kyle's video advised. However, Star and I paid little attention to it, focusing instead on safely leading the group out. We paused by the unconscious bodies, retrieving their guns and ammunition and slinging them over our backs as a precaution.

Knowing that the elevator was not a viable option, we made our way directly to the stairwell. Once inside, we descended with haste. Despite our quick pace, it took us a full hour to descend from the dizzying height. Kyle's voice continued to reverberate on a loop as we made our descent. To our surprise, we encountered no resistance along the way. It soon became evident why we had faced no obstacles. Exiting the building through the emergency exit, we were greeted by a scene of utter chaos in the streets. The city had bigger problems than us.

Chapter 45
The Upper Tower
WIND: Underground Tower #4

I watched as the others scaled the ladder leading up to the next pillar. My nerves had returned, and the last hour of awkwardness between me and the men supposedly guarding me hadn't helped. Bomb had kept a constant dialogue going, so at least it wasn't a silent awkwardness, which would have been a little worse. Only a little.

"That's fifty," Elephant said, cutting off the next group from going up.

"Now we wait," I replied.

"Now we wait," Elephant agreed.

Thankfully, we didn't have to wait long before the signal came of flashing flashlights to send more men. Elephant nodded and sent the next fifty before he would allow me and my guards to make our way up. When my turn did come, I walked over to the bridge and froze. Looking down, I could see just how high I was. Well, not entirely. I couldn't see the ground from here, but it looked like it would go on forever. Fear gripped at me, and I had to fight it with deep breaths before I could put my first foot on the bridge. I gripped the rope, hauling hard as I started to make my way across, my every move making the bridge sway.

One foot after the other, I said to myself, watching Turtle's back as he had insisted on going first in our group. I didn't dare look anywhere else but his back as I put one foot in front of the other and then reached further down for my next grip on the rope railing.

I looked down twice, both mistakes, and it took me a second or two to calm down enough to keep moving. I was relieved when I finally made it to the small platform with the anchor to the ladder that moved up to the next support that spider-legged out from the tower into the cave wall.

"Careful, commander," the soldier that was stationed at the base of the ladder said to me as he held out a hand. I took it and let him guide me quickly to the ladder. "Up you go."

The ladder was much easier as I was looking up the whole time. I put out of my mind how high I was and climbed. The trip up didn't take long, and I soon found myself on the next support, which was six feet across. It had a slight curve to its surface, which was unnerving, but borders and hand grips were placed on it from the men's earlier efforts. I was thankful for the daredevils that had risked their necks to put them there. Again, I focused on climbing up and seeing the light at the end of the tunnel. A large hole had been made in the tower's wall where the support connected. Two of our soldiers stood at the top, helping Turtle in. My eyes focused on that, and I reached for a handhold. Unfortunately, I overextended, and my grip slipped. My body went flat and started to roll, but I hadn't let go of my last handhold, which saved my life. I barely registered the shouting from people who saw me as my mind raced for a way to save myself. Before I could fall too far, I pulled hard on the handhold I still had and flailed for the one I had missed. Thankfully, my hand wrapped around the metal handhold, and I was able to pull myself back into position. My heart was racing, and sweat was dripping off my face, but I hadn't fallen.

"Are you good?" Someone yelled at me from the tower's opening.

"I'm good," I replied as I continued my way to the opening with much more deliberate movements. Thankfully, I made it the rest of the way without incident.

"Thank goodness," Turtle said as I stumbled into the room. "It sounded like someone fell."

"I almost did," I replied as I studied my surroundings. We were in someone's room, but there was a lot more in it than we had in the lower levels. There was a large couch that would fit about eight people that faced a screen that looked like the computer monitor but was much larger. At the moment, it displayed a scene that I had only heard about. A lush green environment with many plants growing and intense light coming

271

from a blue expanse above. Carpets were well kept, and children's toys were piled up in the corner.

"This place is huge," I replied, looking around, my eyes continually returning to the screen.

"I know, right," Turtle replied.

Rat appeared next to me, "Commander,"

"Have we come across any resistance?" I asked, dreading the answer."

"A little, but a kitchen knife is about it. These people, though, have never fought a day in their lives. Taking their improvised weapons from them was easy. We have made it up five floors and down ten so far. We are gathering those we find on the floor below us."

"No weapons yet? No guns?"

"No, we are questioning the people we found, but they said that the higher levels take care of weapon distribution."

"Still, they should have had guards around."

"From the sound of it, they don't have more than a couple dozen guards, and they do what the council tells them to do."

"Only a couple dozen?"

My mind reeled at the realization. That was when the screen turned from the scenic view to something that shocked me. There, on the screen, was someone I knew very well.

"Um… Hello, my name is Reed," Everyone turned to the screen, and some looked between it and me with questioning looks. "And I come from a tower just like the one you live in. Those from my own tower might even know who I am."

"Reed!" I whispered, "You're alive?"

"I used to be a scout, venturing into the tunnels and eliminating zombie hordes."

"Why is your brother on the screen?" Mountain asked as he made it into the building from the outside.

"I don't know, but it sounds like he is alive," I replied, paying attention to every word my brother said.

"However," My brother continued, "we were betrayed by our own tower and sent out to die. But it wasn't merely a death sentence; it was intended for us to become food for the zombies. I've been informed that all tower leadership is essentially the same: corrupt and worthless. And I must agree with that assessment."

My mind reeled as I watched my brother call out Stump and Redwood's betrayal and show where he had been shot. My mind wandered a bit, wondering if Star had lived as well, but that was only for a moment as my mind focused on what he was saying.

"Your leaders bicker amongst themselves," He continued, "and send people out to become zombies simply because they don't align with their own ideologies."

I hadn't seen that in the files. "Those of you from the upper floors who are listening know it. Of course, those who remain unaware of this are the ones battling the zombies on the lower levels. Yes, you heard me correctly: the tower leaderships are dishonorable and should not be blindly followed, as I did for so many years."

"What is he saying?" Turtle said over my brother.

"Shh," others replied.

"Only you possess the knowledge of how to fight and survive in the tunnels. You are the ones who hold hope. The upper tower can not survive without you." My brother cleared his throat for a moment before continuing to describe where he was on the surface. The surface where the sun shown. He described how the Zombies only emerged only for part of the time, and a cure existed. He then described how there was a whole city up there and that it was in danger of being overrun with zombies, but there was another one that we should go to.

"Detailed maps have been sent to your towers, outlining tunnel routes that will lead you to the surface and then to the City of Hope. Your leadership may claim they don't possess such maps, but they do. Retrieve them by any means necessary if you have to. Leaders of the towers, it's time to rectify your ways and cooperate with the people of the lower tower. Only by working together can you survive.

273

"I implore you to listen, for otherwise, you will starve and perish without the support you've received from the city above. Help those around you. Unite as one and fight for each other."

I looked at Rat, "We have a new mission, and we need to get to that information as soon as possible."

"Yes, commander," Rat said, moving toward the door.

Chapter 46
Escape
STAR: Earth's surface: THE CITY
A.K.A
Last City on Earth

Gunshots reverberated in sporadic bursts to our left, drawing our attention to a group of guards armed with guns, firing into an approaching crowd. The distinct deformities on their bodies and their unnatural movements marked them as zombies. Though a few fell under the onslaught of bullets, the sheer mass of the advancing horde made it clear that stopping them was futile.

"Quick, this way!" Kyle shouted urgently.

Without hesitation, we followed Kyle, veering in the opposite direction of the encroaching zombies. As we did, several of those large bugs, which I had learned were called hellcopters from Reed, flew overhead and open-fired on the oncoming Zombies slowing their approach. The whirling of the guns and the buzz of the bullets sending shivers in my spine. It was amazing how they were audible over the engine and wings of the hellcopters.

"Where are we going?" Reed questioned once we had covered a block's distance. "We can't simply run forever. We'll never escape," he added with concern.

"We're heading to my house," Kyle declared.

"Your house?" I inquired, puzzled.

"Yeah, I planned to get you guys out first and then return for my sister. But it seems we'll have to make do with all of us squeezing in together. So, no getting too close to her, okay?" he muttered to Reed, followed by a mischievous grin. "She'd probably enjoy that a bit too much," he added under his breath.

"What?" Reed asked, perplexed.

"Forget it. Just be cautious around her; she's a big fan of yours, Reed," Kyle explained. "She cried for a week when we thought you and Star had perished."

"I have a fan?" Reed exclaimed.

"Is now really the time for this discussion?" Katty interjected as we turned a corner, only to be confronted by a group of thirty zombies blocking our path.

I swiftly raised the machine gun I had retrieved from the fallen guards in the tower and unleashed controlled bursts of fire while Reed positioned himself beside me. Our training ensured that we targeted different zombies, maximizing our efficiency. The horde steadily closed in, but they were easy prey, trapped like fish in a barrel. Soon, all of them lay lifeless on the ground.

"How's our ammo?" I inquired.

"I used four clips. I have only one left," Reed announced.

"I'm down to one as well," I grumbled. "Why is it that there's never enough ammo around here?" I voiced my frustration.

"I know, right? It was our lifeline in the tunnels," Reed muttered in agreement. I halted our progress and asked, "How much farther is it?"

"We have four more blocks to go," Kyle responded.

"We don't have enough bullets to handle another group like that. Why didn't we bring swords anyway?" I complained.

"Swords wouldn't have helped us infiltrate the broadcast room," Kyle replied. "But those knives on your belt have decent lengths. I've seen you maneuver skillfully with those things against a lot of zombies."

"A sword would be preferable," I replied, though I caressed the two knives hanging from my belt, which I also had acquired from the guards in the main tower.

We took another left turn a block ahead, following Kyle's lead. He shouted, "It's the green building, just two more blocks down." As he spoke, a couple of shadows emerged from one of the buildings. I abruptly halted, and the rest followed suit. In front of us lay a group of around twenty zombies, but it was immediately evident that these were not like the ones we had encountered earlier. These were enhanced zombies, displaying intelligence in their movements.

"We've been looking for you," a chillingly familiar feminine voice echoed, sending shivers down my spine.

I whispered to Reed, instructing him to guide the others and conserve their bullets until necessary. Stepping forward, I raised my voice slightly, asserting, "I believe you've mistaken me for someone else. The person you're searching for went in that direction." As I spoke, I held the gun close to my body and unleashed controlled bursts of fire. Five out of the six targeted zombies crumpled to the ground motionless, but the sixth one merely staggered back before growling menacingly in my direction. I knew this was far from ideal. Discarding the machine gun, I swiftly drew my pistol, managing to squeeze off three shots before the horde descended upon me. I did notice the queen zombie and a companion slip back the way they had come, seemingly too busy to deal with me personally.

I brandished a knife in my left hand, continuing to fire bullets with my right while evading and maneuvering through the mass of zombies. Gunshots echoed around me as the battle raged, but I couldn't spare a moment to check on the others' progress. Despite my quick reflexes, only half of my strikes found their mark against the zombies' flesh, hinting at the grim reality that this was a losing fight. Hope began to wane within me, and I realized I had no choice. I lunged at one of the hardened zombies, driving the blade deep into its eye socket as its claws tore at my clothing. It was a desperate move, knowing that I would likely become infected myself. Claws dug into my flesh, piercing my arm and back. I kicked off the creature, propelling myself towards another, firing my pistol at its head. A third zombie kicked me midair, causing me to land directly in front of yet another undead monstrosity. It immediately lunged at me, sinking its teeth deep into my left shoulder. With a gunshot from my pistol, I finally managed to pry the creature off me. Rolling to the side, I quickly rose to my feet, ready to face the remaining four zombies.

"You are one of us now," a haunting female voice hummed from one of the remaining creatures—her voice a little more gurgly than the soft voice of the queen.

I crouched down into a fighting stance while gritting my teeth in reply.

Chapter 47
NO MAN LEFT BEHIND?
REED: Earth's surface: THE CITY
A.K.A
Last City on Earth

Star had whispered to guide the others to Kyle's house while he bought time. I didn't have any time to counter when he stepped forward. As soon as he opened fire, I knew there was no stopping him, so I quickly guided the others to the right, putting my faith in my friend. For some reason, the Zombies were fixated on Star, and the majority moved for him. Only seven moved to block our path, and I quickly unloaded into the group. I was only able to kill five, which took me aback since I knew my bullets had struck true. The two zombie heads only rocked backward when my bullets struck. It didn't even slow them down. I reached for my pistol, which only had a dozen shots in it, but I was too slow. These zombies were much faster than anything I was used to. If it hadn't been for Reyn stepping forward with a rocky fist, the creatures would have had me for dinner. With strong punches from Reyn's stony fists, the Zombies' innards crumpled, sending them reeling back. This allowed the group to get around to Kyle's building side of the zombie group that was now fully focused on Star. I momentarily watched as Star dodged while stabbing and shooting the whole time. I wanted to rush in and help him, but Kyle tugged on my arm.

"He will be fine. Let's go. We need you if others show up."

We ran for all we were worth, following Kyle as he led the group. We made it the last 3 blocks, and it was a good thing I had stayed as four zombies jumped out of the last ally. I fired four shots right after each other, and the bodies only made it a few feet toward us before they were all motionless on the ground. Kyle didn't even bother slowing down, and soon, he made it to our destination. I watched as the others entered the large doors and almost went in myself, but as I stepped forward, something stopped me. I just couldn't step beyond the door frame.

"I need to go back for him," I called out to the others.

Kyle looked over at me through the doorway and nodded. "Go, I'll get the chopper ready. Meet me on the roof."

I nodded, and to my surprise, Reyn joined me as I stepped back into the road. Together, we ran back towards the fight that still persisted down the street. I watched as Star had a Zombie jump on top of him before he was able to blow its brains out. Star jumped to his feet and lunged towards the remaining four creatures with amazing speed before the two could get there. He was moving faster than I had ever seen him before, which was needed because he wasn't the only one moving quickly. These zombies would have easily ripped me apart with their speed.

I stopped in my tracks and looked down the sights of my pistol as Reyn continued forward. Star dropped another creature with a knife in the eye, losing it in the process. He finally had run out of bullets and dropped his pistol. I watched it clatter to the ground as he pulled out his second knife and last knife. He hadn't pulled it fully out when another of the zombies pounced on him. I took careful aim and pulled the trigger in rapid fire, emptying the clip into the two standing creatures as Reyn reached Star. Reyn kicked out with rock-covered legs. The momentum behind the kick sent the creature flying, with parts of its ribs sticking out in awkward locations. It already was dead, though, with Star's knife embedded where its ear should be.

I turned back to see how effective my shots were. I had wasted four bullets on each one. Four on the first because it was so quick I had to predict where it would be. The other zombie just looked big, and I didn't want it to get back up. I was glad to see the speedster of a zombie dead on the ground, but to my dismay, the other zombie I had dropped got to its feet. To my surprise, it didn't come after us but instead ran off. Without bullets, there was no way any of us were going to chase after it.

Reyn helped Star to his feet. "Are you all right?"

Star shook his head, looking down at his ripped and blood-dripping clothing. "I've been infected," he said, accepting the fate.

I ran over to him, "No, no, there has to be something we can do. Where is it?" I pulled at Star's shirt, trying to see how bad the wounds were. If they weren't too deep or in bad locations, we could cut out the infected locations.

Star grabbed me, holding me in place to stop my efforts. "Reed, I already checked, I'm done for now." He gave me a weak smile, "but I can do some damage to these creatures and maybe save some people in the process. I need you to go and keep everyone else safe."

"But we stick together," I protested, not wanting to lose my friend again. I had lost him once, and I wouldn't let that ever happen again.

"Not this time," Star replied, sadly patting me on the face. "Reyn, take him and go." With that, he gave me one last hug before retrieving his knives and running off into the darkness as the clouds above continued to darken and began to send slivers of light down into the city. I watched in shock as he disappeared, engulfed in a city that was still foreign to my eyes.

I would have stayed there all day if it wasn't for Reyn. He gently placed an arm around me and led me back the way we had come. I just followed my mind, reaching for any solution where I wouldn't lose my friend—no, not just a friend but my family—the closest thing to a brother I would ever have.

It didn't take long to reach the top of the building, and it seemed even less to me as my mind was elsewhere. The loud thumping of the hellcopter's spinning propellers brought me back to my surroundings. Reyn didn't even wait for me as he picked me up and put me on the flying contraption. I allowed the others to guide me to a seat and help me buckle in.

"Where is Star?" Kikki yelled over the noise of the propellers.

I just looked back blankly, unable to comprehend the reality of it, or maybe just unwilling to.

"He got infected," Reyn responded when I didn't.

After that, the noise of the helicopter increased as it took off. Headsets were handed out which both blocked out the noise and allowed us to speak to each other.

"Where is Star?" Kyle asked through the headsets from the front of the helicopter.

I still didn't respond, so again, Reyn replied, "He took out the Zombies but got infected."

"What do you mean infected?" Kyle asked.

"He was scratched and bitten all over," I said softly. With the racket from the helicopter, no one could actually make out his words, even with the headsets on.

"What was that!"

"He had bite marks and scratches all over!" I yelled in an angry outburst. "He's gone, infected. I couldn't even cut the bad parts out."

"So," Kyle replied. "He's immune. That was part of what we shot him up with when we swapped his injection before going into the games. You know, that first power that he got. Man, it was hard to act like I didn't know what it was."

"What!" several people yelled.

"Yeah, he was our best bet of keeping the people alive, so I had him put in the games with me," Kyle responded. "But the first thing he got was immunity to the zombie microbodies. That was the first power he received. And even if he was infected, I have the cure in the back with the rest of the supplies."

"I have to go back!" I yelled, trying to undo the buckles but not really sure how. The blasted things were worse than the ones in the van we had driven earlier.

Reyn tried to stop me. "It's too late, man. It's impossible to find him down there."

I looked at him for a brief second before continuing to struggle with the complex buckles. I was not going to leave my friend alone in a city full of Zombies thinking that he was infected. He would fight until his last breath or sacrifice himself to save others. I needed to at least warn him. Let him know he could live. That was when I felt a pain in my arm and looked down to see a puffy thing in it. I reached for it, but even as I did, my senses started to dim, and I lost the ability to control my arms.

"Thank you, sis. Read, sorry, man, Star would want it this way," Kyle said through the headset.

I pulled out the tranquilizer and looked up to see a very pretty girl holding the tranquilizer gun pointing at me, a horrified expression on her face. Blackness started to take me as the girl whispered over the headsets, "Sorry, Reed."

Chapter 48
EXPLORING
Alejandro: Earth's surface: THE CITY
A.K.A
Last City on Earth

We didn't stay on the highway for long and moved off in the direction of the large wall that hugged the city. That is when traffic came to a stop. All the cars in the outer city seemed to have driven the same way we had. The road was full of parked vehicles.

"Everyone out. We are going to have to make the rest of the trek on foot." our armed guard said from the front of the van as he got out himself.

I once again found myself supporting one of the least fortunate people. It made for slow going, but that suited me fine. I just didn't want anyone to notice who I was. We slowly moved for what seemed like two hours, all the time, heading for the towering wall. I didn't know what our destination was, but it looked like it was important as I saw many people heading the same way, caring as much as they could.

I wanted to ask what in the world was going on, but I didn't want to draw attention to myself. Thankfully, someone else asked for it.

"What is going on? I thought you were just rescuing us. This looks like a mass exodus."

"The city is being breached by Zombies sometime today or tomorrow. We are getting as many people out as possible," a guard responded.

"Hence the rescue. We couldn't let our people die at the hands of the horde," another armed man added.

"That being said," the first guard continued, "if there are any amongst you that got a little extra boost from whatever experiments were done to you, we could use all the help we can get guarding the city exit. Mull that over for the next hour. We should get there by then."

Zombies? I thought, now glad that I had insisted on acquiring the cure for myself when I headed the zombie games.

For the next forty minutes, I thought over our circumstances. I knew that it was only a matter of time before I was discovered by someone, so I needed to work on a miracle. That or gain some favor. We finally reached a gate in thé wall that was wide open, but the gate didn't lead through the wall; it went down into the ground below.

The guards who accompanied me ran over to the other guards at the tunnel's entrance. "What is the news?" one asked.

"Not good. The zombies breached about an hour ago on the other side of the city. It's a massacre over there. We are trying to get as many out as possible, but we need more manpower and weapons. Unfortunately, as soon as they get close, we will be forced to shut the gates."

At that moment, something came over the man's radio. I couldn't quite make it out.

"Looks like there is a group coming from Cruise Lane. There are over a thousand, and half are kids. They only have one gun escort with them. I need some men to go and help."

"Will we make it in time?" another guard asked.

"We won't if we sit here. Quick, get some men."

I saw this as my opportunity to gain favor in a big way. "I would like to go. Do you have extra weapons?"

"One of the guards looked me up and down before he reached over to some crates that were just inside the entrance and pulled out a machine gun."

"Do you know how to use this?" He asked.

I picked it up and quickly unlocked the magazine to find it unloaded. I then reassembled it, flipped the safety off, and aimed it up at the sky, away from any people. "Bang," I said.

"It looks like he knows," the other guard replied. "Give him some ammo and get another five people. I want to move out in the next three minutes."

Chapter 49
A KING'S POWER

King Palumbus: Earth's surface: THE CITY
A.K.A
Last City on Earth

An irritating banging was coming from the door that I had bolted shut. Not something with a key that would allow people entry. No, I was the only one allowed to open this door. Everyone knew I wasn't to be disturbed when I came into this room. This was where I thought, experimented, and fulfilled my desires. Yet here was someone causing a ruckus. I might have to send the fool into the tunnels below to die of hunger. As the banging continued, my initial thought of killing the man solidified. The person on the other side of the door would soon find out that a king should never be disturbed. As I approached the door, I thought about how I should proceed. Maybe I would use my heightened reflexes to just snap the neck. Yet if they were causing such a ruckus, I should at least hear them out before I killed them. They might actually have important news. But what could be so important that it couldn't wait for when I was ready for it? No, nothing came to mind. I should just snap their neck and be done with it.

When I reached the door, I unbolted the heavy metal rod from the strong frame. To my surprise, I found Burnington standing on the other side, out of breath. Burnington knew better than to disturb me, so I lowered my hands to my side instead of wrapping around the man's neck.

"What is it?" I asked.

"It's the city, my lord. Zombies got in. They are running rampant."

"Have you sealed the building?" I asked

"Of course, sir. We followed protocol."

"Then why did you disturb me? Take care of it."

"There are too many, sir. We have drones overhead watching, but we don't have the firepower needed to handle the numbers we are seeing."

I sighed deeply. This was the problem with being a king: You had to solve everything yourself. I normally did this by killing those who caused me trouble. That made things simple. I quickly thought about who I would need to kill to make this problem go away. But it was the Zombies who were the problem.

I moved off, determined to see how bad things really were. I knew that if push came to shove, then we could at least live another hundred years inside the walls of my sanctuary without having to worry about this. But then, I wouldn't have fresh supplies or test subjects. I would have to limit myself. No, I would avoid that if I could. Burnington followed me as I made my way to an elevator and then descended to the security office.

When I entered, I looked up at the screens and saw the city in chaos. Zombies were entering houses and pulling people out. Some simply killed the victims, while others rounded the people up. Burnington had been right. The city was lost. My eyes shifted through the screens when my eyes landed on one where a lone figure made its way through the streets with enhanced speed and reflexes. He also had two foot-length daggers in each hand. I watched as he came across a group of twenty zombies. The man didn't pause to take stock but jumped into the fray, sending limbs, heads, and other body parts flying as he moved his way through the group. The knives penetrated eyes and ear sockets skillfully before sliding out again and into the next victim.

"Follow that man," I directed one of the dozen operators in the room.

"Yes, sir."

The man moved forward, and I watched as he encountered hundreds of Zombies. Some had the power of multiple appendages, while others were fast or had hardened skin. Two of the creatures the man fought glided around on thin wings with bulging skin that I knew was full of Helium to make them light.

My eyes narrowed at the sight. I knew that the members who had been turned into zombies still retained their attributes, but I only remember giving one person the ability to fly like that. Yet there were two zombies with that power. How was that possible? My eyes swept over the other screens, and as I looked, the number of zombies with enhancements was several times more than there should be. A moment of fear trickled inside my normally stoic self.

I quickly reminded myself that I had built this tower as a structure that would survive a zombie attack. I had nothing to fear. That was when the warning alarm went off. I looked to see a control panel with a breach warning lit.

"What is that?" I asked.

"They seemed to have broken into the lower floors, sir," someone replied.

"I thought we sealed them off."

"We did, sir. They still got through. I've sealed off the first ten floors from us."

I rubbed the back of my neck in frustration. I had planned for this, but things still weren't going as planned. My eyes turned back to the man who seemed to be able to cut through the zombies. He came across a horde of a thousand and, instead of backing off, started to cut his way through. I blinked to see that he no longer had the daggers but a sword and a machine gun that he was in the process of unloading into the creatures around him.

"Must have picked them up off a dead guard." I mused to myself.

"What was that, Lord Palumbus?"

"Nothing," I said as I watched as the man fought through the zombies and in only a dozen minutes he had killed the whole mass.

Another alarm blared, and someone called out. "Breach on level thirty." someone called out, but as they did, there was the sound of shattering glass and crumbling metal. A blast of wind came in with it. I turned to see three creatures that, as soon as they entered, had started to rip apart the people near them. Anger blared within me as I found three filthy, undeserving creatures in my presence. To throw the icing on the cake, I also didn't have any guards in this room to remove these nuisances for me. They were all down below to prevent any of the creatures from getting up here. A lot of good that seemed to have been done. No, I was surrounded by useless meat. Anger flared up, and I let my body flair with power, power that I had stored up over the last two hundred years. My quick reflexes and speed, along with the strength to crush rock and hardened skin, all came into play as I crushed the creatures before me, their nails scraping ineffective against my skin. I tossed their bodies with crushed skulls back out the window that they had come in.

I looked out the window and when I didn't see anything else, retreated to a position where I could see the screens and the opening at the same time. "Bring a drone over to watch the side of the building. I don't want to be surprised again."

"Ye-s sir," a shaky voice replied.

Several men came into the room shortly after and started to take care of the wounded and hurt as I continued to watch the screen. My eyes kept going to the one with the man. I watched as he cut through a group of zombies and reaching a group of people that the zombies had gathered like cattle. The man led the group away. My eyes flickered to the other scenes, and I saw the whole city in chaos. Groups of people were escaping into the tunnels as the zombies swept through the city. Then, zombies in a large area all started to move at the same time, converging on a single location. I triangulated the destination and realized they were all coming to retrieve the prisoners that the strange man had freed. The drone flew closer to the man, and finally, I got a glimpse of his face. To my surprise, I recognized it. I had seen it before. Then it clicked. The addition to the Zombie games. What was his name again? Sun or Moon or something. He had guided the people to a tunnel system and was guiding them down. As they moved into

289

the tunnels, he moved to the rear of the group. I watched as the horde arrived, and the man stepped forward fearlessly, taking them on as the others attempted to get away. Others tried to help the man, but they only died beside him as he performed a dance of death amidst the zombies. He waded into the horde, asking for death to come to him. Somehow, it never did.

Chapter 50
A MAN'S POWER

Alejandro: Earth's surface: THE CITY
A.K.A
Last City on Earth

As it turned out, seven other people volunteered to help retrieve the families reported coming from Cruise Lane. We had all received weapons and jogged until we reached the new refugees fleeing the city. Technically speaking, we were all refugees at this point. For some reason, I found that funny even though the others didn't.

Evan, the man leading the group, quickly ordered one of the men to lead the way to ensure that the refugees didn't make a wrong turn. He then turned to the rest of us and had us to the back and sides of the mass of people and kids.

I found myself in the far back of the group with Tucker, one other man who had volunteered to come rescue the kids. For the first five minutes, I watched our surroundings. My eyes looked over the deserted cars in the middle of the road and over the buildings. To my surprise, some still had people in them.

"Hey, Tucker, why are there people up there?"

Tucker looked at where I pointed and shrugged. "I guess they don't believe the message that Kyle and Reed sent the city."

"Message?" I asked.

"Yeah, haven't you seen it?"

I shook my head. "Haven't had much time for a screen, and I don't have a phone."

Tucker reached into his pocket and pulled out his phone. After unlocking the screen, he handed it over to me with a looped video playing on it. I listened to it as I continued to survey my surroundings. To my surprise, the rebels knew about the zombie breach before it happened. Well, if it was happening. I wouldn't put it past them to spread fake news all

291

around. But then why would they free us and tell us zombies were coming. No, they must have known ahead of time. But that didn't make sense either. How would they know without the city offices and King Palumbus himself knowing? I just didn't have enough information, but I wasn't going to risk my life and left now. There was nothing for me left in this city. Best to leave with the rebels and make a new name for myself.

Once I had listened to the recording twice, I handed Tucker's phone back. "It sounds legit to me," I replied.

"If you didn't know about the broadcast, how come you are here volunteering?"

"The Rebels saved me from one of the king's experimental facilities and told me zombies were invading."

"Experimental facilities, I thought those were just a rumor," Tucker replied as he continued to survey the area.

"I did as well until I found myself in one," I replied, my eyes drifting over the people we were escorting. Men and women struggled to carry children that were kicking, crying, and screaming. Most of the people in the back with us were there because they were the slowest. This was mostly due to the kids causing tantrums and the heavy load of all the stuff they were trying to carry with them.

"Do you think we will make it in time?" I asked.

"I hope so. Otherwise, we volunteered to die together." Tucker laughed grimly.

"That isn't a happy thought."

"Better than dying alone."

"Is it? I think they both are unappealing. How about we get back and not die?"

Tucker smiled at me, and we continued to walk at a slow pace in the back of the group. We made it a mile without too much difficulty. The worst of that was just keeping the kids moving. They would flop on the ground, yell, cry, walk the wrong way, and ask if we were there yet. I was convinced that my decision not to have children was the right choice right then. Not that there was time for a girlfriend before. The plan for that had always been pushed off.

We were still keeping the group moving when the screaming started. It wasn't anyone in our group but somewhere close by. At the sound of it, everyone tensed up, and the younger kids quieted down fear in their eyes.

"Should you go see what that is?" one of the kids' parents asked us.

I looked at him blankly for a moment as if questioning his sanity before answering. "We don't have enough men to protect this lot, let alone save the city. They were warned, as you were. It's on them."

Tucker nodded in agreement. "Just be glad that they gave us a warning. Keep moving to survive."

The man looked between Tucker and me like we were horrible people before continuing to usher his kids along. Tucker and I started to hurry everyone else to the best we could. The speed increased a little, but I knew we weren't moving fast enough.

Tucker clearly did, too, because he looked at me. "You any good with that gun?"

"I'm proficient, not the best shot, but I at least know how to use it."

"I'm about the same. Just make sure you aim for the head. That is the only way to truly kill them."

"We all have seen the Zombie games," I replied, rolling my eyes. We had all watched people fight zombies for our entire lives. We knew what worked and what didn't.

"True, wait. That is where I know you from. Didn't you run the games or something? Alejandro, right? What are you doing here?"

"The king forced me to run the games, and when I didn't do well enough... Well, he locked me up, and the rebels freed me." I replied, still keeping my eyes keen for the first signs of zombies. That was when I saw them. Six came out from an alleyway and started for us. "Wait till they get closer before shooting," I replied as Tucker and I aimed down the zombies. "I'll take the right and you the left."

293

"Got it," Tucker replied. We waited for the zombies to come within an easier range. Their movement was that of a slow jog, but it was much faster than the speed we were making with the kids and families. It was Tucker who called out when to shoot, though. "Now,"

We both took our shots, then we shot again and again. It took twelve shots to put down the zombies, which I thought was good. I looked over to Tucker, who looked calm under the pressure.

"We should have done it in fewer shots. I called it a little early. We could have let them get a little closer."

"I'm glad you're beside me," I replied, swapping out my magazine and slowly reloading the somewhat depleted mag.

Tucker saw me, nodded, and began to do it as well. "Smart thinking."

"The goal is to stay alive," I replied.

"Then we shouldn't have volunteered to come save this lot."

"It's just another mile," I replied

"Yeah, but we aren't going to make it." Tucker groaned, signaling to another group coming at us, this one thirty-strong. "We need to start shooting at a further range, or we will be overrun."

It got a little hairy, taking on the thirty zombies that came at us. As we finished the last batch, we noticed gunshots to our rear and turned to see that the other groups were taking on their own groups of zombies. As I watched, a fast Zombie, much faster than the rest, sped the distance to one of the groups and started to shred the two men with weapons. I took aim at the creature but missed. It seemed to have sensed the bullet and dodged it. Thankfully, I wasn't the only one that shot. The creature dodged my bullet and ran right into the path of Tucker's. His bullet took it in the shoulder, sending it to the ground. One of the wounded guards it had attacked finished it off at close range.

"This isn't looking good," Tucker replied as we turned to see a hundred zombies come out of an alley the way we had come and start for us. "We aren't going to be able to take on that many."

"Well, I'm going to take as many as I can before they take me," I replied, lifting my weapon."

Tucker smiled at me. "Not a runner?"

"I ran more today to get to these people than I have for years. I'm not going to be able to outrun that lot." I pointed to another group of zombies making their way towards us.

"I bet you could," Tucker replied as three of the zombies broke from the pack and spread in our direction. "Never mind," Tucker grimaced, taking aim. We started to shoot, but together, we only took out one of the three zombies that rushed at us with blinding speed. Their movements were so erratic that I couldn't get a decent shot in. Some of the missed shots swept past them and into the crowd of zombies behind, but it didn't make much of a dent with the large mass.

"Crap, we are dead," I mumbled, taking another shot and missing.

"It was nice knowing you." Tucker agreed.

I took one last desperate shot, which found purchase on one of the zombie's lower legs, blowing it off, but Tucker missed the other. It pounced, and I cringed, waiting for it to tear me apart. The blow never landed, though. Instead, its head exploded, its body falling to the ground at our feet. I looked up in surprise, trying to spot who had saved me, and I noticed something odd. The zombies were no longer pursuing us. Instead, they were being cut down like weeds. Swirling blades flashed through the group, taking limbs, heads, and legs clean off. A single man danced in their midst, moving so fast that none of the zombies were able to touch him. He had two guns strapped to his body, a sword in one hand, and an enforcer's long knife in the other. The zombies swiped at him but missed continually as, one by one, they fell dead to the ground.

"Who in the world," Tucker whispered.

I, on the other hand, knew exactly who that was. I had been watching him for a while now and had done research about him when he had lived in the tower. Somehow, Star had made it here and was killing these creatures to save us.

"He has this. Let's save the others." I replied, turning in the direction of other screams. Several other places up the line of people had zombies approaching them. Tucker moved with me, and we quickly took on another much smaller group of zombies. When we finished with them, we found that only a few people had been hurt or killed by zombies around us. The parents had fought together to take out the ones that had gotten by us. I looked back to see that Star was gone, and only a pile of corpses lay where he had been. After a quick survey of the area, I found Star finishing up another bunch of zombies on the other side that had come from the other side of the street we were traveling down.

Again, we did what we could to keep people moving. People helped the injured while the dead were left behind. A few minutes later, Star approached us. "I wouldn't go that way. The zombies have blocked off the tunnel you were heading to."

"Ahh, who are you?" Tucker asked.

"This is Star," I replied to Tucker before turning back to Star. "You can't cut a path for us?"

"I could cut it, but I'm one man. They would get around me and take you all out."

"But what can we do then?" I asked a little too desperately.

"I found another path. Follow me, and I'll do my best to keep you guys alive. I don't know how long I have, though." He pointed to a wound. "I've been infected as well. So keep an eye on me; if I turn, take me down. Do you understand?"

Tucker and I nodded.

"Good, now get these people to follow me. We need to move this way."

Chapter 51
A KING'S POWER

King Palumbus: Earth's surface: THE CITY
A.K.A Last City on Earth

I was more engrossed in watching the game contestant than I was in the rest of the city. It was mesmerizing, and I hadn't seen anything like it. He had saved several groups and sent them into the tunnels. Even now, he was leading a group made up of half-children to a tunnel entrance.

"Lord Palumbus! We have incoming," someone said, pointing to a screen showing a hundred creatures climbing up the building's walls. They were almost to the breach on our floor.

"I thought we were watching the tower," I said angrily. "How did we miss them?"

"We were. They must have made their way up through the tower before going to the outside wall," someone reasoned.

"Everyone out," I growled as I steadied myself. With the powers I had given myself, this would be a breeze. Even a man with fewer powers had taken on a thousand all on his own. If Sun or Moon could do it or whatever he was called, I could easily do it as well.

I watched as the zombies climbed in through the broken wall to the outdoors like spiders.

"Disgusting," I said, stepping forward, grabbing the first one, and ripping it apart with my bare hands. I was working on my second one when a female voice came smoothly through the room. As she spoke, I felt something stir within me. I turned to see a beautiful woman looking back at me—no, a beautiful zombie.

"How?" I questioned as I realized she was using the powerful attraction power I had created on me. I shook myself, but the moment of hesitation had let the others surround me. "Oh,"

"Oh yes," the woman purred back. "The king himself. O, I look forward to eating my portion of you. With your size, we might get eight or nine portions to go around. Clearly, you took some of the better powers."

"I'll kill you all," I growled, stepping forward to reach out to grab the woman, but as I did, three zombies stepped forward with lightning speed and grabbed hold of me. I pulled with my strength, but their strength matched my own. Their speed did as well.

"How?" I exclaimed, not believing my eyes. I was the most powerful being in the world but here these lesser creatures, these zombies were holding me down.

"You silly thing. Did you think you could hold up to someone like me?" The woman stepped closer, pulling out a knife from her belt. "You can't stop the horde."

She slowly walked over to me, casually looking around the room. Her eyes landed on the screen I had been watching.

"What is this? I thought I had already sent some of my Zs to get him." She ignored me as I continued to struggle. She reached out and caressed the boy's image on the screen. He was just getting to the tunnels with the group he was leading a horde on his tail. "Looks like I have one more that I will have to retrieve personally."

Again, I watched as Zombies stopped on many different screens. They all turned and made their way toward the boy and the group.

"There, that should hold him." The female zombie turned back to me. "Sorry to keep you waiting. I will make this quick. I just wanted to thank you before I dispatched you. I hear it was thanks to you that I was created. So here it is. Thank you. Now let's see if you have the same weaknesses as we do."

Anger flaring and knowing I didn't have any other options, I pulled out my trump card. My entire body burst into flames, searing the zombies that held me still. To my surprise, they didn't let go as their hands and clothing caught fire. Instead, they held me as the woman approached.

"Impressive," she said, moving quickly with a dagger in hand.

The last thing I saw was that dagger coming directly at my eye and the screen that displayed the man I had been watching. Star, that was right, his name was Star. I faintly made out zombies piling on top of him. Then there was pain, and then... nothing.

Chapter 52
Zombies and Trains
Wind: Underground Tower #4

"We need to move up the tower now!" I ordered the hundred men that stood around me. "Work your way up as fast as you can until you reach the 723rd floor. I want that whole floor secured and under our control in the next two hours. Team leaders take charge and move out!"

At my order, everyone started moving, and Elephant made his way over to me. He had just made the ascent from the lower floors. We had secured the elevators and now could bring people up without going outside of the building.

"What's the rush?" Elephant asked.

"Did you see the transmission from my brother?" I asked.

"I heard some of the men talking about it on the way up, but I didn't."

"Well, we have been interrogating the residents that lived on the floors we have taken over and have found that they have communication with the surface. It is from an automated supply train."

"A what?" Elephant asked, confused.

"I don't know; that is what they call it. It is on the 723rd floor, and the loop transmission says that directions will be on it to get to a safe city on the surface—a city with a cure."

Elephant whistles at that. "Sounds like we need to get to the animated supply train."

"Automated," I corrected since I had been corrected myself five times from the individual brought to me with the information.

"Right, automated." Elephant nodded.

"Keep bringing up all the men. I want the whole tower locked down and a supply sweep done as soon as possible. If there is a city with a cure out there, we need to get there."

I didn't do much but talk with more people from the upper tower for the next hour, trying to get as much information as I could. I did get some reports from the lower tower about a message that appeared on the screening computers. I quickly determined it was the same one that was on a loop on the screens in the upper tower. Waving off those reports, I focused on resources and their military power, which was pitiful. As it turned out, they had a lot more food and other resources squandered away. It angered me to find out that they ate as much food in a day as we would consider three days' worth. We often only got two meals a day, but they ate three large ones. It was immediately apparent by their appearances, as their bodies were large and obese, unlike the thin, fit bodies we sported in the lower tower.

Finally, word came that the train floor was secured. Elephant and I both headed up to meet with Rat, who was already up there. We took the elevator, which was a little cramped with my own guards and the five men who accompanied Elephant.

When the doors to the elevator opened up onto the 723rd floor, I was shocked to see such a large open space. The roof above was four stories high, and the floor itself spanned farther than the normal building as if this floor stretched out far into the ground around. As I stepped out, something felt wrong. It took me a second to figure out what it was. The temperature up here was much warmer than I was used to. It also felt wet, as if there was a hot shower going on nearby. In the middle of the room stretched a track that went in both directions.

"Has the train come yet?" I asked Rat, who approached us.

"Not yet. I have men stationed at both tunnels on the lookout. We did come across a little bit of trouble, though. Apparently, this is the floor on which all the guards on duty were stationed. There were a few shots fired when we arrived. Two men are hurt. One dead from our side and five dead on theirs. They surrendered when they realized how outmatched they were."

301

"Are we treating our men?" I asked, concerned. I hated losing people to the zombies and hated it more that we were fighting our own.

"Yes, they are already being taken care of. The men we captured are being kept over there. They say that they are stationed on this floor because when the doors open down the tunnel to let the train in, sometimes a Zombie or two sneak in."

"So we have men doing that?"

"Yes, I have them stationed at both tunnel entrances."

"Should we send scouts out?" I asked.

"Apparently, the train fills the whole tunnel with wheels on the ground and walls. At least, that is what the upper floor guards said when we asked if there was anything we should know. I did emphasize that their lives depended on the outcome of their answers, so I believe it." Rat replied.

"In that case, send some down after the train comes."

Rat nodded and was about to respond when a loud squeaking noise filled the room. It was metal on metal with a background undertone of gears. I watched a hundred spiders move out from the tunnel and into the room just before a large thing entered. It was made of metal and looked like a moving building. It came in quickly and slowed down until its movement was only a crawl. I had never seen anything like it before. The closest would be a combination of an elevator, a cart, and the spiders that always roamed around. I didn't have time to goggle. This is what my brother and his friend Kyle were talking about on their transmissions. It was Kyle who spoke about the trains that would arrive with supplies to help get us to the City of Hope. Still, I felt like it was coming from my brother, though, as he vouched for Kyle. Kyle's transmission had a lot of important information cramped into it but the key was how to get my hands on a phone and then get to the surface where it would automatically work to tell me where to go. I needed to get my hands on one of these magical phones. I just hoped it was as intuitive as Kyle had made it sound on the transmission.

I started to move forward toward the train to look for the device that Kyle had shown on his portion of the transmission.

As I moved, Rat barked orders to get a group to scout out the tunnel from which the train had come. The closer I got to the train, the more nervous I became. I had seen how fast this thing could move. Still, someone had to risk boarding it. I found a spot that looked to be a door and approached. As I did it, a door opened, and I stepped inside. To my surprise, the whole thing was full of boxes. Each had labels on the front, and I quickly read "Military Ration" on over a dozen boxes. There were others, like bullets and guns, but I didn't see one that said phones. I continued to look when another noise came from outside. It was the sound of gunshots. Confused, I made my way out of the train and looked around. All of the men around were heading toward the tunnel the train had come from. Inside were rhythmic shots being fired. I ran as well to see what was going on.

As we all approached the tunnel, one of the men sent down to scout out the tunnel came running back. "It's a horde!" He yelled, "We need to get out of here."

"NO!" Bellowed Rat and Elephant at the same time.

"We need to hold them here." Elephant continued. "Everyone go and support the scout team and retreat as needed. "Rat and Rainbow, go and get more men. I want them all on this floor as soon as possible. Keep making your rounds until they are all here."

Rat, with Rainbow right behind him, practically flew back toward the elevator. The others moved into the tunnel to support the others.

"Wind," Elephant said, "I need you to find those phones and get them to safety. I don't want a horde of Zombies between our people and the map to safety." With that final order, Elephant moved with his men to the tunnel.

I started to move back but remembered just how many boxes there were on the train. I wasn't going to be able to do this all by myself. It would take too long. My eyes searched the area for others to help, but everyone had gone down the tunnel to fend off the Zombies that were coming. That was when my eyes landed on the nineteen men bound to the back of the

303

room. The guards of the upper tower that were stationed on this floor. My mind reeled at the thought, but I couldn't let my anger get the better of me. I needed help; we needed to work together, or we would die alone. With my mind made up, I moved over to the men.

"Listen to me good," I said loudly, getting all the men's attention. "I know that you hate us right now for killing your friends, and we hate you for killing ours. But in reality, we have to work together, or we will all die. Do you understand me?"

There were some hesitant nods.

"So here is the deal: I am going to cut you loose, and you are going to help secure the supplies and, more specifically, the phones on that train. I don't know if you saw it, but my brother sent a transmission that is displaying on every screen in this tower right now. He and his friend have sent us supplies and a map to get to a safe city on the surface. A city with a cure. Now, we lower-floor people are going to go there, and we will take anyone who wants to come along. So are we in agreement to help me save yours and my people?"

There was silence until one man asked. "How do we know you won't just kill us or leave us behind."

"You don't, but I will promise you one thing. I am on the human team. I will not leave more people to become zombies."

"What is a little girl doing promising things like that?" another scoffed.

"I am the commander of the lower floors and now the commander of yours as well." I proclaimed. As I said it, I realized how dumb it sounded. How could I be the leader of the lower floors? I wasn't the only one who thought it sounded off because there was some laughter from the men.

"You the commander?"

"Let the real commander give us the promise, and then we will consider it," another scoffed.

I was reddened with anger and was about to shout back when someone called out to me.

"Commander Wind? Is everything alright over there?"

I turned to see two dozen men who had just got off one of the three elevators that populated the upper floors come over to me.

"Yes, everything is fine," I said, realizing this was my moment to prove who I was to these other people. "Yogurt and Ocean, I need you to wait by the elevator and direct any other people coming up to go down that tunnel to support against the Zombie horde that is coming for us."

"Yes, mam," They replied, moving as ordered.

"Cloud and Truck, I need you two to untie all these prisoners. They will be assisting me in gathering supplies from the train. As for the rest of you, go support our men in the tunnel. Now move!"

They did. Everyone did as I asked from that moment on without any bickering. They had seen the respect from my men. Once all the men were freed from their bonds, I sent Cloud and Truck to help against the Zombies and turned to the newly released men. "Now, follow me to the train. I want all the boxes removed and taken over next to the elevators. I will look for the phones."

We toiled for twenty minutes, moving boxes as I worked on finding the elusive phones. As we worked, more and more armed men and women came up from the floor below to help. Soon, the tunnel leading to the zombies was full, and people were sent back. Lines were formed to unpack the train, while others were formed to supply ammo to the front line, which was constantly shooting. Every now and then, the people in the tunnel would move back, causing more people to join us in the large train room. As more people came to help, the work went by faster, and others started to look for the phones as well. Soon, they were found and brought to the elevator. A special trip was made to move them to a safer floor.

I moved over to Elephant, who was observing the men and women working on all fronts. "Is there any sign that the zombie numbers are dropping?" I asked.

Elephant shook his head. "We don't know how many there are, but the reports so far say that they are endless. They are going to push our men into this room and then overwhelm us."

My stomach turned at that. A large open space, we wouldn't be able to keep them tunneled in. I looked around, and that was when I realized that a wide open space wasn't all that bad as long as the opening to it wasn't large. "Actually, I think this room will be an advantage. We have always been limited in how many guns we could fit in a tunnel. But here." I waved my arm around the room. "We can actually use our numbers for once."

I quickly explained my idea, and Elephant nodded. "It's a good thing we made you commander. You're a natural." He then turned and barked orders. Soon, people lined up in a partial semicircle around the entrance door. We stayed far enough back so that people were hugging the wall. Three layers of people made up the line. The first group lay on the ground while the second kneeled and the third stood. It was enough so over four hundred people fit in the semicircle. Others climbed up on top of the train as well while still more dragged over crates and anything else they could find so that they could also have a line of sight of the cave entrance that led into the room. Even as this was being organized, other people started to ship the supplies from the train down to other floors.

"We are going to need a path for our men in the tunnel to run through," I commented to Elephant, who made the adjustment so that there was a path to the side for them to make it.

"Should we fall back now?" Elephant asked.

"No, we need to take as many out before they reach this. This is our last stand."

Unfortunately, at that moment, people came running out of the tunnel. They took turns turning and firing before running back again. One person ran directly over to Elephant and myself. "There are some creatures that bullets aren't taking down."

"What do you mean?" I asked.

"There are a couple dozen zombies in front of the line that seem to be bulletproof. We shoot them in the head, but they keep getting back up. Only now and then does one fall."

There wasn't time to adjust the plan, so I hoped that the sheer number of guns would overwhelm anything that came through that tunnel.

So we waited a few minutes before our men entirely retreated. That was when the zombies made their appearance. As soon as they did, I yelled out, "Fire," and shots fired filled the room. The bulletproof zombies that were reported fell in a blink under the barrage. Everyone knew to shoot a zombie in the head, so apparently, these zombies weren't bulletproof against a dozen or two at the same time.

"Fire," I yelled, and the second-row shot.

"Fire," the men standing shot.

"Fire," again the first-row shot. All the time, those further back took shots of opportunity.

We shot in waves as we had trained all our lives, and as we did, the pile of bodies grew. Soon, the zombies had to wade through a sea of their brethren just to escape the tunnel. None escaped the barrage, and the pile just kept getting larger and larger, stacking up. The pile started to get pushed out toward us, but we were far enough back in the large four-story room that it didn't even get close to our semicircle. We continued to fire until the pile of bodies became three stories tall. We did have to move back a couple times as the pile was pushed closer and closer to us. Finally, silence came. We all stared in wonder at the pile before us. That was when the screeching noise came back.

"Finally, someone called out. The tunnel door is finally closing."

I turned to see one of the men we had captured, and I had released standing back from the line.

"What do you mean?"

"It's been taking longer and longer to shut as we don't know how to fix it." He replied. It's been worrying us for a while.

We would never have handled a horde like that on our own, but you guys did it easily.

"So more can't get it?" I asked.

"Not until the doors open again." He replied.

A sigh of relief went through the crowd.

"Elephant, post a guard detail in case there are still more on the other side of that pile. As for the rest of us, let's get ready to move out. I want to get to the surface.

Chapter 53
A New City
REED: The City of Hope

I ascended the outer wall of the City of Hope, a routine I had followed for the past six months. The city stood as a testament to resilience, ever-expanding to accommodate the influx of people seeking refuge from The City and its surrounding underground towers. It had taken them about a month to start arriving after our group had flown here. Drones assisted in guiding and protecting the people on their arduous journey. While I felt somewhat helpless, confined to my role on the wall, I knew it was a necessary duty. Someone had to guard and defend this sanctuary. Fortunately, the initial busyness of the city subsided after the majority of groups had successfully made the treacherous journey.

My task involved aiding people through the screening and vaccination processes that the City of Hope had developed. Before our arrival, the city did not possess a vaccine. However, using Kyle's samples, they were able to create ones of their own.

As the sun began to rise above the horizon, casting its gentle rays upon the world, I found myself lost in the beauty and tranquility of the scene. It was in that moment of blissful distraction that I heard approaching footsteps, gradually growing louder and transforming into a run. I turned to see a small brunette, a radiant smile adorning her face, racing toward me. Ignoring the smirk of the man walking behind her, I opened my arms to welcome her.

"I missed you," Julianne Pecoraro said, her voice filled with affection.

"I saw you off last night," I protested, unable to suppress my smile.

"Exactly, it's been nine hours since I saw you," she grinned mischievously. "I wish we were already married. Then we wouldn't have to be apart," Julianne playfully added.

Kyle caught up with us, his smirk still lingering on his face. Sensing the impending comment, I challenged him with a raised eyebrow.

Kyle simply shrugged, his amusement evident. "I warned you about her, and now look. She has you wrapped around her little finger," he chuckled. "Even after she tranquilized you?"

I gazed into Julianne's shimmering eyes, my heart filled with warmth. "Well, some things are just worth it."

She leaned in and planted a tender kiss on my lips as I gently set her back on her feet. The three of us stood there, united, gazing out into the untamed wilderness beyond the protective walls of the city. At that moment, a mix of emotions washed over me. I was undeniably grateful to have Julianne by my side, but there remained a void. A missing piece to my life. Despite the arrival of people from five towers and a significant portion of The City's population, I had yet to see anyone from my own tower. At this point, it seemed unlikely they were still alive, yet every morning, I clung to hope, longing to see them emerging on the horizon, my sister among them. Deep down, a small part of me held onto the belief that my best friend, who had been left behind in the midst of The City's zombie invasion, might still be out there. Star wasn't someone who could be easily killed. He fought with unparalleled determination and possessed an indomitable spirit. But the image of how we had left him behind, aware of his impending transformation into a zombie, dampened my hope. Star would have thrown himself into the midst of the chaos, wielding his weapons with ferocity, determined to take down as many zombies as possible before succumbing to his own fate.

Kyle glanced at me, noticing the expression on my face. "I miss him too," he said, his hand landing on my shoulder in a comforting gesture. "He was a good man, always looking out for everyone else. But it's time to let him go," he added softly.

I let out a sigh, my voice trailing off as I struggled to find the words to express my emotions.

"Why don't we hold a funeral for him?" Kyle suggested, repeating his idea once again. "It could bring some closure."

Unlike the first time he had proposed the idea, I didn't react with anger. Instead, I slumped slightly, feeling Julianne's arm squeezing my own. I looked at her, finding solace in her presence. With her support, I finally felt ready to release my grip on the past. With a slight nod, I spoke, "Can we hold the funeral the day before our wedding? It would feel like he's here with us."

Julianne nodded, embracing me. "As long as it doesn't cast a shadow over our celebration," she smiled tenderly.

"I promise," I said, holding her tightly.

On the designated day, everyone gathered in a spacious building adorned with beautiful flowers. The venue would serve as the setting for both the funeral and our wedding, which was to follow the next day. All the survivors of the Zombie games were present, showing their support. They dressed in vibrant colors, celebrating life and its journey to the next stage. At the side of the room, a large picture of Star, captured from the footage of the games, stood surrounded by flowers. Everyone paid their respects to the image before participating in an open mic session, sharing their thoughts and memories of Star. I took most of the time to recount the humorous moments we had shared. The atmosphere was respectful yet not excessively somber. Most had come to terms with Star's passing months earlier. They had only delayed the service out of consideration for me. When it concluded, the group dispersed.

That night, sleep eluded me, but the next morning, I sprang out of bed, filled with anticipation for my and Julianne's special day. It was the first day since my arrival in the City of Hope that I didn't make my way to the wall. Instead, I headed to check on Julianne. I knocked on the door, only to be greeted by Kyle's familiar face.

"Don't you know it's bad luck to see the bride before the ceremony?" Kyle teased.

311

"Oh... I didn't know. Our ceremonies in the tower were rather simple, more like small parties," I explained.

Kyle pulled me inside the house, his grin widening. "Don't worry, she's not even here. She went to have a bachelorette party at Kikki's," he chuckled.

"Oh," I responded.

"But don't worry, I promised my sister that I'd have you ready and on time," Kyle said, his grin unwavering. "And I might have mentioned the word 'respectable,' so we've got some work to do."

"What's wrong with this?" I exclaimed, gesturing to my current appearance.

"It's my sister's wedding, not yours," Kyle retorted, continuing to grin as he closed the door behind us.

Several hours had passed, and now I stood before a gathering of familiar faces, most of whom hailed from The City, but there were also a few friends from the City of Hope among them. The morning had been more hectic than I had anticipated. Now, as the moment drew near, accompanied by the sweet melodies of the music, there was peace. As the doors swung open at the opposite end of the room, Julianne emerged, dressed in a breathtaking wedding dress. It shimmered under the gentle light, cascading elegantly down to the floor. The top showcased her modesty while accentuating her beautiful figure.

I couldn't tear my eyes away from her as she glided up the aisle until she stood by my side. Her radiant smile melted my heart, and at that moment, Gurney stepped forward, clutching a sheet of paper. "Thank you all for being here," he announced to the room. "Today, we gather to unite two families: Julianne Pecoraro's and Reed's." There was a brief pause, a hint of awkwardness, as I lacked a last name. Such names were nonexistent from where I came from. But Gurney continued, undeterred, "Before we commence the ceremony, I am obliged to inquire if anyone in the audience has anything to say or any reason why this wedding should not take place. Speak now or forever hold your peace."

The customary pause was broken as the doors at the end swung open, and a voice reverberated through the room. "I have something to say," a voice declared.

The crowd's shock turned into audible gasps as they turned their heads to witness the unexpected interruption. Another voice, this one belonging to a woman, echoed the sentiment. "Yeah, I have something to say too."

The first man who entered bore the remnants of old scars on his face, partially concealed beneath the layer of dirt that covered his features. His tattered clothes spoke of the hardships he had endured. The woman accompanying him fared a little better, lacking scars but wearing a worn-out appearance.

My mouth fell open as Star and Wind made their way down the aisle. "You could have at least invited us," Star quipped, his attempt at humor cut short as he was tackled to the ground. Kikki held him in place as he struggled to regain his footing.

I turned to Julianne, my voice laced with an apology. "I'm sorry for my family. They'll grow on you," I said, mustering a weak smile.

Julianne drew closer to me, giving me a loving hug as Gurney made his way down the aisle, loudly reprimanding everyone about maintaining decorum during a wedding.

This is the end of Z.O.M.B.I.E. Games.
I hope you enjoyed it.

Ethan Howatt

Made in the USA
Columbia, SC
01 February 2025

52573121R00188